The Art of Deception

by

CRAWFORD IVIN

'O what a tangled web we weave,
When first we practise to deceive!'

Sir Walter Scott ~ Marmion (1808)

Published by IVIN Productions
St. Helens, Isle of Wight PO33 1TQ UK

Cover illustration of Obernhof village painted by Lollie Ivin

Image of the author © Chris Bamber, www.atlasimages.co.uk

© 2014 Crawford Ivin

ISBN: 978-0-9929009-0-8

All rights reserved. This book or any portion thereof
may not be reproduced or used in any manner whatsoever
without the express written permission of the publisher
except for the use of brief quotations in a book review.

Typeset by Desktop Studio Ltd, St Helens, Isle of Wight PO33 1YB

Also available by Crawford Ivin
Paperback and Amazon Kindle

The story of Four Islands

I am deeply indebted to friends and family for their help, advice and encouragement in the production of this book, with an extra thank you to Sam Hill, Judy Vigors, Margaret Salkeld, Tony Thatcher and Dr James Dearden, and especially Anne Allen who deciphered my handwriting enough to type the first draft. And Brian Cantwell for his valued expertise.

The story was born from an idea I had over thirty-five years ago when reading an article in a jewellery trade magazine. I made a few notes at the time, but nothing further. Those notes were almost discarded when moving house and for years lay forgotten, until recently, when the modest success I enjoyed with 'The Story of Four Islands,' spurred me into action.

A great deal of the content is both accurate and authentic, and was great fun to write. I hope you enjoy reading it.

A detailed list of quotations from various sources appears in the bibliography.

Crawford Ivin 2014

This book is dedicated to the memory of the outstanding men and women of 'The Special Operations Executive' (S.O.E.).

At the height of World War Two, the average life expectancy of a wireless operator in occupied France was six weeks.

One in four agents never returned.

PROLOGUE

Golconda Diamond Mines, India ~ 1650

It was not going to be a good day. It had started badly and but for the intervention of the gods it would end badly.

Ramesh was not a happy man as he made his way towards the mine through narrow streets of impoverished mud and brick dwellings disturbing dust and dirt as he went.

The first rays of dawn were already showing themselves on the horizon to a cloudless sky. It was going to be hot again, and dry and dusty like every day before and every day after.

A dozing dog wisely leapt out of the way at the sight of Ramesh approaching through the half light, somehow sensing his mood and not wanting a kick in the ribs, yet growled in defiance as he passed. But it was wasted on Ramesh, his mind was elsewhere reeling from the news he had just received.

Most men would have been pleased to learn that they were soon to become a father, but not Ramesh. At the age of twenty when he became a father for the first time he had been ecstatic. The second time he was delighted. The third, pleased. This time however he was not pleased. The meagre wage he earned at the mine was not enough to support one child, let alone four, and his wife, the beautiful Renuka. How hard she toiled and sweated in the fields all day and then she had to cook and care for the family. It was not fair. Even though she never complained, accepting life as it came, he could not help but notice the strain on her face, that face once so beautiful and soft and young. It was not fair. May the gods be good to them, this child would have to be the last. There must be no more. There must be no more!

As Ramesh neared the open alluvial mines on the banks of the lower reaches of the Godāvari river, so the noise of people already hard at work grew louder. Today would be no different from any other and he knew well enough the sight that would greet his eyes over the brow of the embankment. It would be the same sight that met him every morning and had ever since he was a young boy. Thousands of men, women and children slaving away trying to earn enough money to survive the day to enable them to return and do the same the following day.

When the mines along the river banks in this part of Southern India were in full production, up to 60,000 wretched souls could be seen fighting against the searing heat and humidity so bad, the sweat was sucked out of you and ran into your eyes so fast you could hardly see. Then there were the clouds of dust to contend with which were cursed by some, but blessed by others, offering at least some protection against the hoards of ferocious biting insects. Life came cheap.

Ramesh was joined by others making their way down to the river bank in the fast approaching light. Nobody spoke, there was no point. The person you worked alongside all day could well be dead the next. The stagnant water and filthy mud they had to stand in infected even the slightest cut overnight sending a person mad before the final blessed release of death. And if disease did not get you, the snakes would.

The men chipped out the rock whilst the women and children dragged it down to the river for crushing, washing and sorting and all for the sake of those tiny little crystal-like pebbles so the rich could make themselves look beautiful. What a waste of a life, and today would be just another day in a wasted life, but at least the family were working in the fields well away from this contaminated pit of death.

Nodding to the foreman who pointed to a south facing bank, without a word Ramesh collected his tools and made his way over to the area where he would spend the next twelve hours.

It was mid-morning and the sun was high before he stopped for a break and took a sip from the tin cup dangling by the water barrel, careful to check first that there was nothing swimming in it.

Wiping perspiration from his face with a neck scarf, he repositioned it over his nose and mouth tying it firmly in place affording him at least some protection from the suffocating rock dust. Forcing himself to forget his problems he continued to chip away at a stubborn lump of rock he had been trying to shift for most of the morning. After what felt like an eternity in that timeless hell, the ball of rock finally came loose and fell to the ground splitting open, capturing the sunlight as it landed between his feet. Suddenly, the whole river bank was flooded with brilliance as if from not one, but a thousand suns.

Ramesh's heart stopped and he gasped as he gazed down at a diamond the size of an orange lying on the ground amongst the rubble.

The huge stone was presented to the Mogul himself, Shah Jahan, Prince of India, whilst Ramesh was rewarded with a day's extra pay.

Encyclopaedia Britannica

'The Great Mogul diamond: the largest diamond ever found in India. It was discovered as a 787 carat rough stone in the Golconda mines in 1650 and subsequently was cut by the Venetian lapidary, Hortentio Borgis. The French jewel trader Jean-Baptiste Tavernier described it in 1665 as a high-crowned rose cut stone with a flaw at the bottom and a small speck within. Its present location is unknown…'

The following is based on real events

CHAPTER ONE

It has been said that after God perfected his skill of creation, he made Norway to sit atop the world like a crown of unsurpassed magnificence.

A sentiment one particular young German tourist on holiday during the long, hot summer of 1923 would certainly not have questioned. Unassuming and unattached, every day the man in his mid twenties could be seen in either the old Viking city of Bergen or more usually out on one of the seven surrounding mountains basking in the beauty of nature, giddy with heady perfumes of pine forests, wild flowers and newly mown hay in high summer pastures, every twist and turn of the mountain trail guiding him to panoramas of fjord, mountain and sky the like of which he had never seen or imagined.

One particular morning the man, Claus Muller, took coffee in one of the many waterfront cafés near the open fish market where he was waited on by a pretty young waitress who had noticed the handsome stranger the moment he arrived, and gave him a smile as she took his order. The following morning he called there again, and for a third time the morning after, when he asked the young waitress to join him. The café was quiet so she agreed, and eventually the young man plucked up enough courage to ask her when her next day off was, as he would greatly appreciate it if she would act as his guide to the delightful city.

The girl, Solveig, told him she was owed a few days leave and forty-eight hours later, the couple could be seen out together enjoying all that Bergen had to offer. They walked together, they talked together. They ate ice-cream and laughed together, and as the days went on they went to the cinema and museums together. They went rambling in the hills and swimming in the chilly waters of the fjord together and eventually he told her how she had captured his heart, filling his every thought, and they kissed and talked of love as they lay in the sunshine under high, dream-like clouds. The pretty waitress had never known such happiness.

But one morning he did not show up at the waterfront café, nor the next day or the day after that. Solveig called at his lodgings only to learn that he had left, leaving no forwarding address. Every day she would pray for a letter, a word, something. But she never heard from him again. She was broken-hearted. There was no way she could have known that the man was a liar and a cheat and had just been using her for his own amusement.

Some weeks had to pass before the girl knew for sure that she was pregnant and wanting to avoid questions and scandal, the pretty young ex-waitress bought herself a cheap wedding ring and hid away in the isolated village of Vadheim, 120 km north-east of Bergen where no-one knew her, with the story that her husband had been killed in an accident.

Eventually she gave birth to a daughter whom she called Ingrid.

*

August 1st 1934: The death of President Hindenburg, and the succession of Adolf Hitler as Führer and Supreme Commander of all the Germans.

*

The night air, heavy with frost, was already leaving its glistening print indiscriminately on nature and humanity's creations alike. All was still except for the occasional leaf of autumn drifting to earth, surrendering forever its fragile right to life.

Though hundreds of S.S. Novices were standing rank upon rank in front of the shrine to fallen Nazis at Munich's Feldherrnhalle, once the clock had struck, not a sound was to be heard, save the occasional spit from one of the many flaming torches illuminating the area with a flickering, menacing glow.

Scarlet banners bedecked with the Nazi emblem hung respectfully still from every available location and from church bells nearby came deep, reverberating, tones which tolled ominously throughout the swearing-in ceremony.

From those most perfect models of pure Aryan humanity who had undergone the most stringent selection and training imaginable, came breaths which rose steam-like into the cold night air. From uniforms, brass, silver and chrome glistened in the torchlight; leather gleamed.

Suddenly, striding onto the portico clutching black leather gloves, advanced Adolf Hitler. His figure contrasted magnificently against the black and scarlet display as he stood between the two impressive stone lions on the steps of the Feldherrnhalle building.

An electric thrill of excitement charged through those who stood rigid to attention before him, as their blood simultaneously ran cold with a mixture of admiration, reverence and fear. This was what they wanted. This was what they believed in. This was the Fatherland at its very best.

The ceremony began.

Later, walking slowly and chatting with staff as he returned to his waiting limousine, Hitler paused briefly by a low wall and fingered the frost as it shimmered in the loom of the torches.

"A cold night, Mein Führer," commented one of his entourage.

"Like little diamonds," he said, "precious little diamonds." Walking on he muttered pensively. "Very precious diamonds."

*

September 30th 1938: British Prime Minister, Neville Chamberlain was photographed standing beside the aeroplane which had just brought him from Europe with a letter promising peace.

The following morning's newspapers pictured the P.M. holding the letter in a manner suggesting he knew it was as worthless as the breeze trying to snatch it from his grasp.

*

April 27th 1939: British men between the ages of twenty and twenty one ordered to report for induction into the military.

*

It was also the day on which Douglas Reid celebrated his twenty-fifth birthday. He had taken a few days off from the British Museum where he was employed in the Department of Geology and had returned to the family home on the outskirts of Guildford, Surrey. The view over the North Downs made a welcome change from his tiny Bayswater flat and his mother's cooking was a joy; but the primary reason for his homecoming was yet to be revealed.

Born to a Norwegian mother and English father, as an only child Douglas was the single most important item in his parents' life. He was the type of son any prospective mother-in-law would have been delighted to receive had an unattached daughter brought him home. Tall like his father, good looking though not extravagantly so, with an open honest face, wavy fair hair and blue eyes, characteristic of his Scandinavian lineage.

Douglas Edward Reid had left school at eighteen to pursue his fascination with rocks by reading geology at Exeter University, which was also where a previously dormant love of sport was awakened. When he wasn't in the laboratory or out hunting for fossils, free time would find him on the rugby field or at the swimming pool or even in the boxing ring, the side effect of which was to make him highly sought after by the opposite sex. Yet it was not until after he had gained a first and started working in London that he met the real love of his life, Dr Jill Johnson. A year older than himself Jill had recently qualified and was in her first year as a junior doctor at St Bartholomew's Hospital in London's Smithfield. As soon as she had, as she put it, at least something in the bank, they planned to marry.

Yet Jill was not the only women in Douglas's life who was important to him. The other woman was his mother, Hanna, which made the reason he had come home all the more difficult.

Hanna was born in a small fishing village on the west coast of Norway but had lived and worked in Oslo where she met her husband Edward who was on a business trip for a UK-based paper company. They were married in 1913 whilst crossing the North Sea, by the Captain of the Newcastle – Bergen ferry, at the exact point mid-way between England and Norway. This, the Captain explained, showed bias to neither bride nor groom.

With no immediate family except for a self-sufficient younger sister, Solveig, there had been no constraints tying Hanna to Norway and once the goodbyes were said and the tears shed, Hanna willingly started a new life setting up home in southern England.

Fortunately for the newly-weds when war was declared in August the following year, Edward was already heavily involved with industrial supplies classified as a 'reserved occupation' and was never called to arms. A fact he always bore with a sense of guilt.

Douglas was born in the first year of the Great War, yet during the ensuing years, every now and again, a sadness would come over Hanna which would manifest itself periodically for no reason other than a particular sound or smell that triggered thoughts of home and the call of the fjords, the scent of wild heather and the crunch of freshly fallen snow underfoot. The usual remedy was the purchase of a new dress or to occupy herself with decorating or housework, yet her motherly intuition told her this time that her son had not returned home solely to celebrate his birthday. Somehow she knew it would take far more than housework to deal with whatever was to follow.

As if to confirm his mother's suspicions, on the evening before Douglas was due back in London, he announced, with ill disguised trepidation, that he had joined the army to train as a junior officer.

His mother had wept as he knew she would. His father had said it would all be over in a few months anyway once the little German upstart had been shown what's what and he wished he had been young enough to join up with him. Douglas had replied that it would have been good to have him along, but both men knew that was not true.

*

The following morning Douglas returned to London, to be met by more tears when Jill learnt of his plans.

"Why didn't you tell me before?"

"I wanted to be sure they'd have me first and I've only just heard."

"You don't have to go. It's not as if they desperately need you."

"Haven't you seen the news? Someone's got to stop this madman. Why not people like me?"

"People like you?!"

"Yes, people like me. We were discussing it at work, and if the balloon does go up it's much better to get in on the ground floor now than wait and be called up as cannon fodder later."

"So you discuss it with your friends, but not your future wife?"

"I didn't want to upset you unnecessarily."

"Well, you have … and besides …"

"Besides what?"

"If you had to join something, you should have joined the Navy."

"Why? Why the Navy?" Puzzled, he looked at her beside him on the settee. She had kicked her shoes off and curled her legs up making her appear vulnerable and fragile, which he knew she was anything but. "Because," she continued trying to mask a grin with a pout, "because navy blue would suit you better than khaki."

It was a long time before he kissed her again the way he did then, and it annoyed him that all he had to remind himself of what she looked like was a small photograph taken on the beach at Brighton, which he taped inside his locker at Sandhurst. She had written across it 'All my love now and forever. J.J. xx.'

For the next few months those long dark wavy curls and deep chestnut eyes were strictly reserved for dreams.

*

September 1st 1939: Germany invaded Poland.
September 3rd 1939: 11 a.m. Great Britain declared war on Germany.

*

After Poland had fallen there followed a period of uneasy quiet, the 'phoney war'.

For Douglas, having already appeared before the War Office Selection Board and been selected for officer training, the months after his birthday were spent at Sandhurst 161 Infantry Officer Cadet Training Unit (RMC). With war like a threatening black cloud building over the horizon, the customary two year training had been greatly condensed and in what felt like a very short space of time he passed out as a Second Lieutenant, assigned to The Suffolk Regiment and stationed in Gibraltar Barracks, Bury St. Edmunds.

No sooner had he arrived than orders were received that the 'Suffolks' were to ship out during the first week of October as part of the British Expeditionary Force, (B.E.F.) in a bid to stop Hitler's rapid advance across Europe. With only a twenty four hour pass Douglas had hoped for a romantic evening with J.J., but his wishes were thwarted as she was on night duty until 8 a.m. and his train left Waterloo for the muster point in Axminster at 08.45.

*

In the corner of the main entrance hall of Bart's Hospital their goodbyes were painful to watch. The duty commissionaire turned away, it was becoming an all too familiar sight. A boy, a girl, one of them in uniform ready to leave. The tears, the painful expressions, the urgent passionate kisses. God alone knowing if or when they would ever meet again.

'This Hitler's got a lot to answer for', he thought to himself as he watched the lad hurrying away continually turning and waving, and the girl in her white coat with a handkerchief, one minute dabbing her tear-swollen eyes, the next, extending it at arm's length in a final farewell.

She stood on the steps looking after him for a moment even though he was out of sight when the man spoke kindly to her.

"Don't worry Miss, he'll be alright."

She looked up at him with a face full of sorrow. "We're going to get married when this is all over."

"Well there we are then. Something nice to look forward to."

*

The B.E.F. numbered an impressive ten divisions yet once in place, there was little to do but wait for Hitler to make a move. When he did however, they proved to be hopelessly outnumbered and out-gunned.

*

April 9th 1940: Germany invaded Norway.

*

Then suddenly, during late spring, lightening struck and caught most of a supposedly prepared Europe with its trousers down. The battle hardened Germans were unstoppable.

*

May 10th 1940: Chamberlin resigned and Winston Churchill became P.M.

*

From their position on the Belgian-French border, the British moved up quickly only to be cut off from behind by rapid Panzer movements smashing through the forests of Ardennes racing for the coast of Northern France.

Suddenly there were Germans to the North, South and East, whilst to the West there was only the sea.

Operation Dynamo swung into action rescuing the ensnared British Army when almost 350,000 British, French and Belgian troops were plucked from the beaches of Dunkirk by an armada of ships and boats. A grateful nation witnessed a miracle and an army had been saved.

Douglas was one of the lucky ones. At the earliest opportunity he put a telephone call through to Bart's Hospital and another to Guildford. That night many a tear of thankfulness and joy was shed on his behalf.

*

June 9th 1940: Norway's High Command ordered the army to stop fighting at midnight, 'It is impossible to continue in this country against a superior power as formidable as Germany …'

*

Once the remnants of the splintered British Army had reassembled and a state that bore some resemblance of organization had been achieved, Douglas was granted a four day pass and returned to his flat in Bayswater, where for three days he enjoyed the therapeutic delights of his own and very personal physician. Before returning to camp, the final day was spent in Guildford with his parents, when his father proudly told him that he had volunteered for the Local Defence Volunteers (later to be known as the Home Guard).

*

June 14th 1940: German troops march into Paris.
June 21st 1940: France surrendered.

*

During the summer and autumn of 1940 not only did the British Army have to lick its wounds after so ignominious a defeat, but as quickly as possible rebuild, retrain and rearm before it could once again assert itself as a successful fighting force. Overhead, in the skies above Southern England, the Battle of Britain was raging.

Douglas Reid was in camp in Suffolk when, on the evening of 1st September, he was told to report to the Officers' Mess where a Captain Silverthorn was waiting to see him.

The Mess was more stuffy and crowded than usual. It was a warm evening and even though the windows were wide open, thick black-out curtains restricted sufficient air flow. Already tobacco smoke was building up and would soon be as thick as a London smog in the depths of winter.

It was not one of Douglas's favourite places yet it helped to go there sometimes and let off steam with his contemporaries.

He had only been there a handful of minutes when he was approached by an officer he did not recognize.

"Ah! Lieutenant Reid I presume." The cultured voice belonged to a tall, gangly man with thin wispy hair and bony features with deep set, dark intelligent eyes. He was not a lot older than Douglas and the badge on his arm announced he was with the I.S.R.B. Neither men saluted as neither were wearing a cap.

"Yes, Sir," said Douglas, unable to conceal his surprise.

Raucous laughter from the general direction of the bar eased the moment. "Cheerful lot aren't they? Silverthorn," said the officer raising his voice. "Alexander Silverthorn." He smiled and held out his hand. "Bit of a mouthful isn't it? This is my first visit but I recognized you at once from your photograph."

"Oh right. Yes I see."

"Good to meet you old boy and right away I can see you're wondering what this is all about. Tell you what," said Silverthorn, "I've reserved a table in the private room over there in the corner," pointing to an unmarked door to the right of the bar Douglas hadn't noticed before. "You go and set yourself up in there and I'll get the lubricants." Silverthorn started to push his way through the throng calling back. "What'll it be?"

"A pint, thank you Sir."

"Two of the best, coming up."

Douglas made his way into the side room which was no more than ten feet square, stuffy and window-less with the only light from a single bulb suspended from the ceiling. The only furniture was a small round table and two upright chairs. The Captain's cap was already occupying one and Douglas sat down on the other and waited.

A few minutes passed and the Captain entered with a tray of drinks, pushing the door closed with his foot.

"Talk about war, it's a battle just to get served! Afraid I've spilt some, but never mind we can soon get some more." Moving his cap he shuffled his chair round until it was exactly opposite Douglas and sat down. "Don't look so worried Lieutenant, you've done nothing wrong and there's nothing to worry about. All will be revealed in good time as they say. Now drink up, it's good for you. Cheers, your very good health."

"Thank you Sir, cheers."

He took out a silver cigarette case and after extracting a cigarette himself offered it to Douglas.

"Thank you Sir," said Douglas, adding "so what brings you to Suffolk?"

"Ah that's what I like. Cut straight to the bone." Silverthorn exhaled a long column of blue-grey smoke watching as it spiralled lazily towards the ceiling. "Well, I could say I wanted an excuse to escape the London blitz and enjoy some sunshine and fresh country air. But, nice thought though it is, it wouldn't be the truth." He lowered his voice, and folding his arms leaned forward on the table focusing on the young officer before him. "The real reason I have come all this way is to meet you."

"I'm intrigued."

"Tell me Lieutenant, how was your Dunkirk?"

Douglas had not expected the question and immediately resented it.

"How was my Dunkirk?!" he repeated, surprised that he should suddenly feel annoyed. The question had sounded so flippant. "Were you there Sir?" he asked.

The man shook his head. "No I wasn't," he said, and took a long, well rehearsed draw of his beer.

"Well, I'll tell you then. It's something I never want to live through again I don't mind telling you. It was bad, really bad. In fact looking back now, it was Hell with a capital H!"

"Yes, I'm sure it was," said Silverthorn, sensing the other man's emotions. "Thank God you made it home." The Captain suddenly became serious. "So what is your next move? What are your orders now?"

Douglas hesitated. "I'm not sure I should be ... "

"It's alright, I have full security clearance. But you're right of course, not to be talking willy-nilly to strangers. I'm sure though, that you're eager to see action again, and right some wrongs, aren't you?"

"I should jolly well say so. I lost some good friends over there – we'd been through a lot together. Some very good friends."

"Yes I'm sure you did."

"We left thousands behind. Did you know that Sir?"

"Yes of course. Terrible."

"Poor buggers."

"Indeed … terrible." He waited to see if Douglas needed to add anything further but he just gazed into his half empty glass. "Well now, Lieutenant, I must say you have been remarkably patient so it's time I came clean and told you what this is all about." He glanced behind making sure the door was closed and then looked Douglas directly in the eye. "I am what you might call a scout, and the people I work for …"

"And who is that Sir?"

"We'll come to that in a moment Lieutenant. The people I work for are looking for men like yourself who have been to hell and back, and now want a chance to even the score – make life hell for the Krauts. We don't usually approach people directly like this but I've come all this way today because we're particularly interested in you. I hear you're good with languages. One of our team reports your file has you down as being fluent in German and Norwegian. Is that correct?"

"It is, Sir."

"Tell me how that is?"

"My mother Sir, she's Norwegian. Before she married and came to this country she was a translator for the Norwegian Government. We used to play a game when I was young and speak a different language each day. My poor father used to get very annoyed as he only speaks a smattering of Norwegian but Mother kept it up. She said it would prove useful one day."

"She's been proved right, and I'm certain she would agree that it's wicked to let all that hard work go to waste."

"Do you want me to do translation work?" he asked, not relishing the thought. "I'm afraid my written work isn't as good as my conversation."

"No, we don't. His Majesty's government has ample translators I'm sure. This is far more serious. What my organisation wants is people who are willing to get involved with cloak and dagger work." He paused to emphasize his words. "You could say we're the British dirty tricks department. We have a mandate direct from Downing Street to 'set Europe ablaze'."

Douglas looked surprised.

"I know it's not much to go on but I'm afraid that's all I'm at liberty to say for now, but you're a clever chap, you don't need me to spell it out for you, do you?"

"No, of course not. Overseas work then Sir?"

"Almost exclusively."

"So what does I.S.R.B. stand for, I've not heard of them before?"

"The Inter-Services Research Bureau. You wouldn't have heard of us, it's a cover name."

"But exactly who are they?"

"Primarily, we're made up of all branches of Secret Intelligence Services and Military Intelligence, but we include everyone who's relevant; War Office, Home Office, Foreign Office, et cetera, et cetera, all working together."

"I'm impressed."

"You should be."

"Real cloak and dagger."

"War is a very real and a very serious business Lieutenant as you have already discovered. But we only take volunteers, mind you. No-one is press-ganged. No-one will force you to do anything you don't want to do. And the training of course is the best, the very best there is."

"What I'm going to do, is to leave you my telephone number Reid, and I want you to think things over for a few days. Then, if you would like to know more, we can meet again and go into a lot more detail before you make any commitment. You can either stay here with this lot outside doing what you're told, when you're told, or you can be trained to stand on your own two feet and act on your own initiative and really make a significant contribution to the war effort. The choice is yours. I say again though, you are under no pressure, but remember this. The evil that's knocking at our door plays dirty, very dirty, so it's time we too took the gloves off and gave Jerry a taste of his own medicine, otherwise this war will run on for years."

"Well Sir, what can I say? I'm flattered that you should come here specifically to see me … "

"It isn't something we usually do."

" … but frankly Sir, if I'm honest, it's not me. I'm not cut out for cloak and dagger work. What do I know about that sort of thing? I'm a geologist for goodness sake."

"I know you are. And I used to work for Martin's Bank, but we're all fighting for the same thing. The British way of life and liberty. Remember that. Think it over for a few days, sleep on it. But Hitler's got to be stopped one way or another by fair means or foul. My task this evening, is to introduce myself and to plant a seed, something for you to think about."

"You've certainly done that alright."

The Captain pencilled down a London Welbeck telephone number on the back of a beer mat. "Can you remember that?"

"Got it."

"Good." The Captain slipped the mat in his pocket. "Just one thing. If for any reason you ever received a letter from me, it won't be from me. We don't send letters."

"I understand."

"And another thing," the Captain paused and drained his glass. "No-one must know about our meeting, no-one. Not your mother, father, Jill Johnson, no-one. Is that perfectly understood? It's for their safety as well as yours and ours."

"Yes Sir," he said, not knowing quite how to react to such an invasion of privacy. "You certainly know all about me don't you?"

"Oh yes, all about you. And we like what we see. You're just the sort of chap we're looking for to join our merry little band." He stood up sharply, the meeting over, and stubbed out his cigarette, collecting his cap. "It was nice to meet you Lieutenant," and they shook hands for the second time. "I hope we meet again soon. Think it over, only volunteers remember."

"Goodbye Sir."

"Goodbye Lieutenant, and have a story ready for your friends outside if anyone asks who I am. Tell them anything but the truth. You know what they say, don't you? Be like Dad; keep Mum."

"You can rely on me Sir."

"Yes I'm sure I can. Oh and keep up the sport it's very good for you. Keeping fit's very important. I was watching you on the football field this afternoon."

"We won."

"May you always be on the winning side Lieutenant. I'll go out first, you follow in a few minutes. Goodbye." So saying, Captain Silverthorn turned and left, closing the door behind him and made his way through the crowded Mess, out into the darkness leaving Douglas with an empty glass, his thoughts and the cheerless prospect of a sleepless night.

*

The early evening summer sun was already casting long shadows through the forests of Southern Bavaria as the black staff car negotiated the winding mountain roads around Berchtesgaden, Obersalzberg, a mountain retreat area in the Bavarian Alps. The car gently glided to a halt at the Guard House blocking the access road at the entrance to The Berghof. Through the car window the passenger got his first glimpse of the typically Bavarian painted render and stone L-shaped house, made famous on the news reels, with window boxes festooned with deep red geraniums, and surrounded by trees and greenery, and manicured sloping lawns.

S.S. guards were in abundance and though bathed in gentle sunlight, their intimidating presence could not stop the occupant of the car from feeling uncomfortable.

An officer of the S.S. in the familiar black uniform with the name of Adolf Hitler woven into his left cuff as proof that he was part of Hitler's elite personal body guard, S.S. Begleitkammando, looked through the car's open window at the driver and his single passenger. Behind him a guard stood armed with a machine gun and on the opposite side, another guard moved forward. They were taking no chances.

"Your papers. Please." The officer made a lengthy and exaggerated show of examining the passenger's paperwork, making sure it corresponded exactly with his own information.

"Good afternoon Major," he said eventually. "Welcome to the Berghof." He smiled but his pallid blue eyes remained cold. "Your first visit I think?"

"Yes, thank you Untersturmführer."

Returning the papers, the officer told the driver where to park the car once through the gate, and the Major that he would be met directly.

"One moment!" The way his command startled the visitors amused him. "Your weapon Major. No-one enters the house armed. It will be returned when you leave."

The Major unclipped his Luger and passed it through the open window. "And your briefcase Major. Please open it."

Obligingly, the Major held it so the contents were clearly visible.

"Danke," said the officer, and stepped back smartly. "Heil Hitler!"

"Heil Hitler," repeated the Major. The gate opened.

*

Major Walter Baum stepped down from the car and took a deep breath. How clean and fresh the air was here near the Austrian border, very different from that in the city and it helped to clear his head. It had been a long, hot, drive and he was thankful at last to be able to stretch his legs.

A Scharfüher came towards him, saluted and asked if he'd like to freshen himself before the meeting. Making certain he still had his briefcase, Baum followed the Sergeant up the steep flight of steps, turning right through a series of stone arches at the top, and into the residence of the leader of all the Germans, which Hitler had purchased in 1933 with funds from the sale of his political manifesto 'Mein Kampf'.

They passed through the Great Room, decorated with impressive works of art, where a group of uniformed officers were seated in front of a large black marble fireplace around a low table discussing the map spread out before them. They paid Baum no attention as the Scharfüher lead him directly through into a hallway and indicated the washroom.

Left alone, he was able to collect his thoughts, yet as he looked at his reflection in the wall mirror he knew he looked as tired as he felt. He had not been sleeping well of late and perhaps that was why there were more lines on his face than there used to be. His hair had turned a streaky grey and now he had eyebrows to match and he knew he looked more than his fifty-five years. But he was proud of his nose. He considered it almost Roman, aristocratic.

He felt nervous, much more so than at their first meeting but was determined not to reveal the fact to the great man. He used the toilet, combed his hair and smoothed his uniform, deciding to tuck the briefcase under his arm, along with his cap, in the belief it made him appear more business like. He knew that on Hitler's special instructions his confidential presentation would not be reviewed by the Führer's staff as were most documents entering the house.

With one final glance in the mirror he left the washroom and was lead upstairs through to a large, well furnished room, boasting a number of fine oil paintings and opening directly out onto an extensive terrace with magnificent views over the surrounding mountains, hills and forests all in a hundred gentle shades of green.

Adolf Hitler was sitting enjoying the evening sunshine on a low perimeter wall which ran on three sides of a rectangle around the edge of the terrace. On the other side of the wall the ground fell steeply away into the valley below. He was wearing a brown jacket and dark trousers with a red and black swastika arm band and was rolling a ball along the paving stones for the amusement of a German Shepherd dog.

As the Major walked out into the sunshine he was announced by a small man in a white staff jacket, who then discretely withdrew.

"Ah, Major Baum. How nice to see you again."

Baum gave the salute of his career. "Heil Hitler!"

Hitler half raised his arm in response but then much to Baum's surprise walked over to him and warmly shook his hand.

"How are you? Do come and sit down."

"It's an honour to be with you again Mein Führer," said Baum. "Thank you Sir, I am quite well. What a beautiful situation you enjoy here."

"It's inspiring isn't it?"

"Yes, inspiring."

"Come and sit down and we'll talk."

Baum respectfully waited until Adolf Hitler was seated before seating himself in one of the comfortable garden chairs beside a white painted wooden table under a sun umbrella. As the dog came and joined them, stretching out at the Führer's feet, Baum placed his cap on the table and removed the contents of his briefcase ready for the dialogue to begin.

"So, Major," Hitler opened congenially "how are you getting along with the task I set you?"

"I am delighted to report, Mein Führer, that I have been successful in finding the right man for the job."

"Let us hope you are right. Who is it?"

"Claus Muller. Major Claus Muller." He paused, expecting a response of recognition but there was none.

"What do we know about him?"

The Major focused on his notes and, clearing his throat, began reading. "He's forty-one years of age, formally of the Seventh Panzer Division where he rose rapidly through the ranks, distinguished himself in the battle for France for which he was promoted and awarded the Iron Cross, first class. It was there that he also lost an eye and received the Wound Medal.

"A widower for the past five years, his wife died of tuberculosis in 1935 leaving him to bring up two children; a son now in the army, and a daughter, nineteen, who until recently was a member of the Union of German Girls."

"And what of his professional qualifications?"

The Major continued reading. "He studied at Universities in Berlin and Vienna and before enlisting into the army, was employed at the University in Berlin in the department of archaeology and antiquities, where he specialized in precious metals and jewellery. He has been involved in digs in Egypt and India, and led an expedition himself to Greece. He has also written a number of papers. He is a member of the Deutsche Gemmologische Gesellschaft. Even before his accident, he was showing a considerable flair for intelligence work, and subsequently it was decided to transfer him into the Abwehr where his input has been of some significance. I should add there is a note in his file that states he isn't particularly social. He doesn't readily make friends."

"Nothing wrong with that."

"But he is loyal and daring, and respected by his comrades."

"Sounds like he's our man."

"By coincidence, Mein Führer …"

"Yes."

" A short while ago he was transferred to your staff at headquarters in Berlin."

"That is a coincidence. What a shame you spent so much time looking for the right man when all the time we were almost falling over him."

The Major went to speak, but the Führer continued. "Is he the one with the eye patch?"

"That is the one."

"Yes, I thought so, I've seen him about. That eye patch makes him look quite menacing."

The Major grinned respectfully.

"So do you think he will find what we're looking for?"

"I believe so Mein Führer, he's certainly well qualified."

"I hope so Major. I do hope so. As you know I have had this in mind for some time. The British have their beloved Crown Jewels. The Romanoff's had jewels beyond … beyond dreams and as Germany reaches its zenith, now is the time when the people of the Third Reich deserve to have something they can look to with pride, a symbol they can focus on for the exciting days ahead.

"This is the time when I want the purest race of people on earth to have as their own, the finest and largest diamond the world has ever known. They deserve it. It will be a triumph," his voice had started to rise. "I am the people's Messiah and this diamond will be a new star lighting the path forward to greater and greater accomplishments. With pride, the people will christen it 'Light of the Reich'. It will be a triumph. It will mark a new dawn. It will be a sign to wise men of the world that the brightness of the Fatherland is unquenchable. It is to be the centre piece of my dream!"

He paused, and leaning forward continued almost in a whisper. "This is to remain our little secret you understand. I want to surprise the people. They will love me all the more. And be sure to tell this Muller I expect results. As you know Major, failure is not a word that appears in my vocabulary. Be sure not to come back to me in a few months time with your tail between your legs and a list of excuses an arm long, complaining that you cannot find it. I am holding you and Muller personally responsible for the success of this mission. Do I make myself perfectly clear?"

"Crystal clear, Mein Führer."

Hitler suddenly tossed his head back and let out a short sharp laugh. "Ha! You mean diamond clear Major. You should have said clear as a diamond. Ha!"

A few minutes later as Baum left the house and made his way down the steps to the waiting car, he wiped a handkerchief across his brow and murmured to himself, "God help us all."

*

In the days after Captain Silverthorn's visit, Douglas found himself in a paradoxical no-man's land. Wanting to do the right thing, yet not knowing which way to turn. His position was made all the more difficult as he could share his predicament with no-one.

He decided to give it a week before telephoning London with a final decision, inwardly knowing all along his answer would be 'No'.

*

September 7th 1940: A raid of 1,000 enemy bombers over London sets the capital ablaze.

*

As soon as Douglas heard the news on the wireless, he immediately tried putting a call through to Bart's Hospital, but the line was dead. It was not until the 9th of September having managed eventually to contact a friend of Jill's, did he learn that she had worked a double shift the night prior to the raid as the hospital was frantically busy. Being exhausted to the point of collapse she had returned to the digs she shared with three other girls near the hospital and must have slept through the air-raid warnings. The house had received a direct hit and Jill had been killed outright as she slept.

*

Lifting the receiver, Douglas dialled the number from memory. How many times had he stood like this and waited for her soft voice on the other end? 'Duggie I knew it was you, I was just thinking about you.'

The phone continued ringing. Her perfume filled his head, the smell of her hair.

"Yes." The voice was short, abrupt.

"I need to speak to Captain Silverthorn. Will you put me through?"

"Who is that?"

"Douglas Reid."

"Why Lieutenant Reid," the tone changed to what Douglas remembered. "Silverthorn here. Good to hear from you old boy."

"The offer you made me the other evening, Sir …"

"Yes."

"I'd like to take you up on it. As soon as possible."

CHAPTER TWO

"Will you join me in a little schnapps?"

"That would be most agreeable." The two men watched as equal measures were poured into crystal glasses by the steward.

"Leave us now." Major Baum spoke as one used to giving orders and the steward respectfully withdrew, closing the tall mahogany door silently behind him, leaving the two military men alone.

"What is the toast?" asked the Major's guest.

"Of course. Our dear and glorious leader." They raised their glasses simultaneously.

"Heil Hitler!" And, following a time honoured tradition, drained the contents of the glasses in one movement and then zealously hurled them into the fireplace, sending up a shower of tiny crystal splinters. There was no fire in the grate in mid-September; there would be time enough for log fires when winter came to this part of the Loire Valley in Central France.

"This is a beautiful building Major. I'm very jealous."

"Why so?"

"Whatever is it that you do that affords you such lavish surroundings? By comparison my office is quite poverty-stricken."

The two men moved away from the elaborately carved marble fireplace and sat each side of an antique desk littered with papers, as well as a large bronze of a lion rampant, holding a lamp in its claws, casting a circular pool of light onto the green and gilded leather top.

The Major offered his guest a cigarette from an engraved silver box and taking one himself, struck a match and held it steady. "American," he said "finest Virginia."

The surrounding walls were covered from floor to ceiling with row upon row of books, many antique and leather bound, the pale light highlighting a gilt binding here and there like the wink of an eye staring down at the men who were themselves, print on a new page of history.

Behind the desk, a small balcony could be seen in the twilight through a pair of French doors over-seeing immaculately tailored lawns and hedges, shrubs and gurgling fountains. The air hung heavy with opulence.

"Yes, it's difficult to remember sometimes that this château, and many more just like it throughout France, is now part of the Third Reich and though I may refer to it as 'home' sometimes, it is not, of course. I have to continually remind myself that my real home is far away in Frankfurt."

"Life in the lap of luxury, all be it temporarily, is agreeable though surely?"

"Indeed it is. I could so very easily get used to all of this but, as you say, it's only temporary and yet it's all for a very good cause. Yes, I will tell you what it is I do because I am permitted now to take you into my confidence. But I must also tell you, warn you, that what you are about to hear is absolutely secret. Top secret."

"I quite understand."

"I do hope so. There are not many officers, if any, of my rank who can say they answer to no-one but the Führer himself, at least in relation to what I am about to share with you. Yet that is my unique position. My orders come from him alone and any breach of that trust will have very, very serious consequences."

"Of course."

He lightly tapped ash from his cigarette before continuing thoughtfully. "The Führer, as you may or may not know, is an avid collector of art. Treasures of every form imaginable. He is also a very far-sighted man and back in the early summer of 'thirty-nine his vision of a new Europe was already firmly in position. He realized then that all the vast treasures of Europe were about to fall into his lap and he considered it his duty, his calling, shall we say, to rescue them. To protect them.

"You are naturally aware that the Führer is Austrian, born in Linz in Upper Austria, and he has a vision to make Linz a city of international renown. It should, he feels, be the name on everyone's lips and what better way to accomplish that than to make Linz the centre of art and culture for the new western world on a scale that would exceed Vienna or Paris or even Rome? He can foresee a time when art and the name of Linz will be spoken of in the same breath and with equal admiration and respect. I believe it to be his way of honouring Linz for what it has done for him. I can tell you that I had the honour of accompanying him on a visit to Linz in 'thirty-eight and he was treated like a god! Already his vision is on the way to becoming a fantastic reality.

"However, to build a new city is difficult enough, but to construct a city of beauty and joy to the honour of art and culture is an undertaking of monumental proportions. The building of galleries and museums, theatres, wide boulevards and parks. The mind boggles. The logistics are frightening. And yet on the 26th June last year an order was given from the Berghof. I have a copy here to show you. Here we are," he resumed. "From the Führer. Do read it, please." And passed it across the desk.

Baum's guest read aloud.

> " I commission Dr Hans Posse, Director of the Dresden Art Gallery, to build up the new art museums for Linz.
> All party and state services are ordered to assist Dr Posse in fulfilment of his mission.
> Signed. Adolf Hitler."

The man looked up. "This is remarkable. I knew nothing of this," he said handing the order back "but nothing surprises me in these times."

"You were not involved so why ever should you know? You see the Führer had found the right man for the job. Dr Posse is a very clever man and on that day in June the Sonderauftrag Linz [*Linz Special Mission*]. was born. It is without doubt the greatest art rescue mission the world has ever known."

"And do you really believe this will happen?"

"I have to believe it! But what I believe is of no importance. What matters is what the Führer believes. And whatever the Führer believes, the people will also believe, and with the people behind him anything is possible."

"That I do believe."

"Strangely enough, though the Führer is an avid collector, he is not, and perhaps I should choose my words carefully, he is not a lover. He's a hoarder. Do you know what I mean?"

"I think so."

"Whereas Reichsmarschal Göring, for example, is quite the opposite. He is a genuine art lover with an insatiable passion for possessing, but Hitler stores his treasures away for safe-keeping and his collection is by far the greater of the two, by far the greater."

"I had no idea any of this was going on. I knew works of art were being collected up, as everyone does but I presumed they were being stored for safe keeping. Now I know why."

"That's right, and all of that is a very lengthy answer to your question 'why is my office so grand?' The reason is we simply take what it is we want and move swiftly on. Other times we need a large building such as this as a base, where we can catalogue and store each item before crating and transporting them to secret repositories in other parts of this country or Austria, or Germany, all ready and waiting for the new Linz.

"We have experts in every field you can think of, art of course, the great masters. China and porcelain, furniture, jewellery, sculptures, coins, books, armour, the list is endless. Even vintage wines and champagnes."

"I'm sure that goes down well with the hierarchy."

"Needless to say. My orders are to rescue works of art and treasures from the hands of our rivals and redirect them into the hands of those who would care for and appreciate them.

I consider myself a caretaker."

"Without too much emphasis on the 'taker'."

"Well quite," he said, following through with a grin. "Sometimes of course they will insist on hiding their treasures away and then we have to encourage their release which can be very tiresome and time consuming. Other times though we buy at auction, needless to say at a knock down price. We clear museums and galleries, and so on and so on. But what can I say to you? I am a humble administrative cog in a giant wheel that all goes to make up the glorious new Fatherland."

"You underestimate your own importance, Major Baum. I think perhaps you are a very important cog."

"How very generous of you to say so. All of this is close to your own field of expertise, is it not?"

"I am an archaeologist Major. All of this," and he waved his hand in a general encompass "charming though it is, is at least a thousand years too young for my taste. However, unless I am mistaken, I believe our two paths are about to cross. Is that not why I was ordered to report to you? It's a very long way from Berlin simply to discuss your work. Fascinating though it is."

Major Baum slowly eased himself from his chair and turned to look through the French doors. The light had almost gone, enveloping the gardens in unrecognizable shadows.

"Some time ago," he began, still looking out "I was summoned to Berlin by the Führer. I had met him before of course because of all I've just told you, but at this particular meeting he told me of something I had not previously heard of, which disappeared a long time ago and how good it would be for the people of the new Germany if it were rediscovered."

He turned around, inhaling deeply on his cigarette and leant both hands on the edge of the desk. "The problem was it would take a certain type of person with very specialized talents to find what it is the Führer is looking for, and he asked me with my contacts if I knew of someone suitable. Unfortunately, at the time I did not, but I promised not to rest until the right person could be found.

"Then, a few weeks ago, I went to see the Führer again, this time at the Berghof. Very beautiful … " he held up his hand to stop his guest from interrupting and resumed his seat. " …And I was able to report that at last I had found the right man for the job." His slate black eyes suddenly looked sharp and alive.

"So where exactly do I come into all of this?" The man asked, sensing the sudden mood change.

"That's simple. You see, you are that man, Major Claus Muller."

"But you have not told me what it is I am to rediscover."

"Unfortunately that is not so simple." Baum looked pensive and lent his elbows on the desk, arching his hands, finger tip to finger tip, and looked deeply at the man opposite. He knew him to be in his early forties, well educated, efficient, achieving his rank through merit. Yet other than that, Baum suddenly realized he knew very little about the man the Führer was willing to trust on his recommendation. Should Muller fail, it would put Baum in a very difficult position. Very difficult and very dangerous.

He looked tough though, fit, perhaps a little overweight. 165 cm tall, fair hair, blue eyes and certainly what the ladies would call good-looking. Strange he had not remarried after the death of his wife; the war, who knows? More likely the ladies were frightened away by the black eye patch. The Führer was right, it did make him look menacing. Cruel even. And the ugly scar extending from the patch to the centre of his cheek didn't help.

"Correct me if I'm wrong Major Muller, but I believe you are an expert in precious metals and jewels of antiquity?"

"That is correct."

"So I presume you are quite conversant with diamonds?"

"Of course."

"All types of diamonds?"

"There is only one type of diamond, Major. They are all made of crystallised carbon."

"I meant, are you familiar with famous diamonds?"

"Reasonably so. I am conversant with most principal stones, but where is all this leading?"

"It is leading, Major, to the name of Claus Muller becoming one of the most famous names in Germany. In fact I don't think I would be exaggerating if I were to say your name would go down in history. You could be world famous."

"You're making me nervous. Please get to the point."

"The point is that the Führer would like you, to find for him, the diamond known as the Great Mogul."

For a moment both men remained quiet, the only sound a regular tick from an ormolu clock on the mantle above the fireplace. Eventually the silence was broken by Muller breaking into guffaws of laughter. He threw his head back and laughed more than he had in a very long time.

Baum didn't know what to do. This was not the reaction he had anticipated at all. But Muller caught the Major's set expression and stopped laughing abruptly.

"Oh my God!" he exclaimed. "You're serious aren't you? Please tell me this is a joke!"

"A joke?! This is no joke Major. I fail to see what you find so amusing. The Führer is in deadly earnest."

"Do you seriously expect me to find, to rediscover as you put it, the Great Mogul diamond? It's been missing for God knows how many hundreds of years. I can't just go out and, and, dig it up!"

"You have been selected Major because of your special talents and qualifications, and at this time in our history it is very important for Germany to possess the largest diamond in the world. It is a great honour that you have been chosen. I do hope you realize that."

"An honour!? It's the equivalent of an archaeological suicide mission, that's what it is. It's ludicrous. A total farce. Madness!" He was up now and pacing the floor. "Of all the ridiculous schemes I have ever heard, this is by far the most ... the most nonsensical, absurd, that's ever been conceived. It's a joke and a very bad joke."

"You must be careful what you say Major. I must warn you this is a direct order from the Führer himself."

"Well you can go back to the Führer and tell him that it's gone! Lost for ever in the dusts of time like the Ark of the Jews or the city of Atlantis. Gone forever."

"I think not. I know for a fact there was such a stone."

"Precisely. Was. Past tense. Look, we're talking at cross purposes here. Don't you understand? It's a legend. It's the thing dreams are made of. Look," Muller sat down on the edge of the chair. "I am an archaeologist. Lately I've been trained to drive tanks, destroy buildings and kill people and I became quite good at it. In fact in the end, I even began to enjoy it which I'm not particularly proud of but they gave me a medal none the less. But now because of this," and he flipped his eye patch, "I'm behind a desk compiling intelligence reports. Now how can any of that be useful to the Führer in finding a dream, eh? I'm not a magician. I don't do magic tricks – wave a wand and make things reappear. It's a nice thought owning virtually the biggest diamond in the world but it disappeared aeons ago and no-one, no-one, least of all me, knows where it is."

" But I'm afraid you don't have a choice Major. You are ordered to find it."

"But whereever would I begin!?"

"You're the archaeologist; that's why we chose you."

"Dear God this can't be happening. And you say I'll be the most famous man in Germany? I'll be a laughing stock, an object of ridicule everywhere I go. This is the ramblings of a crazy man!"

"Enough!" Baum slammed his fist down on the desk. "I must warn you Major Muller to be very careful what you say. Remember treason has very serious consequences."

"At this precise moment, death looks far more agreeable than chasing after myths."

"There will be no more talk Major! Orders are not open to discussion. If you had been my subordinate I would have had you arrested."

"Well I'm not your subordinate, I'm your equal."

Major Baum moderated his tone suddenly. "Yes you are, and you are also a highly intelligent and respected officer and as such you underestimate yourself. The Führer has every confidence in you as have I, and all the resources of the Reich will be put at your disposal. You will be given unlimited assistance whenever and wherever you so desire. The only condition is that you keep me abreast of how your search is progressing, to relate to Berlin. That is all I ask of you for now. You will of course, have access to a generous expense account for your own requirements and should you need any larger amounts of money, that can easily be arranged too."

Muller's head fell forward as he let out a deep and considered sigh. It was an admission of defeat. "If it's anywhere, the damned thing's in India."

"Yes, well I can see how that would be a problem. But all problems have their solutions do they not?"

"I can't believe this is happening to me, I really can't."

"No more talk. Come now," Baum stood up abruptly "come and enjoy my hospitality. Let me show you the château's extensive wine cellar. They produce quite a pleasing Muscadet locally."

"I need something to drown my sorrows." Muller stood up slowly, already feeling the pressure of his new burden. "Major Baum," he began, realizing it would be more advantageous to work with the man than against him and extended his hand. "Forgive my outburst. I know orders are orders and we all have to submit to a higher authority, but you'll appreciate an order such as this has come as a shock."

"I do understand and if there is anything I can do to help, I'm easy to find." The two men shook hands across the desk. "I wish you every possible good fortune."

"Believe me, I'm going to need it."

"You may be interested to know that the Führer has already decided to rename the diamond 'Light of the Reich.'"

"Then I can only hope the light of good fortune shines on me."

"I'm certain it will Major Muller. It has got to. The diamond is to be the centre piece of the Führer's dream for the new Linz collection. We're making history here you know. Years from now you will look back on this day with gratitude for all it started for you."

But Muller did not respond.

*

Later that night before Muller left the château he was presented with an envelope containing details of a specially numbered Swiss bank account opened for his exclusive use, supervised jointly by Major Baum and Berlin, which would give him access to any necessary funds.

He was ordered to make regular progress reports for Major Baum to forward to the Führer, and when his endeavours were successful, to use the single code word 'STARLIGHT'. Nothing more. Secrecy and security were to be of paramount importance. If such optimism had not been so ridiculous it would have been quite amusing.

There was also a letter of authority from the Führer, written in his own hand, demanding complete co-operation with the entreaties of the bearer.

Surprisingly there was no clause to stop the fund being abused, but Muller knew well enough how they would guarantee that.

*

It does not take long to travel by underground from Liverpool Street to Charing Cross, but long enough for a young man to review how his life had changed in a little over eighteen months. Sandhurst, Dunkirk, Jill, and now this. Whatever next?

He wished the train on, not liking idle moments when his mind would slip back to the funeral. How it had rained. And he recalled with a shudder the mud and pools of water as mourners stood silently around the open grave, as the dripping coffin was slowly lowered to its final resting place, the Vicar's voice almost lost in the deluge. 'Ashes to ashes, dust to dust …'

'Please don't let me die in the rain'.

What really cut deep was when he overheard a couple whispering that the coffin was almost empty; the bomb had done its awful work well, leaving virtually nothing of J.J. left to bury. The coffin had to be weighted with bricks.

Any doubts he may have harboured about whether he had made the right decision regarding his future were at that moment, completely washed away.

He wished the train on.

Douglas may have decided his future but the organization to which Captain Silverthorn introduced him had not. Entry into H.M. Secret Service is not conducted over a pint of beer, and Douglas was told to report for interview to the Northumberland Hotel a few yards behind the War Office which had been requisitioned for the duration. Passing a pair of armed M.P.s he was met by the familiar lean features of Captain Silverthorn and taken into a small lounge.

"I was so sorry to hear about Miss Johnson," he said. " It must have come as a terrible blow."

"Thank you Sir. Yes, it did. We'd planned to marry when this was all over, you know."

"The most awful bad luck."

Douglas looked about. It was strange being in a hotel without any guests, everything was in place yet in a state of limbo, which he felt wasn't far from his own circumstances. "Is there anything you people don't know about me?" Douglas spoke without malice.

"I'm afraid not. That's one of the reasons we invited you here."

Douglas shifted unconsciously in the leather arm chair.

"Relax, Lieutenant, it's all very low key here. In a few moments I'll introduce you to the gentleman who'll be conducting the interview which will all be over very quickly, I assure you."

"What is his name Sir?"

Silverthorn smiled wryly. "You don't need to know."

"I see, like that is it?" and added "Is Silverthorn your real name?"

The Captain did not answer. "I'm afraid that's something you'll have to get used to around here. However I can tell you I'm a Staff Officer and I can also tell you who we are."

"That's something at least."

"We are known as the S.O.E. which is The Special Operations Executive. We are a secret organization and as I explained when we met, we're made up of personnel from the Special Intelligence Service, now usually known as MI6, MI5, the Home Office and so on. And of course, we draw from all three services."

"Men and women?"

"Oh rather, and all ages. The S.O.E., which is also known in some corners of Whitehall as 'the ministry of ungentlemanly warfare', is like a huge tree which is growing all the time and, you'll forgive the pun, we have branches everywhere. I consider myself just a leaf on one of those many branches."

"So what does that make me? A little bud or barking mad?"

Silverthorn laughed. "That's a new one. It's good to have a sense of humour." He checked his watch. "I'll take you up now to the interview room. Oh and don't be put off by the surroundings. It's just something M likes to do."

"M?!"

"Head of Operations Section. You'll get used to it. If you don't know names you can't spill the beans. Simple really, but it works. He likes to vet all the new intake himself. I know it's a bit daunting but relax. He's on your side remember. We're all on the same side. This way."

M was a cloak used by Colonel Sir Colin McVean Gubbins, Deputy Director and one of the founding fathers when S.O.E. was formed in March 1939. Gubbins was fluent in both French and German and possessed a good command of Russian; well-read and well-travelled, he brought a daring spirit and original mind to an organisation that was still in it's infancy, but which was to play a vital role during the dark days ahead.

Douglas was taken up to the first floor and into what must originally have been a guest room, yet once inside, any guest in their right mind would have run a mile. A black-out screen had been placed over the window and a naked light bulb cast an eerie light over a room which was completely void of all furniture, save for two folding chairs which faced each other.

Douglas glanced at Silverthorn, trying to conceal what he was feeling.

"Looks like I'm going to be interrogated."

"Relax, you'll be fine old boy. Sit here."

But before he could sit a short, bald gentleman in a double breasted grey lounge suit entered, carrying a buff coloured folder.

"Douglas Reid, Sir," the Captain informed him, as Reid brought himself smartly to attention.

"How do you do Reid? As you were. We don't stand on ceremony here. I'm very pleased to meet you." His voice was sharp, official, yet moderated by a distinct Highland lilt.

"This is M, Lieutenant."

"How do you do Sir." His hand was fat but firm in Reid's grasp, tell-tale of a military history, along with a bearing to match. His face exuded experience and wisdom and supported a ruddy complexion and a toothbrush moustache; dark alert eyes under bushy brows and a furrowed forehead. Douglas guessed his age to be in the high fifties.

"Thank you Captain," said M.

"Sir." Silverthorn withdrew, quietly closing the door behind him.

"Do sit down, Lieutenant." M sat opposite, crossed his legs and laced his fingers over one knee. "Now tell me about yourself. In German." And Douglas proceeded to tell him all that he knew the man knew already.

When he had finished M told him. "It's your languages that we're particularly interested in. I'm certain we could put those to good use. But what concerns me is that you're only twenty-five."

"Twenty-six, Sir,"

"Quite."

"Still old enough to fight for what I believe in."

"And what do you believe in Lieutenant?"

Except for the sound of traffic outside, the room was silent for a moment until Douglas spoke again. "The right to determine my own future, and the freedom and liberty regardless of race or creed that's been the hallmark of this country since Norman times."

M's expression revealed nothing of what he may have been thinking. "I don't know how much Captain Silverthorn has told you but we haven't been up and running all that long, although we do already have a network of agents all over Europe causing as much trouble as they can for the enemy. Sabotage, labour unrest, training and fighting with resistance groups, all that sort of thing. And we're constantly looking to enlarge our network. How does that sound to you?"

"It's what I expected Sir."

"If we do decide to adopt you, once you've been through the training programme, with your languages we could well place you deep behind enemy lines. You would probably have to work alone. Does the thought of that worry you?"

"Not excessively Sir." He answered simply.

"You'd be trained to kill, maim and destroy. You'd be dropped at night by parachute. You might even have to live off the land for a while. Then of course, there's the very strong possibility that you might be discovered and captured and only God knows what would happen to you then."

"I understand."

"I'm not trying to frighten you Reid, but I do want you to understand quite clearly what it is you're letting yourself in for. Better to know now rather than regret later. Are you fit?"

"Comparatively, yes I think so."

"Good. We'd soon bring you up to scratch anyway." M gathered his papers together in a way suggesting the interview was over. It had lasted forty minutes.

"I confess I'm still concerned about your age. I think what I'd like you to do is to return here again this time next week when I want you to meet a colleague of mine. That sound agreeable to you?"

"Next week? Yes, Sir."

"It will also give you time to decide whether you're doing the right thing or not."

They said their goodbyes and as if responding to an unseen cue, Captain Silverthorn entered holding the door open for M as he left.

"How did it go?"

"It was all over very quickly."

"Told you. Let me guess, he wants to see you again in seven days?"

"How did you know that?"

"Standard procedure, old boy."

"He said I was too young."

"Believe me if you weren't too young, you'd be too small, too thin, too anything. It's just his way of getting you back here again and keeping you on your toes. It's a good sign usually though." He failed to add the real reason being that seven days was just enough time for MI5 to run a complete security check on Reid and his immediate family.

Silverthorn led the way down to the main vestibule and before they parted company reminded Douglas. "Not a word remember. No-one. Farvel på gjensyn."

"Yes, goodbye for now. I didn't know you spoke Norwegian."

"How could you old boy? Take care of yourself."

*

On the other side of the English Channel, Major Claus Muller had decided that he was not a man on whom fate smiled. He had lost his wife and apart from two children, was quite alone. He had lost an eye and gained an unsightly scar and now to top it all, had been given a task which would without doubt prove totally fruitless as well as hazardous.

Baum had made it perfectly clear that failure was not an option and Muller knew well enough that orders, however ridiculous, were without exception always to be executed. Accordingly, the consequences for failing to realise an order from the Führer himself would put him and those close to him, in a very perilous position.

As he made his way north to Paris, he determined not to waste time and energy trying to find the stone for he knew it had vanished forever, but to devise a scheme which would somehow placate the idea's originator as well as afford him and his family some security. But how? Hitler wanted the diamond and Muller knew he would never be able to give it to him.

He checked in to the splendid Hotel Meurice on the Rue de Rivoli, which had been requisitioned by the German occupation authorities, affording a unique view of the Tuileries Garden beside the Seine with the Eiffel Tower in the distance, and immediately wrote two long and overdue letters, firstly to his son in the military, and another to his daughter who was living with friends in Berlin, telling her to leave the city at once and move in with her aunt in the country. It would, he encouraged her, be protection from air-raids and at the least keep her out of harm's way for however long the war lasted. Country life and fresh air would be good for her. He also wrote a short note to his wife's sister explaining his wishes and that he only wanted the best for her niece. The rest of the day was spent in contemplation in the company of a bottle of brandy.

The new day however found him at the Musée de l'Histoire de France, but too many exhibits had been withdrawn for safe keeping and the morning was wasted. Changing tack, after lunch back at the hotel, he made his way along the Rue de Richelieu arriving at the Bibliothèque Nationale, the nation's premier library.

Though now a legend, Muller knew from his university days that the Great Mogul diamond had indeed at one time existed and had been shown by its owner the Shah Jahan, builder of the Taj Mahal, to an early French explorer and jewel trader. But any more than that would need researching. He proposed to investigate as much information as there was available and compile an extensive report which would, he hoped, put the matter to rest once and for all in the Führer's mind when it could be proved beyond doubt that the diamond was a casualty of history.

The Principal of the Bibliothèque was an agreeable man though Muller was at once confronted with a problem he had failed to take into consideration. The language barrier. Eventually though it was understood and agreed that Muller should return on the Monday, five days hence, to consult with the Assistant Principal, a Monsieur Charles Le Mar, who it was understood was excellent in French, German and English and who would help him with whatever it was he sought. Apparently, Le Mar was an elderly gentleman and did not enjoy good health, hence his absence.

Muller knew he had no choice but to settle for the suggestion, annoyed with himself that his French had such very definite limitations.

*

As Douglas Reid made his way to London for the second time, Great Britain was experiencing its second autumn of war. In little more than a year, much of Europe had been brought under the Jackboot and the German army was now within twenty-one miles of the coast of England. Already invasion plans were underway on the other side of the Channel. The news was grim but Prime Minister Winston Churchill was doing his best to keep the country's morale high.

As Douglas walked along Northumberland Avenue, past the buildings with their taped windows and sandbags, he could not help but marvel at the stoicism of the British people. Down they may have been, but out, they were not.

The interview room was as bleak and bare as he remembered, only this time there was the addition of an extra chair. Right on time M entered wearing the same grey suit but was accompanied by a tall and immaculately dressed gentleman, porting a red carnation button-hole and smoking a cigarette in an elegant black holder.

M spoke first. "Good to see you again, Lieutenant."

"And you, Sir."

"This is my colleague who's joining us for our little chat."

"How do you do?" said Douglas knowing better than to expect a name.

"Ah! So this is the young man you were telling me about. Unusual combination Norwegian and German. I'm delighted to make your acquaintance, Lieutenant Reid." He had a kind voice and as he spoke the ends of his thick moustache twitched in time with his voice. "I've heard a lot about you and now I believe we are to hear even more."

The gentleman lived up to his name, Major Robert Splendid, a gifted member of the 'think tank' of S.O.E., known as D Section.

"I'm pleased to meet you too, Sir."

Once seated the questions began in earnest as the two men probed Reid's character and searched the person behind the mask. They tested his relationship with his parents, his private life, friends and relationships. His former employment. How did he feel coming under fire for the first time in France? Did he consider himself reckless? They were particularly careful to avoid candidates who showed signs of impulsiveness. Quick impulsive characters were all very well and good on the field of battle where decisions were needed instantaneously, but prudence would prove an agent's most valuable asset.

Then followed questions as to why he wanted to join the S.O.E. Was it because of a healthy contempt for Nazism and all that it stood for or was he seeking revenge for the life of Jill Johnson?

Was he courageous? Yes, they would train each candidate in every aspect of secret warfare, from building a bomb from nothing to knowing how to kill without making a sound, but if courage was not the bedrock of an agent's personality everyone was wasting their time and risking lives unnecessarily. (Douglas had no way of knowing that his C.O. had already been questioned in this respect.) How did he cope with pain?

"You told me last time Lieutenant, that you believed in the freedom this country enjoys, but you won't feel very free when you're strapped to a table screaming for death under torture will you?"

"Of course not. But then who would, Sir?"

"That's what they do when they capture spies and saboteurs. They torture them and when they're finished they kill them and dump their bodies without a Christian burial. Have you really thought this through?"

"We want you to understand," interjected the gentleman with the carnation "exactly what it is you are getting yourself into. You are still young and we're concerned that the excitement and attraction of it all may have prevented you forming a realistic picture. It's only right to tell you that we estimate one in four of our agents will never return. Are you prepared to accept those odds?"

The room remained quiet before Douglas spoke slowly and deliberately. "When Captain Silverthorn originally came to see me, he told me his job was to plant a seed of thought. He did his job well as I've thought of nothing else since that night. My original answer was to be no, but since then as you know I lost the love of my life, which means I am now alone, no ties. At first, my instant gut reaction was quite frankly revenge. A life for a life. But since then all of this has reminded me that I possess a … ," he hesitated "a valuable talent for languages and for me not to use that talent and play my part would be very remiss of me. Yes, I have thought it through thoroughly, and yes I am prepared to take those odds."

"What about leaving your parents?"

"I love my mother and father dearly, Sir but I left the nest a long time ago."

The two men exchanged the briefest of glances before M spoke again. "Go back to your regiment now Reid, and give yourself seven days before coming to any final decision."

"I …"

"That's an order."

"Yes, Sir."

"Those seven days won't be the easiest of days because you won't be able to discuss matters with anyone. You'll be entirely on your own, which could well be something you'll have to get used to."

Douglas made no response, disappointed that the matter could not be finalized immediately.

"Is there anything you would like to add?" M asked the other gentleman.

"That's jolly sound advice you know, Reid. Go away and think about it. This is a life and death decision for both of us. We have to decide whether we can risk your life and you have to decide whether you're willing to risk it. And remember, what's gone on between these four walls stays between these walls. You're a sensible fellow Lieutenant, no point in putting lives unnecessarily at risk."

The interview was terminated, having lasted a little over ninety minutes.

*

It is said that everyone should see Paris in the spring, but for Major Claus Muller his time came during the autumn of 1940. Not that he had any cause for complaint, for as an officer of the occupying power, he could enjoy privileges denied lesser mortals. Yet with an enjoyable few days behind him, at a little before nine o'clock Monday morning he mounted the steps of the Bibliothèque Nationale and asked for the Assistant Principal Monsieur Charles Le Mar. He had chosen to wear a lounge suit considering it less antagonistic to a gentleman whose knowledge and experience could prove invaluable.

Muller had been warned that Le Mar was elderly, but even so had difficulty concealing his surprise when a wizened man with a pronounced stoop, completely bald except for two white tufts above each ear, a pair of pince-nez perched on the end of a pointed nose and wearing a crumpled black suit topped by a winged collar, stepped forward to meet him.

"Guten Morgen, Herr Major. I am Charles Le Mar, Assistant Principal here at the Bibliothèque." He may have been old but his voice was strong and his German flawless. "I understand from my colleague that my services are required. My apologies for not being on hand when you called before. A slight malaise, you understand. Now, how is it I may help you?" Le Mar led the way into a small and secluded office. "Come and sit down Major, I'm sure you don't wish your business to be aired in public."

"I am interested in tracing the history of a certain diamond, the Great Mogul. Have you heard of it?"

"Oui. I have."

"I seem to recall a French traveller saw it at some stage and wrote about it, but I cannot remember his name."

"Nor I, Monsieur, but rest assured together we shall find it." Le Mar peered at Muller over the top of his pince-nez. "You must be wondering why an old man like me has not been put out to pasture."

Muller did not respond knowing he was about to learn why.

"I have been employed here all my working life Major, and now even though I should have retired long ago the Principal, a gentleman, has agreed that I may stay because, you understand, I am alone now. My wife died eighteen years ago, and if I have no interests then I fear I too will quickly go the same way. The Bibliothèque is my life. Take it away and that will be the end of Charles Le Mar. Tell me, Major. How old do you think I am?"

"I'm not very good at that sort of thing," he answered honestly.

"Please, guess."

"Seventy then."

"I'm eighty-eight."

"That's remarkable!"

"Thank you. Now I want you to know Major that I will help you in any way I can, but if we are going to work together, I would like to make my position perfectly clear. Will you permit me to speak freely?"

"Please."

"I want you to know that I think what your countrymen have done to France is a disgrace. A crime against humanity. The people and the land will forever bear the scars. Did you know that your people have already seized many thousands of books from this library alone?

How many more are they to rob us of?"

"I know nothing of such things. I assure you Monsieur, that I am here to read, to learn, not to steal."

"I just thank God that I will not live much longer to see my beloved country torn apart as it has been these past months." Le Mar shifted in his chair. "However," he pondered "such great affairs have nothing to do with an ancient old man and you, I think, are under orders from a higher authority and must obey whether you agree or not. C'est la vie." The old man shook his head. "There now, I have said my piece. Is there anything you would like to say to me in return?"

Muller thought that had Le Mar been twenty years younger he would have said a lot. Instead he answered simply. "No."

"Bon. Then let us commence our search. Follow me Monsieur, s'il vous plaît. I think we shall begin in the Eastern Section."

*

For the third time, Douglas found himself seated in the austere surroundings of the Northumberland Hotel, the only difference on this occasion being that M wore a heavily decorated Colonel's uniform of The Royal Artillery.

"As a prospective agent, this will be your final interview," he announced. "You must decide to take the plunge or withdraw. For our part we have decided we would like to have you on board, but the final decision must rest with you."

"I think perhaps you know what my answer will be, Sir."

"Excellent. Well done."

"Thank you. So, what now?"

"Just give it twenty-four hours and report to 64 Baker Street."

"What do I tell them at my end?"

"Nothing, leave all that to us. We'll liaise with your commanding officer. You just pack your bags and go. The fewer people you say goodbye to the better. There'll be a travel pass waiting for you at the gate and we'll tell you what to do next when you get here. Good luck, and welcome to The Special Operations Executive."

*

Major Muller looked out of his hotel room window as flakes of snow brushed gently across the glass. The Eiffel tower, usually dominant on the sky line, was lost to swirling flurries and down in the street everything was already covered in a white blanket as pedestrians hurrying by left footprints which were quickly erased.

He sat down again in front of the typewriter, removed the last sheet of paper and added it to the others. Months of work stared back at him. Down in the hotel's reception a special courier was waiting to take the papers directly to Major Baum, but Muller kept him waiting whilst he sifted through salient points for the final time.

SECRET

TO: Major Walter Baum   PARIS
                                            10th November 1940

FOR: The Chancellor, Führer and Supreme Commander of all the Germans, Adolf Hitler.

REPORT ON THE INVESTIGATION AS TO THE SITUATION OF 'THE GREAT MOGUL' DIAMOND.

Heil Hitler,
I wish to commence this report with my thanks to the Führer for conferring on me the honour of trying to discover the whereabouts of the missing 'Great Mogul' diamond, and to assure you that at every step of the investigation every possible source of information which might prove useful, however miniscule, has been thoroughly examined and evaluated and that throughout the assignment I have remained loyal to both yourself and the Fatherland.

THE GREAT MOGUL DIAMOND ... is thought to have been found between 1650 and 1658 in the Kollur mine near Golconda in Hyderabad, India. Originally weighed 787.500 carats; the largest stone ever discovered in India. Its name is derived from its owner, the Great Mogul of India.
It was entrusted to the Venetian cutter Hortentio Borgis, who attempted to give it a rose cut in the shape of half an egg. However it was so badly done, that the stone was reduced to a mere 280 carats.
What is important to remember at this point, is that the stone had a definite place of origin and a certain history.
We are extremely fortunate in so much that approximately twenty years after its discovery, it was seen and described at great length by an eyewitness, Jean-Baptiste Tavernier, a wealthy French jewel trader who spent much of his life travelling Europe and Asia as a representative of Louis XIV of France.
In his publication, 'Voyages en Torquie, en Perse et aux Indes' (1670) translated by V. Ball, we read (along with a sketch I have reproduced below) ...
'This diamond belongs to the Great Mogul of Delhi, Shah Jahan, whose son Aurangzeb did me the honour to have it shown to me with all the other jewels ... As I was allowed to weigh it I ascertained that it weighed 319½ ratis, which are equal to 279$\frac{9}{16}$ of our carats. When in the rough it weighed 907 ratis, or 793$\frac{5}{8}$ carats. This stone is of the same form as if one cut an egg through the middle.
A high crowned rose-cut with a flaw at the bottom and small fleck within.'

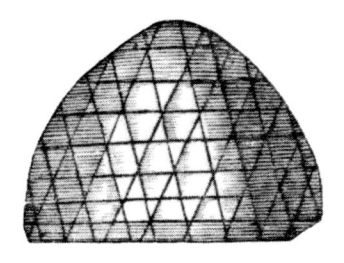

Taken from Tavernier's original drawing (not to scale).

Nothing else is known of the stone and all traces of it appear to have been lost after the 17th century.
Here for a moment we must branch off at a tangent, for I encountered too many references to discredit, to the fact that the famous Koh-i-noor and Orlov diamonds possibly being remnants of the Great Mogul. This opinion is voiced by numerous experts so therefore it was necessary to investigate in depth the histories of both of these diamonds.

THE KOH-I-NOOR DIAMOND (meaning 'Mountain of light'). The history of this stone appears to have begun amidst a mist of uncertainty in the 14th century when it was a clumsily Mughal-cut stone weighing 186 carats. (The term Mughal-cut refers to a native Indian cut exhibiting a large flat base and table separated by an array of smaller facets.) Again it is important to remember that its early history is a matter of some conjecture and does not become a known fact until after the date when the Great Mogul was discovered. In any case, it most likely formed part of the loot of Nādir Shāh of Iran when he sacked Delhi in 1739.
In Ball's translation of Tavernier's book we read, "no-one can examine the authentic sketches and models of the Koh-i-noor without feeling a strong presumption that it must have been mutilated, after cutting, and that it cannot have been left in such an incomplete condition by the jeweller who cut and polished it. In addition to its possessing defects similar to some of those described by Tavernier as having been in the Mogul's diamond, Mr Tennent (lecture on Gems and Precious Stone. London. 1852), records that 'the Koh-i-noor had a flaw near the summit which, being on a line of cleavage parallel to the upper surface, may very possibly have been produced when the upper portion was removed … "

THE ORLOFF DIAMOND is shaped like half an egg with facets covering its domed surface, and is nearly flat underneath. This diamond was first heard of as one of the eyes of a temple statue of Brahma at Mysore in India. It is said to have been stolen by a French deserter who gained admittance to the temple one night by disguising himself as a religious fanatic.

As has already been mentioned, some experts suggest the Orloff may, in fact, be part of the vanished Great Mogul as it is similar in shape to Tavernier's descriptions.

Again, as with the Koh-i-noor, its early history proved to be at the very least uncertain so I arrived at a point where I had to revise my thinking. The question I set out to answer was, 'where is the Great Mogul now?' Yet these readings and many, many others prompted me to change the question to, 'when looking at the Koh-i-noor and Orloff diamonds are we justified in thinking that we are looking at fragments, indeed all that is left of the Great Mogul?

I trust the following chart will simplify matters.

	GREAT MOGUL	KOH-I-NOOR	ORLOFF
Found:	Golconda, 1650	Questionable Legends	Questionable Legends
Weight:	787cts	186cts	189cts
Cut:	High crowned rose cut with a flaw at the bottom and a small speck within. Shaped like half an egg.	Originally a lumpy Mughal-cut, or clumsy rose cut.	Rose cut. Shaped like half an egg with facets covering its domed surface and nearly flat underneath.
Currently:	Missing	British Crown Jewels England	Romanov Crown Jewels Russia

SUMMARY

I arrived, therefore, at the point where we no longer seek the 507cts lost when the Great Mogul was cut, for there surely (yet even this is supposition) lie the Koh-i-noor and Orloff. We look for the 280cts approximately (allowing for cutting loss) that were left; the remains of the stone which can truly be called the Great Mogul. I have ascertained, I believe as far as it is humanly possible, that the Koh-i-noor and Orloff diamonds are indeed all that is left of the Great Mogul. A principle adopted by such eminent experts as Professor N.S. Maskelyne, (Royal Institute of Great Britian 1860), Professor Nicol and Dr. H.A. Miers. But even if these, and many other experts are wrong, that such a stone should remain 'lost' for hundreds of years is most highly improbable. Yet what did happen to it?

It is my deepest regret to have to answer my own question in so negative a manner, but I do not know. It is impossible to discover the truth out of so myriad a number of possibilities, uncertainties and legends.

There is also some consideration given to the belief that the Mogul's diamond could, in fact, be the diamond known as Bābur's Diamond, as there are some distinct similarities. This I discounted however, as Bārbur's diamond has a history extending back many hundreds of years prior to the discovery of the Great Mogul.

We must, therefore, console ourselves that when looking at the Koh-in-noor and Orloff we are looking at possibly two thirds of the largest diamond ever found in India. Yet we may be wrong, maybe one day the Great Mogul will reappear. That will truly be a great day, and it did occur to me that with the Führer's excellence in military campaigns the Koh-i-noor diamond in Great Britain and the Orloff in Russia will both shortly be included among the many treasures of the new and glorious Third Reich.

I await your further orders.

Your most humble and loyal servant.

Major Claus Muller.

There was nothing else to say. That would have to do, and should be the end of the matter. He sealed the envelope and placed it in a black leather pouch embossed with the Nazi gold eagle and locked it. Baum had a duplicate key. Putting on his jacket he went downstairs and gave the courier his instructions. All there was to do then, was wait.

*

By 24th December Muller had received no word as to whether his report was accepted or otherwise. Regretting not using the time to visit his daughter he decided instead to call on Charles Le Mar.

"Charles, I want you to know how grateful I am for all your hard work. I don't know what I would have done without you, especially in the translations we spent so many hours over."

"Monsieur Muller it is I who should thank you. I don't know why you wanted to know so much about the Mogul's diamond, but it has been a pleasure to work with a gentleman of your knowledge and calibre, and it has given me an interest for the past few months. You have made me feel almost like a detective. It's been fun."

"Well, that's nice to know. Tell me, do you have any plans for this evening?"

"I have no plans Monsieur."

"The Hotel is putting on a special Christmas dinner and I thought perhaps as a mark of my appreciation you might like to join me as my guest. We may come from very different backgrounds with differing reasons for being in Paris, but I see no reason why the two of us should be alone at Christmas."

"You are most kind."

Whilst the rest of France celebrated its first Christmas as best it could under German occupation, later that evening the two men could be seen enjoying Christmas festivities along with other guests and listening to a children's choir the hotel had arranged to sing carols.

At approximately ten p.m. a courier arrived and, asking for Major Muller, handed him an envelope marked 'OFFICE OF THE REICH CHANCELLOR, BERLIN, which he tore open, swiftly scanning the contents.

'REPORT UNACCEPTABLE. RESUME SEARCH IMMEDIATELY.
ADOLF HITLER.'

Muller told the courier there was no reply and returned to his table.

"Not bad news I hope, Major."

"No, not at all. Nothing I hadn't expected. I know now what I have to do in the New Year."

"Let us raise our glasses Major, to peace on earth and may life exceed your expectations."

"It will have to Charles," he frowned. "It will have to."

CHAPTER THREE

The village of Vadheim, nestling at the foot of the mountains along the northern shores of Sognafjord Norway, has, according to it's handful of residents, two primary qualities; it is both beautiful and peaceful. There is but little industry except for fishing and forestry on a very humble scale, along with a small hotel for visitors seeking their portion of precious, undisturbed calm. Watching the waters of the fjord gently lap the coastline which runs in a large crescent shape, it is possible to see clusters of painted timber houses, dotted at random along the shore, before the ground starts to climb steeply, into lush pine forest for as far as the eye can see.

In summer when the sun remains in the sky for almost twenty-four hours, the people focus on outdoor life. When winter arrives and wraps the village in a blanket allowing only four hours of daylight, they take to their wooden homes when family life is in itself a full time occupation. For centuries from the time of the Vikings, this unity has helped to breed a tough, yet home loving people, both deeply patriotic and proud of their country and its natural beauty.

Yet all of that was in happier times. Now Norway's Nazi masters heaped restriction upon oppression in a bid to crush that inherent spirit, making everyday existence hard and life cheap, quickly and ruthlessly suppressing any resistance to the new ruling authority.

In the village, German soldiers knowing the people were suffering serious food shortages would find perverse satisfaction in spreading butter on chocolate from their own abundant stores and eating it in front of hungry children, whilst the women folk were reduced to making a poor quality flour type substitute from seaweed simply to stay alive. Peace, calm and tranquillity had been replaced with oppression, hatred and fear.

As members of the great and all-conquering army stationed in Vadheim, six young infantry men and their C.O., a junior Lieutenant, considered the posting a bore as there was never anything to do. One particular evening towards the end of January, the boredom became all too much for one young man. He felt he had to get out and even though he knew the temperature outside was more than 20ºC below freezing, he did not care.

Dressing in his special issue heavy protective clothing and head gear, he swung his rifle over his shoulder and left his companions to their singing and drinking. But once outside, away from the protection of the insulated wooden hostel, the freezing air hit him like an iron bar flung hard against his chest, forcing him to stand still, gasping, while his lungs adapted to the sudden change of temperature. Once he could breath again, he trudged off leaving heavy prints in the deep powdery snow.

Walking on down the main street with its three shops – a general store, hairdresser and bakery all locked and shuttered – he paused for a moment by the small hotel to look out across the fjord. The air was deafeningly silent, except for the out-of-rhythm swish of salt water against the icy shore. The occasional gap in clouds heavy with the next fall of snow allowed moonlight to sweep across the landscape, highlighting glistening crystals on the surrounding snow packed peaks and reflecting on the mirror-still surface of the fjord like a huge silver football.

"How I hate this place," he shivered, and longed for the excitement of his home town.

The hotel was closed as it had been ever since Norway surrendered. No tourists visited Norway now. He had walked around to the rear of the building which backed almost directly onto the edge of the fjord, when suddenly he noticed a light coming from one of the downstairs rooms. Walking over he peered in through the window.

The room seemed to act as a small store room, for stacked up against three walls, were bare wooden shelves from floor to ceiling with a naked light above the only door. Inexplicably, he felt as if he shouldn't be there. As if he was about to witness something he was not meant to, and his heart started to beat a little faster. The thought irritated him. There was no fear of being heard, the triple glazing made sure of that, and with snow piled halfway up the window he certainly could not be seen. He waited expectantly.

Abruptly, into the room from the door at the far end, came a young girl carrying a bucket and cloths. She was not beautiful but attractive in an adolescent way, and he put her age between fifteen and seventeen. Her hair was tied up in a head scarf and her clothes were hidden under a floral patterned overall. She placed the bucket in the centre of the floor and proceeded to wash the shelves, ignorant that she was being observed.

The German soldier watched her for nearly ten minutes, then remembered he had seen her before, serving in the store. He forgot how cold it was, excited by her slender body as it pressed against the shelves and could not have been more excited had he seen her undressed. He glanced around quickly, looking for a way in and, noticing a side door, made his way quietly inside. Following the light, he burst into the room.

"What are you doing?!!" he stormed. The girl screamed at the sight of the German uniform and a look of horror fell across her face.

"Answer! What are you doing here? The hotel is closed."

"I was told … to keep it clean," she stammered.

"Clean? Who by?!"

"The owner."

"The owner, what owner? I don't know any owner. Get out. Get out. Schnell!"

"I'm not doing anything wrong."

"Don't speak," and he grabbed her arm, pulling her from the room out into the darkness of the corridor.

"Don't … you're hurting me." She was crying now, terrified.

"Silence, don't speak!" He pushed her up against the wall, forcing her head back as he cupped her chin in his leather glove, delighted by the tremble of her youthful frame.

"You have been very bad," he told her, and leaning his rifle up against the wall started to unbutton his coat. "So now you must be punished." Even in the poor light she could see him smile in a way that sent a bolt of alarm shooting through her brain and without further thought, as he opened his heavy coat, with all the strength her young body could muster, she brought her knee up hard into his groin.

Instantly he let out a shriek of agony and as he keeled over, the girl bolted for the outer door and raced off into the night, as fast as she could wearing only her thin overalls. But the cold went unnoticed when she heard the soldier call after her. "I'll get you … I'll get you!"

*

Solveig, the girl's mother, reported the incident to the Lieutenant the following day, and was assured that he would speak to the man concerned. However, it was put down to youthful exuberance and no further action was taken, but from that moment Ingrid Nielsen lived in constant fear.

*

In France, a memorandum crossed Major Walter Baum's desk, stating that Major Muller's daughter had left the family home in Berlin.

"How long ago did this happen?!"

"We do not know, Herr Major," his aide told him cautiously.

"Well, where has she gone?"

"To the country is all we know."

"Well find out! She's my only insurance."

*

For Douglas Reid, the winter months had been eventful. Though he had been adopted as a candidate into the Special Operations Executive, it was by no means certain that he would pass out as an agent, as many obstacles had to be overcome along the way and failure at any stage would mean certain rejection. He had shown he was willing, now he had to prove he was able.

After reporting to the S.O.E. Headquarters, he was immediately sent for initial training along with other men and women of all ages and all backgrounds. At Wanborough Manor, south-east of Guildford, his abilities were tested as he passed through the first of many sieves which rarely failed to sort out those unsuitable before they could harm themselves or others.

With many thousands of domestic servants throughout the country away in the services or involved with war work, numerous large country houses were closed by their owners for the duration, and let to various government departments, who undertook their upkeep yet rarely divulged the precise purpose the house was used for. The villagers around Wanborough were satisfied with the view that the Manor was being used for special commando training, a notion supported every morning at 6 a.m. by the sight of men and women out on cross-country runs.

Douglas soon realized why he had been asked if he was fit, as the first three weeks at Wanborough were primarily concerned with physical fitness, along with basic arms training and map reading which, after Sandhurst, he found no strain. However, not all candidates had an ex-service background and already faces were disappearing as the sieve did its work.

Those who did pass this initial stage moved on to Arisaig on the western coast of Inverness-shire for an intensive four weeks of paramilitary style training. The S.O.E. had requisitioned a group of fine, and more importantly, deserted country houses in a prohibited area completely screened off from prying eyes. The shores of Lochailort and the Sound of Arisaig were wild, bleak and hard, and at the same time, grand with a beauty all of their own. Over the weeks, the men and women being taught how to stay alive, came to know every inch of them.

Much more time and effort was devoted to arms training here, than at Wanborough, and each candidate was drilled in all well-known weaponry including German, Italian, as well as British and American, with special emphasis on the Sten sub-machine gun, which was to prove invaluable, as it was tough, deadly and cheap to produce. Students were taught how to strip, reassemble, load, fire and maintain all principle weapons in total darkness and trained in accuracy on the firing range, as well as competing in mock attacks when they were shown the importance of firing two quick shots into a target and not to rely on one. A wounded enemy could still fight.

They also learnt that it was not only cowboys who needed to be quick on the draw; shoulder holster, pocket, hip and even handbag were all used to maximum effect.

Great attention was paid to self-preservation and protection which involved the 'art' of silent killing with the commando knife, garrotte or bare hands. Within a short space of time the self-confidence of each candidate was boosted to the point where he or she could face the possibility of combat without fear or anxiety, knowing for certain that they were capable of killing easily and swiftly, in a dozen different ways. Yet they were reminded that once trained in the 'art' of killing, they were never to lose control in a sudden row which could so easily result in serious injury or even death at their own hand.

There was always a well-stocked bar and not only for recreational purposes. Even here, students were closely monitored. An agent who couldn't hold a drink or two could easily let slip information endangering lives, not least their own, without even being aware of what they were doing.

Overseeing each candidate's progress were 'conducting officers,' who would befriend each student, and be willing to listen to any problems and offer help when needed. They would also specialize in particular languages, the use of which was constantly encouraged throughout the course. Where possible, these officers were made up of returned agents whose experiences were inestimable.

Towards the end of the four weeks, not only had the staff decided who was promising, but it was also the point at which students could, without shame or recrimination, decide for themselves that an agent's life was not for them. At this time, those who wished to continue were split into two groups, A and B. Those who remained at Avisaig, group A, were trained in demolition, sabotage, ambush and the like, with a view to causing as much trouble for the enemy as possible. The London, Midland and Scottish Railway were encouraged to donate track, engines and rolling stock for use in training with live explosives. This proved to be a popular course with many adventurous types.

Group B was moved to other country houses; this time, in and around Beaulieu in the New Forest, including Beaulieu Manor itself. This group focussed on the day to day life and survival of an agent, but with additional technical emphasis.

It had been determined that Douglas Reid would move to Group B. A decision which was supported by an event which took place at the S.O.E. headquarters in London.

Part of the work of the S.O.E. was to gather and process incoming intelligent reports from its various agents in the field, and one evening, deep in the basements of the Baker Street building, highly trained specialists were working late, processing a package which had recently been smuggled out of Germany. The package contained details of troop movements, arms production and changes in command, along with a roll of photographic film. The reports were forwarded to the relevant departments and the film to the laboratory. The film proved to be photographs of a number of top German military personnel, which eventually found their way to the office of the head of Operations Section.

The following morning as always M was at his desk bright and early, and at once focused his attention on the reports his agents had risked their lives to send. It was whilst he was going through the ten or so photographs that suddenly a face stared back at him that he recognized at once, sending an icy shiver coursing through his veins.

He spoke to his secretary over the intercom. " Find Captain Silverthorn will you. I want him here. Now."

A few moments later, Silverthorn was handed a photograph.

"Take a look at this."

"Good Lord!"

"Isn't it incredible?"

"If I hadn't seen it myself, Sir, I would never have believed it possible."

"Where is he now?"

"I believe he's just left Arisaig and moved to Beaulieu."

"B section, good. For now we'll leave him where he is. I don't want him alarmed or warned in any way that something's up. Understand?"

"Of course Sir."

"I can see we're going to have to give this a lot of consideration. A lot of very careful consideration indeed."

*

Life in Beaulieu was different in so much that it was not quite so cold and damp as in Scotland, yet the training continued relentlessly. Immediately they were shown the importance of working with indigenous peoples where at all possible. The Poles were known to shown unreserved co-operation with agents, whilst in Norway and France, help could be more complicated.

Scotland Yard was brought in to give advice on handling police controls and what it was like to have one's papers checked regularly. It was important to remain as nonchalant as possible, even bored, and never to offer any more information than absolutely necessary. If asked, for example, why they had not drawn their full food ration for the past week, they should simply say they had been ill, rather than go into lengthy explanations which could lead to trouble.

More than once, students were woken in the dead of night and marched off for interrogation by men in Gestapo uniforms, who went as far as possible to create what a real interrogation would be like. No torture was used but being questioned and re-questioned again and again, shouted at and verbally abused made it all frighteningly real, especially when they were told at what point they should swallow their lethal cyanide pill.

Students had to learn how to live their cover. Each was given a cover story to memorize which they had to live down to the smallest details, even to the point of not holding a knife and fork and eating the way the British did.

Nothing was overlooked or left to chance, and the principle rules of security were drummed into all students.

Don't share accommodation with another agent.
Don't commit anything to writing.
Don't talk about operations.
Don't ask what is happening in other districts.
Don't go direct to meetings, or home.
Don't get drunk in public.
Don't keep a mistress.
Don't sit in a public vehicle – stand by the entrance.
Don't disclose your identity card name.
Don't recognize other agents in public.
Don't undertake more than one type of activity.
Don't go out with another agent, except on operations.
Always have an alibi (i.e. be able to explain your presence).
Use code names only.
Look for safety signals.
After ringing a doorbell, move away and be ready to run.

They also learnt how to spot if an agent was being followed. How to lose a tail. How to exchange an arranged password during a casual bar room chat. Did students talk in their sleep? If they did, which language did they use and what did they say? To find out, rooms were fitted with tiny microphones. This examination alone meant the end of the course for a number of students.

Some of those who eventually completed the course to their instructor's satisfaction were then sent for wireless training to Thame Park, east of Oxford. Douglas was amongst those who were thoroughly grounded in the practice and theory of wireless techniques, as well as coding and ciphering.

Other courses were available such as safe-breaking, printing and even aggression advancement for those who were too genteel, but for Douglas and a handful of others, the only course remaining was parachute training.

This took place at Altrincham near Manchester, with drops into the grounds of Tatton Park from Whitley aircraft stationed at Ringway.

Douglas passed through the preliminary mock jumps without any problems and was looking forward to his first true jump, when on the morning of the jump he was withdrawn at the last moment, without explanation, and told to pack his things and report as soon as possible to Baker Street.

*

Major Walter Baum's aide knocked on the door of his office at the château in the Loire Valley.

"Enter. What is it?"

"Major Muller's daughter, Sir. We have found her."

"About time. Where?"

The man went over to the large wall map and after a pause, pointed to the place. "Here, Sir."

"Do we have an agent there?"

"No, Herr Major. But there are people in the village we could use."

"Do that. I want her watched. We must be sure not lose sight of her again."

*

At the headquarters of the S.O.E. at 64 Baker Street, Captain Alexander Silverthorn had just informed M that Douglas Reid was waiting downstairs.

"Right. Yes, we still have a lot of thinking to do regarding this young man. I have already commissioned a feasibility study to be confident we explore all possibilities, and the Director and Major Splendid have requested a few minutes of the Prime Minister's time the day after tomorrow. It's only right he's made fully aware of the seriousness and staggering potential of this situation. If we were to act without his knowledge and something go wrong, we'd spend the rest of our lives in the Tower of London."

"How do you think Mr Churchill will react, Sir?"

"I don't know. But I do know this is the stuff nightmares are made of, so I want Reid handled with kid gloves. He must not suspect a thing, so not a word until I say so. Do you understand?"

"Understood, Sir."

"Right. Send him up."

Moments later Reid entered M's office. A square room, with wood panelled walls. Reid looked slightly perplexed, but well enough, considering he had obviously lost some weight.

"Ah. There you are Lieutenant. Come in and sit down."

"Thank you, Sir."

"You're looking well."

"Thank you Sir."

"So how did it go? Would you like some tea?"

"Tea?"

"Yes, don't look so surprised. I'm sure Mr Churchill's government won't mind if we indulge ourselves."

"Well, yes please. Thank you Sir. I'm just a little puzzled. I thought because I was taken off parachute training and told to report to you, that I had done something wrong. Ready for the chop."

"Not at all. Nasty things, aeroplanes. Can't have you falling out and doing yourself a mischief, now can we? But how did you get on other than that?"

"Well, I don't know what to say. Fascinating, exciting, very interesting, even frightening at times. 'It was the best of times, it was the worst of times.' I think that just about sums it up."

" 'It was the age of wisdom, it was the age of foolishness, it was the epoch of belief, it was the epoch of incredulity, it was the season of light, it was the season of darkness, ... ' and so on and so forth."

"Well that's the last time I quote Dickens to anyone!"

"A little hobby of mine."

"What was the real reason you stopped me making a jump, Sir?" He asked wanting the truth. "Surely, if I'm to drop behind enemy lines, that would have been an invaluable experience?"

"We've put a lot of effort, time and money into your training, Lieutenant. I can tell you those courses don't come cheap. But I've seen your instructor's reports and we're very pleased with your progress. You've done well and learnt a lot, I'm sure ... "

"I certainly have Sir."

"So I won't have you putting all that at risk for the sake of jumping out of an aeroplane and probably breaking a leg, or worse. For now, I want you to take fourteen days leave, relax and unwind. Your parents live in Guildford, don't they?"

"Yes, Sir."

"Well go and spend some time with them. Drive down to Brighton for a day, and then report back here when you're fully refreshed and we'll find something for you to do."

"Any idea what, Sir?"

"No, not yet. But nothing for you to worry yourself about unduly," he lied. "Any questions?"

"No Sir. Thank you Sir." And he stood ready to leave.

"That's all, then. Sorry about the tea. Have a cup before you go with Captain Silverthorn downstairs. And Reid ... "

"Sir?"

"You do know, you still can't talk of the S.O.E. with your parents?"

"I haven't forgotten Sir."

"Take good care of yourself, Lieutenant," he said, and smiled father-like "that's an order."

"I will, Sir. Thank you."

As M watched Reid leave, his heart went out to the young man's parents who within the next few months would have no idea where their son was or what he would be doing. And then one day they would more then likely receive a telegram stating simply that he had been killed in action.

He spoke to his secretary. "I think I'm in need of a cup of tea, if you would be so kind."

When it was brought in he said to the middle-aged woman. "We will never surrender you know, never."

"I'm very pleased to hear it, Sir."

"I will not have any of my agents dying in vain. They're heroes, every last one of them. Heroes."

*

1st January 1941 found Major Claus Muller on the observation platform of the Eiffel Tower, wrapped deep in thought, oblivious to the strong and bitter north-easterly wind whistling around the famous iron structure. The icy gusts helped to clear the thinking process blocked ever since the arrival of the Führer's terse order, as Muller knew for certain the only way out of the ridiculous situation was to make it clear beyond doubt in Hitler's understanding, that the Great Mogul diamond as a whole no longer existed. There was no other way. His first attempt at reason had failed, so now he would have to try again, but harder. Only when Hitler gave the order could a halt be called to the futile search. Only when Hitler changed his mind would Muller and his daughter be safe from any reprisals and life return to some semblance of normality. Muller knew what he had to do. But how to do it?

Needing to be alone and conscious of a group of German officers enjoying the views and laughing with their lady friends, he moved away, around the platform, allowing his imagination to see a very different army, in a very different time, and the cheering crowds and celebrations when Napoleon had arrived back in the city from exile. One army after another surrendering to his charms without a shot being fired. And as he stood there with uninterrupted views to north, south, east and west, suddenly the laborious work of the past few months began to fall into its rightful place in his trained methodical intellect and he saw it all as a prelude, an initiation into whatever was to follow. Like a mist clearing, problems started to tumble one after another without a hostile argument being fired and with a jolt he realized what the next step forward would have to be. 'Of course! On any archaeological investigation, always unearth the lives and secrets of those who have gone before.'

Casually regarding the Parisian skyline, his eye fell on the Arc de Triomphe and his spirits immediately lifted. 'This could still be a triumph. There's still an honourable way out of this mess. Tavernier must hold the answer. He must!'

After the long walk it was late afternoon by the time Muller arrived back at the Hotel Meurice, yet he couldn't wait to re-read the few notes he had made on Jean-Baptiste Tavernier, the only Westerner to have seen the Great Mogul diamond. He decided to call at the Bibliothèque the following morning and seek Charles Le Mar's valuable assistance and examine Tavernier's life in as great a depth as possible, certain it would hold a clue, an answer, something.

Unexpectedly later in the evening, he received a telephone call.

"Charles, what a coincidence, I was just thinking of you."

"Good thoughts, I hope Major."

"Of course. I'm coming to see you tomorrow."

"Any particular reason?"

"Yes. I want to examine the life and times of Jean-Baptiste Tavernier in greater depth."

"I remember. The man who saw the Mogul's diamond."

"I'm certain there's something there we have overlooked."

"It is on this very subject that I call you now, Major."

"Oh?"

"I have found something which may be of interest to you."

"And what is that?"

"The Musco di Storia della Scienze in Milan recently made a life-size crystal replica of the Great Mogul for display purposes."

"Did they indeed?" his interest aroused. "How did you get to hear about it?"

"The Bibliothèque recently acquired a modest collection of books and I took some home to study. Strictly speaking I shouldn't, but the Principal turns a blind eye. He knows I always return them."

Muller's thinking process suddenly tingled to a thousand different commands. "That's very interesting, Charles," he said calmly, "thank you so much for calling. I look forward to seeing you tomorrow. Good night, and a Happy New Year to you." Replacing the receiver he immediately sat down and wrote to the Curator of the Milan Museum, stating that he was compiling information about the Great Mogul diamond for inclusion in a book on famous diamonds and requested photographs, measurements and estimated weights along with a plaster cast mould of the reproduction stone and any other relevant material which might prove helpful. On receipt of the data he promised the Museum a sizable donation.

Once the porter had taken the letter for posting, Muller sat back, satisfied with the day's unexpected bonus. He knew he could have trusted the letter to the swifter and more reliable military postal service, but risked it being opened. This way may have been slower, but it was safer and the fewer people who knew, the better.

The following morning started weeks of reading and re-reading, along with translations of French to German and English to German, as everything available on the life of Jean-Baptiste Tavernier was examined in minute detail. All over Paris, as the buds of spring awoke from their winter slumbers, so a forgotten life that had ended over two hundred and fifty years earlier, was resurrected and lived again as Muller began to compile a new report.

*

"I'm anxious to hear how your meeting went with Winston," asked M.

The gentleman briefly smelt his red carnation before carefully inserting it into his button-hole. "The bottom line, as the Director told him, is that it's just too good an opportunity to miss. Which is right of course. But Reid's completely inexperienced for a mission of this magnitude, Sir. It's an enormous responsibility for someone who's still green." He waited for a moment before continuing and lowered his head, giving the impression of studying the bottle-green linoleum in M's office. M knew better than to interrupt his colleague and did not have long to wait before he looked up.

"He's only recently completed training you say?"

"Yes. I had him withdrawn from parachute training in case he injured himself."

"That was sensible, if I may say so? No, in that case it's far too soon. We do have a responsibility towards these people and I refuse to agree to sending them on exceedingly dangerous missions when they're obviously not fully prepared."

"Unfortunately we can't afford to delay for too long."

"I know you only want to bounce some ideas off me, Sir, but this is what I would suggest. We send him into Germany on a simple uncomplicated task, for a week or ten days or so, then get him back again. I'm sure there's something your department wants done, but the task isn't important. What is important is to build the lad's confidence in himself, help him to find his feet behind enemy lines. There never has been, and there never will, be any substitute for experience. Then when he's back, and providing all goes well, we'll tell him what it is we really want of him. But to send him cold directly into the lion's den … well it simply won't do.

"Put together a water-tight cover story for him, and as he speaks Norwegian he can go in via Norway and use the same route out which will also prepare him for the second mission. I doubt if they'll expect an operator to run north."

"They'll be watching every port, station, road junction, aerodrome, everything. The whole country will be on the alert."

"Which only goes to support my point. We cannot send him to almost certain death on his first mission."

"Agreed."

"Fortunately the P.M. didn't set a time-scale and is happy to leave the details to us, but he insisted on being kept informed of progress. Do you think Reid can pull it off, Sir?"

"I'm not a betting man as you know," M reminded him "but if I had to, I'd put my money on him to win."

"Yes, having met him, so would I. Can your people handle the disguise he'll need for the second mission?"

"No problem."

"What do you think he'll say about that?"

"If I know him as well as I think I do, it should not be a problem."

"What about our agent in Berlin, can he be trusted? Is his cover still good?"

"We haven't heard from him since the package with the photographs arrived but he's one of our best."

"And the first mission, is there something useful you can find him to do in so short a time?"

"As a matter of fact there is. We've been watching the village of Obernhof just east of Koblenz. There's a hill in the centre of the village with a large church on top and we suspect the hill has been excavated and is being used as an arms dump. We need on the ground intelligence before we send in the R.A.F."

"Excellent, Reid can be in and out in a week or so."

"Yes, I like it. Well done, it's a good plan. It makes sense."

"I have my moments."

"We'll put both missions on an operational status. Since it's your idea perhaps you would like to suggest suitable code names?"

The gentleman looked directly at M and gave him a half grin, but his eyes betrayed the very real concern he felt. "Why don't you call the first operation David, and the second, Goliath?"

"Now I call that divine inspiration."

"Let's just pray the outcome is a repeat of the original." He stood and took a step towards the door. "Do keep me informed of events, Sir, and I would suggest maximum security for both tours. The fewer people who know about this, the better. We can't be too careful. When is he due back from leave?"

"In forty-eight hours."

"Just gives you time to sort out a cover story. Good luck."

*

Major Muller sat at the end of the bed in his room at the Hotel Meurice and flipped through his latest report once again.

SECRET

TO: Major Walter Baum   PARIS
10th November 1940

FOR: The Chancellor, Führer and Supreme Commander of all the Germans, Adolf Hitler.

SECOND REPORT ON THE INVESTIGATION AS TO THE SITUATION OF 'THE GREAT MOGUL' DIAMOND.

Heil Hitler,
I am pleased to announce that a new line of investigation concerning Jean-Baptiste Tavernier, the only Westerner to have seen the Great Mogul as mentioned in my previous report, has proved to be, as far as I can ascertain at this juncture, the correct line to pursue as the following précis of his life with quotes from various writings, will present.

Jean-Baptiste Tavernier: Born Paris 1605. Died Moscow 1689.
Father: Gabriel. Occupation: Geographer; inspired Jean-Baptiste to travel. By the age of 25 visited most of Europe and spoke most of the principle languages …
Eager to visit east … first journey reaching Ispahan … next five years of life uncertain, possibly became controller of household of Duke of Orleans.
September 1638. Started second journey east to Persia and India as far as Golconda where the Great Mogul was mined in 1650 …
His visit to the court of the Great Mogul and to the diamond mines was connected with plans realized more fully in later voyages, in which Tavernier travelled as a merchant of the highest rank, trading in costly jewels and other precious wares and finding his chief customers among the greatest princes of the East. The second journey was followed by four others. In his last three, he did not proceed beyond India. The details of these voyages are often obscure, but they gave him an extraordinary knowledge of the routes of overland Eastern trade, and brought the

now famous merchant into close and friendly communication with the greatest Oriental potentates …

He was presented to Louis XIV … in 1662 he married Madeleine Goisse, daughter of a Parisian jeweller … during 1684 he travelled to Berlin at the invitation of the Great Elector who commissioned him to organize an Eastern Trading Company; a project never realized …

The closing years of Tavernier's life are obscure, the time was not favourable for a Protestant and it has even been supposed that he passed some time in the Bastille. What is certain, is that he left Paris for Switzerland in 1687 …

It appears that he still had business relations in the East, but the neglect of these by his nephew to whom they were entrusted, had determined the indefatigable old man to undertake a fresh journey …

SUMMARY

I hope it may be seen that a careful attempt has been made to disentangle the threads of a life which is still in many parts obscure.
It is my belief that further information regarding Tavernier may possibly be obtained from interviewing any descendants of either his or his wife's, (I am uncertain if there was any issue from the marriage). The 252 years since his death may appear some considerable length of time, but is in fact approximately only three or four life-spans and with so famous a relation, doubtless a number of rumours, stories and perhaps even artefacts connected with his travels would have been passed down.
I shall also closely examine the life of his friend and constant companion Pepin de Roehmers.
This direction is in my view the best to follow for the time being, for not only do a great number of Tavernier's writings speak at length of the Great Mogul, but his regular contact with the Kings and Princes of India may well have produced tokens, gifts, maps etc. which may lead us forward and help our case.
Your most humble and loyal servant.

When he had finished, he read the last two paragraphs again, in disbelief of what he had just typed. Could there be the slightest chance … ? Suddenly he realized, no longer was he searching for proof that the Great Mogul diamond was nothing more than a legend, but was in fact trying to produce evidence that it really did exist! How could his objective have changed so subtly? How could all those hours of deliberations completely have changed direction without his knowledge? Had he succumbed to the Führer's hypnotic powers of suggestion?

Annoyed with himself for being so blind to what was happening, he bundled the report into the leather pouch and locked it ready for collection and went downstairs to the hotel bar. Passing through the reception area he was called to the desk. A parcel had arrived from Milan.

"I had almost forgotten about it."

"Pardon, Monsieur?"

"Nothing. I'll collect it when I've had a drink, or three."

*

Douglas had been pleased to find his Bayswater flat undisturbed by the Luftwaffe and spent a week in town and the second week with his parents. Whilst it was good to see them, relationships were strained as he was constantly on guard against letting slip any hint of his real activities, and he left a day earlier than planned, and then regretted it.

They knew all was not well but put his distant manner down to losing Jill and the ravages of war on a young mind. Their goodbyes were painful.

*

Captain Silverthorn was sitting in M's office at the S.O.E. Headquarters.

"I know you're not usually involved with missions, Alex," began M "but you get on well with Reid and I want you to look after him. You've seen all the details of his cover story and what he's got to do so you can fill him in and test him thoroughly. We're using the Shetland Bus a week from today and then when he gets back I'll announce what we've got planned for his next trip."

"The big one."

"Yes, the big one," repeated M seriously. "But not a word until he's ready and I say so."

"I understand, Sir. Leave it to me."

*

There followed five days of intense effort as Douglas took on a new identity, that of Frederic Kutzner, an agricultural machinery representative from Minden working for Koch Engineering in Hanover. Fortunately an authentic travelling salesman touring the British Isles during the spring of 1939 before the outbreak of war, had been careless enough to leave his bag along with all its contents on the Dover train, which British Intelligence snapped up as soon as war looked imminent, in anticipation of putting it to good use along with all 'foreign' lost luggage.

Douglas was young enough to pass as single which made his cover easier to work without family complications. His identity was typed out for him and he learnt it parrot fashion until he lived the part, and was quizzed on it by a special tutor both day and night. Once Silverthorn was satisfied his cover was flawless, the details were destroyed.

Experts in forged papers (a number of whom were taken from the underworld or prisons around the country and employed by the intelligence agencies for the duration), produced excellent facsimiles of German identity papers, ration books and travel permits all suitably stamped and dated, and as dog-eared as thought necessary.

Then followed checks on what he would be carrying and wearing. He was to rendezvous with a Norwegian fishing vessel off the coast of Shetland, so he would start by wearing well- worn and aptly-smelling, fishing togs. The Shetland station had a supply of these which he would collect en-route but he would need to take a change of clothes for use once landed in Bergen. When he had been measured and suited, all items were closely examined to be sure there was no link with the U.K. Every label and style had to be synonymous with the continent. Even the soles of his shoes were checked to be certain they bore no British manufacturer's mark.

In the unlikely event the fishing boat was stopped, he would need to carry a Norwegian identity, that of Harald Arnstad of Bergen, whose identity papers he could safely leave on board ready for the return trip, rather than risk being found in possession of two different identities.

The watch he was to wear was of Swiss manufacture and unengraved. The leather holdall containing German farming magazines, papers and orders from the Hanover factory had a well-worn Frankfurt label stitched onto the lining and in addition, he was given a collection of leaflets on the very latest farming machinery which he had to learn thoroughly. All the cash he carried was in used notes, both Norwegian and German. He was allowed to carry a map which a travelling salesman would have referred to regularly, and pinned to the map and in his own handwriting were a number of names and addresses of large farms in Norway and Northern Germany he would have been expected to visit. Some were circled on the map. A miniature compass looking no more significant than one from a souvenir shop and stamped Leipzig on the reverse, was hooked onto a small bunch of keys like a trinket, which he was to keep in his pocket; everyone carries keys and he would find it very useful in an emergency. Leaving him finally with the unsavoury task of writing his last will and testament, which was then locked away for safe-keeping until such time it might be required.

He was not given a firearm for if he was searched the game would be up at once; however he was permitted a 3-inch double-edged, steel blade, razor sharp in a slim sheath, which was sewn into the reverse of a coat lapel. Once stabbed into the jugular vein, it would have messy but instant results.

On preparation day six of 'Operation David,' Reid was called to M's office.

"I just wanted to wish you all the best Douglas."

"Thank you, Sir," he said, surprised at having been addressed by his Christian name.

"I'm sure Captain Silverthorn has taken good care of you?"

"Indeed he has."

"Is your cover story quite clear in your mind?"

"Absolutely, Sir. Do I get commission on any machinery sales?"

"Ha! You know what you've got to do, but don't take any chances." He moved around to the front of his desk and they shook hands. "Take good care of yourself."

"I will, Sir."

"Send Captain Silverthorn to me will you. Goodbye, and good luck."

When Silverthorn arrived, M questioned him. "Does he know you're riding shotgun as far as Shetland?"

"Yes, Sir. I told him I had to attend to a problem at our station there."

"Do you think he smelt a rat?"

"No, not at all. He seems in quite high spirits."

"Good. Just as long as he isn't overconfident. That young man is extremely valuable to this country right now, and I don't want anything going wrong. When do you think you'll be back here?"

"Ten days, twelve at the most."

"I'll see you both then."

As Silverthorn was about to leave he turned and asked. "Any sightings of our German officer yet, Sir?"

"Not yet. But our people are on the job. I'm optimistic."

*

It was a bright but frosty spring morning when Reid and Silverthorn left central London, before the rush hour traffic combined with the clearing of air-raid damage could delay them, and were driven to R.A.F. Northolt where a pre-arranged flight was waiting to take them north. After a refuelling stop at R.A.F. Catterick near Thornaby-on-Tees, there were no further stops and the Avro Anson eventually broke cloud late afternoon above Sumburgh Head on the southern most tip of the Shetland Islands.

Below them the sea was dotted with ships of the Royal Navy, upholding the Islands' role as gatekeeper between the North Sea and North Atlantic. Huge gun emplacements at strategic points along the coast supported the islands' defences, along with 20,000 British troops, as well as Canadians and Norwegians. But the island itself remained unchanged, known to its inhabitants as 'The Old Rock', barren and exposed to the most violent weather in the British Isles.

There followed a bumpy landing in a strong cross-wind at RAF Sumburgh and when the aircraft finally taxied to a halt beside a collection of wooden huts at the end of the single grass run-way, a scruffy looking giant of a man with a ruddy complexion, a thick beard and dressed in oil skins and rubber boots came out to meet them. He was introduced as Hamish, and Silverthorn appeared to know him well, greeting him like an old pal. The Scotsman knew better than to ask the reason for their arrival, and was introduced to Douglas simply a new operative.

After a brief exchange of news from the capital and progress of war on the island, they passed through a military checkpoint, and in the rapidly fading light, Hamish drove them north along a winding road to a small cottage overlooking Lerwick harbour which he shared with his wife Martha, and where the two Englishmen were to spend the night.

Martha was a chubby lady with a moon face and a quick smile, who welcomed them in a rich island accent as they stooped to pass under the low lintel. "Aye, come in and warm yersel by the fire. Ye must be frozen." She took their coats and hung them on the back of the door which opened directly into a compact but cosy room, with light coming from a single oil lamp on a centre table. Flames from a log fire bathed the room in a cheerful amber glow.

"Ye men sit and talk the King's business while I see to the stew," she told them. "It'll be ready soon."

"Sounds wonderful Martha thank you so much."

"Yer welcome, Cap'n T. Hamish has been looking forward to yer visit. He's bin saving a special bottle."

"Relax mah dear, 'tis all in hand." And Hamish produced three glasses and a bottle of Highland malt whisky.

"Only the best, Hamish."

"Oh aye Cap'n T. Only the best. Ye men deserve it," and reverently poured three equal measures. "Here's to ye. Kick the Devil 'n make him cry."

"Cheers."

"Your good health."

"Hamish and Martha run the best 'secret' guest house on Shetland, Douglas. They've been with us right from the start."

"Aye, we have that. But there are few secrets here on the island. We all do our best to fight the Bosch." He failed to mention how fearful the islanders were of an imminent German invasion from the Norwegian mainland.

"I must tell you Douglas, that they take great care of all our agents, and a lot pass through here, don't they Hamish?"

"Aye, they do that Cap'n T. To catch the Shetland Bus it is."

"Bus?" Questioned Douglas.

"The trip to Norway is used so frequently it's like a bus service. In fact Bergen is nearer to Shetland than Edinburgh."

"Aye. Now I must tell ye there's been a wee change o' plan for the morrow."

"Oh!" Douglas immediately looked concerned.

"Nothing for ye to be worrying yourself aboot, young sir. 'Tis simply the boat from Norway we were goin' to tak ye oot to meet will now be calling in the harbour."

"Is that safe, wise?"

"Oh aye. There are no strangers on the island barring yer good sel and the military. I would have heard otherwise."

"That's good news for you, old boy. Having to change boats at this time of year can be a bit dicey, even just off-shore."

"There's something I think you should know," began Douglas hesitantly, "I should have mentioned it before."

"Oh dear. What ever is it?" The Captain asked apprehensively.

"I very easily get sea sick."

Silverthorn let out a sigh. "I thought there for a moment you were going to say something serious."

"Dinnae worry yourself now, young sir. I've known Cap'n Rune Olsen for over twenty years. He's bin in 'n oot o' this harbour like a Jack-in-the-box. He'll see ye safely there and bring ye safely back again. On that ye can depend."

"That's good to know. Thank you."

"But," he added with a wide grin "he might nae be able to stop ye goin' green along the way."

"You'll be fine old boy. Just relax."

"Another drop o' best Highland spirit will wash yer fears away, young sir. I may nae be able to know yer full name, but I kin tell when a man enjoys a wee dram." And he carefully refilled their glasses. "Am I allowed to ask if ye huv been to Norway before?"

"Once, when I was a lad. Though I don't remember much about it. I have an aunt living there."

"Have ye now, and where aboots?"

"I don't know I'm afraid. We've lost contact over the years."

Martha entered with the supper.

*

Hamish woke Douglas at four a.m. whilst it was still dark and gave him a pile of fisherman's gear to wear.

"Be sure 'n wear it all now. The wind blows doon off the ice this time o' year 'n goes straight through ye."

He had finished dressing and was about to go downstairs, when he heard the two men talking.

"Is it his first mission?"

"Yes." Silverthorn told the islander.

"Aye, I thought so. Ye can always tell."

"He's a good man. We've got great things planned for him."

"Aye, nice lad."

Coming downstairs they were waiting for him at the breakfast table.

"Good Lord, you absolutely stink, old boy!"

"Thanks very much, Sir."

"No self respecting German would come within a mile of you."

"I think that's the general idea."

"Sit yesel doon Sir and enjoy a real Shetland breakfast." On cue Martha appeared with a tray of porridge and pancakes.

"The pancakes are made with powdered eggs, I'm afraid. 'Tis the rationing, ye know. But we do our best."

"Eat that lot 'n ye wull sink the boat."

"Leave him be, Hamish," said Martha. "Ye eat all ye can young man. And there's one o' two more where that came from."

"I'm sure they'll be lovely, Martha. Thank you."

"I heard that ye boat arrived during the night, but there's time enough to eat before we leave."

"How do the Norwegians know when to call, or do they visit here regularly?"

"We send instructions in the form of cryptic messages over the B.B.C. news broadcasts" Silverthorn told him.

"Is that safe?"

"Aye 'tis safe enough. Although the local people hereaboots know what's goin' on 'tis generally a well-kept secret."

"And are the boats armed?"

"Oh yes," Silverthorn told him "they carry a number of light machine guns usually concealed in an oil drum on deck."

When they had eaten their fill, Hamish checked the hour by the wall clock and announced it was time they were away, and called his wife to join them.

"Will ye all please stand." Douglas looked at Silverthorn unsure what was about to happen as they all stood around the small square table, but was unable to catch his eye.

"Young man, this is yer first visit here and yer first mission, so you'll nae know 'tis our custom when ever an agent leaves mah hoose to commit them into God's good care and what ever be your persuasion, ye will be no exception. Please bow yer heads."

Douglas glanced at Silverthorn again but his eyes were already closed.

"Oh Lord our God," began Hamish, his deep tone filling the little room "we place this young gentleman into thy mighty and powerful hands. We pray ye will bless him and guide him in what he has tae do, and bring him safely home when his work is done. Amen."

"Amen," they all repeated.

"Right. Lets be aboot the King's business. I'll fetch yer oilskins for ye. We keep them outdoors, on account o' the smell."

Martha returned to the kitchen and Hamish left Douglas and Silverthorn alone.

"I'm sorry, I forgot to warn you about the prayers. He always does it. They're a very devout lot up here."

"That's alright. It was rather nice. No-one ever prayed for me before, besides I've a feeling I'm going to need all the prayers I can get."

"He'll give thanks when you return too."

"What about those who never return?"

"That's not something you have to concern yourself with. But tell me, how are you feeling?"

"Nervous."

"Well, that's good. I'd be worried if you weren't. Nerves keep you on your toes."

"Now tell me something, Sir. What would happen if Olsen didn't return to Norway?"

"Simple. They shoot his family."

Just as they were about, to leave Martha handed Douglas a small packet.

"For Cap'n Olsen," she told him "he's crazy aboot mah pancakes. He says it's the only reason he comes here."

"I'll see he gets them. Thank you for your kindness."

Collecting his holdall which would be concealed on board, they joined Hamish outside, and with the first hint of day visible on the distant horizon, the three made their way along the Esplanade in the direction of the harbour.

"It'll be a fine day. Cold but fine, mark ma' words. I knew by the sunset last nicht."

"I'll hold you to that Hamish. And the sea?"

"Like a pond, Sir. And in less than twenty-four hours ye wull be safe ower the other side."

The deep and sheltered inlet was well used by both the Royal and Merchant Fleets with a number of mine sweepers and supply vessels either docked or anchored in deeper water off shore. A number of fishing boats of various size and colour were huddled together in the small harbour, protected from the wrath of North Sea gales by a sturdy sea wall. Already crews were showing signs of activity.

"There she is. There's Cap'n Olsen's boat." And pointing to a medium-sized trawler rising and falling on the swell; Hamish walked on ahead.

"I couldn't help overhearing you talking with Hamish earlier Sir" said Douglas.

"And what exactly was it you heard us talking about?"

"That you had great things planned for me. What sort of great things?"

"You'll find out in good time, Lieutenant. In the meantime, your orders are to get there, do the job, and get yourself safely back again, which you won't do by eavesdropping other people's conversations!"

"Sir."

"I expect my business here will detain me for a few days so I'll be waiting for you. No point in flying back alone. But good luck, Douglas. We're all rooting for you," and gave him a reassuring pat on the back.

"Thank you Sir. I'll do my best."

"I'm sure you will."

They didn't speak anymore. As they neared the boat in the ever increasing light, a strong smell of diesel wafted towards them on the strengthening breeze and immediately Douglas began to feel queasy, but he quickly determined not to look the fool by being sick before they had even cast off. The sight of the waves and white horses out beyond the protection of the harbour however, told him it may not be too long before he was ill.

The boat's engines were already idling when Captain Olsen saw the group approaching along the quay, and stepped down the narrow gangway to meet them.

Captain Rune Olsen was the original Norwegian seaman. Tall, tough and thick-set with fair hair protruding from beneath a woollen hat and a thick beard to match; light blue eyes that came alive when he smiled and a sing-song Bergen accent.

"My friend H'mish. 'Tis good to see you again," he said. Maybe it was the early hour or the half light or the clandestine nature of their meeting, but instinctively voices were subdued.

"Rune, welcome to Shetland mah friend."

"Where is the lovely Ma'tha? Has she at last left you for me?"

"Ha! She's more sense than to fall for ye, ye auld Vikin'."

"One day I come take away her."

"This is yer passenger, Rune," Hamish told the Norwegian.

He had a vice-like grip as he shook Douglas' hand.

"God dag Keptein Olsen. Takk for at due tok meg til Norge."

"Du er velkommen. Are you Norwegian?" the Captain asked surprised. "You talk good."

"No, my mother is."

"This is good man you have here," he said turning to Hamish "I know. I see many come, go. This man has strong face like Viking warrior. And what about you Capt' Silve'orn," he said shaking the man's hand. "Long time not see you."

"You look well, Rune."

"No thanks to filthy Bosch. Life hard in Norway. Much suffer. This is good man you send. What name they give you use, Englishman?"

"Harald Arnstad," Douglas told him.

"Good name Harald. My father Harald. You have papers?"

Douglas nodded.

"We make you like Norwegian man and kill Germans for us. Ja?"

"Martha gave me this for you," said Douglas in answer passing him the package.

"Always the cakes. You lucky man H'mish. Give her big kiss from me."

"I'll let ye kiss her yersel' when ye get back."

"Ja! I do it."

The note of the boat's engines changed suddenly and a member of the crew called out.

"Ja. Come," said Rune "we go now. Tide is good. Come English Harald. Farvel!"

*

To a man like Hamish, used to being surrounded by the worst storms in nature, the sea that day was as he had said it would be for early spring. Yet to a land-lubber like Douglas Reid it was as if the gates of Neptune's cave had been flung wide open to let loose his wrath on a warring world. He was violently ill.

With a stiff tail wind they were making good time but at 17.00 G.M.T. at approximately 2° of longitude, when they were a little over half way, the accident happened.

CHAPTER FOUR

The contents of the parcel from the Science Museum in Milan were strewn about on Major Muller's bed in his room at the Hotel Meurice. Everything was there exactly as he had requested; weights, measurements, drawings, photographs along with a rubber mould of the Italian copy of the Great Mogul diamond.

Muller was on the telephone listening to the tone waiting impatiently for someone to pick up. Eventually someone did. "This is Major Claus Muller. I want to be put through at once to Inspecteur Rosaria. He's expecting my call."

"One moment, Monsieur," responded a woman's voice "and I'll see if he's available."

"He will be."

Moments elapsed when another voice spoke. It sounded tired, weary. "This is Inspecteur Rosare." He spoke German.

"Inspecteur, this is Major Muller. I believe you have been expecting me to make contact. I spoke to the office of Military Commander General Otto von Stülpnagel. You should have heard from them."

"Yes Major, I did. What is it I can do for you?"

"It's an inquiry of a personal nature Inspecteur, too delicate to discuss over the telephone. We will need to meet, and as soon as possible."

"Can you not give me some indication as to the nature of the inquiry?"

"That isn't possible now. We can meet at my hotel, I'm staying at the Meurice. I presume you know it?"

"Of course, Monsieur."

"So when is the earliest you could be here?"

"This evening?"

"Good. Shall we say six o'clock?"

"Very well, six o'clock."

"I look forward to it."

*

It was not a perfect plan Muller told himself, but it would do. Involving someone else could be risky but the man need know only the barest of details, and the Sûreté would certainly know where to look and get the job done quickly.

He checked the pile of notes which had grown considerably over the past few weeks as, together with Charles Le Mar, they had studied the life and times of Jean-Baptiste Tavernier and watched as a fascinating picture emerged of his life.

Muller flicked through the pages and read aloud as he paced the room.

"Highly intelligent merchant traveller, made himself a fortune from travelling the world." 'You certainly don't get rich by being stupid.' He reminded himself. "Early journeys Europe, Germany et cetera with regular visits to Switzerland with constant friend and companion Pepin de Roehmers. Eager to visit East. Visited a dozen different countries by 1631 and seen action with Colonel Hans Brenner, Viceroy of Hungary. Was friend of dukes and spoke many languages. At twenty-six teamed up with two French priests, M. de Chapes and M. de St. Liebau, who had received a mission to the Levant and arrived in Constantinople. Spent eleven months there, then on to Persia, Ispahan then returned to Paris 1633. Did not reach India.

"1638, journeyed to Persia, India as far as Agra and Golconda, birth place of Great Mogul diamond. Four further journeys east.

"1684, travelled to Berlin at invitation of Great Elector. Left Paris for Switzerland again 1687, as always with de Roehmers; died Moscow, 1689, leaving affairs in the hands of his nephew."

"Yes!" He exclaimed "I know I'm right. What a fool I've been not to have seen it before."

The study of Tavernier's life, fascinating though it was, revealed nothing to suggest that he was guilty of any impropriety, or that he had died in the knowledge that the Great Mogul diamond was in anyone else's hands other than its rightful owner. Though many famous stones had passed through his hands in the course of business over the years, the mere fact that his business interests faltered so soon after passing to his nephew, was proof enough that the Taverniers did not possess the vast wealth the Great Mogul would undoubtably have brought. Yet the life of his friend and companion, Pepin de Roehmers, was not so distinct. It was in fact an enigma and shrouded in mystery.

*

Inspecteur Rosare relaxed on the back seat of the black Citroën as it made its way through the wartime evening traffic of Paris. It made no difference to him who he worked for; the French Government, German, all were the same to him. A job was a job, just as long as whoever they were remembered to pay him at the end of the month. He was good at his work and he knew it, that was why he, above others, had been instructed by the Commissaire de Police to do whatever it was this Major Muller wanted.

The car eventually came to a halt outside the multiple arched facade of the Hotel Meurice and the Inspecteur told his driver to wait.

The habit of a lifetime made him pause before entering the building and look around. Nothing unusual for the time of year, yet two years ago it would all have been inconceivable. Germans everywhere, going in and out of the hotels with pretty French girls on their arms, girls most patriots would call collaborators, or strolling along the banks of the Seine relaxed, laughing with their painted paid women whilst sober Parisians had little to laugh about, all the while living in fear of what tomorrow may bring. He inhaled the last breath of his Galoise cigarette and, stubbing it out on the sidewalk, strode into the hotel.

Inside, if it had not been for the many military uniforms, one would never have guessed there was a war on. In the corner of the large and opulent entrance hall, a string quartet was playing for early evening guests and hotel staff buzzed to the demands of their patrons. Business was booming, and he felt sick at the remembrance of those who had died in vain for a country that could no longer call itself free.

He told the desk to advise Major Muller of his arrival and lit another cigarette before being informed he could proceed upstairs.

Stepping over to the lift waiting for it to descend, he caught a glimpse of his reflection in the mirrored doors but abruptly turned away not needing a reminder of his appearance. He looked like every other Frenchman, conquered, beaten, tired and hopeless. And he knew he looked pale, gaunt even. The few days in the country hadn't done him much good and he was still smoking far too much. But just ten more years and he could retire, just ten more. But a lot could happen in ten years. If Britain should fall?

His thoughts switched to the people around him, foreigners mostly. Years ago he would have felt uncomfortable amongst such affluence and glamour, but not now, not since the death of his son. Now nothing mattered any more. Was it three years already? Maybe in a strange way it was for the best. If he had lived to see the new France it would have broken his heart, like it had already broken the heart and soul of every loyal citizen. And poor Mimi, she had cried herself to sleep again last night. It could all have been so different. Who knows?

The lift arrived.

The Inspecteur only had to knock once before the door was opened.

"Ja?"

At the sight of Muller's eye patch and disfigurement Rosare was caught unaware, yet his trained expression remained stoically fixed.

"Bonjour Monsieur, my name is Rosare. Inspecteur Maurice Rosare."

"Come in Inspecteur, thank you for being so punctual."

"Not only Germans are efficient Monsieur," and Rosare entered, habitually absorbing in a single glance all that the room had to offer.

"I'm pleased to say your army doesn't think quite the way you do, Inspecteur." Muller could not resist the jibe but Rosare wasn't ruffled and instead smiled ironically.

"I'm sure you have not invited me here to discuss warfare, Monsieur." He stubbed out his cigarette in the cut glass ash tray on a small coffee table. "May I?" he said, and sat down in one of two high-backed chairs obviously positioned for their meeting. "It's been a hard day."

"Of course. Let's get down to business," Muller sat opposite him. "I wouldn't wish to detain you any longer than necessary."

"What is it I can do for you, Monsieur?"

"I want you to find someone for me."

"Major Muller," the Frenchman began, obviously annoyed. "I am an Inspecteur of Police. With the country at war, there are thousands of refugees and missing persons, literally thousands. If you have brought me here simply to find someone, I wish I had known in advance, because I would have sent one of my juniors."

"Relax, Inspecteur," said Muller, knowing he would catch more flies with honey than with vinegar. "You're jumping to all the wrong conclusions. This is no ordinary missing person's inquiry. The person I have in mind lived a long time ago and for certain reasons I need to trace any living relatives."

"Am I permitted to know why you need this person traced?"

"No."

"It could help."

"It could, but no matter what, the reason remains confidential."

"So who are we talking about?"

"A man by the name of Pepin Udo De Roehmers. He lived in Paris during the seventeenth century."

"Interesting name. Germanic and French. But the seventeenth century? Monsieur have you any idea what you are asking?"

"Inspecteur, I am perfectly familiar with the procedure for tracing families of antiquity but I also know that with all the resources available to the police you could find someone far sooner than I."

"There's something you have obviously overlooked but I'll come back to that in a moment. But the seventeenth century … why there could be hundreds of descendants, thousands even."

"Possibly yes, but on the other hand, there could also be very few, if any." He handed Rosare a paper. "I have prepared this for you with as much information as I have about the man, but you will observe there are two names. The other is that of Jean-Baptiste Tavernier." Rosare held the sheet at arm's length and quickly glanced down the close typed data as Muller continued. "Now, De Roehmers was Tavernier's friend and constant companion and accompanied him on most of his travels which I have listed, and as you will see, were extensive.

"Unfortunately I don't know where De Roehmers was born or died but I have included Tavernier's details because being contemporaries they would more than likely have been of a similar age. That may help you. As far as I know there was no issue from Tavernier's marriage but I can't tell if De Roehmers was married or not. I suspect, though I may be wrong, that he was a priest."

"Catholic or Protestant?"

"I can't say but I do know Tavernier was Protestant and they were inseparable friends."

"What you ask of me, is," Rosare shrugged "with a good helping of luck, possible, I suppose. But as I say, you're overlooking one very important event."

"Which is?"

"The Revolution, Monsier."

"Of course, the Revolution! You're right, I did forget. How very careless" he said, fingering his scar, annoyed with himself for the oversight. "But what possible difference can it make to the search for this man's family?"

"A great difference. Many books, family papers, family histories, details of births, marriages, deaths and much more were thrown into the flames. Was this De Roehmers or Tavernier nobility?"

"Tavernier was extremely wealthy by all accounts and was on excellent terms with Louis the fourteenth, and dukes, and noblemen from a number of countries."

Rosare nodded. "He was nobility. What of De Roehmers?"

"I don't know. But does that make a great difference? He was dead long before the Revolution."

Rosare glanced down at the paper. "When did Tavernier die?"

"1689, he was eighty four."

"So we can presume De Roehmers died late sixteen hundred or early seventeen if they were of a similar age. The Revolution was around 1790 but you see, the homes of the nobility were particularly targeted Monsieur; who knows what evidence was lost." Rosare read down the paper Muller had prepared for him. "This is very thorough," he commented.

"You see Inspecteur, we Germans are efficient."

"Touché."

"Is there anything else you need to know?"

"Only what I am to do if I find any descendants."

"You do nothing. Do not attempt to make contact in any way. You report back to me with your findings and I'll take it from there."

"As you wish."

"I want this handled discreetly, Inspecteur. Will you be working alone?"

"From the way the Commissaire was speaking, yes. We are very low on manpower of course, but I have been assigned to help you Monsieur. You obviously have friends in high places."

"It helps to get things done."

"What you have asked of me is no quick task, you understand."

"Of course, but I'm sure you will give it your best and should you need access to files or information from other countries …"

"Other countries! You didn't say you wanted the search extended outside of France!"

"Why yes, of course. I want a thorough search. The whole of western Europe. People migrate, Inspecteur."

"But that makes it an enormous task."

"Indeed it is, and will require all your expertise, but should you need help you may always contact Colonel von Stülpnagel's office and mention my name."

Rosare knew any further protest would be futile and resigned himself to his fate. "This is all most unusual. I shall need all your influence Monsieur, I think."

"These are unusual times, Inspecteur."

"Oui, indeed. But it will make a welcome change from chasing criminals, I suppose."

"I'm sure it will. I shall be away for a while so if you should need to contact me be sure not to leave any of your findings with anyone. Just wait until I return."

"Here?"

"Yes."

"As you wish, Monsieur."

As the Inspecteur returned to his car, he looked up, imagining he could pick out the windows of the room he had just vacated, and muttered "Vive la France."

"Did you say something, Patron?" asked his driver.

"It'll keep."

*

Even though it was bitterly cold, the sun had been with them from soon after they left Lerwick harbour, and was only now beginning to lose its strength. The wind was blowing a constant westerly but nothing stronger than a force four, which helped to push Captain Olsen and his crew nearer Bergen, and home. Yet even though conditions were ideal every second was a living hell for Douglas Reid, laid out on a soiled damp bunk behind the wheel-house, painfully conscious of the boat's every movement, his only companion a bucket into which he constantly retched with every lift of the prow until his stomach had nothing left to surrender.

The swell eased somewhat around 5 p.m. when the boat's motion lessened. Douglas forced himself off the bunk and into the adjoining wheel-house, being sure not to look out at the vast expanse of lead-grey ocean rising and falling, breaking over the bow, sending sheets of spray smashing against the glass screen like machine-gun fire.

"Ah! English Harald." Captain Olsen was at the helm. "Feel better?"

"I must have some water to drink. I mustn't dehydrate."

"Water we have," and pointed to a small rusted tank on the back wall of the cramped and cluttered wheel-house. Along side was a chipped enamel mug that dangled on the end of a piece of string and banged against the wall with each lurch of the vessel.

"No German boats today, no."

"That's good."

"Ja, is good."

Even though the water tasted stale, it was at least wet. Douglas felt no better, but he felt no worse.

"I think some fresh air might help."

"Air ja, good for sick man. You hold on to rail."

Dressing in one of the oilskin jackets hanging on the back of the door, Douglas cautiously ventured outside, where the sudden rush of freezing air and salt spray had an immediate effect. Forgotten were the heady diesel fumes that had plagued him all day, together with the thump-thump-thump of the engine, and the strong wind helped clear his head of the clinging odour of vomit.

Still feeling groggy but on the mend, in the rapidly weakening light he gripped the wooden hand rail which ran around the wheel-house and made his way to the rear where the three man crew were busy gutting the last catch of the day. Soon it would be too dark to fish and Olsen had said how suspicious it would look to arrive in Bergen with an empty hold. Watching them as they deftly separated bone from flesh, for the first time in twelve hours Douglas forgot his sickness and found himself almost looking forward to the second half of the voyage, which could only be better than the first.

One of the crew known as Leife, who was shorter and older than the other two, with a deeply weathered and tanned skin was the first to speak.

"You try cut fish?"

"No, not me thanks. I have enough trouble just standing still."

"You try. I show."

The men were standing working around a blood-stained wooden slab, connected to the rear of the wheel-house, and as each fish was gutted, the head was retained while the tail and entrails were tossed over the side to be eagerly snatched by flocks of screaming gulls fighting for the best prize.

With a flick of the knife the cod, skate, herring or mackerel were opened, cleaned and then packed into boxes of ice or salt. They made it appear so easy.

"Try." Leife encouraged him, offering the handle of a vicious-looking narrow-bladed knife which Douglas reluctantly accepted, steadying himself as best he could, as Leife banged a large cod down onto the slab. The other men looked on in amused silence.

"First, head off," Leife told him, which Douglas managed without much trouble triumphantly flinging it into the scraps bin.

"Is good! Now from tail to head."

But Douglas hesitated.

"Ja, you do it. Make good fish man."

Without answering, Douglas pressed and held the fish firmly down with his left hand as he had seen the men do, and inserted the knife a little way behind the tail.

"Push in, ja." The knife went in half way to the hilt.

"Pull towards now."

Douglas did as he was told, precisely as a freak wave hit the bow sending the knife off in the wrong direction, causing a gash to appear all the way along the side of his index finger and down to the bone at the base of the thumb.

He dropped the knife and stared at his hand in disbelief. There was no pain and for a second, there was no blood. Then the crimson flow began, dripping onto the wooden deck, mixing with discarded fish guts as a fog of nausea enveloped him. Only this time, the motion of the sea was not to blame, but a deep nervous sickness as the ghastly ramifications of what he had done began to dawn on him. Everything was ruined. Then the pain arrived, and he started to sway, Leife catching hold of him shouting to one of the men who scrambled into the wheel-house. A second later, the Captain appeared immediately realizing what had happened.

"You fool! Letting him play with knives! Get him inside."

The Captain grabbed his wrist - attempting to stem the flow of blood - squeezing so hard Douglas thought it would break, and led him back into the wheel-house where one of the men already had a first-aid box open, but it was pitifully inadequate.

Still clasping his wrist, Olsen guided Douglas onto the bunk he had left only moments earlier and looked at his English passenger. His skin was clammy, sweaty yet cold and what little colour he had regained, had now drained completely leaving him deathly white. And the cabin air was still heavy with the stench of vomit. It did not help.

"This is bad, English Harald. I must sew. You want we should go back, or go on? This cut bad but you must decide."

Douglas had difficulty focussing and Olsen's voice appeared to be coming at him down a long tunnel. "Go on," he said, "we must go on."

Olsen nodded and spoke to one of the men who reached for a bottle of whisky from an overhead locker. "Drink this, Englishman. What I must do is not good; this will help." He pulled the cork with his teeth and, still squeezing Douglas's wrist with one hand, held the bottle to his lips as Leife, looking on anxiously, raised Douglas up enough to let him drink.

"Drink deep, will help."

The spirit burned his mouth, throat and gut as it slipped down into an empty stomach but he didn't care. He just didn't care … any … more … not at … all …

The captain gave an order. "Get the glass screen covered up or we'll be seen from miles away."

Once the Englishman had passed out, Olsen worked quickly and by the light of a swinging oil lamp tied a tourniquet bandage around Douglas's wrist. One of the crew fetched a fresh reel of the finest fishing line they had, along with a set of sewing needles which were usually used for darning socks and jumpers. Olsen filled a glass with whisky and dropped the newest looking needle in whilst pouring more of the liquid over the fishing line, his hands, and the open wound. Removing the needle from the whisky, he threaded a prepared length of line and without hesitation, as Leife held Douglas's hand still, jabbed the needle into the pale flesh and began to stitch, working as fast as he could, oblivious to the half-conscious man's moans.

Within minutes the powerful hands more used to mending fishing nets had closed the six inch cut with craftsmanship of which any surgeon under similar conditions would have been proud. Pouring the remains of the whisky over his finished work, he dried it with cotton-wool and applied the best pressure bandage he could, with what the first-aid kit allowed. Tying a length of bandage to a hook on the wall, he quickly rigged up a cradle to take the weight off Reid's arm, and once secure, he gradually released the tourniquet thinking to himself the last place this English agent should be was in the middle of the North Sea when he should be in hospital. If he ever regained the use of his thumb it would be a miracle.

As the final light of day dipped below the western horizon so Douglas slipped in and out of consciousness, with every waking moment acutely aware of the excruciating throbbing in his hand, along with the dilemma he now found himself in, thanks to his own stupidity. Should they have turned back? To return a failure on his first mission would be unthinkable. No, he had made the right decision to go on, and certainly had not gone through all those weeks of training for nothing. Yet what would he say if he were stopped? The huge bandage with only the tips of his fingers showing was hardly discreet. An accident at one of the farms en-route. That would do. And waiting until home in Germany to get seen to properly. But what about the return journey, what excuse could he use then? He would worry about that nearer the time. For now, lives depended on completion of the mission ready for 'greater things' later. Whatever that might mean. Oh for terra-firma!

*

The ancient Viking harbour of Bergen is buried deep behind countless islands and exposed outcrops of rock, and at night most small craft take between forty-five minutes and an hour from the time they leave the open sea until the tricky waterways have been successfully negotiated, and are able to dock. The journey across from Shetland had been so timed that Captain Olsen would arrive in Bergen on a favourable tide and under the cover of darkness, at approximately 5 a.m. local time. It was only after leaving the North Sea that Hamish's prediction of a 'pond-like' sea proved accurate, as the waters of the huge fjord were always 'pond-like', and so the change in Douglas was immediately noticeable.

Captain Olsen throttled back on the engine until it was no more than a gentle murmur, giving them as much time as possible before reaching the quay, but not wanting to stop altogether and arouse suspicion or a possible boarding by a patrol vessel. Handing over the helm to one of the crew, Olsen anxiously checked on his passenger's bandages which, miracle of miracles, had not shown any new signs of blood.

"Before we dock you eat and drink, or too weak to travel."

"I can feel the water's much calmer now."

"We now in fjord. No more waves, all calm."

"I'm feeling better. I'm sorry to have caused you so much trouble."

The Captain looked down at the young man lying in his bunk who was willing to risk everything for the fight against oppression.

"Next time, you use this," he said pointing to his head "before you use these," holding up his hands.

"I will, sorry."

"You have long way to go?"

"Yes, a long way." Douglas knew Olsen would know nothing about the mission. It was S.O.E. practice that the less those involved knew, the better.

"Then now English Harald, you must eat. Then you change so can leave boat quickly when people come for fish."

*

Captain Rune Olsen's boat slipped quietly into Bergen's Vågen harbour along with six or so other fishing vessels at a little after 5.30 a.m. The outlines of eighteenth-century wooden trading houses on Bryggen Torget were only just visible through the gloom, behind a row of quay-side lamps which cast pools of light into the deep, motionless, waters of the dock. The stillness of the night was only now being broken by the first sounds of a city awakening to another day of life under occupation.

The boat's return was acknowledged, but as a regular sight on the quay, received little attention other than from a pair of guards who checked the docking and fishing permits and enquired as to their catch. "The usual," they told them fleetingly. Once satisfied, and as was the usual practice, the German quota of the catch was commandeered and unloaded onto the dock to be collected later, leaving a pitiful balance for the fisherman to do with as they wished. Most boat captains kept a secret, second hold for Black Market trading as it was the only way to survive.

It was raining heavily so the guards did not stay around to investigate further, but moved along to check on the arrival of other boats quayside.

Douglas rested on the bunk, fully recovered from seasickness but with his hand still throbbing until 7.30 a.m., when the first of the town's womenfolk began to appear, to inspect the remaining fish the crews had arranged along the dock. With strict food rationing, even scraps were in demand.

By 8 o'clock the rain had stopped, and dark clouds had given way to patches of blue. A weak sun was already reflecting in the puddles of the night as people milled around the fish stalls, with only the occasional guard, wearing a very indifferent expression, to be seen.

With his Norwegian papers suitably hidden away on board, and dressed appropriately for an agricultural machinery salesman, Douglas bade Rune farewell.

"We'll be here for you, English Harald. You know the boat. Remember to keep hand up. Good luck Englishman."

Checking the quay through the wheel-house screen and seeing an opportunity when a number of people gathered close by their stall, Douglas collected his holdall and stepped off the boat. With only the slightest of nods to the crew, he assumed his new identity of Frederic Kutzner and disappeared into the crowd.

*

"Hello." The voice on the other end of the telephone was that of an elderly man.

"Is that Willem Beck?"

"It is."

"My name is Claus Muller. You probably don't remember me."

"No, should I?"

"I was a student at the Frederick William University in Berlin, and I remember you as a guest lecturer when you spoke on diamonds and diamond cutting."

"That I do remember, but it was many years ago. Wasn't it as part of an archaeology course?"

"That's right, it was."

"Did you graduate?"

"I did."

"Good. Must have been a good lecture. How did you get my number after all this time?"

"From the D.G.G., the German Gemmological Association."

"I didn't know I was still a member."

"Tell me Herr Beck, are you still working at diamond cutting?"

"Yes and no. Officially I'm retired. I'm almost seventy, you know."

"Really?"

"But I take special commissions when something interesting comes along, which isn't very often these days of course, but it helps to pay the bills."

"I'm glad you said that, because I have a very special commission for you if you would be interested."

"I could be, but I'd like to know a little more about it before I commit myself."

"It's impossible to discuss it over the telephone. I think it best if I were to come and see you."

"Yes, if you wish. Do you know the address?"

"Yes, they gave me that too. Tell me just one thing before you go."

"If I can."

"If I were creating something to look like diamond what would I use?"

"To look like a diamond but not?"

"As near as humanly possible."

"Well, there's a difference of opinion on that. Some would answer zircon to your question, but I wouldn't. I would say corundum."

"I thought so."

"Colourless corundum, of course. It doesn't have the fire of a diamond but I've seen some nice stones in my time, and providing they're cut well, they can look quite convincing."

"And there's definitely nothing closer to diamond?"

"Only zircon but as I say, I'm not that taken with zircon, I never have been. It's not as hard as corundum for a start. Naturally, there are one or two differences between diamond and corundum of course, such as their refractive index. Corundum, which as you know includes sapphire and ruby is, I seem to remember, 1.76 against diamond 2.42."

"That refers to its reflective qualities?"

"Yes. Though on a hardness scale they're very close with diamond at the top of the scale at 10.0 and corundum just behind at 9.0, and providing a so called colourless stone isn't completely void of fire, as I say, they can look quite good."

"Excellent."

"Is corundum what you want me to work with?"

"I won't commit myself now but I know you'll be fascinated when I tell you."

"So when should I expect you? I'm sorry I didn't catch your name fully."

"Muller, Major Claus Muller."

"You're in the German army now then?"

"Yes, does that make a difference?"

"I suppose not. I knew you weren't Dutch."

"I hope to be with you within a day or two."

"Until then, Major Muller."

"I look forward to seeing you again after all this time."

Returning the telephone to its hook on the wall, Muller looked very pleased with himself and made his way from the small room at the rear of the café out into the restaurant, and spoke to the proprietor.

"Thank you, Monsieur for the use of your telephone." He placed a pile of coins on the counter far in excess of what he had spent, knowing he would need the 'safe' telephone again.

"A coffee, Monsieur?"

"Yes, I will. To celebrate."

*

In watery sunlight, Douglas Reid walked the deck of the Oslo-Kiel ferry, thankful that it was larger than Captain Olsen's boat, as well as for the fact that the waters of the Kattegat were so much calmer than the North Sea, at least on this occasion. Even so, he was careful to do whatever he could to keep well. He breathed deeply, the fresh salty air filling his lungs, then slowly exhaled. It helped.

After leaving Shetland, he was already three days into the mission. Having said goodbye to Olsen in Bergen, he eventually caught the train which took him on a spectacular route over the mountains to Oslo where, after some considerable delay which he used to have something to eat, he boarded the passenger ferry for Kiel on the northern tip of Germany. Another half-hour and they would be there.

The ferry itself was carrying less than fifty percent of its passenger capacity, yet still no-one spoke to him, an air of mistrust and suspicion prevailing. These were dangerous times for everyone.

So far there had been no difficulties. His papers had been checked regularly along the way, as was to be expected, and twice his bag had been searched. Then, before he could purchase a ferry ticket, he had been told to produce a travel permit. The forgers back at S.O.E. had done their work well and at every occasion those painful weeks of training were recalled, reminding him to appear as nonchalant and unconcerned as possible. Though what things would be like once inside Germany remained to be seen.

Only one traveller on the train had mentioned his bandaged hand, and when Douglas had responded in German, the man had quickly lost interest. Remembering to elevate his hand as much as possible meant the bandage had continued to show no signs of blood, even though the throbbing had not abated.

The ferry had already passed close between the Danish islands of Fyn and Sjaelland, and coming into Kiel Bay, it was obvious from the distant columns of smoke rising through the early morning mist, that the R.A.F. had paid the German naval installation a visit during the night. No doubt another agent would report on the various warships at anchor and the submarine-producing shipyard, the thought of which made Douglas feel both proud and humble that he was playing his part in the network that went to make up British Secret Intelligence.

Entry into the Fatherland was certainly different from his arrival in Norway. There were guards with dogs, military police and port authorities checking and rechecking everyone who disembarked. Handbags, luggage, briefcases, everything was thoroughly scrutinized and some individuals were taken aside and body-searched. Not carrying a gun proved to be a wise move, for to be caught in possession of an unauthorized firearm would have proved difficult to explain.

Douglas continued to look unconcerned by it all, even to the point of yawning (which was genuine enough even though he had managed a nap during the twenty-hour crossing). He passed through the checkpoint without incident, managing to answer all the questions, and was about to make for the railway station when suddenly he was hailed.

"Halt!"

Heads turned, but hurried on when they realized the shout was not for them. An officer standing aside from the main body of personnel walked over, looking the stranger up and down as he came towards him. He was younger than Douglas, an Oberleutnant and smartly turned out. Douglas remained calm and slowly put his holdall down, purposely presenting a picture of someone who had no reason to run. But he couldn't help fingering the lethal thin blade inside his lapel. Not here, not now.

"What have you been doing to yourself?" the soldier asked directly.

"What, this? It was my own stupid fault, I caught it in some farm machinery."

"By the size of the bandage and the colour of your thumb you should get it seen to at the hospital, and soon." The man looked genuinely concerned.

"Now that I'm home again, I will. Thank you."

"Take care of yourself."

With his heart pounding, Douglas picked up his holdall and walked on. It was 8.30 a.m. on a fine morning of day four of 'Operation David'.

Once he had breakfasted at a water-side café, he made his way through the old town to the railway station which, like many parts of the town, bore heavy scars of the Royal Air Force who were also to blame for delaying the train to Hamburg which, when it arrived, was packed with relocating troops. He found himself a seat and pretended to be asleep rather than get involved in conversation. Once in Hamburg, Germany's second largest city, he changed trains and without further hold up, passed through the lowlands to Hanover and then on to Kassel where he had to change again. At every town he passed through, the sight of destruction and devastation was appalling, and on a scale he would never have believed had he not witnessed it himself. The German's were certainly getting as good as they gave in Britain.

After yet another frustrating delay spent pacing up and down the platform, grumbling along with other travellers, the train that was to deliver him to his destination eventually ground to a halt amidst a cloud of steam. With Kassel behind him, the train pushed on to higher ground and the countryside around the old towns of Merburg, Lahn, then Limburg and finally the village of Obernhof.

His identity papers and travel permit had been examined again and again, yet never once had they aroused suspicion, and his bandaged hand had proved an unexpected asset even though it attracted regular glances.

Who would suspect a foreign agent in his condition? He was exhausted, but relieved when at last he stepped down from the train, although no-one else alighted with him. As he looked around, he understood why. Obernhof was nothing more than a small hamlet, the peace time population of which could not have exceeded more than three hundred souls at the most. Much smaller than expected.

Running through the centre of the pretty village, under the eye of the all seeing Nazi flag, were the waters of the river Lahn. Clusters of neat wood and brick-clad houses ran along both banks, from where the land climbed gently to tree covered hills surrounding the whole area like a wall of natural protection. Then, lifted above the trees on one particular hill like a shepherd guarding his flock, stood the white and grey stone building of the church he had journeyed so far to investigate. Could the Germans really be using this backwater as an arms dump? It was up to him to find out.

Already the sun was falling behind the hills, and rather than start wandering around in the twilight when as a stranger he would stand out like the sore thumb he already was, he decided to find a pension. He could then carry out his reconnaissance under the cover of darkness and, all being well, catch an early train out the following morning.

A short way from the station he was presented with a choice. The road to the right ran under the railway bridge then up and over a humped back bridge, across the river to the south side of the village, whilst the road to the left climbed slowly as it rose up to the hill with the church. He chose left, nearer his objective, and had walked only two hundred yards when he saw a sign in the window of a pleasant two storey house advertising bed and board. He knocked on the door. It transpired that the landlady was away with a friend in Lahn and, as her elderly husband explained, she would not be back for a couple of days but if he did not mind preparing his own bed and having a simple sausage and potato supper, he was welcome to stay. Douglas willingly accepted the terms. The house was simply furnished, and clean, and offered him the welcome prospect of his first bed for three nights. However, whilst he was eating the simple meal, he learnt something that upset all his arrangements for the return journey. The following day was Sunday, and no trains had stopped at Obernhof on a Sunday since the outbreak of war.

He retired early having first checked the lock on the front door, which was just a simple latch. He determined just to doze until midnight when he could creep out and follow the path up to the church to try to find out just what was going on. If it was an arms dump as expected, there would be guards and barbed wire and God knows what else, which alone would give the game away. But his rest was troubled by thoughts of what the next day would bring. There was nothing else for it but to walk to Limburg however far it was, - six, eight miles - and catch a train from there. He had been drilled that once a mission was completed, to get out as quickly as possible, by whatever means available and not to hang around. Also he could not afford to keep Captain Olsen waiting in Bergen.

When the house had been still for a couple of hours and he could hear the rhythmic snoring of the old man in the room next door, he soundlessly went downstairs and at a little after midnight crept out into the darkness, leaving the door on the latch.

The road continued on for about another five hundred yards with houses at irregular intervals on both sides, and then veered to the right starting to climb steeply and narrowing, until it eventually became no more than a wide path, too narrow for any motor vehicles. The night sky was heavy with cloud completely blocking out any moonlight, yet even so, he kept to the edge, ready to dart into the trees should anyone suddenly appear. But there was no-one. The whole area was still and undisturbed, save for the occasional bird or rabbit scurrying through the undergrowth. Even the air was still, though heavy with dank scents of the country by night.

The path continued winding its way up the hill, eventually opening out into an area resembling a courtyard surrounded by trees in front of the entrance to the church known as Kloster Arnstein. Keeping to the perimeter, he made for the door and silently tried the large iron handle. Locked, of course, but it was already Sunday so surely the church would be open for worshippers during the day. He would return later and investigate the inside.

Retracing his steps, he made his way down the path but instead of following the road back, branched off passing through the trees and behind the hill. Nothing at all. No guards, no wires, no concealed entrances, nothing. The whole journey had been a waste of time and effort, yet he resolved to check inside just in case. Who knew, maybe the priests were in on the secret? History told of stranger things.

*

He awoke with a start to the sound of bells, so loud they could have been directly above his head. The sun was streaming in through the little window at the foot of the bed and he glanced at his watch. Seven o'clock, but what was that other noise? He jumped out of bed and crossed to the window, shocked by what he saw in the street below. Walking slowly past the house was a long continuous column of elderly men and women and some children in single file, the women and girls all with head scarves or shawls, making their way unhurriedly, reverently, past and up the hill.

'Matins. They're all going to the church', he told himself 'the whole village'. The bells continued zealously calling the faithful to prayer. 'Now's my chance to see the inside'. Shaving as quickly as he could for the first time in days, he dashed out and joined some stragglers towards the tail end of the line. The old man of the house had obviously left already.

Slowly, he followed the route he had taken only hours earlier, only this time the huge studded double doors of the Kloster were wide open and once inside the snake of people broke up, filling the pews down both sides of the aisle.

The doors banged shut and the bells fell silent.

Being one of the last in, Douglas took a seat at the back and during the short service used the time to look around as much as he could from his vantage point, without attracting attention. The building was illuminated by hundreds of candles and all looked quite as one would expect the interior of a church to look. When the call for communion was sounded he walked down to the altar to receive the holy sacraments, following the example of the villagers. His head however, was not bent in reverence, but in inspection of the marble floor for trap doors. There were none.

An hour after it had started, the service ended and as people filed out he slipped to one side pretending to read the various wall plaques as he slowly made his way around the exterior walls. When he had finished he was totally convinced there was nothing in or around the building to suggest any military involvement, and feeling both discouraged and annoyed that all his efforts had been in vain, walked quickly to the exit, conscious that he was the last to leave. The huge heavy doors were closed and as he tried them only the right one gave way. As he squeezed through it fell back much faster and harder than expected and, unable to pull his bandaged hand free in time, the iron studded door banged shut trapping his hand in a vice like grip.

The bells had been loud, but never had Obernhof heard a sound like it heard then. From deep within his body every fibre joined together emitting a cry that sent shivers through all those who heard it amplified against the stillness in the confines of the courtyard.

Instinctively, he forced the door open and removed his hand, as people who had been standing talking together after the service rushed to his aid, realizing what had happened. Douglas was at the point of collapse when he felt strong arms around him guiding him to a bench on the perimeter under the trees. It was one of the priests, a tall elderly man with a thick dark beard. Some of the womenfolk fussed around and were at the point of removing the bandage when he noticed it was already damp with blood. Obviously the stitches had burst. "No!" He told them anxiously. "Not here."

"I know," a young voice in the group spoke out. "My house is the nearest. He can go and rest there. I'll take care of him."

Douglas looked up to see who had spoken. The voice belonged to a girl in her late teens, or early twenties. He had only ever seen a girl like this before in his dreams. She was wearing a pink headscarf around hair so fair it was almost white, which only added to her air of serenity.

He managed a smile. "That's kind of you, but I think it'll need stitching."

When she smiled back her deep blue eyes were full of concern. "I have done a first aid course, I'm sure I can cope," she told him confidently. Before he could respond, the girl had already said something to the priest who helped Douglas to his feet. "I will help you to this girl's house; it's directly at the foot of the hill. She will take good care of you, I know. Then tomorrow, when the doctor visits the village, you must see him."

Further discussion was pointless and by now most of the bandage had soaked red. Something had to be done and quickly.

The girl lead the way down the path followed by the priest with his arm around Douglas more for comfort than support, whilst a few women followed on behind. At the base of the hill passing through a white gate he had not noticed in the dark the night before, Douglas was helped along a narrow footpath, past a small cluster of trees, to the door of an old two-storey white painted house, which was mostly covered by ivy and creepers. The priest helped him into the kitchen where the girl was already filling a kettle and sat him down beside a well-scrubbed wooden table.

"You must rest now, young man," he told him. "I think you have lost a lot of blood," and reassuringly rested his hand on Douglas's shoulder. "You are in good hands here. What brings you to Obernhof? I haven't seen you here before."

"I'm involved with farm machinery, that's how I got this," but the priest was watching the girl laying out clean towels and bandages.

"What can I do to help you, Astrid?"

"You can," she lowered her voice "send those women away." Neither of the men had realized that four or five women from church had followed them in and were clustered around the kitchen door, eagerly watching the proceedings.

"Come now ladies," began the priest, "nothing more to see here. I'm sure this young man doesn't want an audience." And he shooed them along the hall.

"I think I need a tourniquet." Douglas told the girl.

"I think you do too." Working quickly, a bandage was looped around his wrist and tightened. "Too tight?" she asked.

"No, it's fine."

"I'll fetch some scissors and things. Don't go away." And she smiled at him for the second time, bringing her face alive with warmth and tenderness.

"I promise you I won't go anywhere," he said wearily. Sitting alone in the kitchen, he listened to her go upstairs as the front door closed and the priest returned.

"That's better, quiet now. Are you feeling alright?"

"Mmmm. I have felt better."

"A drink of water, perhaps?"

"Please, yes."

The man let the water run cold from the tap, filled a glass and passed it over. "I feel so bad that this has happened in my church."

"Please don't concern yourself, it's just unfortunate that it's opened an already bad cut."

"We'll soon have you fixed up. Are you staying in the village?"

"Yes, at a place just along the road here."

"I know. They always have rooms for visitors."

"Is it true there are no trains on Sundays?"

"That is correct. Not since the start of the war you know. But there'll be no travelling for you today anyway, not now. You must rest and regain your strength. Your systems had a nasty shock, you look very pale."

The girl returned with an enamel bowl and some first aid implements.

"Can you help me Father?" she said pouring boiling water into the bowl.

"I can my child."

"Are you alright with the sight of blood?"

"You forget I came through a world war."

"And you, …. what is your name?" She asked him kindly.

"Frederic, Frederic Kutzner."

"And are you alright Frederic? If you feel faint tell me."

"Oh I will," and he gave a nervous little laugh. "I promise."

She had removed her scarf, revealing her hair in all its glory. It was so fair it glowed in the sunlight which filtered in through the trees and lattice windows. As she busied herself he noticed how slim she was, and realized he hadn't really looked at another girl since Jill. How far away that all was now. Her enchanting smile and those deep brown eyes, the laugh he would hear no more.

"What are you thinking about, Frederic?" she said noticing his far away expression. "You look very sad."

"What am I thinking about? Another time, another place." How different this girl was. Not dark but fair, so very, very fair. Astrid.

"Well concentrate and hold still now. I'm going to unwrap the bandage." And she threw him a quick reassuring glance.

With the bandage removed the full extent of the damage caused by the door was visible. Fifty percent of Captain Olsen's stitches had burst and in addition the hand was now badly bruised, but other than that it looked intact.

The priest said nothing, he didn't need to, his expression spoke for him.

"This is a bad cut, Frederic," Astrid's voice was compassionate and the gentle way she dealt with him helped him forget the pain. "Can you move your fingers?"

He could. "That's good. However did you do this in the first place?"

"Farm machinery." He answered a little too quickly.

"You must take more care, young man. There's enough unnecessary blood being spilt these days without adding to it."

"The stitches look like … fishing line?" As she spoke she gently wiped away lumps of congealed blood.

"It is. That's all there was available."

"On a farm? Where ever was this?" asked the priest.

"In Norway, near a fjord."

"Norway." She sounded impressed. "My, you have come a long way. Now, Father, hold the hand nice and still, because I'm afraid this will hurt Frederic. I have to remove the broken stitches and put in some new ones." From where she sat across the table she glanced at the handsome young man who had come so unexpectedly into her day. "Keep an eye on him Father, he looks very pale."

He may have looked poorly outside but inside his senses were alive to her every movement, every look, each flick of her hair. Her every touch became like a spark longing to be fanned into flame.

"Look the other way, my son. It'll all be over soon enough."

*

The priest was right; soon enough the broken stitches were replaced by much neater ones and his hand disinfected and re-bandaged.

"There's no sign of infection Frederic, but you will have to be careful."

"Tell me, where is your home?" asked the old priest.

"Er … Minden," he remembered in time. "I must leave tomorrow at the latest."

"Well, there's certainly no way you can get to Minden today, so I suggest you rest here if that's alright with you, Astrid?"

"I'll look after him Father."

"I'm sure you will dear child – you were kind hearted enough to offer in the first place. Bless you for it. I'll call at the house where you're staying Frederic, and tell of what's happened. When your aunt returns there'll be a lot to tell her, Astrid."

"She's away in Lahn with Olga."

"I know." The priest turned to Douglas. "Olga is the wife of the man you're staying with," he told him, adding with a grin, "this village gets smaller every day. But now I must be away. God's duties to attend to as always."

"Thank you for your help," said Douglas.

"I have done nothing, in fact it was all my fault. If I had left the doors open just seconds longer none of this would ever have happened. Fate, who knows?"

"I'll see you out, Father Brant."

"God go with you Frederic. Come and see us again soon."

He listened to their goodbyes when suddenly he realised that the thought of being alone in the house with so beautiful a girl had completely turned his mind from his injury. When she returned she asked if he would like a drink. "I know it's a bit early in the day but you look as if you need it, if you don't mind my saying so. I'm afraid we don't have anything stronger than home-made wine. My aunt makes it."

"That'll be fine."

"Elderberry or raspberry, that's all that's left?"

"You choose, surprise me."

She smiled broadly at him. "Alright. But don't stay in here, go and sit in the front room, it's much more comfortable. Are you alright to walk?"

"Thanks to you I'm just fine, excellent."

The room was typically German with a wooden floor covered in places with rugs and a few pieces of dark antique furniture which had been painted with floral designs. On the wall were a number of photographs of people with solemn expressions and a tapestry of a mountain hunting scene. Douglas sat in a leather arm chair which had seen better days, but was at the least comfortable.

When she appeared carrying a tray with a bottle of wine and glasses, he was on the verge of standing up, but checked himself in time; too English.

"Have you lived here long?" he began for something to say as she filled the glasses.

"Well, this isn't really my home at all. I'm from Berlin, but with my father away in the army he thought I'd be safer here away from the bombing, so my aunt agreed to have me. It's nice for her too as she's on her own." She passed Douglas his glass. "Talking of my father, I haven't told you but you look so like him it's extraordinary. It's like looking at the father I remember from my childhood. I wish I had a photograph to prove it to you, but I left them all behind."

"They say everyone has a double somewhere don't they? And your mother?"

"My mother passed away some time ago."

"I'm sorry, I didn't mean to pry."

"That's alright. I have an elder brother, Stefan, he's away in the army too."

"Whereabouts?"

"Scandinavia. I'm not sure where, exactly. He may even be in Norway where you have just come from. I send any letters to my father and he forwards them on through the army post. We get on well but letter writing isn't one of my brother's talents."

"So which one of your aunt's specialities have you surprised me with?"

"Oh yes, it's elderberry. I hope that's alright?"

He took a sip, feeling the delicious warmth slipping down. "It certainly is."

"Have you had any breakfast?"

"No, as a matter of fact, I haven't."

"Neither have I. We always go to church first and eat afterwards. When you've finished your drink I'll get us something."

"I can't thank you enough for your kindness I don't know where I'd be without your expertise."

"All girls are taught first aid in the League of German Maidens."

"What you performed on me is far above basic first-aid."

"Well yes," she admitted modestly. "I did go a bit further with the course."

He looked at her seated opposite. She was really quite beautiful, with a cute little nose and high cheek bones under a dusting of freckles that sent a thrill of excitement racing through his body. Hair like he had never seen before framed her face handsomely, and fell about her slender shoulders and her green floral dress. He allowed his eyes to follow each pleat and fold all the way down to her slim and tanned legs. She noticed him looking at her and spoke up quickly. "How's your wine?"

"It's good. Please tell your aunt from me I think she's very clever."

"She'll be pleased." She stood up suddenly. "I'll get us something to eat."

As he sat waiting, he thought of what M and Captain Silverthorn would have said had they known what he was doing as this was hardly what they had in mind for him. But he must get away tomorrow.

Astrid returned shortly, with dark bread and cheese and German sausage.

"It's very simple I'm afraid. Rationing you know. Are things difficult where you are?"

"Oh you know, much the same."

"Are you busy with your farm machines? What is it that you do exactly?"

"I'm an agricultural rep. Busy? Oh yes, we're always busy. Food production's very important – we all need to do our best."

"Norway must be lovely at this time of year. I've always wanted to go."

"Yes it's very beautiful, the mountains the fjords. Lovely."

"I hope you don't mind my saying so, but your accent, there's something there that's not quite …"

"You've spotted it! Well done." he got in hastily.

"Oh dear, have I said something I shouldn't?"

"Not at all, but you see my mother was Norwegian, that's what you can hear. I lived there for a while."

"But isn't there a problem with the authorities over mixed race marriages? Or doesn't that include Scandinavian countries?"

"What can I say … ? Yes, you're right of course, but my mother proved her loyalty to the Fatherland long ago."

"Is that why you're not in the army because of something to do with your mother's bloodline?"

"Well, there again, you're right and you're wrong. Because I was already involved with food production when war broke out, they said I should continue in the vital work and everything else was overlooked." He changed the subject rapidly. "But what do you do Astrid, apart from ministering to strangers in need?"

She gave a little laugh. "I work on the farm nearby much the same as you really, food production. All doing our bit to help the Führer be victorious. But look, I'm keeping you from eating and I'm talking far too much. Eat up, please, then afterwards you should take a little nap. I must say you do look very tired."

He inwardly relaxed, the danger having passed, for now at least.

"I do feel tired actually, I must go back to my room."

"I won't hear of it. I said I would look after you, so you stay and relax here and I'll find us something for lunch later."

Alarm bells rang in his head and the training manual flashed before his eyes. Get out! Go! Now!

"Well, if it's alright. That's very kind, I accept." 'You fool, you fool what have you done? This girl is the enemy. What have you done?!'

In so short a space of time, Astrid had proved herself kind and capable, as well as astute and correct, in so much as he *was* tired. He had been up most of the night and needed sleep, but the only sleep he could manage was the fitful sleep of someone knowingly in the wrong, plagued by his conscience. He was playing with fire and knew it.

He awoke to the sound of her working in the kitchen, unaware that as he had dozed in the chair more than once she had looked in on her handsome visitor, and had been well pleased by what she saw. Yet was it because he reminded her so much of her absent father, or was it because she had already surrendered her head to the will of her heart? She found her thoughts perplexing.

They ate a simple lunch together under the trees in the garden, enjoying the spring sunshine, and then she took him on a short tour of the village.

"No wonder your father wanted you to come here after Berlin, it's very beautiful."

"The war could be a thousand miles away."

"I haven't seen anyone in uniform since I arrived."

"Nothing much happens here," she told him gloomily "occasionally one or two of the men return on leave, but other than that life goes on as it always has. Where do your parents live?"

"My parents? I lost both my parents."

"I'm sorry. Recently?"

"It's not something I like to talk about, you understand."

"I do. I know exactly how you feel. Memories of parents are very private and personal."

"This has been a very unusual day for me Astrid. It didn't start well, but it's going well now. It's not every day an ordinary farm machinery salesman gets to take a stroll with the most beautiful girl in the village."

"Why Frederic, I do believe you're flirting with me!" she said with a girlish giggle.

"Yes, I do believe I am."

"As your nurse I can tell you that positive thoughts aid speedy recovery."

"Then I'll have lots of positive thoughts concerning a certain young lady."

"It's been lovely having you here Frederic. I thought the weekend was going to be very dull with my aunt away. Not that any weekend is lively, mind you. You're the youngest man I've spoken to since I can't remember when. Except for one of the priests, but he doesn't count."

"And if that church door hadn't slammed shut, we probably would never have met."

She looked at him as they walked by the river. "Father Brant said it was fate."

Douglas held up his bandaged hand. "I wish fate could have found a kinder way of introducing us."

The girl laughed. "At least the other hand's alright."

"Oh yes, that's working well, see." And he slipped it into hers.

"Yes, it's working very well" she said, avoiding eye contact but making no attempt to separate.

They didn't talk for a while as they continued along the bank of the river. They didn't need to, just a touch spoke all that was needed to be said for now.

Returning through the village they passed some people she knew but still she didn't let go of his grasp, proud to be seen with him regardless of what others may think. Nearing the house she asked him why he had come to Obernhof. "I know you work with farm machines, so have you been visiting farms around here? Perhaps you called at the farm where I work and I missed you."

"Er … no, no … I, well I simply didn't want to go home." He said, digging a hole for himself.

"Oh that sounds so sad. Why?"

"Well, it was the weekend and I live alone, but I just didn't want to be alone this weekend. Don't ask me why, I don't know. Who knows? So I just got off the train and well, here I am."

"It really was fate that brought you here."

"It must have been."

"Do you have to go back tomorrow? Couldn't you stay another day then you could see the doctor and I could show you some more of the area. You could meet my aunt, she'd like that, I know she would."

"It all sounds wonderful, but I really do have to go back tomorrow. There are people waiting for me." As he listened to his own words, his mind was brought up sharply to what he was doing. He let go of her hand quickly, and then regretted it and ran his hand nonchalantly through his hair hoping she hadn't noticed.

'Oh God,' he cried inwardly, 'what am I doing? I should be on my way back to England. I'm a spy for God's sake, a British spy!'

"Is everything alright Frederic? You look concerned about something suddenly? It is your hand?"

"Astrid, dear Astrid."

"Whatever's wrong?"

"Nothing's wrong. Yes, everything. No," he fumbled. "What I am trying to say is you have been so kind to me, so very kind, and I will never forget what you have done for me, or our lovely day together. It's been wonderful, wonderful. But the country is at war and we all have our different parts to play and we're all answerable to someone, and my work takes me far away …"

"Farm machinery?"

"You'd be surprised. It's been just lovely, but it must end, sadly it must end. It can never be."

The blue eyes he had noticed for the first time outside the church looked at him again, only now they looked painfully unhappy and tore at his soul.

"I thought …" she stopped herself.

"What is it?"

"It doesn't matter."

"No, what were you going to say?"

"It's just that I thought something special had happened here today. I was going to ask if you would like me to write to you."

"Oh yes, yes of course but … oh dear … the trouble is, I'm hardly ever there and … I'm in the middle of moving so, well you know what it's like."

She let her head fall forward, hiding her face from his gaze. "It's alright, I understand." She spoke so quietly he only just caught her words.

"But I can write to you though," he told her "I can at least do that, somehow."

She smiled, but not with her eyes. "That would be nice I'd like that."

They walked on, holding hands again until they arrived at the house where he was staying and went inside. There was no sign of the old man. She wrote her address on a slip of paper.

"I'll write to you. I will. I promise," he told her.

"What time are you off in the morning?"

"The first train, whenever that is."

"Seven-thirty. What will you do for supper?"

"Don't worry, I'm sure my land lord will have that in hand."

"You could easily come back. I can fix up something for us, it's no trouble."

"No Astrid. It's better this way, believe me."

"Alright. Well, it's goodbye then. Take care of that hand."

"I will, and thank you again for all your care and for a lovely day. I will never forget it."

She reached up to kiss him and he badly wanted her to but, struggling against a natural longing and commitment to duty, he turned away at the last moment. "I'm sorry Astrid. I am so, so sorry but it's for the best, believe me. You must believe me."

Without another word, she turned and left leaving him feeling thoroughly rotten and deceitful. He watched her walk quickly away, up the hill, until she was out of sight. "Forgive me Astrid but how can I ever tell you the truth?"

*

The following morning he was up early, and after breakfast paid for his room and board and made his way down to the station. The previous day's sunshine had been replaced with low, dark clouds which brushed the tops of the hills, reflecting his mood. He had not slept a wink disturbed by the events of the day and the way he had unwillingly hurt the girl. If only he had not played around with that fishing knife, if only Jill had not died, if only Hitler had not invaded Poland. If only. It could all have been so different.

It was a little after 7.15 a.m. when he reached the station. By the time he had bought his ticket there was just ten minutes before he would be away, starting the long trek home. Other than a lady with a small child, he was alone on the platform.

"Did you sleep well, Frederic?" He was so engrossed in his thoughts he had failed to hear footsteps behind him, and spun round to see the girl standing there looking just as beautiful as he remembered. "Astrid!"

"How did you sleep with your bad hand?" Her eyes were full of care and affection.

"How did I sleep? How did I sleep? I didn't sleep. I couldn't help thinking of you." He let his bag fall to the ground as his words came tumbling out. "I thought about you all night. I'm so sorry for yesterday. I know I hurt you, but believe me I didn't mean to." Without thinking he stepped closer, brushing caution aside and wrapped his arms around her, pulling her tight to his chest.

"Oh Frederic," she sighed with undisguised emotion. "I knew it was fate that brought you to me and now nothing can keep us apart."

"Dear God, I never meant this to happen, but I can't stop it." He stroked her golden hair kissing it again and again, then her cheek and, cupping her face in his one good hand, spoke softly. "Why did you come? I don't know what to say. Oh Astrid, Astrid what are we going to do?"

"Kiss me before you go, Frederic." And he did. Hard and longingly, releasing months of pent-up emotion and suppressed desires. Her lips were soft and sweet and dangerous, but he didn't care.

"I knew how you felt," she said "when first you touched my hand."

"Yes you're right, so right I can't deny it. I've been in love with you since the moment I first set eyes on you. I just refused to believe it. I wouldn't have thought it possible for two strangers to feel this way so quickly."

"I knew you felt the same way. I just knew you did."

The train whistled as it came into view, right on time, and the sound of the engine grew louder and louder, with smoke and steam escaping in all directions as it neared the couple all too quickly.

"I made some sandwiches for you," she said, putting them in his hand, adding "promise you'll write?"

"You're so kind to me. Yes, I will write. Somehow I will," and pulled her address from his pocket. "You see, I kept it. But you didn't put your full name down. What's your other name?"

"It's Muller. Astrid Muller."

CHAPTER FIVE

Before Douglas was back in London, a message had been received in the office of Major Walter Baum in the Loire Valley.

"Our agent in Obernhof reports that Muller's daughter has been seen with a young man from Minden, a farm machinery salesman. Apparently he stayed in our man's house", Baum's aide informed him.

"The girl's romantic liaisons are of no interest to me. All I want to know is exactly where she is at all times."

"The girl is still in the village, Herr Major."

"Good. Make sure that I'm informed the moment that position changes."

"There is something else, Sir."

"Well?"

"Major Muller has left the Hotel Meurice in Paris."

"When did you learn this?"

"The report has only just arrived Sir."

"Well, where has he gone?"

"We don't know."

"What's his forwarding address then, surely we know that?"

"He didn't leave a forwarding address, but he did tell the clerk that he would return in a week and he's left most of his belongings in the room."

Major Baum rose from behind his ornate desk and turned to look out at the gardens. The view frequently inspired him, but on this occasion it only helped to fan the sense of misgiving he had been harbouring for some days. "Left his things behind you say?" he queried after a pause.

"Almost everything, Sir. Typewriter, shoes, suits."

"But he'll be back within a week?"

"That is what he told the desk when he left, Sir."

"I wonder what he's up to?" He thought for a moment, letting his eye follow the line of the neatly trimmed lawns. "Alright, we'll give him ten, no fourteen days. We don't want to look too jumpy. But if he hasn't returned to the hotel by then, bring his daughter in. In the meantime, I want that girl watched like a hawk. Do you understand?"

"Yes, Herr Major."

"I'm not interested who she's sleeping with, but I will personally execute whoever lets her slip away unnoticed."

"What if Major Muller makes a dash for his daughter and then together they make a run for it?"

"That will be the day I land in very, very serious trouble and that's why I want her watched day and night. This agent in Obernhof, is he any good?"

"We're using a husband and wife. They're elderly, but on the ball and loyal, and nothing happens in the village without their knowing about it. They also have good contact with the girl's aunt, Muller's sister-in-law. We could put an agent in of our own but frankly Sir, in such a close community, it would not be a good idea. They would close ranks immediately. Outsiders these days arouse too much suspicion."

"So who is this machinery salesman from Minden? Is he a stranger?"

"We don't know. Apparently he was only in the village two nights, spent some time with the girl and left. He cut himself badly while he was there."

"Doing what?"

"Shut his hand in a door I believe."

"Don't we know anything about him at all?"

"Only what our man gleaned from going through his bag. We only know his first name, Frederic. He works for ….. one moment, Sir I have it here." He checked his notes. "He works for Koch Engineering in Hanover and apparently he had just returned from Norway on a sales trip."

"Norway? I wouldn't have thought the Norwegians were very eager to buy German machinery. I think you should ask this couple in Obernhof to discreetly try and discover who this man is, a name. Then get on to Koch Engineering and have him verified. You never know, he could be a go-between for Muller and his daughter, and the more we know, the better."

"I'll see to it at once, Sir."

*

The early evening Bim-Bam chimes of five o'clock from a musical clock nearby went unnoticed as Major Claus Muller sheltered from a torrential thunderstorm which had caught him by surprise, along with office workers hurrying home for the evening. Dressed in civilian clothes, he took an address from his suit pocket and read it again; Van Bree Straat behind Vondelpark. He asked the woman sheltering next to him in the doorway if she knew where it was, but she only spoke Dutch. When he showed her the slip of paper she indicated he should go right and then left, but then she ran off quickly despite the rain, distrusting the German stranger with the nasty scar.

The rain eventually eased to a fine drizzle and, lifting his collar, he walked off in the direction the woman had indicated. The charm of Amsterdam was lost on him, focussed as he was entirely on his mission. After ten or so wet minutes the woman was proved right, and he arrived at his destination, a three storey block of apartments. Pushing open the communal entrance door, he stepped inside. He needed the top flat, but there was no lift.

The bell made an irritating buzz but the door was opened punctually by a man of slight stature and a pronounced stoop, but crowned with a full head of silver grey hair and a beard to match; the man Muller had come to see.

"Herr Beck?"

"Yes." The man failed to conceal his surprise at the sight of a stranger sporting a black eye patch.

"I am Claus Muller. Please forgive my disfigurement. I didn't mean to startle you, I should have warned you."

"I'm sorry Herr Muller. It just took me a little by surprise, that's all. Please come in, I've been expecting you. Let me take your coat, it's very damp out there today."

The apartment was small and cluttered with a lifetime's memorabilia and in places, thick with dust. The man obviously lived alone, no self respecting woman would live in such disorder.

"Come through and sit down."

Removing a collection of newspapers from an armchair Muller sat down and looked around. There were piles of pictures, photographs, magazines, newspapers, books and more books, very little of it in its rightful place. The room was gloomy, the curtains not having been opened fully and over all, hung the stench of musty paper and stale tobacco.

Beck must have read his visitor's thoughts. "Excuse the flat," he said "one day I promise myself I'll have a tidy up, but not today I think. Let me offer you a schnapps, Herr Muller."

"Thank you, that would be good."

"What would you prefer I call you? I remember you said you are now a Major. Should I call you Major?"

"No, no please call me Claus."

"Very well, Claus it will be and my name as you know, is Willem." He settled a bottle and glasses on the low table between them and sat down.

"I must say Willem, you haven't changed from when I remember you at the university."

The old man gave a wry grin. "All those years ago, and you say I haven't changed! If only, that is what I say, if only. You know what they say, don't you? Every time a diamond cutter makes a cut he gets another grey hair."

"Then I can only think that your hair speaks very highly of your experience."

"Thank you. I didn't have this back then, I think." He said, stroking his Van Dyke beard.

"Perhaps not."

"I must be honest but I cannot say the same of you. I don't remember you at all."

"Of course not. I wouldn't have expected you to. I was just one of many faces at a lecture, but I never forgot what you said and I remember being very impressed by your enthusiasm and the way you obviously enjoyed your work."

"Yes, that's true. A man who is happy at work is a lucky man. But drink up."

"Good to see you again." And they emptied their glasses.

"Now tell me what brings you to Amsterdam. Something other than the war I imagine."

"A special mission, or rather a special commission for you, if you would be interested."

"Has it to do with the corundum we spoke of?"

"Yes it has. I need a replica of a diamond, a very famous diamond, and in corundum."

"Yes, that's quite possible," he nodded thoughtfully. "Which diamond? The Kimberley, the Tiffany, the Blue Tavernier ……..?"

"What did you say?!" Muller almost jumped in his chair.

"Excuse me?" Muller's sudden reaction startled the old man.

"You said Tavernier. You used the word Tavernier."

"Yes, the Blue Tavernier. Also known as the Hope Diamond," he said, wondering what this was all about.

"I … I've never heard of this stone."

"Is everything alright, only you look shocked?"

"Yes, yes of course. Excuse me, but I've been conducting very extensive research recently into diamonds and I've never heard of the Blue Tavernier."

"I have a book here somewhere on famous diamonds. I'm sure it's mentioned in there. Would you like to see it?"

"Yes I certainly would."

Beck rummaged through the books piled on the floor muttering to himself until eventually he found what he was looking for.

"Here we are, Now let me see …… The Blue Tavernier, page ten …… yes."

" 'The Hope Diamond,' " he read. " 'The history of this famous diamond is linked with that of another, the "Blue Tavernier", which weighed 112.50 carats in the rough. It is likely that both names refer to the same famous gem – a diamond of a rare blue colour.

The "Blue Tavernier" was found in the Kollur mine, Golconda, and was bought by the French gem expert of the same name in 1642. On his last return from the East in 1668, Tavernier sold it with some other jewels to Louis XIV. The stone weighed 67.50 carats after cutting and polishing, and it became the showpiece of the French Regalia. During the French Revolution the "Blue Tavernier" was stolen from the Garde Meuble with the rest of the French Regalia, and all trace of it was lost.' Should I continue?"

"Do."

" 'In 1830 a diamond of a similar colour to that of the "Blue Tavernier", weighing 44.50 carats, came on to the London market. It was bought by Henry Thomas Hope, a banker and keen collector of gems, for £18,000, after whom the stone is now named. It was probably the "Blue Tavernier", smuggled out of France and recut to escape detection.

In 1908 the Hope was acquired by Abdul Hamid, Sultan of Turkey, who is reputed to have paid £80,000 for it. Three years later, the stone was sold at Cartier's in Paris to the late Mrs Edward B. McLean of Washington. U.S.A.'" He closed the book and looked across at the German.

"Fascinating.," said Muller "I had no idea Tavernier named a diamond after himself. In all my research there was never any mention of it."

"Is this the diamond you wish me to copy? Because of its colour it would be extremely difficult to … "

"No, not that one. It's blue you say?"

"Yes, a very rare blue."

"No, then that's of no use to me at all. No, the diamond I want you to copy is the Great Mogul."

"The Great Mogul," repeated Beck impressed "but why ever do you want a copy of that?"

"Please don't ask."

"Very well, that's your business I appreciate, but the Great Mogul, correct me if I'm mistaken, is missing, is it not?"

"It is, that's quite correct."

"Major Muller, forgive me if I should sound naïve, but how can I produce a replica of something when no-one knows what it looks like?"

"Ah, but there you're wrong Willem. The same Tavernier you were just reading about, Jean-Baptiste Tavernier, made an extensive examination of the stone and supplied history with weights and diagrams and a firm description. And in addition, I've managed to obtain photographs and more useful material from the Science museum in Milan along with a mould of an exact copy they made themselves of the Great Mogul."

"What was their copy made of?"

"That was only in quartz, it was simply for display purposes."

"But you want something to look like the real thing?"

"I do."

"Well," he said, stroking his beard "what a very unusual commission. I've never been asked to do anything quite like this before. You do understand that usually I work exclusively with diamonds but this is so out of the ordinary, how could I possibly turn it down? Ah, but wait a moment."

"What is it?"

"How big was the Mogul? How many carats?"

"In the rough it weight 787.50. Finished, approximately 280 carats."

"Then I need a piece of corundum at least 400 to 500 carats. Whereever will I get that, good quality too and in war time?"

"Before I answer that, I agree with your weight estimates but do you agree to undertake the assignment because once started there can be no turning back?"

"If you can somehow lay your hands on the material then yes, I'd be pleased to."

"Needless to say, you would be well rewarded."

"I was waiting for you to get round to that. How well exactly?"

"Shall we say, one thousand Reichsmarks per month whilst you're working and a bonus of ten thousand on completion of a top quality and authentic job?"

"For that Claus, my friend," beamed the old man "I will make you a stone that is better than the original and fit for a King!"

"That is exactly what I want. But there's one other thing."

"And what's that?"

"No-one, repeat no-one must know what you are doing. This is strictly a private arrangement between you and me. Do I make myself clear?"

"You do, and I see no problem in that direction. Since I retired I have set up a small workshop in the room next door, so no-one will know what I'm doing."

"Excellent, so on that basis we shall proceed. I will call on you again within a few days and deliver what you need. In the meantime, I have brought with me all the measurements and details I mentioned and the mould for you to study."

"But wherever will you find such a huge piece of corundum?"

"A problem is no longer a problem when it has a solution, and I have the solution, believe me."

*

Douglas's return to his homeland proved arduous yet uneventful. He arrived in Bergen a day later than expected, but as promised Captain Rune Olsen was waiting. They sailed for Shetland immediately, arriving twenty-six hours later, after the type of crossing that proved nightmares can come true. After Hamish had given thanks for his safe return and Martha had fed him, the doctor in Lerwick took a look at his hand which revealed no signs of infection. Rather than disturb the unorthodox stitches the doctor decided to leave well alone and let nature take its course with the aid of regular, clean dressings. Then, together with Captain Silverthorn, he shared the flight south to London, where he was debriefed and reported to M that the mission had been a failure.

"Nonsense! How can you call it a failure Lieutenant? You did exactly what we asked you to do; determine whether or not the church was hiding anything. Mission accomplished."

"I'm sorry it wasn't what you expected Sir."

"This was just your first mission, young man. You'll get your share of excitement I'm sure, but for now you're no good to us with that hand of yours. The M.O. tells me it will be at least a month before it's back to normal, so what I want you to do is take a week's leave, and then report back here and we'll sort out something else for you to do when you're A.1 again."

"Can you give me any idea what that will be, Sir?"

"No, I can't," 'I even lie with a straight conscience now,' thought M 'how low have I sunk?' "That's all then, but I don't like the idea of you remaining a 2nd Lieutenant. I think you have earnt an extra pip on your shoulder. I'll speak to the powers that be but you may take it as gospel."

"Thank you very much, Sir." Douglas sounded more than a little surprised.

"See you in seven days Lieutenant. And look after that hand."

*

Later that day M was called to the office of the Director, head of S.O.E., former Member of Parliament, Sir Frank Nelson. Known by the initials, C.D. A deeply intellectual man who's abilities were well suited to the intelligence service.

"Come in Colonel. Do sit down. Sherry?" he asked, focusing his sharp eyes on M.

"Not right now, Sir, thank you."

"I hear Reid's back. How did he get on?"

"He did what was asked of him Sir, with no problems except that he cut his hand badly."

"How come?"

"An accident on the boat going out, but a sixth sense tells me we haven't been told the whole story."

"Do you think he's hiding something?" queried C.D.

"No, not at all, Sir. If I understand the situation correctly, it was his own carelessness. Perhaps that's why he's being reticent with the truth."

"Why was he a day late returning?"

"Delay with the trains apparently."

"Understandable. So when will he be operational again, only we've got a bit of a problem?"

"At least a month, why?"

"Had a call from Downing Street. The P.M. wants it brought forward."

"Oh dear," said M, shaking his head. "That's not good news. To when?"

"He hasn't set any date but made it perfectly clear it's got to be sooner rather than later."

"Well, we can't send him back with his hand as it is and then he's got to have surgery which will also take time to heal. He looked all in when I saw him earlier so I gave him seven days leave."

"Alright, we'll leave things as they are for seven days, but as soon as he returns you must put the plan to him and see what his reaction is."

"I don't think there'll be any problem."

"I do hope not. His answer could change the course of the entire war. Has the man been seen in Berlin yet?"

"I'm sorry to say no."

"Let's pray he pops up soon. How very strange this should happen. Truth certainly is stranger than fiction."

*

Spring arrives late in Norway, but eventually winds rolling down from the polar ice cap give way to warmer air from the North Atlantic and the snow recedes, the ice melts and buds appear. The land changes from white to green once again. The people hang up their skis and furs and try to enjoy the longer, warmer days even though now their country was part of the Third Reich.

The events of the night when Ingrid Nielsen was attacked in the old hotel in the village of Vadheim remained fresh in her mind and each time she passed a German uniform she would be overtaken with fear, terrified that next time, as the man had promised, 'he would get her'. She could only pray he would not.

April 3rd 1941 dawned bright and clear, the sun glistening across the still waters of Sognefjord bringing a much needed glow. At a little after eleven o'clock, Ingrid, along with three girlfriends each carrying a knapsack and meagre lunch, made their way from the village up into the forest and hills. It felt good to get away, no soldiers here, no reminders that life had changed so much.

As the sun rose higher, the girls walked on up through the forest rich with the scent of pine and out onto the mountain thick with wild heathers and bushes which in a few months would be laden with berries. After two hours they arrived at a mountain lake where they rested and ate their few simple smørbrød sandwiches.

The sun was the warmest since winter had ended and the girls rolled up their trousers and paddled in the cold, still water laughing and splashing, all cares forgotten. Two of the girls were for walking further, spurred on by the glorious day, but the other two, including Ingrid, wanted to stay by the lake and relax. Amicably they parted.

About three o'clock when the sun had lost most of its strength, Ingrid and her friend Elsae started the descent back to the village, retracing their steps over the hills and down through the forest by which time shadows were already lengthening and a chill was returning to the mountain air. They sang at the top of their voices as they walked, patriotic songs which had long been forbidden.

Had they been walking quietly they would probably not have been seen, but as it was the noise they were making attracted the attention of a lone German soldier in full kit walking quickly, furtively even, following another track up the hill as they were coming down. He stopped and peered through the trees to see who was singing and laughing, and some way ahead of him to the right he saw the girls. As he recognized one of them a wicked smirk passed across his face. Unseen and moving swiftly, he crossed through the undergrowth over to the other track and hid some way ahead, waiting for them to appear. He did not have to wait long. He sprang out onto the path in front of them, making them jump in alarm.

"Halt!" They both froze at the sight of the uniform and the young soldier brandishing his rifle.

"You!" cried Ingrid, with a sharp intake of breath recognizing at once the man from the night at the hotel.

"I promised I'd get you, and now I have you all to myself." He let out a dirty laugh and waved his rifle, indicating she should move into the trees. But she stood her ground, strengthened by the fact that this time she was not alone. "It's him!" She warned Elsae. "He's the one I told you about."

"Get out of the way!" he shouted to the other girl. "Or you'll get it too." But the girls clung to each other, linking arms, terrified but determined not to give way.

"I said get out of the way!" Fired with revenge he swiftly brought his rifle butt down on Elsae's head before she had chance to move. She sank to the ground without a sound. Ingrid began to tremble and scream, yet saw her chance and was about to run for it when, anticipating her move, he stuck out his foot and sent her sprawling to the ground with a groan.

"Just where I want you." He told her, and grabbing hold of her wrists pulled her into the undergrowth. Before she realized what was happening he had flipped her slim body over, slipped off his backpack and dropped to his knees, straddling her.

"I won't let you! I won't let you! Get off me!"

"You can shout and scream all you like, no-one's going to hear you up here. How about a goodbye kiss. I'm getting out of this dump. Come on. A nice kiss to send me on my way." And he bent down forcing his lips to meet hers as she tried to wriggle free.

His breath stank of beer and she punched out wildly with her fists but he was oblivious to any protest and tried to force her slacks down, but in his eagerness forgot to undo the belt. He let out a roar of frustration. "Ahhhhh!!" Reaching over, he unclipped the bayonet from the scabbard hanging at his waist and slipped it under the girl's belt, slicing through the material like a knife through butter. Letting the bayonet drop into the dirt he ripped open her trousers as she screamed and punched him frantically.

"Keep still and keep quiet or when I've finished, I'll slit your throat!" And he grabbed hold of both of her arms, forcing them behind her head. "Understand?!"

Ingrid was sobbing uncontrollably between gasps for air as he tried to make her lie still with a palm pressed firmly over her mouth, but she continued to fight and thrashed out wildly, when suddenly her right hand hit the hilt of the discarded bayonet. Without a second's thought as to the consequences, she picked it up, gripped it tight and plunged it between the ribs under his arm, with all her might.

The effect was instantaneous. He froze as a look of horror paralysed his features with disbelief. Reaching round he tried to touch the blade which had only half gone home but as he did so, she pushed hard, once again forcing the long steel in as far as it would go, right up to the hilt.

"You bitch ... you ... bitch ......" But his life was already ebbing away, causing him to fight for every breath. "Curse you ... curse ... you." Blood was beginning to bubble and flow from his mouth, dripping onto her face but she lay still, instinctively knowing that his end was near. And then he flopped forward, covering her in the final throws of death, as his butchered lungs let go of their ultimate breath. It was all over.

Ingrid, weighed down by the soldier's lifeless body, wriggled and squirmed with what little strength she had remaining, until finally he toppled off her and landed at an unnatural angle beside her.

She lay there paralysed with exhaustion as slowly the realization of what she had done began to dawn on her. It was then that she heard a moan coming from nearby and forced herself up on one elbow. "Elsae! Elsae! Help me!"

"What happened? ... Oh my head ... Ingrid, where are you?"

"Over here! Over here." Watching as her friend crawled through the undergrowth. "Oh Elsae something terrible's happened," she cried.

"Whatever's happened? My head feels terrible ... Dear God! What's wrong with him?" she said, spying the young soldier's body.

"He's dead."

"Dead?!"

"I killed him, Elsae. I had to. He would have killed me. It was terrible. He stank … !" And she broke down shaking and sobbing uncontrollably.

"But what are we going to do? … We'll be shot!!"

*

It was dark by the time the girls got back to the village, but within twenty minutes of hearing their tale of events Elsae's parents, and Ingrid's mother, got together and determined what they would have to do, knowing that if the truth should ever leak out, the girls, and probably their parents as well, would face a firing squad.

Back on the mountain the truth lay hidden beneath layers of spruce branches, the body still punctured by the bayonet.

It was decided to send the two girls away up into the mountains to relations of Elsae's for as long as necessary, and they left Vadheim before dawn the following morning.

Three days passed before the body of Stefan Muller was discovered. The news was immediately reported to the office of The Commander of German Forces (Norway), in Bergen. Without hesitation he ordered that if the perpetrator or perpetrators did not come forward within twenty-four hours, on the basis that one German was worth ten Norwegians, ten residents of Vadheim of various ages and gender would be rounded up and executed.

Suddenly the usually peaceful village was in the grip of terror, everyone petrified that they would be selected. Protests were made and ignored. Pleadings were heard and dismissed. No-one slept that night and the twenty-four hours ticked by all too quickly. When no confession was forthcoming as the time limit expired, ten residents were dragged screaming from their homes, businesses and farms. In front of the whole community, which had been ordered to assemble in the square, they had their hands tied and were forced to stand against a wall. In the stillness of the early evening, the mountains echoed to the sound of gun fire.

*

Major Claus Muller pressed the door bell which responded immediately with its irksome buzz. He waited.

"Why Claus, I didn't expect to see you so soon. Come in."

"Thank you, Willem. Are you well?" enquired Muller, clutching a box under his arm.

"Yes, quite well. Come though into my workshop, I'm just having a tidy up."

The workshop in Willem Beck's apartment had unmistakably been a bedroom at one time, made apparent by the floral wallpaper and curtains. Yet over the years, the patterns had faded until walls thick with polishing dust resembled any other jeweller's workshop, especially when combined with the many different tools and machines of the trade which were littered about indiscriminately. Like every other room it was a mess to which Muller's orderly mind reacted badly, but he kept his opinions quiet conscious only that this man could liberate him from serious trouble.

"I have something for you," he said with a satisfied grin, and placed the box down carefully on the workbench.

"Don't tell me you've found the corundum already?" said Beck. " I don't believe it."

"I have, just as you ordered."

"But when you said you'd be back in a few days, I thought you were joking. I didn't think I'd see you for months. You Germans really are efficient."

"Ha! Someone else said that to me recently."

"But it's true. Wherever did you get it from?" Beck stood stroking the sides of the cardboard box as if postponing the moment of pleasure.

"Have you heard of Bonebakker?" asked Muller.

"On Rokin?"

Muller nodded.

"You're asking an old diamond cutter if he has ever heard of Bonebakker? Why every cutter in the northern hemisphere's heard of Bonebakker. Is that where you got it?"

"Long before I came to see you, I remembered reading somewhere that they had a huge piece of corundum on display, so I paid them a visit and there it was."

"They've been trading in Amsterdam for hundreds of years you know," said Beck, surprised that such a thing had not already been confiscated by the Germans as had most precious gems. But he kept his thoughts private.

"Yes I did know, and I think for most of those years this has just been sitting there on display."

"May I enquire what you paid for it?"

"You may certainly ask my friend, but you'll understand if I don't tell you. Let's just say the negotiations were absorbing."

"May I open it?"

"But of course."

Reverently, the old craftsman lifted the lid and, parting the tissue paper, peered inside while simultaneously sucking a long breath through his teeth. "Just one moment." He hurried out of the room suddenly, only to return moments later with a sheet of white paper which he placed on the workbench beside the box. "I want to see it in all its glory" he explained, and after wiping his hands down his shirt front, he slowly raised the stone out of the box and placed it carefully on the paper. It was the size of a small grapefruit and shaped like a snowball that had started to melt. He said nothing but scrutinized it with trained eyes.

Eventually Muller broke the silence. "So, what do you think?"

Willem slowly nodded his approval. "It's magnificent, magnificent."

"I was hoping you'd say that."

"See how it almost glows against the white background."

"The light in here is exceptionally good."

"Look up. I had the ceiling opened up and a fanlight fitted when I first moved in. Good light as you know is extremely important for cutting stones; I couldn't possibly work without it."

"And stops nosy neighbours looking in."

But Willem was not paying attention. He had already taken an eyeglass and was beginning to examine the stone more closely.

"Willem, I must leave you to it now, I have to get back."

"Of course, of course, I understand. I shall have to study it in very great detail for days before I can even begin to think of cutting anyway."

"Right. Now one final thing" said Muller.

"You have my undivided attention." But still he couldn't take his eyes off the stone which even in its unsightly, raw, state was radiant with fire.

"You must never contact me."

Beck turned and looked directly at the German. "Never?" He queried.

"Never. Under any circumstances whatsoever. I will always contact you. That is extremely important."

"Very well, if that is what you wish. Come to think of it I don't know where you're based anyway."

"It's best that way."

Muller pulled a buff coloured envelope from his pocket. "Here's the first instalment of the monthly payments we agreed on, and I have made arrangements with my bank to send you the same amount, each month, starting next month until further notice."

"Thank you."

"Roughly how long do you think it will take?"

"I really can't say. Contact me in four months and I'll have a better idea. I've been reading the information you gave me the other day. Someone's gone to a lot of trouble to get this exactly right."

"Indeed they have, a lot of trouble."

"I notice part of the Mogul is Jubilee-cut."

"What is that exactly?"

"It's a style of rose-cut, so called after the Jubilee of Queen Victoria of England. It has a flat base but a pointed top and is covered with facets. But the Mogul of course, has a cut all of its own and every one of its facets has to be polished individually. A very long and exacting job I must tell you."

"I'm sure it is."

"But before you go there's something I would like to show you." He nodded in the direction of a free standing small chest of drawers. "See the cloth on top of the drawers? Lift it carefully."

Intrigued, Muller slowly removed the cloth. "Well! And there it is." He exclaimed, delighted.

"I made the mould yesterday from what you left me. It's only plaster of Paris. It's alright, you can pick it up it's quite dry. That's what the copy of the Great Mogul diamond will look like in a few months from now."

Muller held the white moulded plaster in his hands, suddenly seeing an end to his problems. "This is most encouraging," he said "a real step in the right direction."

"A schnapps to celebrate your magnificent find before you go, Major?"

"Yes surely, but then I really must go."

*

An elegant column of smoke rose from an equally elegant black cigarette holder as its owner tapped it gently in the crystal ashtray on the edge of M's desk.

"Downstairs now?" he asked, fingering his red carnation.

"Yes Sir." Captain Silverthorn told him.

"Well, there we are my friend," he addressed M. "The end of 'Operation David' and the start of 'Goliath'. Does he have any idea do you think Alex? You get on well with him?"

"As far as I know, Sir," began Silverthorn "it will come as a complete surprise."

"He's seen the M.O. and the hand's healing nicely, so that at least shouldn't be a problem" put in M.

"Let me know what he says right away, won't you, Sir?"

"Of course."

"Only the P.M. wants to know if it's a goer or not. But the all-important question is have there been any further sightings of the man in the photograph?"

"Not yet, which frankly is a worry." M told him.

"So we don't know where he is then?"

"All our agents in Germany are on the alert but so far nothing."

"You don't need me to remind you, but if he isn't seen soon, very soon, the operation's off."

"That would be a shame, but yes there's nothing else we could do."

110

"However, I feel we should proceed on the assumption he will show; but if by the time Reid's ready to move, again presuming he's willing, and the man still hasn't shown, we've no choice but to pull the plug. To proceed then would be far, far too dangerous. And another thing, I don't think you should tell Reid that the plan might be scrapped at the last minute, Sir. Poor chap won't know whether he's coming or going. Literally."

"Well," said M, "let's have him in and put it to him."

"In that case, I'll get out of your way and leave you to it. Too many cook's, don't you know."

When the gentleman had left, M remained quiet and looked pensive, seated behind his oak desk.

"A penny for them Sir," offered Silverthorn.

"I was only thinking. Don't you think it's strange that here we are in the centre of London, ordinary people doing their best and battling on to keep Hitler at bay, when downstairs is a young man who through an accident of nature completely beyond his control, could single-handedly alter the entire course of the war, even history?"

"If you read it in a book you wouldn't believe it."

"No, you wouldn't. A chance like this comes once in ….. I don't know how many hundreds of years. The chance to destroy our enemy from within. Our own Trojan horse right into the enemy's camp."

"Shall I bring him up?"

"Yes, you'd better, otherwise I'll procrastinate all day." M unlocked the top drawer of his desk and removed a file marked 'GOLIATH/MOST SECRET.' He placed the file face down in front of him and waited, surprised to feel his heartbeat quicken.

He didn't have to wait long.

"Ah, Lieutenant Reid. Come in and sit down."

"Thank you, Sir."

"Cigarette?" he asked, pointing to a silver box.

"No, thank you, Sir."

"Well it's nice to see you looking refreshed after your week."

Silverthorn took a chair and sat next to Douglas, opposite M across the desk.

"So how are things?"

"Quite well, Sir thank you. The hand's mending nicely. The M.O. says the stitches can come out tomorrow."

"That's good. So you're feeling on top and ready for anything are you?"

"More or less. Why, what have you got planned for me?"

"We'll come to that in a moment, but firstly tell me about your last mission. Do you feel you learnt anything from it?"

"Without a doubt Sir," he glanced at Silverthorn conscious that something was 'in the air' but his expression was giving nothing away. "I had a first rate cover story, and to be behind the front line as it were, and see how Jerry lives and the country its self, was a real education."

"Good. And do you feel you learnt anything about yourself?"

Douglas took a moment before answering, and remembered the many checks made on his papers, at any one of which he could have been arrested. "The danger, Sir. I almost enjoyed it. Does that sound strange?"

"No not at all. You didn't get on too well with the sea crossings, I hear."

"Er, no," he admitted shyly.

"Sadly Lieutenant," smiled M "the force of nature is something beyond our control."

"But you got there and did the job and got back safely, that's what counts," joined Silverthorn.

"I was just annoyed to think that so many people had put so much effort into a mission which in the end drew a blank."

"Listen to me," began M. "If we had sent in the R.A.F. without ground intelligence, the consequences could have been far more serious than a few wasted hours. Some of the crews may never have returned. Anyway," he said dismissing the subject "that's all history now" and sat up close to the desk facing the task in hand.

"Now I'm going to show you a picture of a German officer and I want you to tell me who he reminds you of." He turned over the file and removed an eight by ten black and white, head and shoulders photograph of a German officer standing talking with another man, and passed it across to Douglas.

No-one spoke for a moment, M and Silverthorn watching Reid closely for his reaction.

"I can't believe it." He said finally. "I really can't believe it. Whoever is this man?"

"Never mind that. Who does he remind you of?"

"Who does he remind me of? Well, it's obvious. He looks like a slightly older version ... of me!"

"Exactly. That's what we thought as well."

"I've never seen anything like it." Douglas couldn't take his eyes off the picture. "If it wasn't for the eye patch and the scar, and a few years difference, it could easily be me in a German uniform. What is he, I can't quite make it out?"

"A Major." Silverthorn told him.

"So he's roughly, what forty?"

"Yes, that's right."

"But wait a minute. Oh my God!" A horrified look moved across his features suddenly as the implication of what he was looking at dawned on him. "Oh no! You want me to impersonate him! A German officer. Oh my God!"

"Hold your horses young man." M held up his hand and spoke firmly. "Let's not run off in the wrong direction. You don't know what it is we've got in mind, so please do not go jumping to conclusions."

"But I'm right aren't I?" Looking at Silverthorn for confirmation.

"Listen to the plan first," said the Captain calmly.

"I can't believe it," he was studying the photograph again "he looks like my older brother." Suddenly he looked up, seeing something new.

"But I couldn't impersonate him. Look at that scar."

No-one said anything, they didn't need to. "Oh no, you're not serious! You don't expect me to have a scar like that do you?!"

"Please Lieutenant, let's take one step at a time."

Douglas fell back in his chair. "I'm ... Sir? For goodness sake ... "

"We obviously have a unique situation here, but it will be handled correctly and sensitively and in a controlled manner. So let's not run on ahead before we know where we're going." M paused, toying nervously with the file. "We will present you with our ideas to maximize the situation, but the decision, the final decision to proceed or not, will rest entirely with you and no-one else. Do I make myself clear?"

"You do."

"If you don't like what we tell you, then it will be scrapped, and on that basis we shall continue."

"Who is this man Sir, what's his position?"

"I'll come to that shortly. We received this picture along with others a short while ago and at the time we knew only that he was a Major in Intelligence with the Abwehr at the German High Command in Berlin. Since then we've received more information from our man on the inside, who's done a fantastic job, risking his life helping us build as near possible a complete picture of his life. His name is Muller. Major Claus Muller."

Douglas took a sharp intake of breath but it went unnoticed.

"He's forty-two and before losing an eye was with the Seventh Panzer Division and awarded the Iron Cross. A widower, with a son Stefan in the army and a daughter Astrid. Normally we wouldn't ... I say Lieutenant are you alright? You've gone quite pale?"

"Yes ... I ... yes, I'm fine thank you Sir," he wiped his hand across his brow which was already damp. "It's all come as a bit of a blow, that's all. Must be delayed reaction or something."

"I'll get you a glass of water old boy," offered Silverthorn.

"Why don't we all have some tea? Would you arrange it, Captain?"

"Indian or China, Sir?"

"I couldn't care less. Just get some tea!"

Douglas meantime had gone from pale to grey.

"Put your head between your legs Reid, you look as if you are about to pass out. I don't think you're quite as well as you make out."

"I was alright when I came in, Sir. As I say delayed reaction, discovering I've got a double. A German double at that." He stared down at the green flooring but all he could see were the trees around her house, the church, her green dress and fair hair and those longing, blue eyes as she looked up, imploring him to write. 'She said the likeness was extraordinary,' he said to himself, 'well it's extraordinary all right. The whole situation's extraordinary'.

Silverthorn returned with a secretary bearing a tray of tea.

"Very good." Said M, trying to sound in control.

"Here we are old boy. Nothing like an English cuppa to pick you up."

Douglas gratefully accepted the refreshment.

"Sugar?"

"No thanks."

"Oh you should, you know, especially when you've had a bit of a shock."

"A bit of a shock?! Is that all you think this is, Sir?" But he didn't complain as the Captain dropped two lumps into his cup. "So what is it exactly you want me to do then, Sir?"

"Alright, we'll move onto that," M cleared his throat. "It is our hope to place you directly in the enemy camp with a view to assassinating Hitler." He paused, anticipating a reaction but Douglas remained speechless. His expression spoke for him. M continued.

"Our people have noticed that of late, for obvious security reasons, Hitler has become very unpredictable in his movements. Not even his staff know until the very last moment which mode of transport he will use, be it train, aeroplane, car, whatever, so for the boffins in 'planning' to put together a feasible plot has been extremely difficult. Alright it might be possible for you to destroy one of the above, but with Hitler's arrangements so erratic, to synchronise his movements with yours would be virtually impossible, requiring a great deal of work and considerable danger, with very little hope of a guaranteed result. However, as I've said already, we know that Muller is with the Abwehr, and once a week he and fellow officers report directly to the Führer. In the past these meetings have been held in Berlin, but more recently at Hitler's new command post, the 'Wolf's Lair' in Eastern Prussia, where he's spending an ever-increasing amount of his time and where he meets in conference with his inner circle and top brass."

"It gets worse."

"What you have … what we would like you to do, or rather what you will have to do first of all, is to kill Muller."

"Kill him?!"

"Why, yes of course," said Silverthorn "we can't have two of the same person wandering around, now can we?"

"I suppose not. Go on Sir."

"We propose you kill Muller the night before one of these meetings takes place, and with him out of the way you'll be free to join the group to the Wolfsschanze, the 'Wolf's Lair'."

"So how will I kill Hitler?"

"Yes. Now initially we had thought of a bomb concealed in your briefcase, but with security tight even with a false bottom the chances of it being discovered are too great to warrant the risk. Then one of our people had a brain wave. A real stroke of genius."

"Oh?"

"Hitler has a dog, an Alsatian called Blondi. It was a gift from Martin Bormann, his secretary, vile man, and, if what I'm told is correct, Hitler's besotted with the creature. Now, the plan is to get one of our agents already established in Germany to arrange for a painting of Blondi which can easily be copied from pictures of the creature in the newspapers. The painting, a watercolour, will bear your signature and I understand will be quite … acceptable from an artistic point of view. But, and this is the genius part, the ornate wooden frame will be extra deep and extra wide and packed with over two pounds of plastic explosive. You will present the painting to your beloved Führer as a belated birthday gift, which you will only have missed by a few weeks. But, as you present it to him, you accidently knock the bottom left hand corner of the frame on something nearby - a table or even the floor if necessary - breaking a glass file of acid concealed in the frame's edge, which will burn through a thin copper wire at a set rate before releasing a pin to strike the detonator cap, and so trigger an explosion. You'll be familiar with the rudiments of all this from your training."

"But surely the picture, … how big is it … ?"

"Roughly two foot square."

"Surely it will be extraordinarily heavy?"

"We've thought of that. It'll be covered by a thick piece of glass. Should Hitler comment on the weight you simply put it down to the glass. Two pounds of high explosive will be more than enough to cause total carnage."

"So do try not to drop it on the way there," put in Silverthorn. "It would rather give the game away."

Douglas let out a sigh.

M continued. "Hitler likes to appear the animal lover so you will be the blue-eyed boy par excellence. And while everyone is standing around admiring it, you make a very hasty retreat saying you've left your briefcase outside or in need of the toilet, a runny tummy anything, but just get out."

"I probably will need the toilet. And then?"

"Get back here A.S.A.P. through the route you are already familiar with."

"I see. Simple as that." Douglas shook his head in disbelief.

"It's far from simple and the details have yet to be ironed out of course, but that's the bones of the plan. I know it all sounds far-fetched, Lieutenant, and I am tempted to say ridiculous even. But that is it's unique appeal. It's great strength. Who on earth will suspect a painting of a dog?! What could be more innocent?"

"So, if I may just recap. Firstly, I get my face mutilated and a scar like Muller's," he glanced at the photograph "very nice. Then I 'become' Muller. I'll have to learn his identity inside out. Anyone could ask me the simplest of questions but if I don't know the answer … well, that would be that. Then I go to Berlin with my scar and my new I.D., find Muller wherever he is and kill him, as you say, the night before one of these meetings. Then I dress up as him, eye patch and all and … wait a moment! Don't tell me you want me to lose an eye as well?"

"No. That won't be necessary."

"Well, that's something at least. Where was I? Yes, and go to the 'Wolf's Lair' with my new-found friends whom I shall also have to learn everything about, praying I don't let something slip which could get me shot. Then I present my painting of the dog, knock the fuse into life and run like hell before it goes off. And then just pop back to jolly old Blighty."

Put like that it sounded farcical. If it had not been deadly serious it would almost have been funny.

"Well, am I right, Sir? Is that what you want me to do?"

"I think you are drastically over simplifying it Lieutenant, but yes. I have to admit in a nutshell, that is correct." M tried to hide his annoyance, his team had already put hours of planning into the operation and now in a few seconds, Reid had reduced it to a pantomime.

Unbeknown to Douglas, weeks earlier the Director of S.O.E. had met secretly with the head of S.I.S. (Secret Intelligence Service) known as 'C', to discuss the situation. Shortly after their meeting all the top bass of S.O.E., known as The Council, were brought together and a feasibility study was conducted using the latest intelligence collected from agents in the field. Eventually the plan to assassinate Hitler was hatched, presented to the Prime Minister and approved. Yet not every voice was raised in agreement concerned by what Germany without Hitler would be like.

British Intelligence were aware of the fact that the Führer had a contingency plan in place to suppress public unrest should anything happen to him. A new government would be installed within six hours, the incalculable consequences of which Mr Churchill and his government would have to deal with. But that was a headache for the future. For now S.O.E.'s direction was plain and simple. Eliminate Hitler.

"But you're forgetting the single most important reality." Silverthorn added quietly.

"Which is what, Sir?"

"Single-handedly, you would have brought the war to an end."

Douglas looked directly at Silverthorn, speechless. The awesome truth hit home hard, and it hurt.

"That's right, Lieutenant," agreed M "with Hitler dead, Germany would seek an honourable surrender. There is no-one suited to replace him now that Hess has crossed over and been arrested. Goebbels, Göring and Himmler, even Admiral Donitz, are not national leaders. Without Hitler, they would be like fish out of water. The war would be over within weeks. Months at the most. Countless thousands of lives would be saved."

Douglas put his face in his hands. "Oh dear God. Whatever have I done to deserve this?" Eventually, slowly, lifting his head. "I don't know what to say. You can't expect me to say yay or nay now, surely?"

"No. But neither can we postpone for very long. We have the Prime Minister breathing down our necks."

"The Prime Minister!" He repeated. "Does he know about it?"

"Of course. This is of national importance."

"What did he say?"

"He wants to know your reaction the moment we do."

"Does he think it's a good plan?"

"Lieutenant," M leaned forward "there is no other way. This is our one and only chance to send an agent literally into Hitler's lap and blow his brains out."

"And mine too, probably."

"The nub of the whole operation," M moved quickly on "is that Muller is a familiar face. A new face would not get anywhere near the 'Wolf's Lair' in a million years, but Muller's face could just walk in. His face is the key to the success of this whole operation and you, like it or not Lieutenant, wear that key. It's important you appreciate exactly why this has to take place at the 'Wolf's Lair,' because it is there where he is most vulnerable, since he is surrounded by those he believes to be the most loyal. And besides, not only will you eliminate Hitler but also half of his 'High Command'! Our enemy will be in total confusion." He nodded at the thought. "It really is the perfect plan."

"Don't think you'll be alone Lieutenant," Silverthorn tried to sound reassuring. "On your last mission we sent you in 'blind', no reception committee, but this time we have agents all over Germany, experienced agents, just waiting for instructions."

Douglas sat still for a moment, his brow deeply furrowed in concentrated thought whilst his superiors remained silent. This was something he had to decide for himself.

"I'm sorry," he said after a while "but I must have some time."

"I'm sorry too, but I can't give you very much time," said M. "I have to have your answer by the end of this day."

Douglas nodded, almost trance like. "Very well, if that's what it's got to be I will give you my answer today. But not right away. What time do you leave here this evening, Sir?"

M checked his watch. "It's three now, I'll be here at least until eight."

"Very well then, I'll tell you one way or the other by eight o'clock tonight."

"Perhaps you would like to talk," offered Silverthorn, "I'll willingly listen."

"No, thanks all the same Sir, I'd rather be alone if you don't mind. In fact I think I might go for a walk."

"As you wish."

The three men rose together and the meeting adjourned.

*

It was a pleasant May afternoon with just a light breeze lifting off the River Thames when Lieutenant Douglas Reid stood on the steps of the Special Operations Executive building and let out a deep sigh.

'What a mess', he thought 'what a dreadful, bloody mess'. And took a deep breath in an effort to clear his head. It did not. Stepping down onto Baker Street, he threw his gas-mask case over his shoulder, and started to walk, not knowing where he was headed or what his answer would be.

Orchard Street, Oxford Street on to Marble Arch and down Park Lane. Due to petrol rationing the afternoon traffic was light, but even so it went unnoticed, people hurried by unseen, the noise of a city at war drowned out by his own agonizing thoughts and concerns.

'How can I tell them the truth? Oh yes Muller, I know all about him. I've already met his daughter and we've fallen for each other'. 'And what would she say if she knew I'd been ordered to kill her father, her only remaining parent? What a mess'.

On he walked; Hyde Park Corner, Buckingham Palace Road, crossing the River Thames over Chelsea Bridge, pausing to stare at the turbulent dark waters before moving on and into Battersea.

'If only Jill hadn't died, I would never had signed up, but if my hand hadn't caught in the door I would never have met Astrid. Dear God, that sounds terrible. I'm playing the girls off against each other'. Oblivious to time and place, on and on he went. 'It's a suicide mission that's what it is. I was just being prepared for it last time. The chances of getting in are slim enough but getting out, virtually zero. But how many lives would be saved with Hitler dead? Hundreds of thousands and all because of my face! But where would I be? In little bits all around the room with Hitler probably. But if I do make it back, well. Churchill's waiting for my decision is he?'

He stopped dead in his tracks on the pavement and looked up as if appealing for divine guidance, receiving strange looks from passers by. "Oh God, what am I going to do?!" It was then he remembered his parents. What would they say if they knew of his impossible dilemma? Thanks to security he couldn't mention it. They didn't even know he was part of S.O.E. How would they feel if the remains of their only son were soon to be hosed off the walls of a bunker deep inside Germany? But if he succeeded the war would be over and if he got back … imagine.

On he walked for hours, neither knowing nor caring if he turned right, left, crossed a road or walked on with the general flow. On and on, deep into the East End, going over and over in his mind again and again all the ifs, buts and perhaps, but was still none the wiser.

'Other agents would help. They'll need to. I'm sure to need all the help I can get but what about that terrible scar? That's for life! And what will Astrid say, if I ever see her again, that is? "Where did you get that scar, Frederic, it's exactly like the one my father had?" "Oh it's nothing; I got it just before I killed him and blew up Hitler."'

On he walked, unconscious of where he was or the time of day.

At a set of crossroads ahead, there appeared to be a small assembly of people standing quietly by the curb blocking the pavement. About twenty or thirty people, each side of the junction, but all looking in the same general direction, down the street, as if waiting for something to appear. They were quiet, sombre even, speaking in hushed tones. The situation puzzled him and dragged him out of his thoughts.

He followed the gaze of the bystanders and a little way off could just make out a line of horse-drawn hearses, the air suddenly echoing to the sound of hooves, the horse's black-feathered headdresses gradually drawing into view. 'A funeral! That's all I need.' But he remained there none-the-less for there was something different about this procession which held his attention. A respectful hush fell over the crowd, some were weeping openly.

The open hearses rolled unhurriedly by. One, two, three, four, five hearses carrying a coffin each, followed by a car for the mourners. From the size of the coffins it was obvious that many of the deceased had been children. "So many coffins." He hadn't meant to voice his thoughts aloud. A middle-aged women standing next to him turned, immediately noticing his uniform, and asked. "Did you know the Parkers?"

"No," he said "I didn't."

"The whole family took, they was. Three kids, mum and dad. He'd only just come home on leave from the Navy too. She'd stopped 'em being evacuated knowing he was on his way. Direct hit. Took the lot of 'em." She opened a hand-bag that had seen better days and removing a handkerchief, dabbed the corners of her eyes.

"The whole family. How ghastly."

"The whole family," she repeated and sniffed heavily. "I wish someone'd drop a bomb on that Hitler, I do, for all what e's done. They were good, decent living, people too."

"Yes, quite." The last of the hearses which contained the smallest coffin of all, an infant's, moved adjacent to where they were standing and his mind flashed back to Jill's funeral. Did they manage to find all the body parts or was that weighted too?

He turned back to the woman. "You must excuse me, madam," he told her "only there's something important I have to attend to."

*

Taking a taxi to Baker Street he arrived there a little before 20.00, just as it was getting dark and took the stairs two at a time to the first floor, anxious to get it over with before he changed his mind. Knocking on M's door he went straight in without waiting for a response.

"Do come in, why don't you, Lieutenant." M looked up from his work over horn-rimmed glasses.

"I'm sorry Sir, but I've made up my mind."

"And?"

"I'll do it but on one condition." he said, striding boldly over and standing directly in front of M's desk. "There's absolutely no way I'm going across that North Sea ever again! I don't mind doing it on the way back, but I flatly refuse to start a mission as important as this feeling like hell warmed up."

M looked up at him from his chair with a face a mixture of respect, compassion and admiration, and the sides of his mouth rose in a crooked grin. "We're one jump ahead of you Lieutenant. You won't have to go 'on' the water, we're sending you under the waves in your own private submarine, courtesy of His Majesty's Royal Navy. You are a very important man." Before Douglas could respond he stood up and offered his hand across the desk. "Let me shake your hand. You, Sir, are a truly courageous young man and you have my deepest respect, and I promise you that I will do everything within my power, as will everyone in this organization, to ensure that this mission is a resounding success and you get back home again safely."

*

As Douglas made his way back to his flat, M knocked on the door of an office a little further along the corridor from his own.

"Come!"

He didn't go in but put his head around the door. "Glad I caught you."

"I couldn't go before I knew. Well?"

"David is willing to face Goliath."

"Thank God. What a sterling young man he must be."

"My sentiment exactly."

"Now, we must get the ball rolling. C.D. will want to call into Downing Street on the way home and inform the Prime Minister personally. He'll be delighted."

Outside, air-raid sirens began sounding their regular dreadful warning.

CHAPTER SIX

"Some interesting developments, Sir."

"Go on." Major Walter Baum sounded impatient at having to stop what he was working on to listen to his assistant.

"Two things, Sir. Firstly Major Muller has reappeared in Paris."

"Has he indeed!" he said tapping his pen on the desk. "Do we have any idea where he has been?"

"No Sir, none at all."

"That's a shame, but still if we don't know we don't know; no doubt time will surely tell us though. At least we know where he is now so we can keep an eye on him. What was the other news?"

"Yes Sir, news from Obernhof."

"Our mysterious machinery salesman?"

"Previously known to us only as Frederic, but we know now his name is Frederic Kutzner. I contacted the company he supposedly worked for, Koch Engineering in Hanover, but they had never heard of him."

"This is becoming very interesting, go on."

"It's interesting especially since they stopped producing agricultural machinery at the end of nineteen thirty-nine and now devote their entire production-line to arms manufacture."

"Well, that is interesting." Baum's eyes widened suddenly. "Just what is going on here? I can't believe I'm hearing this. One minute we had someone called Frederic, a farm machinery salesman from Minden, who we imagined to be Muller's daughter's boyfriend paying her a visit. Now, we have Frederic Kutzner, a man never heard of by the company he supposedly represents, and who don't even make what he's selling. So why should this Frederic Kutzner call on Muller's daughter at precisely the time Muller disappears for a few days?"

The other man shrugged, his face a blank.

"You're perfectly sure Kutzner wasn't Muller?"

"Without a doubt Sir. Major Muller is recognizable immediately with his patch and scar."

"Exactly, and why should Muller go to the trouble of disguising himself simply to visit his own daughter? Which leaves us with the question, who is this man, that he should go to all this trouble pretending to be someone he obviously is not? You say Koch Engineering produces arms. What type of arms?"

"I don't know, Sir but I could find out."

"Yes do. If they're producing small arms may be, just may be, Muller's daughter is somehow involved with smuggling arms to discontents and may not be quite the patriotic little country girl we all imagine her to be."

"But arms from inside Germany?"

"Stranger things have happened. She could be a connection for any one of hundreds of Resistance groups. German weapons are highly prized, remember."

"Do you want her brought in for questioning?"

"Certainly not!" His thoughts moved quickly, concerned more for his own skin than the identity of the stranger.

"I have a feeling," he continued "that if this Frederic Kutzner called once, providing he isn't frightened away, he will call again, so we'll play the waiting game for however long it takes. Like the crocodile unseen beneath the surface, patiently watching its prey. Suddenly," clapping his palms together "we've got him! Now I want a good agent set up in Obernhof right away. We can't rely on this geriatric couple any longer. Things are moving unexpectedly. I want someone who can think and act quickly on their own initiative."

"I'll see to it at once Sir."

"If this Kutzner or whoever he is shows up again, the jaws will bite and we'll learn who he really is." But after his aide had left Baum, remained deep in thought. 'Gun running in Obernhof? No. Yet where did Muller disappear to, and who is the mysterious Frederic Kutzner? If any of this should leak….'

But the following day matters took a turn for the worse.

"There's been another development Sir."

"Now what?"

"I contacted Koch Engineering again and they only produce parts for tanks."

"So that rules out guns for the Resistance."

"But there's more, Sir."

"Go on." The Major slumped back in his chair, sensing bad news.

"I spoke to the same person as I had the day before and he told me my call had triggered his memory. Apparently, a little while before they switched from producing machinery to arms, he remembers a serious row in the office when a salesman returned from a trip to Ireland and the United Kingdom in disgrace."

"Why?"

"It appears he left his luggage and everything relating to his work along with all the orders he had taken, on a train in England, and it was never recovered."

"So?"

"So what he described to me from memory as the contents of the salesman's 'kit,' very closely resembles the contents our man in Obernhof reported having seen Kutzner with."

"I cannot believe I am hearing this! Whatever have we stumbled into? Does this mean our Frederic Kutzner's a foreign agent? A British spy? You're sure Koch Engineering does not recognise Kutzner's name?"

"Sure."

"Then it's obvious what's happened. The British have given one of their agents a bogus name, but they must have found the real salesman's bag and kept it as a useful cover story, yet failed to check what Koch Engineering does now."

"The times tie in perfectly. The bag was lost around the middle of 'thirty-nine and the British declared war on us in the beginning of September."

The Major was on his feet now. "But whyever does a British agent come all the way from the United Kingdom to see Muller's daughter and at exactly the same time as Muller himself disappears?"

"What action would you like me to take, Sir?"

"Action? You'll take no action at all, that's what you'll do. We do nothing or we'll scare him away when he could turn up again at any moment. Even the hint of a trap will scare a professional agent away. Is our new agent in place yet?"

"Tomorrow, Sir."

"Make sure he's got a perfect description of Kutzner or whatever he's calling himself. I want that man apprehended the moment he surfaces and I want to know exactly what's going on. Whyever are the British interested in Obernhof of all places?"

Once again, as soon as he was alone he found there was no shortage of questions in need of answers. 'This was supposed to be a methodical search for a famous diamond, but now suddenly the British are involved. But that just doesn't make sense. And wherever does Muller come into all of this? Could his daughter be some sort of go-between? Whatever do the British want with the Great Mogul? Could they have learnt about the Führer's dream for Linz, and plan to sabotage it by hijacking the centre piece? There's something here that does not add up. And precisely who is Frederic Kutzner?'

*

An official envelope marked 'Berlin' (which had perceptibly been opened and resealed), awaited Muller on his return from Amsterdam. He ripped it open with disdain, knowing he was not the first to read it.

REPORT IN PERSON TO WOLFSSCHANZE WITH PROGRESS OF SEARCH. ADOLF HITLER.'

"When did this arrive?"

"Yesterday morning, Monsieur." The Hotel desk clerk told him.

"From tomorrow I shall be away for a while in Berlin." 'There', he thought 'that will save Baum looking for me'. "Keep my room exactly as it is until I return."

"Of course, Monsieur Muller."

Once in the room and before removing his coat, he lifted the telephone receiver and gave the operator a number. This was official so it didn't matter if it was overheard.

"Inspecteur Rosare, this is Major Muller."

"Bonjour, Major."

"Are you well?"

"As well as can be expected, Monsieur."

"I wondered as I hadn't heard from you, how you are getting on?"

"What can I say? I am making headway, that is all I can tell you for now. You set me an enormous task looking for this De Roehmers. It's a process, and a very lengthy process, of elimination, not only in this country, but most of Europe, as you requested. I will get there but it will take time. You will have to be patient with me."

"Can you give me any time scale?"

"I would rather not Monsieur, and then have to let you down. I will contact you just as soon as I'm satisfied that I have done the job thoroughly."

"That's what I wanted to hear Inspecteur. I would much rather wait and have the search done thoroughly, than a haphazard approach and miss vital evidence. But I had to call, my superiors are demanding a progress report."

"I'll get back to you just as soon as I can, as we arranged. You have my word."

*

It was a long way from Paris to Rastenburg, and the sight of Hitler's new Headquarters, Wolfsschanze, the 'Wolf's Lair,' hidden deep in a corner of Eastern Prussia free from enemy surveillance, amidst thick and ancient forests, never failed to fill visitors with a sense of trepidation.

The air was damp from the many inland lakes nearby and tasted of salt blown in off the Baltic. The forest floor added a tang of earthiness which was both irksome and depressing. Security was tight and Muller's pass was checked and rechecked; his firearm surrendered.

It had been a long journey and even after an overnight stop at his home in Berlin, Muller was tired and irritable at having been kept waiting. With an open-ended appointment he had chosen to arrive at 15.00 hours allowing the leader time enough for one of his regular extensive lunches, which should have put him in a good mood, but it was now 16.00 and no matter how Muller protested to Hitler's Adjutant, he was to wait. The Führer was occupied.

He idly walked around the long single storey barrack style building used as a conference room, leaving foot prints in the soft earth, hoping to catch a glimpse of the Führer to remind him of his presence, before he descended to the underground bunker. He could make out various familiar figures inside, busy talking and leaning over tables covered with maps and charts, but he went unnoticed and continued to pace up and down impatiently, all the while carefully observed by the guards.

"Major Muller?" It was the voice of a small and insignificant middle-aged man.

"Yes. Why?"

"Haven't seen you here in a long time, Sir." It was one of the drivers who, like he, was hanging around waiting for his superiors to make their decisions.

"Cigarette Sir?"

"Thank you."

"Back here again now then?" The man asked, holding a lighted match. The smoke tasted good, but Muller wasn't in the mood to talk.

"Looks like it, doesn't it?" he said.

The driver got the message and wandered off.

A more authoritative voice called his name moments later. "Major Muller!" It was a member of Hitler's staff. "The Führer has told me to tell you that he will see you at the same time, a week from today."

"A week! But I have things to attend to."

"This time next week Major. Heil Hitler."

There was nothing for it, but to return to Berlin and repeat the performance seven days hence.

Having spent so much time in Paris which was comparatively untouched by war, it came as a shock to see the damage that had been caused by air-raids on Berlin and the conditions that people had to endure. Yet even so Muller's own home had remained intact and he spent a frustrating week in and around the capital, when he knew he could have used the time more profitably on a long overdue visit to his daughter and sister-in-law in the country. It would have to wait.

At 08.00 hours exactly a week after his first journey to Prussia, the staff car arrived to take him to the railway station to board the fast, non-stop train run exclusively for officials, for Rastenburg, and a repeat journey. He arrived at 15.00, precisely and reported his arrival, but was curtly informed he was early and to wait. He waited, repeating the previous week's episode. The same driver offered him another cigarette, which he refused, and resumed pacing up and down the now familiar ground.

At 16.00 he was ushered into the Führer's presence, only to reappear at 16.10 looking decidedly displeased; the plan of a good lunch making for a good mood had plainly failed.

The Führer was growing impatient for results and had made his feelings abundantly clear. His plans for the Linz project were on target but frustrated by the absence of the all important centre-piece. Muller expounded his efforts to date and his plans to pursue connections of Tavernier's associate De Roehmers as the best avenue of investigation. But the Supreme Commander of all the Germans was not interested in history, only in results and told Muller time was running out. He returned to Paris deeply disturbed by events on his visit to the 'Wolf's Lair.'

*

At S.O.E. Headquarters, the development of Operation Goliath and the plot to assassinate Adolf Hitler was progressing. All relevant information and intelligence from agents in the field was correlated, scrutinized and then re-examined, first by one team of experts then by another to be sure nothing had been overlooked or left to chance.

Once Muller had been eliminated, the main area of concern was Reid's entry into the fortress-like Wolf's Lair, and great attention was given as to what he could expect to find.

The Wolfsschanze had been constructed deep inside the Masurian forest north of Warsaw, as an impregnable field command-post, consisting of eighty buildings, including a massive bunker with walls 8m thick, for high ranking officials. Two thousand troops guarded the Führer and the self-contained infrastructure; two airports, electric power station, railway station, waterworks, barracks, shelters and fifty huge bunkers. The surrounding dense forest (reeking of rotting vegetation from the marshland nearby and alive with biting insects so intense, troops wore netting protection), was littered with 10,000 land mines and a series of heavily armed trenches which were manned twenty-four hours a day both summer and winter, along with a succession of walls and barbed wire fences.

Added to all this were three secure entry check point zones where every visitor's pass and I.D. were inspected and where even the slightest discrepancy would be exposed.

*

"Well, there we are Captain Silverthorn," began Arthur Powell, "one fully prepared agent, His Majesty's Secret Service for the use of." The two men studied Douglas as teachers might a student.

"You believe him ready, Mr Powell?" Asked Silverthorn.

"I do. He knows all he's got to know, inside and out."

"As always you've done an excellent job. If you say he's ready, your word is good enough for me."

"It's Douglas who's done all the hard work remember, not me." Arthur Powell was the S.O.E Chief Tutor who had been with them from the outset. Drawing on his past experience as a retired headmaster of one of the country's top public schools, as well as being an ex-army man, he had developed ingenious ways to ensure that agents embarking on a tour of duty were thoroughly schooled in their cover stories, local knowledge and objectives. Not usually based at Baker Street but at one of the S.O.E.'s many 'schools' around the country, Powell had been brought to London as this was no ordinary tour. Secrecy was paramount and the more preparations were contained, the better for security. He was highly intelligent, well-travelled and popular with his students (as well as bearing a striking resemblance to Charles Laughton), and in addition to schooling Douglas, Powell had also prepared the two agents who were to assist him known only by their code names 'Seagull' and 'Willow'. Yet that was some time ago, and both men were now well integrated into German life. They had received their new instructions via special courier, as the use of wireless transmissions, however well-coded, could be traced within minutes by German operators who maintained a 24-hour watch over every conceivable frequency. Douglas had not met either agent but had seen their photographs and a few short sentences of recognition would be all that was necessary to establish contact and trust.

"Yes thank you, Mr Powell," said Douglas, "we must do this again some time."

"You like to joke I know, but if all goes according to plan we won't need to do it again."

"Just remind me of what you have covered together." Silverthorn's respect for the man was transparent.

"Certainly. The route in, cover story, the plan whilst undercover, including rendezvous with additional agents already in position. Muller's history and family, as much as is known, and Muller's colleagues known to be working in intelligence from our files and photographs, as well as some of their backgrounds. Most of the top brass he's likely to bump into in Rastenburg. The plan of attack and familiarization with the type of explosive used in the bomb, and finally the route out. I believe that's everything."

"Excellent."

"I must say it hasn't been easy, as we didn't have a great deal to go on as you know, but we made good use of the intelligence we had already, plus the more recent reports and overall I'm satisfied with the results," adding "and his German is faultless of course." He gave Douglas a nod of approval. "Which just leaves me to wish you every possible success. When you return you will be famous and I'll be able to tell my grandchildren I knew the man who killed Adolf Hitler."

"I hope I live up to your optimism, but thank you, anyway Sir," Returned Douglas, stifling a yawn, as Powell left the two agents alone.

The strain of the past few weeks was beginning to show. This was far and above any usual mission and the arrangements had been both myriad and difficult, yet when Silverthorn spoke again he was full of enthusiasm, obviously in his element.

"We have decided that your code name will be the same as the operation title, Goliath," he said. "May as well keep it all as simple as possible. I can tell you Lieutenant, that at one point we were mindful of scrapping the mission because our Major Muller vanished into thin air for some considerable time. However, he's back now and we've had two confirmed sightings of him at the 'Wolf's Lair' as usual, and always on a Tuesday afternoon at 15.00. Obviously he's resumed his weekly intelligence reports. Our man has noticed one important difference though; whereas before he was one of a group, on the last two occasions he's been quite alone. Which of course makes things much easier for you, not having to mix with other officers."

"Especially as Muller's story has so many gaps."

"Especially as Muller's story has so many gaps, yes. But I wouldn't worry too much about that. It's extremely unlikely that anyone will ask you detailed questions about his, that is your, family history."

'Little do you know what I know about his daughter,' thought Douglas.

"Unfortunately, our chap in Berlin has not been able to come up with any more information. He risks his life with every communication as it is." He leant back against the school-style desk at the head of a room which bore every resemblance to a small class room. Behind him stood a blackboard with as much as was known of Claus Muller and his associates chalked across it. Outside, the sun was setting over the London skyline at the end of a busy day.

"I would like to hear your itinerary once more and then we'll call it a day." He knew his pupil was tired but he also knew accuracy saved lives.

Douglas contemplated the grain in the oak desk top, simultaneously drawing in a slow, and deep breath.

"Car to Southampton," he began, looking up "03.00 hours board His Majesty's submarine 'Seadragon' and up the Channel to Vejers Strand on the Western Denmark coast. Forty-five hours later at 00.00 hours, take dinghy ashore where I'll be met by the Resistance and taken to the German border to catch the train at Flensburg for Berlin, via Hamburg, travelling as before, as Frederic Kutzner agricultural machinery salesman from Minden." He stopped mid-flow. "Are you sure it's wise to use the same cover a second time, Sir?"

"Certainly, whyever not? It worked well enough once and there is no reason to suspect it would not work a second time. Besides, you've had enough to learn with Muller without adopting a new cover story. Continue."

"In Berlin, I'm met at the central railway station by 'Seagull' who'll respond to my 'where can I buy a return ticket on Sunday?' with, 'you can't, there are no trains this Sunday'. Together, we'll go to an address from where we can watch Muller's house, and where I shall also take delivery of the watercolour of Blondi. When we're sure Muller's alone, we both go in and silently kill him. Disposing of the body somewhere in the house; a wardrobe anywhere. We spend the rest of the night there. If for any reason Muller does not show, and he could be anywhere, 'Seagull' will radio London for further instructions. But all being well, in the morning I dress in Muller's uniform, not forgetting the eye patch, and at 08.00 the staff car should arrive as it always has in the past apparently, to take Muller, now me, to the railway station where, accompanied by the painting, I catch the non-stop express train to Rastenburg and the Wolf's Lair on my weekly trip. Remember not to talk unnecessarily to drivers, guards and so on and read or doze on the train; avoid conversations.

"Remember to include Muller's identity papers and security passes and the documents he would have brought home with him the night before, and use every opportunity to familiarise myself with the contents. We should arrive approximately at 15.00.

"From then on I'm on my own. Once having passed through all the security checks looking bored and arrogant, I'll be shown in and will undoubtedly meet some of Hitler's Generals most of whom thankfully I am now familiar with. I greet Hitler with a click of the heels and salute, Heil … and so forth, and present him with my work of art, being sure to catch the bottom left-hand corner on something to trigger the sixty second fuse. Then excuse myself with a case of the runs. God willing I'm able to surreptitiously make my way outside where 'Willow', a driver for one of the Generals – a regular member of the Führer's staff - will have his car running with the bonnet open and will be tinkering with the engine. If I hadn't already met him the night before he will confirm his identity by saying 'these engines are good but they sometimes play up after a long run'.

"I get in, and we drive off at a leisurely, but not too leisurely I hope, pace. When over the border and back into Germany proper, I change back into my own clothes hidden in the boot along with my Frederic Kutzner holdall, which would have been collected the night before on our arrival at 'Seagull's' address. All by which time Hitler's brains will hopefully be decorating the walls of his headquarters.

"We drive all the way to Berlin, if possible. If not possible for any reason, we dump the car, split up and use the railway. If we do get to Berlin, we dump the car and 'Willow' disappears, his cover blown, and I catch the train for Kiel eventually boarding the ferry for Oslo as before, and all in the hope that by then all of Germany will be looking for a one-eyed German Major called Muller and not yours truly.

"Oslo – Bergen by train. In Bergen I meet Captain Olsen after dark and board his boat for a trip that is guaranteed to make me as sick as a dog all the way to Shetland, and home. How's that Sir?"

"Perfect. Well done. And you return a hero."

"I'll be more than happy just to get home."

"You will, I'm certain. Any questions?"

"Yes. Just one thing's been puzzling me. I know Muller and I are roughly the same height and build, our people worked that out from the original photograph, but how did you manage to discover we share the same shoe size? Only I've got to wear his boots."

"When no-one was around our man measured his foot print."

"He was that close to him?"

The Captain nodded. "I see you've had your hair colour toned down."

"I had to go to our disguise hairdresser people. I was the only man in the place. I felt a real Charlie I can tell you."

They were both too tired to crack any jokes and the occasion didn't suit any.

"All in the line of duty, old boy," Silverthorn nodded approvingly. In fact, all those involved with drilling, guiding and training the young man had been impressed with his hard work, devotion to duty and unrelenting attention to detail. Attributes that would help keep him alive. "You've come a long way, Douglas."

"It seems we only met the other day."

"Yes, and now here we are, 'Operation Goliath' is go. Just remember to rest and sleep whenever you can, it helps to keep the brain alert. And be mindful of your cover story. Know it inside out and backwards and forwards.

Whenever you get a moment in the sub or on the train go over it again in your mind. You cannot know it too well."

"Indeed I will."

"And do try not to drop the painting in transit. You don't want to blow yourself up."

"Indeed I don't, Sir."

"Well, you've worked very hard and we're all very proud of you but tomorrow's a big day so now I order you," he smiled "to unwind, have a good meal and get some rest."

*

A month to the day after Douglas had agreed on an attempt to assassinate Adolf Hitler brought him to the night before his departure. He was prepared as much as it was possible to be and lay on top of the bed in a room assigned him on the top floor of the S.O.E. building, trying to relax, but finding it impossible. No matter how hard he fought to reassure himself that nothing had been overlooked, the myriad details continued to run around inside his head.

He looked at his left hand and flexed the fingers and thumb, thankful he still had complete use of it and no lasting damage had been done, even though the scars of Captain Olsen's unorthodox stitches would not fade for years, or so the M.O. had told him, if ever. He touched the suicide pill in his top pocket and a nervous shudder ran through his body, wondering if he would ever need it. If he did, the end would be instantaneous. Not far away in Guildford were his mother and father, and he wondered how they would feel if they knew what he was about to embark on. He felt relieved that he had made time to write to them even if it was only an 'everything's fine, hope you're well' letter. 'I wonder if I'll ever see them again?'

Before his imagination could lead him to dark places, there was a sharp rap on the door. "Yes, come in."

"Excuse me Lieutenant." It was M's secretary.

"Hello. Come to tuck me in?"

She laughed. "It's been a few years since I've done that. M wants to see you, and right away."

"Now? he said, swinging his legs off the bed. "It's nine o'clock whatever can he want?"

"I don't know Sir but it sounded urgent."

*

"You're not serious, Sir?!"

"Oh yes I am. We have just received the call and he wants to see you right now."

"Well I'd better go and spruce myself up."

"And double quick, there'll be a car outside in five minutes."

As Douglas hurried off, M felt pleased for him. Everyone should have their moment of glory. God knew he would earn it.

With Douglas as the only passenger, the waiting car sped through the blacked out streets of war-torn London, over the river Thames and on towards Kent and Chartwell, the country residence of Prime Minister Winston Churchill.

*

Douglas remained seated in the back as the Wolsey came to a halt in front of a pair of large wooden gates in a high brick wall, watched over by two members of the Kent Constabulary. The driver gave their particulars, and a policeman scrutinised their passes as a torch-light beam searched the interior of the vehicle. The gates swung open, and the car moved down the short drive and parked to the right of the main entrance under a tall lime tree silhouetted against a starless sky.

There was surprisingly little security at the home of the leader of the British people, which he used very infrequently during hostilities, as it was felt not to be a good security risk for the P.M. and family to stay so close to the Kent coast, usually spending weekends at Chequers, the official residence. Yet the armed trooper patrolling the lawn did not go unnoticed, and no doubt there were more covering the extensive grounds and woodlands. Another policeman stood by the front door, his features lost in the darkness, and politely touched his helmet.

"Good evening, Sir."

"Good evening constable."

"All quiet so far."

"Excuse me?"

"Air-raids, Sir."

"Yes of course, all quiet. I'm sorry my mind was miles away."

The door was opened by an unseen hand, and passing through black-out curtains, Douglas stepped inside.

"Lieutenant Reid?" enquired a man obviously used to dealing with a diverse range of callers.

"Indeed."

"Allow me to relieve you of your cap. You are expected. May I enquire if you are carrying a firearm Sir?"

"No, I'm not."

"Then follow me Sir, if you please."

Passing through French doors into the hall, Douglas was led upstairs and into the Prime Minister's study, put at ease by the prevailing air of calm and homeliness helped by soft lighting and thick carpets. He was silently instructed by the man before he disappeared, to stand on a certain spot and wait.

The study was large and rectangular, with a high ceiling of exposed timbers; photographs, books and pictures covered the walls, including a large oil painting of Blenheim Palace hanging above the fireplace at the end of the room, in front of which lay a small and somnolent brown poodle.

Winston Churchill was seated writing by the light of a small lamp at his desk, facing the fireplace, wearing shirt sleeves and open waistcoat, and continued to puff heavily on a stub cigar without looking up.

Douglas didn't know quite what he was meant to do and nervously straightened his uniform, deciding to remain still and silent. But after a few moments cleared his throat.

"What is it, Inches? I specifically told you I was not to be disturbed." That familiar gruff voice, yet still he didn't raise his head.

"It's Lieutenant Reid, Sir. You wanted to see me." His words brought a quick reaction and Churchill turned, glancing over the top of his glasses. Even though he looked starved of sleep, that indomitable bull-dog spirit still burned in his alert blue eyes.

"They didn't tell me you were here already!" He raised himself awkwardly. "Put the light on won't you, by the door. Let me look at you………Yes, just as I imagined. Come closer and sit down." And they shook hands.

"It's nice to meet you, dear boy, and thank you for coming."

"My pleasure, Sir."

"I wanted to meet the man who's going to rid the world of this evil dictator. Tell me, when do you leave?"

"First thing tomorrow, Sir."

"Tomorrow!? They didn't tell me. Why you should be resting. If I had known I would not have bothered you."

"It's no bother Sir. I couldn't sleep anyway."

"I suppose not. I understand. I remember. Please do sit down."

"Thank you Sir," And took a chair on the opposite side of the desk.

"They told me about the scar. How do you feel about it? Scars are socially acceptable in Germany I believe."

Douglas allowed his fingers to find the mutilated flesh beneath his left eye which he was only just beginning to accept. "I'm just thankful the man I'm to impersonate didn't have a wooden leg."

The Prime Minister laughed. "It would be very wrong of me," he said "to keep you the night before your departure, but before you leave I want to say this.

"To suggest that the outcome of the horrendous conflict we find ourselves in depends on you, would be a gross exaggeration of the truth and we both know that not to be the case. Such matters rest with an authority far mightier than you or I. Yet I believe this is an opportunity which, were we to let it pass, would forever be a source of regret. Should it succeed, thousands of men, women and children will own their continued existence to your fortitude. Should it fail, then I will know you gave of your best, and no Prime Minister could expect more."

"Thank you Sir. I'll bear that in mind during the days ahead."

"Needless to say, the wets in Whitehall are concerned what Germany will be like post-Hitler. I say I don't care! You just blow his brains out, Lieutenant, and come home safely. I'll deal with things at this end."

"I'll do my best, Sir."

"Without doubt, and you have my deepest admiration. But now it would be grossly inappropriate of me to detain you a moment longer. Thank you for coming all this way." Churchill moved around to the front of the desk and as they shook hands, he spoke again.

"When you return, dear boy, I shall be honoured if you would accompany me to Buckingham Palace. I know His Majesty will want to meet you."

"It is I who will be honoured, Sir."

"Goodbye, and God speed."

*

"Take her up to periscope depth nice and slow, I don't want to pop up like a duck in a shooting gallery."

"Aye, aye, Sir."

Douglas watched the dial's trembling needles and steadied himself as the deck began to tilt, unconsciously leaning into the angle of ascent. Fifty feet, forty-five, forty, thirty …. and steady. The young Commander positioned himself almost on his knees and snapped down the periscope handles as it hissed up from the well. Foam cleared from the glass and slowly his eyes grew accustomed to the darkness whilst shapes began to form. Carefully, he moved around the well, turning the lenses to full power as he scanned one hundred and eighty degrees, and then reversing along the other direction.

"We should be about a mile from shore, Sir." The Navigation Officer told him tapping his chart nervously.

"That we are. Time?"

"Twenty-three fifty-nine. You should see a red light followed by two white."

The Commander continued to scan the shadows of the low lying mainland. "Nothing yet."

"Ten seconds to midnight Sir."

"There! Red … white … and another." The periscope descended and the Commander stood upright. "Punctual lot, these Danes." He sounded relieved. "Right, pay attention everyone. There's no moon but it's as still as the grave up there, and the slightest noise will be heard five miles away, let alone one, so let's all be very careful how we move about. Only speak in whispers and even then only if absolutely necessary. Gun crew stand down, we won't be up there long enough to use the Browning and the noise setting it up isn't worth the risk." He turned to his passenger. "You all set, Lieutenant?"

"All set," repeated Douglas "and thanks for everything."

"My pleasure. Right, well good luck. Give 'em hell from us. You'll need to move down to the forward hatch, the dinghy's all ready." He turned back to the crew and with trained eyes, ensured everyone was where they should be.

"Ready everyone? Stand by to surface. … Surface!"

Suddenly the boat was alive. Like sprinters off the mark, men moved quickly in well rehearsed precision to their various stations, as 'Seadragon' lurched violently to the surface. Hatches were thrown open spilling sea-water onto the waiting crew as they scrambled up ladders, anxious to get the job done and return to the safety of the deep before shore batteries spotted them and opened fire.

Down at the forward hatch two seamen had already pulled the inflatable dinghy onto the dripping deck, had it over the side and into the water as Douglas, passing up his holdall, climbed up to join them. Even after the confines of the pressurized sub, the fresh air went unnoticed, for within seconds he had scrambled down the slippery hull and was in the dinghy paddling away. As he listened to a rush of air being expelled from the tanks, he allowed himself a backward glance and saw his last connection with England and home disappear beneath the waves. There could be no turning back now.

*

Berlin Zoologischer Garten railway station was crowded with travellers and men and women in uniform, the air thick with the hiss of steam, trains and noise. Bomb damage was everywhere.

The man was leaning against a pillar, smoking, giving any observer the impression he was absorbed in his newspaper. He recognized Douglas long before Douglas saw him, but stood his ground; these meetings could be dangerous as you never knew who might be watching. He could have been tailed. He followed Douglas with his eyes as he passed through the exit gate at the end of the platform and continued to hold him in view, watching as he made his first mistake.

Douglas looked around in such a bewildered manner he may just as well have shouted out 'I'm a stranger here, anyone seen my contact?' Green amateurs! But then the man noticed the terrible scar running down one side of his face. Anyone who would agree to that couldn't be all bad.

Eventually Douglas spotted 'Seagull' and made his way towards him via a visit to a newspaper kiosk.

"Where can I buy a return ticket on Sunday?" he said.

"You can't, there are no trains this Sunday." The man aged about forty-five was short but solidly built, with close-cut dark hair, parted in the centre, and had a small pointed moustache.

"Seagull," said Douglas quietly.

"Welcome to Berlin, Goliath. And whoever gave you such a ridiculous name?" Without waiting for an answer he started to point and behave as if he were giving directions. "You don't know who's watching. Two men meeting like this could easily arouse suspicion these days, everyone's very jumpy." He spoke quickly as his dark eyes moved this way and that all the while testing, searching. "Walk out of the station, turn left and keep going straight. I'll catch you up in a short while." And with that, he walked quickly away, lost in the crowd.

There were guards, sand bags and gun emplacements outside but Douglas was neither challenged nor his papers examined, and walking casually he left the station behind, instinctively knowing he was being followed but denying himself the urge to turn around. After a while 'Seagull' was beside him.

"Take the next left and continue on until you come to a baker's, then turn right and right again. The house has a pair of brick pillars but no gate. They took that for the metal. Got it?"

"Got it."

'Seagull' hastened on by a different route.

The house was a typical middle class three bed semi, similar to that of any in the U.K. and cluttered with dark, heavy furniture. All Douglas was told was that the owners had moved out for the duration and now 'Seagull' rented it, yet all importantly, from the upstairs front window, anyone could watch Muller's house directly opposite, day and night, without being observed. Douglas agreed to begin the surveillance whilst 'Seagull' made them sandwiches and tea. It was 4.30 p.m.

As he probed the house opposite through a pair of power binoculars, Douglas found his thoughts drifting to Astrid and how she would have felt had she known what he was about to do. 'How strange to be looking at the home of the woman I love, yet be unable to knock the door. I wonder when I'll see her again? Never did write. How could I from England? But I could from here though'.

When 'Seagull' appeared with the tea, Douglas questioned him.

"When does Muller usually return?"

"When he worked here in Berlin and made his weekly reports here, he would normally be back anytime between six and eight most nights. But since giving the reports in Rastenburg, he used to appear around seven and the car would collect him at eight the following morning. Always a Tuesday, tomorrow. Then for months he didn't show at all, no idea where he went, but then suddenly for the last two weeks, it's been back to his old schedule and business as usual."

"Is that what you do, watch Muller?"

"He's just one of many assignments, one of the more recent ones. I've been here some time now. You certainly do look like him, don't you?"

"Don't I know it."

"Good bit younger, though."

"I've brought a small amount of cordite with me to swallow. It makes you feel sick but gives the skin an older, greyish tone. Feeling like I do at the moment, I won't be needing it."

"By the way, that package in the corner. That's your painting. All wrapped up and ready to go."

"Is it any good?"

"It's good enough, that's all you need to worry about."

"I didn't know I was so talented."

"Don't drop it though. Be the last thing you ever do."

*

By 7.30 p.m. there was still no sign of Muller.

"He's later than usual and it'll be getting dark soon, but don't put any lights on. Apart from the black-out rules it's better the house looks empty."

By nine o'clock Muller still had not shown and the house opposite remained dark and the tree lined street deserted.

"You go next door and get some rest. You've got a big day tomorrow. I'll call you the second he shows, don't you worry. No lights remember."

Douglas was thankful for an opportunity to rest and flopped out on the bed, nervous exhaustion having drained him far more than he realized. He soon dozed off.

He awoke with a start in what felt like moments later, to find 'Seagull' standing over him.

"Wake up! 'Willow' is here. He wants your bag and clothes."

"What's the time?" he asked, swinging his legs to the floor.

"Eleven-fifteen. There's still no sign of Muller."

"Are you sure? You should have called me before."

"Of course I'm sure. Do you think I've been asleep too?!"

"But I can't give him my bag if I'm not certain it's a 'goer' or not. How am I ever going to get back otherwise?"

"You'd better come and talk to him yourself, he's in a bit of a hurry. I'll watch the house. We don't want to miss Muller now."

Goliath hurried downstairs, startled to be confronted in the gloom by a man in a German military uniform standing in the hall.

"Goliath?" Questioned the stranger.

"Yes," Douglas told him "and you must be 'Willow'."

"I've got to have your bag and kit quickly. I've got the General's car outside."

"What do you make the time?"

"Just after eleven-twenty. Please hurry! I've got to collect him at midnight right across the other side of town and we've got a very early start in the morning."

"Damn!" Douglas tapped his watch impatiently as if it were lying to him. "Wait there," he said, and ran up the stairs, two at a time, bursting into the front room.

"Has he ever been this late before?"

"Not to my knowledge," responded 'Seagull'.

"Could he be out socializing perhaps?"

"He's not the type, he's more of a loner. But then again it's not impossible. Who knows?"

"There's nothing for it, you'll have to radio London and ask for instructions; he's obviously not going to show. Damn, what a bloody waste of time this all is."

"It'll take a few minutes to get the transmitter rigged up it's hidden in the attic."

"Just do it, please!" Douglas moved quickly downstairs as the other man climbed up into the roof.

"You'd better come upstairs so I can watch the house and we can talk," he said. "You can fix yourself a drink."

"Look mate. I've risked my life coming here and I can't wait a moment longer!" It sounded so strange to hear an English accent coming from someone looking like the enemy.

"Please," appealed Douglas "come up and I'll explain what's happening as quickly as I can."

From the upstairs front room Goliath kept one eye on Muller's house and the other on 'Willow'.

"You can tell the General the car broke down, anything, but if I give you my cover for goodness sake, I'll have nothing to support my reason for being here or my exit route, and may just as well give myself up now."

"He'll help you out," said 'Willow,' with a nod of his head "and I understand what you're saying, I've been doing this a lot longer than you, remember. But what you've got to understand is that any minute one of the city patrols will find the General's car outside, then you, me, and him in the loft 'll cop it. Right?!"

They were interrupted by a voice calling down from the attic. "I'm through to London! I'm to wait."

*

Six hundred miles away in London, the brief wireless telegraphy Morse code message (too short to be traced by the Gestapo, the Secret State Police who maintained a 24 hour watch on every conceivable frequency), had been received at the headquarters of the Secret Intelligence Service by Women's Auxiliary Air Force wireless operator, Mary Wilson. Having been forewarned of the possibility of an urgent incoming message, she immediately recognized 'Seagull's' unique style of transmission and responded quickly by transmitting the recognized acknowledgement codes with instructions to stand by.

The message passed swiftly into the hands of a decoder and within minutes was relayed to Baker Street and the Deputy Director of S.O.E., M.

Despite the hour, M and Captain Silverthorn had stayed behind, anxiously following every step Goliath would take, knowing exactly what his position would be at any given time. But suddenly their worse fears were realized.

"From 'Seagull' Sir, 'DADDY DIDN'T COME TO THE PARTY'."

"Blast!" M hit the desk hard. "Then where the hell is he?!"

"He could be anywhere," responded Silverthorn "he could have travelled a day early and stayed overnight at Rastenburg. If Goliath should arrive tomorrow and walk straight into him ... ."

"Do you imagine I haven't considered that?!" The tension was showing.

"Alternatively, and I hate to say it Sir, but there could have been a leak."

"Dear God, I do hope not. They'll all be like rats in a trap."

"It's a possibility we have to consider."

The minutes ticked by while M formed his decision.

"'Seagull' is standing by, Sir." It was not difficult to imagine what the agents were going through.

"I know, I know. All that planning," he sighed "but there's nothing for it. We must abort. What else can we do? What a shame. What a wicked shame! Reid must be furious. Send the message, but warn them to watch their backs."

*

Meanwhile in the enemy's capital 'Willow' could wait no longer. It was now 11.55 p.m.

"I'm sorry mate, but I've worked bloody hard for my cover and I'm not going to blow it all for the sake of your plans. I was willing to do it for the mission but not now. You may enjoy having your finger nails pulled out one by one and your wedding furniture wired up to a thousand volts but I don't. I'm off!"

Deeply discouraged Goliath heard the front door slam and watched as the shadowy figure climbed into the staff car and sped off into the night. Still Muller had not shown. It was all over now, surely. But he continued to watch the house fully aware that his exit plan was wrecked if Muller did now appear and the mission went ahead, but forced the ramifications to the back of his mind.

Staring out into the darkness across at Astrid's family house, he was not aware of 'Seagull's' movements behind him.

"I've heard from London!"

"And?"

"ABORT."

"Bugger!"

"There's more though, 'POSSIBLE TRAP'."

"Great! That's all I need."

"We must take the warning seriously, someone could have talked. Muller may have been warned and the Gestapo or the Police could easily be watching us even now, and they'll see us long before we see them. This is their country remember and they're not fools, they know all the tricks of the trade believe me."

"So what do you suggest we do?"

"We stay here. It'll be far too risky to go out this late - we'd be questioned immediately. There's a hidden cellar under the kitchen floor downstairs, so we hide there if there's a raid and just hope for the best. There's a couple of machine guns and some ammunition there too. My security pack. In the morning, I suggest you take the train and get as far away from here as possible."

"What will do you?"

"It's better you don't know, but for now we just sit it out in the dark. It'll be light in six hours."

"And the painting?"

"Forget about it. I'll destroy it."

Douglas however had already determined that the trip would not be a complete waste.

*

The rest of the night proved uneventful. There was no air raid, Muller did not show, nor were there any further callers or unwelcome visitors, and slowly the dawn forced the darkness aside and the great city began its daily motions.

Douglas washed and shaved and ate a simple breakfast. Just after nine a.m. he said a brief goodbye to 'Seagull,' each man knowing they would not meet again. Anxious to catch the busy commuter period when he would become just another face in the crowd, resuming his identity of Frederic Kutzner, Douglas hurried to the station and purchased a one way ticket, but the train on which he eventually found a seat was not going north as arranged, but west. The journey brought ample time for reflection. Should he have continued with the mission regardless of London's orders? Failure would mean the war would run on for years, countless lives lost. Surely it would have been better to try, than to return home with nothing to show for everyone's efforts? Undoubtedly he would have been captured, and he gingerly touched the suicide pill in the top pocket of his shirt. If he had gone to Rastenburg independently, he would have needed it. The car had not shown up at eight so Muller had either been scared off or was away. But where?

He sat bolt upright suddenly, startling the woman beside him, as a dreadful thought dawned. Was he about to come face to face with Major Claus Muller at his journey's end?! An involuntary shiver ran through his body as the countryside flashed by and the train hurried on, unconcerned by the worries of its passengers.

*

Obernhof was Obernhof. On the surface quaint, quiescent and unaffected by the troubles and tribulations of the world, yet beneath the tranquil façade ominous designs were already in play as Douglas, oblivious to them all, stepped down from the train. He briskly began the short walk in the direction of the church, as the last of the afternoon sun cast long shadows through the trees by the side of the road.

Unbeknown to him, twenty-five miles away to the west, as the crow flies, at the end of the line in Coblenz, S.S. Obersturmbannführer Otto von

Mehren and his entourage were boarding a special section of the train for Berlin reserved exclusively for V.I.P.s. There was however, a problem with the engine and much to the Lieutenant-Colonel's annoyance, the train was delayed whilst repairs were undertaken.

Douglas made his way through the village, eventually passing the house where he had spent the night and as he did, a face looked out at him. But this was not the friendly face of the old man he had known before, but younger, threatening and he felt it watching his back all the while he made his way up the hill.

The white gate, the path, the door. He hesitated before knocking but then let the knocker connect and waited. Was Muller lingering on the other side?

The door was opened by a woman who must have been in her mid-fifties. This was obviously the aunt because of the family likeness, yet though she wore her grey hair in a bun, maintained a youthful air, her face bright and flushed with health, evidence of an outdoor life. She was wearing a floral apron over brown work trousers and top. She took one look at Douglas and knew instantly who he was.

"Good God! You don't need to tell me who you are. It's like turning the clock back twenty years." Her blue eyes were wide with surprise. "All you need is an eye patch."

"Good afternoon," he said taken aback. No sign of Muller obviously.

"No doubt you've come to see Astrid?" She said with unmasked joy.

"Er yes, if that's possible."

"Oh yes, its possible alright. She talks of no-one else," she told him, smiling. "If I were to send you away she'd never forgive me but then why ever would I want to do that? Come in Frederic, come in, you're very welcome. I'll tell Astrid you're here, she's out in the garden. She won't believe me, she just won't believe me. She didn't tell me about your … never mind."

She led Douglas into the room he knew already and left him to sit in the chair he had used before. Nothing had changed.

Suddenly there were squeals of delight and muffled voices emanating from the kitchen, then someone running quickly upstairs. The aunt reappeared after a pause minus her apron. "Astrid's coming, she's only just got back from the farm. She's gone to pretty herself up, won't be a moment." She was excited, her movements quick, nervous. "She'll be so pleased to see you."

"I do hope I haven't called at an inconvenient moment?"

"No, no of course not. Can I get you a drink, coffee perhaps?"

"A coffee would be very nice, thank you. I remember how much I enjoyed your excellent elderberry wine last time I was here."

"Would you prefer a glass of wine, we've plenty left?"

"No, coffee would be just fine thank you."

"I'll go and make it then. Why don't we all have some?" And she left him alone pleased to have something to do.

Moments later someone was running downstairs. The footsteps paused for a second outside the room and Douglas jumped up in anticipation. And then Astrid appeared, hesitating for a moment in the door way, framed like a study in happiness, her face aglow with joy and expectation. Neither of them spoke but held one another with their eyes. The same green dress he remembered covered her trembling body, and with every movement, hair rippled about her shoulders like dancing sunlight.

But suddenly, a cloud passed over her face as she took in his dreadful scar and her expression changed to a complicated jigsaw of mixed and confused pieces. She hesitated momentarily, then went to him.

"Oh Frederic, you came. How I've dreamt of this moment."

He touched her gently as if she were a dream that might abruptly end, but then pulled her close, kissing her tanned face again and again. Just holding her, the fears and disappointments of the past days dissolved like the release of a terrible burden, and he knew whatever the future may hold, they had to be together.

"I knew you'd come back to me," she told him.

"I had to, I couldn't stay away another day."

"I was so worried when you didn't write."

"I couldn't, believe me, I couldn't, but can you still love me with this face?"

"You look more like my father every day. In a way I've been loving you for years and I always will, no matter what you look like," and she let her lips brush the torn flesh. "My father has a scar exactly the same."

She couldn't have known but her words came like a knife to his heart. A few syllables and the war, Hitler and the S.O.E. all came flooding back and he started to lie once again.

"Flying glass," he told her. "I was caught in an air raid."

"My poor darling man, how terrible for you." Tenderly she kissed his damaged cheek.

"It'll heal in time I hope."

"It looks very painful."

"How is your father, have you heard from him lately?"

"I had a letter he's fine but I haven't seen him for a long time. How nice of you to ask."

"Where is he stationed these days?" He probed.

"I've no idea, security, you know what it's like."

Douglas visibly relaxed, the mission really was over.

There came the sound of footsteps in the hall and the aunt brought in a tray of coffee.

"Here we are, my dears. You must stay and have supper with us, Frederic. We're eating early all this week as I'm on the night shift at the farm. Packing eggs, very boring. But do stay, I'm sure you've both got plenty to catch up on."

*

With the supper cleared away, Astrid's aunt left for work and no sooner had the door clicked shut than once again they fell into each other's arms, hungry for love.

"I want you so badly," he whispered, running her hair through his fingers. "I can hardly breath."

"Well, we can't have that. That will never do," and with a flash of her blue eyes took hold of his hand and led him, without another word, out into the hall, upstairs to her room, and closed the door.

The curtains were open, allowing sufficient luminescence into the small square room as he drew her close and with trembling hands began to undo the buttons of her dress, one by one, delighted when it fell away, revealing her slender body protected only by a flimsy slip.

"My turn now," she said, and proceeded to unbutton his shirt letting it fall to the floor where his suicide pill fell unnoticed and rolled under the bed.

They held each other close savouring the moment, touching, feeling, neither of them conscious of a creak on the stairs.

Suddenly the door burst open under the force of a heavy boot and a man brandishing a hand gun stood threateningly in the doorway. Astrid screamed as Douglas spun round, automatically shielding her body with his. "What the … ! !"

"What a touching sight!" The man was tall and powerfully built, with close cropped hair and even in the half-light he looked dangerous, brutal. "Make a move and you'll regret it!"

"Who the hell are you?!" Douglas felt Astrid's arms tighten around him.

"That's a very good question, Frederic Kutzner, who the hell are you?" And he edged cautiously into the room, all the while training the gun directly at Douglas's chest. "Get dressed. You're coming with me."

"What ?!"

"You heard me. Get dressed. I'm taking you away for questioning." Suddenly Douglas remembered where he had seen the callous face before; it had looked out at him as he'd walked up the hill.

"Who exactly are you?!"

"Never you mind Kutzner, get dressed! Or would you rather come half naked?"

Douglas knew there was nothing he could do, he was unarmed and any scuffle could all too easily result in Astrid getting injured. He would have to go with him, whoever he was.

"What's happening Frederic! Tell me? Who is this man?!"

"I don't know. I don't know what's going on."

"Don't leave me!"

"Stop chatting and get moving. No tricks or the girl gets it."

Douglas finished dressing, all the while looking for an opportunity to jump his assailant, but the man was a professional knowing to keep just out of reach. When he was ready the man produced a pair of handcuffs and threw them on to the bed.

"You, girl. Put them on him."

Astrid looked at Douglas, her eyes full of fear and filling with tears.

"It's alright," he tried to reassure her "just do as he says. I'm sure it's all a terrible misunderstanding."

Still half undressed she picked up the handcuffs and glanced again at Douglas. Whoever this man was he was taking her Frederic away; she had to do something. She fumbled with the handcuffs for a moment, her mind racing, and then flung them hard at the stranger who dodged aside in time. But as he did, the gun went off with a loud crack. Astrid let out a shriek of pain and made a grab for her thigh.

Douglas was about to pounce but the man already had the gun trained on him again.

"You bastard, what have you done?!"

"I told you, no tricks!"

Douglas went to help Astrid who had fallen across the bed, her slip already red with blood.

"Stay where you are! Put the cuffs on."

Douglas hesitated. "For God's sake, man!"

"Quick! Or I'll finish the trollop off."

Reluctantly he did what he was told and was about to click the second cuff home when …

"Wait. I'm not stupid. Put your hands behind your back."

Douglas held his hands together behind his back as the man moved closer until he felt a small circle of cold metal pressing hard against his neck.

"Flinch, and you're history." The voice was guttural, thick, menacing.

The second lock snapped shut. It was too late to do anything.

"Move!" And he waved the gun in the direction of the door.

"I'm not leaving her here like this!"

In agony, Astrid remained curled up on the bed, all the time bravely not making a sound as she squeezed her thigh as hard as she could in an attempt to stem the flow of blood.

"Get out, I said!"

"Astrid!"

"I'll be all right," she spoke through gritted teeth "I think the bullet passed right through."

"I've got to help you!" he cried, leaning over her, powerless to move much. As he did, the butt of the gun came down behind his ear, connecting metal with bone, and he collapsed on top of the girl as she let out a scream, believing him dead.

"You've killed him! You've killed him!" She yelled.

The man grabbed Douglas by the collar yanking him upright and gave her a mocking laugh. "It'll take more than that," and shook his prey like a lion.

"Get out, you. Downstairs!"

All Douglas knew was the pain behind his right ear and the fist on his collar dragging him, almost falling down the stairs. And then he was outside in the darkness.

*

In the Loire Valley, Major Walter Baum's dinner guests were being entertained with tales of his most recent acquisitions from the world of art, when his assistant quietly entered the dining-room and respectfully approached his superior.

"Excuse me, Herr Major."

"What is it? This had better be important – you know how I hate being disturbed during dinner."

The man spoke confidentially in the Major's ear. "We have just received a message from Obernhof, Sir. Frederic Kutzner has shown up."

The Major's look of annoyance rapidly changed to a self-satisfied grin.

"Excellent. Bring him to me. It's time to learn some answers."

*

Baum's man in Obernhof meanwhile, was not experiencing quite the same feeling of self- gratification as his master. From Astrid's house, Frederic had been forced at gunpoint down the hill to the station, the plan being to catch the next available train for Lahn, where he could be detained overnight in a Police cell, there being no suitable facilities in Obernhof. Then the following morning, he would be escorted under guard as the military prisoner of Major Baum into occupied France.

The sensitive internal workings of a steam locomotive however, had already determined a very different course of events.

S.S. Obersturmbannführer Otto von Mehren had eventually departed Coblenz following a lengthy delay, whilst essential repairs were carried out to the engine, only to be further frustrated when just outside Obernhof, he was informed the repairs had proved unsatisfactory. The train had limped into Obernhof's tiny station, and died.

*

The long line of carriages sat impotently on the track, adjacent to the handful of low level buildings which functioned as Obernhof's solitary station.

A gentle hiss of steam could be heard leaking from the engine where the engineer and fireman were standing, looking forlorn, and shaking their heads. Some passengers remained seated on the train, whilst others chose to stroll up and down the platform in the darkness, periodically checking their watches in a vain attempt at hurrying time along.

Otto von Mehren paced up and down with them, smoking and slapping an ivory handled riding crop against his boots in frustration, furious at the delay whilst a replacement engine was brought from Coblenz. Powerless to do anything, no matter how angrily he barked at his subordinates and Station staff alike, he tried to resign himself to the postponement with a sense of stoicism.

*

Unaware of the reason why a train should be standing idly in the station and people milling about, Frederic's captor, with a tight grip on his prisoner's arms, marched him quickly into the station office, anxious to board the waiting train and be away.

He soon learnt of the delay and demanded a secure room in which to hold his prisoner until the replacement engine arrived, but the only room with a lock of any consequence was the waiting-room. It would have to do, and Frederic was unceremoniously propelled in its direction.

"Wait!" The unmistakable voice of authority stopped the man dead, and he yanked Frederic to a halt beside him.

"What is this?" The Lieutenant-Colonel nodded contemptuously in Frederic's direction.

"A prisoner, Herr Colonel," answered the man respectfully at the sight of the uniform.

"I can see that, I didn't think you were out for an evening stroll. Whose prisoner?"

"Major Baum's, Herr Colonel."

149

"Major Baum, Major Baum, I don't know any Major Baum."

"In France, Herr Colonel. I am to take the prisoner to Lahn for the night, then tomorrow we journey to France and Major Baum."

"Why? What is he accused of?" The riding crop started to beat faster against the gleaming black boot.

"He is suspected of being a foreign agent, Herr Colonel."

"A foreign agent, indeed!" Even in the dim light emitting from the station office, the Colonel's expression was clear, as boredom gave way to stimulating involvement. "And since when has this Major Baum been responsible for the interrogation of foreign agents?"

A small number of travellers had started to gather, wondering what all the commotion was about.

"I am only acting on orders, Herr Colonel. I was told to apprehend him…"

"Yes, of course you are only acting on orders, and so here's a new order for you. Tell your Major Baum that the prisoner is now under the jurisdiction of S.S. Obersturmbonnführer Otto von Mehren, and will accompany me to Berlin where, you may assure your Major, he will be thoroughly interrogated by experts." He turned to Frederic who had remained silent, but seriously alarmed. "What is your name?"

"Frederic Kutzner, Herr Colonel. I am a representative for Koch Engineering in Hanover. We produce agricultural machinery. This is all a terrible misunderstanding. I am not a foreign agent. Do I even look like a foreign agent, Herr Colonel?"

The Colonel raised his crop and, planting it directly under Frederic's chin, lifted his head into the light. "As a matter of fact, you don't. Only a fool would masquerade as an agent with an ugly scar like that. How did you get it?"

"Flying glass, Herr Colonel, an air-raid."

He turned back to the other man. "So tell me, why does Baum suspect he is an agent?"

"Koch Engineering, Herr Colonel," began the man slowly "no longer exists."

Of all the words in the German language, only those could have filled Douglas with absolute horror as they did at that moment, and he knew his fate was sealed. He felt sick to his very soul.

"No, that's not true!" He shouted in protest. "My salesman's bag is back at the house." But it was too late.

"Ha!" Scoffed the Colonel. "Put him on the train, we'll soon get to the truth. Not you," he said to the man still holding Douglas. "You're not coming."

"But what shall I tell Major Baum, Herr Colonel?"

"I have already told you what you are to tell him. Tell him he can have his prisoner back when we've finished with him. What's left of him, that is."

The man relented obediently. "As you say, Herr Colonel."

"While we're waiting for this cursed train, you will give all the relevant details to my adjutant and we will take it from there. Remember to surrender the handcuff keys. I'm quite looking forward to talking with this Kutzner myself, it will help pass the time."

The sound of a train whistle in the distance broke up the gathering and Douglas was moved onto a waiting carriage by S.S. guards, who undid the handcuffs and then secured him immediately to a steel and immovable roof support pole in the goods section. A guard settled down nearby, resting a submachine gun across his lap with a hard fixed expression on his face. It was hopeless.

Again, the whistle could be heard getting closer and Douglas slipped back to when he had stood on the same platform with Astrid in his arms, as they had hungrily kissed their goodbyes. What of Astrid now left lying on the bed covered in blood?

It was all a terrible nightmare.

Outside, rain had started to beat heavily against the carriage roof.

CHAPTER SEVEN

Major Claus Muller was seated in the lounge of the Hotel Meurice reading an out of date copy of 'Das Reich', when a bell boy handed him an envelope.

"This has just arrived for you Monsieur."

Muller gave the spotty youth what small change he had and quickly opened the unexpected delivery.

> Major Muller.
> I am sure you will be pleased to learn that my enquiries on your behalf concerning Pepin De Roehmers are almost concluded and all being well I hope be able to present you with my results within the next day or so. I think you will be pleasantly surprised.
>
> Maurice Rosare.

Muller folded the note away and called the waiter over.

"A cognac, s'il vous plait. Make it a double."

*

South of Paris in the Loire Valley, the news was not so good.

"What?!" Major Baum jumped up out of his chair sending it crashing to the floor. "The S.S.!" Blood rushed to his cheeks suddenly, flushing them red. "How the hell did that happen? What kind of a fool is this man you installed?"

"As far as I know, Herr Major everything went according to plan." His assistant responded calmly, the Major's outbursts were nothing new. "Kutzner was apprehended and was about to be taken to a secure position in a village nearby when they were intercepted by S.S. Obersturmbannführer Otto von Mehren."

"Von Mehren, I've heard of him. What was he doing in Obernhof? It's becoming a very busy place suddenly."

"They were on the same train. He told our man that as a foreign agent Kutzner would be taken to Berlin for questioning. There was nothing he could do."

"Dear God. Of all people, he has to fall into the hands of the Gestapo. If Kutzner is a British agent and if he knows what I suspect he knows about the Linz project …"

"He might not talk."

"Oh, he'll talk. The S.S. have very imaginative ways of making people talk and when he does, I'll be finished. Linz and the diamond were supposed to be a secret. The Führer will hear of it and I'll be finished." He crossed to the window and stood gazing at the manicured grounds. "All of this will be history and I'll be sent to the Russian front." He turned and looked contemptuously at the man standing before him, always looking so neat and well turned out and pointed at him accusingly. "And so will you!"

*

Eventually the replacement engine shunted into position and drew the defective engine into a siding. It then connected with the carriages and in cloud of steam, the whole train pulled slowly out of Obernhof station and into the night.

Burdened with self-recrimination, Douglas examined his stupidity, choosing to visit the daughter of the man he was meant to eliminate, instead of returning directly to the U.K. Now under torture he would undoubtedly endanger the lives of many; the S.O.E. training had warned him what to expect.

He brushed his arm against his chest, searching for the suicide pill. Gone! Now he was totally without hope. The lowest point of his life.

As the train trundled on, he made himself as comfortable as possible against the rough wooden side of the windowless goods wagon and tried lying down, but the splintered floor dug into his face and the awkward position stretched his arms until the handcuffs bit into his wrists and he lost sensation in his hands. But while shifting around, he realized he was still carrying his identity papers. In all the commotion no-one had thought to check. And he also had some money, and most importantly of all the tiny 3" blade was still safely stitched into the lapel of his jacket.

Sitting upright, he watched the guard by the light of a single weak bulb, looking menacing in his black uniform and following every move he made. Those men were brutishly tough and even if he were to somehow break free, the chances of overpowering the man before he was riddled with lead were as good as zero. It was going to be a long and uncomfortable night in every sense.

The train had been travelling for almost three hours, making slow progress with occasional stops at various stations along the line, and Douglas estimated their position to be somewhere between Kassel and Hanover, when another guard entered the carriage. The two men spoke quietly for a few moments then the new arrival moved across to their prisoner.

"The Colonel wants to see you. Stand up!"

Was this an opportunity to make a break? He threw the other guard a quick glance but the machine gun was already pointing in his direction.

"Well, I'm very pleased to hear it. Perhaps now we'll get this sorted out and I can return home."

"Shut up! You're not going anywhere."

Douglas stood up as the guard unlocked one cuff releasing him from the pole and pushing his hands behind his back, snapped it shut again quickly. One guard led the way whilst the one with the machine gun followed immediately behind and they passed through the low doorway of the goods wagon, over a ramp and into the passenger section of the train. Having been cramped for so long, walking was difficult especially with the rocking motion and he repeatedly fell against the carriage wall only to be reminded by a poke in the back not to try anything.

They continued to the back of the train collecting curious glances from passengers, when Douglas noticed a toilet.

"Can I?" he asked. "I haven't been for hours, I'm bursting."

The two men looked at each other. "Very well," said one, pushing open the cloakroom door "but no tricks."

"My hands, I can't ..."

"Ha!" One of the guards took a quick glance inside the cramped washroom and, unlocking one of Douglas's hands, pulled him in with him snapping the cuff shut around a brass bar supporting the wash hand basin, testing it for strength. "Don't lock the door." He ordered, and squeezed past shutting the door behind him.

Inside, a snatched glimpse of the window frame and the base of the bar he was connected to told Douglas all he needed to know. He did need to use the toilet but it would have to wait, time was more precious. With his free hand he bent his jacket lapel forward so that the tip of the thin steel blade appeared which he carefully pulled free.

Kneeling down, jamming himself tightly between the wall and the toilet against the rocking of the train, he proceeded to scrape years of verdigris away from the three brass round head screws securing the bar to the floor. Holding the blade like a screw-driver he tried the first one, but because of the blade's fine point nothing happened, so he turned the blade sideways and tried again. At first nothing, but after a few attempts the screw began to turn and slowly moving backwards and forwards the first screw was removed. He repeated the procedure again, and again for a third time, but the final screw proved more stubborn.

"You're a long time. What are you doing in there?"

"What do you think I'm doing? Do you want to come and watch?"

"Hurry up!"

Eventually the third screw gave way and pulling the bar towards him, he was able to slip the handcuff free.

With unrestricted use of both hands he soon got to work on the window frame. Eight screws in all, two on each side in mahogany beading.

"Oh, I'm so constipated." He called out, and broke wind which wasn't difficult, fear doing strange things to his bowels.

"If you ….." but the guard was interrupted by the sudden sound of heavy gun-fire from outside, and not far away and growing nearer with every revolution of the wheels.

It was anti-aircraft fire, but Douglas had other problems on his mind. The window screws were countersunk and buried too deep for the blade to work sideways and the pointed tip was useless. Then he had an idea. Covering the pointed end with the hand towel he was able to use the rounded end-part of the knife which fitted snugly into the screw head giving him excellent leverage.

Even above the noise of the train and ever increasing gun fire, he could still hear the guards talking outside, when one of them said he would see if he could discover what was going on, and left.

'I can tell you that,' thought Douglas as he worked on his escape 'our brave boys in blue are bombing Hanover,' and gave the remaining guard a reassuring moan and broke wind again.

One screw left and the glass could be prised out.

"You must come out. Now!"

"Yes, yes I'm just finishing." The single remaining screw dropped into the toilet bowl and Douglas was able to pull the beading away and lift out the two foot square pane of frosted glass which unexpectedly split in two at the very last moment. Laying the first piece down, he went for the second but was jolted suddenly as the train braked sharply, and all the lights in the train went out simultaneously.

Explosions could be heard clearly now and the anti-aircraft fire was close by, but all Douglas was concerned with was working in the dark on the final piece of glass.

"I'm coming in!" Announced the guard.

"No, I'm … " but it was too late. The door burst open and the S.S. guard put his head round, unable to open the door fully with Douglas pushing against it.

"What's … ? !" The man's impatience sealed his fate. There was nothing else Douglas could do and swiftly slashed the remaining piece of glass deep across the German's throat.

The man's head was trapped between the door and the wall, unable to move, and for seconds he gasped for breath which never came as his life's blood spurted everywhere; frantically kicking and battling against the inevitable, his efforts drowned by the noise of gun fire. Gurgling and choking, he fought to hang onto life as Douglas waited all the while pressing hard against the door, pinning him down praying there was no-one outside in the corridor.

Even in the darkness the whites of the German's eyes were clearly visible as eventually his terrified eyes rolled back in their sockets and he fell quiet. Douglas grabbed his shoulder and, pulling him into the cramped closet, quickly locked the door, dumping the body over the toilet. He knew he was covered with the guard's blood but he couldn't worry about that now.

Fortunately this was the same man who had secured him to the basin, so somewhere on his person should be the key to the handcuffs. He quickly rummaged through the uniform pockets until he located the small metal key, then freed himself from the restraints.

The train was almost at a standstill. It was now or never, and clambering over the lifeless body, he thrust his legs through the window, just managing to snatch his tiny blade from the windowsill in time before dropping down onto the tracks.

Once outside the noise was deafening, as explosion after explosion mixed with anti-aircraft fire reverberated against his eardrums, and dashing across the parallel track, he threw himself into the nearest clump of bushes.

The night sky was bright with fires from a hundred different locations as the city blazed beneath lethal rain from wave after wave of British bombers, so low their markings were clearly visible. Some were caught in the glare of enemy search lights. The air was thick with the stench of spent cordite.

In all the confusion, just the sight of a familiar Lancaster filled him with hope and he looked back at the motionless train, still without lights, but illuminated by fires, to check he had not been followed. All clear. The guard couldn't have been missed, yet.

Taking a moment to check his bearings, it was evident the train had stopped on the outskirts of the city and he was at the edge of a field with the railway track following the perimeter. Roughly five hundred yards away, a small wood began and continued on down a slope to a river at the bottom which, at that precise moment was alive and dancing to the colours of the sky. It would be safer in the wood, and with a final glance over his shoulder, he made a dash for the cover of the trees. The air-raid was still in progress and while he was running for his life, the train was hit as bomb after bomb fell in line, following the course of the track until the train received two direct hits, sending huge columns of flames, sparks and dense black smoke high into the night sky. The energy of the combined explosions was powerful enough to lift him off his feet and drop him yards away with a thump, winded but intact.

Dazed, he looked back at the train now a mass of burning twisted metal. There couldn't possibly be any survivors. Even the bushes along the edge of track were on fire. If he had stayed there seconds longer, he would not have stood a chance.

With his ears ringing from the force of the blasts, he picked himself up off the damp grass, staggered into the trees and collapsed, exhausted. It was then he started to shake, uncontrollably. From head to toe his whole body shook violently and no matter how hard he fought against it, it would not stop. His training warned him what it was; a combination of shock, fear and delayed reaction to extreme trauma, especially a first kill. All the same it was scary and he wiped his eyes, ashamed of his emotions yet powerless to control them.

Only gradually did his nervous system return to normal and his body quieten, and as it did he realized the rain that had started in Obernhof had stopped. In a flash he was back beside Jill's open grave in the pouring rain, remembering his plea 'don't let me die in the rain'. "Thank you," he said quietly. He didn't know who he was addressing, if anyone, but he repeated it again. "Thank you. I don't want to die in the rain."

His thoughts turned to Astrid and the sight of her distorted face fighting the pain of the bullet wound. The remembrance of the efficient way she had dealt with his hand that fateful day somehow told him she would pull through.

The noise of the raid had been overwhelming, but now that it had passed the aftermath was equally intense and abruptly brought him back to his precarious situation. He checked his watch, two forty-five; in three hours it would be light. Wiping his cuff across his face, he immediately picked up the pungent scent of blood and knew what he had to do. He made his way through the trees and down to the river, still conscious of muffled explosions emanating from what was left of the train.

Escape from Germany would be impossible if he was found covered in blood, and on arrival at the shallow river, he stripped off his jacket, shirt and trousers and kneeling on the bank rinsed and squeezed away the incriminating evidence being careful not to spoil his identity papers and paper currency. When he had finished he splashed himself over, the cool water helping to lift his spirits. He took a drink in the hope the water was not contaminated. Having wrung as much water out of his clothes as possible, he pulled them back into shape and dressed. They would have to dry along the way.

If this was Hanover and he was south of the city, he could either pass through it or skirt it but either way he needed to go north and back on the original course.

Keen to avoid being seen so early in the day and attracting attention, keeping to the west Douglas skirted the city extremities, just as the sun began to rise in the east, presenting him with a good sense of the direction he would need to follow. Remaining as inconspicuous as possible by sticking to the course of hedgerow or wood, he made good progress. But as the light increased, so the full extent of the night's raid gradually became apparent.

Columns of acrid smoke rose from fires raging all over the city and even from his position on the outskirts he could make out the charred shells of building after building, roofless and windowless. The remains of unsupported walls and churches minus their spires stood defiant amidst a haze of ash and dust, with scorched possessions scattered indiscriminately by the blast, and the air thick with the sickly odour of death and destruction.

*

By the end of the day he had arrived in Kiel. As there had been no trains out of Hanover, he had taken a bus to Nienburg from where it had been possible to catch a train north.

He bought a tie and comb and smartened himself up, and having also purchased a razor, had a shave in a public toilet where someone had questioned him as to why he hadn't shaved at home. He replied that as a resident of Hanover, he no longer had a home.

Now he was about to board the ferry for Oslo, which he should have done a day earlier.

A mature official of Port Security read his papers and travel permit thoroughly, but then eyed him up and down with a distrustful expression.

"Why are you travelling to Norway?" The man questioned.

"Some of the agricultural machines I sold on a previous visit are quite complicated to operate and now that the farms have taken delivery, I'm to show our customers the correct way to use them. For maximum efficiency, you understand. An after sales service you might call it."

"And where are these farms?"

"One in Bergen, the other in Haugesund, and if I've got time one final call in Kristiansand." Douglas thought it all sounded quite convincing, but the man was not satisfied. This was the last ferry of the day and Douglas wanted to be on it, at all costs avoiding another night on German soil, but one little slip now and a guard would be called and that would be that.

"I see you work for Koch Engineering."

"Yes."

"What type of farm machines are you to demonstrate?"

"The one that's been giving owners problems is the XR9. A wonderful machine that's designed to cut harvest time in half but if the automatic cutter isn't calibrated correctly the result …"

"Alright, alright." The man knew when he was beaten. "You have no luggage?"

"No, I always travel light and besides I'm being met the other side by a lady friend. She always takes care of my needs." And he gave the man a knowing wink who nodded in return.

"Yes, I've heard about these Norwegian girls," he said, and stamped and returned his papers "enjoy yourself Herr Kutzner," indicating he could board.

Climbing the gangway Douglas allowed himself a smile.

'The XR9. Ha!'

Once aboard he was able to eat for the first time in twenty-four hours and then slept like a baby.

*

It was first light before the ferry docked in Oslo's deep water harbour, when passengers were allowed to disembark and pass through yet another check point. Ever since the summer of 1940 all Norwegian authorities acted under direction of the German High Command and as Douglas filed past he knew that trained eyes would be watching for signs of anything out of the ordinary.

A functionary examined his papers, throwing him a quick glance and was about to stamp the travel pass when an official standing behind him spoke. The official was older than the man at the desk, and as soon as he opened his mouth it was obvious he was no native of Norway.

"Why are you here?" he asked.

Douglas repeated at length his story of the previous evening and was subsequently allowed to pass through unhindered, and within a couple of hours boarded the train for Bergen.

*

Arriving in Bergen well before dark, it was simply a question of treading time until he could slip aboard Olsen's boat and head for home. He had a bite to eat and played tourist for the rest of the day until six p.m., when he converged on the fish market and dock keeping a look out for Captain Olsen. And there he was in his usual place, on deck smoking a pipe and mending nets. Douglas made his way to the quay side and catching Olsen's eye, gave him an almost imperceptible nod, knowing there were eyes everywhere. He would return under the cover of darkness as arranged.

The market area was beginning to empty, stalls packing away, pavements washed down. Not wanting to look obvious he too walked away, encouraged knowing home was in sight.

A little way ahead two German Grenadiers were seated on a low wall looking bored, their guns leaning carelessly beside them. The pair could not have been more than nineteen or twenty years old and appeared to be aimlessly watching the comings and goings of the harbour traffic. They had in fact been on duty all day, yet had nothing to show for their efforts and were looking forward to the night off.

As Douglas passed by one spoke to him. "No fish then?" The voice was friendly enough.

"Excuse me?" said Douglas.

"You're not carrying any fish. Didn't you buy any?"

"No, I … I only came down here for a stroll."

"Ah you're German!" The young soldier sounded genuinely pleased.

"Yes."

"Whereabout's are you from?"

"My company's in Hanover, but I'm … "

"Hanover! I come from Hanover too."

Douglas instinctively knew he was on dangerous ground and made to walk on. "You'll have to excuse me," he said.

"I say, just a moment." The young man jumped up and came towards him. "Is it true what I hear that Hanover was bombed badly the other night?"

"Yes, it's true. Very badly."

The young man shook his head. "I thought so. Dear, I hope my mother and sister are alright."

"I'm sure they're fine. Now I'm sorry, but I'll be late if I don't … "

But the guard continued. "It's nice to meet someone from home. Who do you work for?"

Before he answered he remembered the words of his captor, 'Koch Engineering no longer exists'. "Well," he said, suddenly conscious of a chill breeze coming off the water, "I used to be with Koch Engineering, but now I'm freelance."

"I know the Koch building. They used to make machines for farms didn't they?"

"That's right."

"It's really nice to talk to someone from home."

Douglas glanced at the other man who was still seated on the wall, unconcerned by the exchange.

"Is your friend from Hanover too?" he asked – obviously they just wanted to talk to someone from back home.

"No, not him."

"What!?" exclaimed the other soldier. "You talking about me?"

"I told the gentleman you're a country boy."

"And what's wrong with that?" he answered defensively "rather that then live in a town and get bombed every night." And he turned away.

"So how are things back home? I haven't been home for almost a year. Can you believe it?"

"Oh, you know, much the same. The raids go on but we give them as good as they give us."

"It's nice here now, but 'wow' does it get cold in the winter."

"I'm sure it does, you're a lot nearer the Arctic Circle than in Hanover. Well, it's nice to talk with you but I must be off. Take care of yourself."

"Thanks, nice to talk to you too. Give my regards to the homeland when next you're there."

"I will." Douglas felt he could relax again.

"Sad about old Herr Koch dying like that wasn't it?"

"Yes awful, those English bombers have a lot to answer for."

The man looked puzzled suddenly. "How do you mean?" he said.

"The raid," Douglas hesitated, conscious he had suddenly trodden on thin ice.

"Old Herr Koch died in a terrible accident at the factory back in 'thirty-nine, he lost both his legs. It was in the local paper. Surely you knew about that, working for them?"

"Oh yes everybody knew about that of course, poor old chap."

"You said you worked for them until recently, how recently?"

The other man had picked up the change in the tone of the conversation and slowly reached for his gun, bringing it to bear in Douglas' direction.

"Check his papers," he told his friend.

"Yes, show me your papers." The guard took a step back and picking up his rifle, slung it round his shoulder.

"Of course, my pleasure." Douglas sounded as casual as he could, suppressing his indignation at being questioned by a pair of overgrown school boys, and handed over his papers. After a moment the soldier looked up. "This states you're employed by Koch Engineering."

"Well, there we are then. I am. I told you."

"No you didn't. You told me you used to until recently, but now you're freelance."

"Now look here soldier. I am a German citizen here on business. What's the problem for goodness sake?"

"I don't know what the problem is but there's something here I don't like the smell of. You didn't even know about the man you worked for." And he swung his weapon round sharply, pointing it directly at Douglas. "But we'll soon find out."

162

Douglas considered making a dash for it but both guards had their guns trained on him now; he could bring down one but not two simultaneously.

"This is ridiculous! I told you I'm here on business. I used to work for Koch Engineering but now I'm self-employed. Is that a crime these days?"

"Whatever the truth is we'll find out with a few simple telephone calls. Get moving!"

Douglas's spirits collapsed as he started to walk ahead of the two young guards back in the direction past the boat waiting to take him home. Olsen was still on deck having witnessed the whole confrontation and for the second time they caught one another's eye.

"Don't try any tricks," came a voice from behind Douglas. "You won't be the first person I've shot in the back."

*

News of the air-raid over Hanover and the destruction of the train carrying Frederic Kutzner had reached the ears of Major Walter Baum.

"There were no survivors, Sir," his aide informed him. "The train was completely devastated."

"This whole business goes from bad to worse, it's unbelievable. Now with Kutzner dead we're none the wiser. We still don't know who he was, or who he was working for, or anything else about him and we probably never will now."

"At least he didn't have an opportunity to talk to the S.S."

"There is that." The Major was silent for a moment, as he thought about the way ahead. Eventually he gave his instructions.

"I want you to continue to keep a watch on Muller's daughter. Whoever Kutzner was with may replace him with another contact. And you'd better replace our man there. If he can lose Kutzner, he'll probably lose the next one too. I want that girl watched twenty-four hours a day. Let me know at once if any strangers start appearing on the scene."

"Yes, Herr Major."

"Is Muller still in Paris?"

"He is, Sir."

"Maintain the watch on him too, of course." He shook his head. "This is all very puzzling. Not at all what I had envisaged."

*

Douglas had been kept standing for almost two hours, a bright light shining directly in his face, his bare feet cold and swollen. He had not slept for three nights, ever since arriving at the former industrial building which now served as Gestapo Headquarters, Bergen. Deprived of food and allowed only sips of water, locked in a cell under a glaring light making the atmosphere intolerably hot and now having lost all sense of time, he was close to the point of collapse.

Two Nazi officers were seated behind a table in front of him, smoking and considering his case as they had ever since he had been brought before them for the sixth time. And the questions kept coming. The same questions repeated again and again, begging him to incriminate himself.

"So, let's recap shall we?" The younger of the two continued the cross examination. A nasty little man with glasses and a pointed nose not unlike a hedgehog. "You tell us you are Frederic Kutzner, an agricultural representative from Minden, working freelance for Koch Engineering in Hanover. Is that correct?"

"I've told you again and again that's who I am." His voice was husky, his mouth dry.

"Then how do you explain they have never heard of you!?" He sounded condemning, accusing.

"I don't know, I've told you they're obviously mistaken."

Now the other man joined in. He was older and obese and was sweating freely. "Why do you suppose Koch Engineering told us that someone else had been asking if you worked there?"

"I have no idea."

"Why is it the farms you told us you're going to visit have never heard of you, or Koch Engineering and know nothing about any machinery?"

"Maybe you spoke to the wrong people. I've come all this way simply to demonstrate our machines. I wish I'd stayed at home."

"But I just told you no-one's heard of you!"

"When the young soldier spoke to you he said you were unaware how the owner of Koch Engineering, Herr Koch himself, died."

"I misunderstood him that's all."

"So how did Herr Koch die?"

"He lost both his legs."

"How!?"

"There was a terrible accident at the factory."

"What sort of accident? Surely you know that!?"

The room was beginning to swim and the two men appeared to be moving backwards.

"Answer! How did he die?!"

164

"An explosion I think. I may be wrong."

"Wrong, yes! He was caught in a cutting machine."

"Yes, yes that's right I remember now. It was in all the papers."

"How could any employee forget the terrible way his employer died?!"

"I'm tired. I forgot that's all. I remember it well really. There was blood everywhere."

"So, suddenly you remember you were there and what you saw, but you forget how he died!"

"I told you, I forgot; that's all."

"You're lying. You were never there at all!!" He shouted, in a cascade of saliva.

The questions continued without a break.

"If you're a company rep, where's your bag of samples, leaflets? Where's your order pad?"

"I left them in Germany because I didn't need them this trip. I'm only here for a few days visiting the farms."

"You're lying!!"

"You're a liar! You're not a company representative at all but a spy!" yelled the two Nazi officers in unison.

"That's ridiculous."

"Ridiculous? Then explain why you only purchased a one-way ticket!"

"What?!" He instinctively put his hand in his pocket, but the trousers he was wearing were not his own.

"We found the stub of a one-way ticket from Kiel in your pocket. Why?"

"Because …"

"Well? Answer. Why?"

"Because I wasn't sure when I'd be returning."

"Liar! It's because you've no intention of returning to Germany at all, but to Sweden or England!"

"No that's all wrong."

"No, that's all right! Where do you come from? Tell us!" yelled the fat man excitedly.

"I've told you already. I come from Minden."

The two officers exchanged a glance and the questions stopped abruptly and a guard was called in. The hedgehog-like man spoke quietly but what he said sent a bolt of horror through Douglas's exhausted frame.

"You stand accused of being a foreign agent and as such it has been decided to transfer you to Gestapo Supreme Headquarters in Oslo for," the corners of his mouth turned up in the beginning of a sadistic grin, "serious questioning."

"You'll enjoy that," added the other man with an exaggerated laugh. "You'll wish you'd never been born."

"Take him away!"

"This is a wicked miscarriage of justice I demand … " But no-one was listening.

To Douglas the news was like a sentence of death, the reputation of the feared Gestapo H.Q. was renowned. But he was too tired to care and was frogmarched back to his cell and dumped on the stone floor under the powerful light which continued to glare down unrelentingly. He had thought of smashing it but the wire netting cover was too strong and the ceiling too high. The heat was almost overpowering.

The cell was void of any furniture except for a wooden bench bolted firmly to the floor. It was too short and narrow to lie on, but better to sit on than the stone floor. Whatever he did though, he could not stop shivering despite the heat. The room was windowless, airless and hopeless. A single bucket acted as a toilet.

He sat on the bench and rested his head on his knees, too weak to think, too uncomfortable to sleep, even though his throbbing brain cried out for rest. And then the strangest thing happened.

The cell door opened and a guard entered. Douglas wearily raised his head believing his time for transfer had come, but the guard was carrying a tray.

"Herr Kutzner. The Commandant sends his compliments. There has been an unfortunate misunderstanding and he hopes you will enjoy your meal." He handed over the tray and left.

Douglas could not believe either his ears or his eyes. The tray was laden with bread, sausage, cheese and a bottle of beer. What was going on? Was this some cruel trick? Either way, he ate hungrily before they changed their minds and took it away.

He had almost finished when suddenly the cell door was flung wide open and a hose nozzle appeared, instantly erupting into life, sending a powerful jet of ice cold water in his direction. The tray went flying, the plate and bottle crashing to the floor as Douglas was physically lifted off the bench and hurled against the wall.

It was designed to shock and it worked. From sweating with heat to shivering with cold took only seconds, but the effect psychologically, as the water jet followed him whereever he went around the cell, was devastating and as his life flashed before him he started to scream louder and louder, terrified, knowing he was looking death in the face.

Eventually an unseen hand turned off the flow and Douglas collapsed in a heap into a pool of icy water.

A hand grabbed the collar of his shirt and yanked him to his knees.

"Well?!" The voice shouted close against his face. "Are you going to tell us who are you?!"

Douglas didn't or couldn't answer but reeled back suddenly, hitting his head on the floor as a fist hit him full on the mouth and a gentle flow of warm blood began to trickle down his chin.

"I've … told … you … already … ."

Again the fist connected with his chin, and that was the last he remembered.

*

"Inspecteur Rosare, how very nice to see you again. Do come in."

Muller opened the door to his hotel room for Inspecteur Maurice Rosare of the Sûrete, immediately registering how tired the man looked, dressed in a dark and crumpled suit, the front of which was stained with cigarette ash.

"Monsier Muller. I trust you are well."

"I find Parisian life agreeable, Inspecteur."

Rosare did not respond.

"I have the information you require," he said, sitting himself down.

"Excellent. Was it a laborious task, I know these things can be sometimes?"

"Yes, and no. You are a very lucky man, Monsieur. If I may say so?"

"And why do you say so?"

Rosare removed a large folder from his briefcase and placed it on the small table between them.

"This Pepin Udo De Roehmers whom I have studied extensively for the past few months and now know more about than my own mother, was an interesting character. As you told me he was friendly with Jean-Baptiste Tavernier and together they travelled extensively."

"That is correct."

"But did you know that De Roehmers was Swiss?"

"Swiss!" he answered surprised. "No I did not know that."

"He was the younger son of a wealthy landowner living in Switzerland."

"How did you discover that?"

"It wasn't difficult, I knew roughly which dates to look at."

"But what led you to look to Switzerland in the first place?"

"Two things. Firstly the, as you call it, laborious bit. All Western European countries were investigated to see if the name appeared anywhere. Tax records, registration of births and deaths, electoral registers, all the usual. That's why I said you are a lucky man because I would not be sitting here now if the name had appeared, but it did not. If it had, the investigation would have taken years but I know now that it's a very rare name and does not appear in France, Belgium, Germany, Holland and Luxemburg, with the exception of Denmark, but I'll return to that in a moment."

"You have obviously been very thorough."

"I have. Only in Switzerland did the name appear at all."

"That's very interesting."

"Again you were lucky, because the family all but died out some time ago during a plague or something, and what few survivors there were kept the family to a minimum. It is all detailed in my report here," he said tapping the folder. "I remember you weren't sure if De Roehmers was a priest or not."

"That's right."

"Well I can tell you now that he was, a Catholic Priest. Consequently he never married as far as I know and died without family. What sexual peccadillos he may have committed though" and he shrugged his shoulders "is anyone's guess."

"How did you discover he was in the church? Church records?"

"That's right. The family name continued not through him, but his older brother Edsel. It's all in my report. So in a nutshell, and to answer the original task you set me, as far as I can ascertain, today the name of De Roehmers appears only in Switzerland. As I say, the name all but died out and there are only a handful of survivors."

"You said two things lead you to Switzerland."

"Yes. The name De Roehmers of course is French, but Pepin and Udo are German. I don't know why but I immediately thought of Switzerland. I suppose you might call it a policeman's intuition, a hunch that paid off. But as I say, all Western European countries were examined. Tell me Monsieur Muller, are you aware of what the names mean?"

"No, do they mean anything?"

"Pepin means 'enduring', and Udo 'prosperous'. Put the two together and you have 'enduring prosperity' or 'enduringly prosperous De Rohemers'."

"Good Lord," Muller was genuinely surprised. "I had no idea. That's fascinating, fascinating." He thought for a moment. "You mentioned Denmark."

"Denmark yes, I was coming to that. Denmark is not a country you would immediately associate with a name like De Roehmers yet in my investigations, and the Danish authorities were very obliging, I came across what you might call an irregularity."

"In what way?"

"The name De Roehmers does currently appear in Denmark but only once or rather twice, a single surviving couple. But the details are very sketchy as if something's not quite right. You can blame my policeman's nose perhaps."

"I see. I shall have to look into the Denmark link."

"Yes, there's something peculiar there. I can't make out what exactly but it's all in my report. It makes for interesting reading."

"I'm sure it will. You've done an outstanding piece of investigative police work Inspecteur."

"Thank you, Monsieur."

"Did any countries hinder your investigations?"

"What can I say? You gave me some strings to pull and sometimes, only sometimes, I had to give them a gentle tug. But all in all I quite enjoyed it. It made a pleasant change from playing cops and robbers."

"You have admirably completed what I asked you to do and I shall be writing to your superiors to tell them so."

"I'm sure they'll be delighted to hear from you."

Muller let the remark go. "Now, I insist you be my guest for lunch."

"What can I say? The likes of Maurice Rosare has never been fortunate enough to dine at the Hotel Meurice. I think your invitation sounds far more appetizing than the cheese sandwich sitting curling in my desk drawer."

"Bon."

As the two gentlemen went down to lunch, Muller mentally gave himself a pat on the back for having the good sense to call on the police, who were obviously given far greater co-operation than he would have experienced as an alien. Over lunch, his mind was already planning what his next move should be to placate the Führer, impatient as he was for his diamond.

*

Eight hundred miles away in Bergen, Douglas continued to drift in and out of consciousness. After the initial drenching, he was left lying on the wet stone floor from which he eventually managed to ease himself up onto the bench, yet he could not stop shivering, even in the oppressive temperature. He shook violently and ceaselessly from head to toe, whether from cold, fear or exhaustion he could not tell, nor did he care but instead prayed for death. The thought of further degenerate abuse at the hands of the Gestapo in Oslo filled his exhausted mind with terror.

'O God help me. Take me away from all this.'

He lost all sense of time and could have been sitting there for five minutes or five hours as there was no way of knowing and sleep was impossible, when suddenly the cell door opened and he instinctively braced himself for another dousing. But instead, a guard brought in another tray of food only this was better than the last, and carefully placed it on the floor at the prisoner's feet. It looked like a roast chicken dinner and to add the final insult, on one corner of the tray a red carnation sat elegantly in a tall vase. Someone had a very cruel sense of humour.

They couldn't have known, but the last time Douglas had seen one of these was in the buttonhole of the man at S.O.E. Headquarters.

Nauseated at the sight of it all, he kicked it across the floor, too tired to eat, too fearful of what dessert would follow.

He was soon proved right. Moments after the guard had gently closed the door it was flung open and a hose appeared. Again, he was saturated and beaten. Again, he refused to talk. Again, they left him alone, for how long he did not know. Then the process was repeated a third time; the food, the hose, the water, the beating. Only when mercifully he finally lost consciousness did they leave him alone.

*

Completely ignorant of time, Douglas had no way of knowing that it was the following day when he was transferred to a different cell with a bed, all-be-it without blankets, and a tiny barred window instead of a powerful ceiling light. He was given food, water for washing and some dry clothes and told to sleep and prepare himself for transportation later in the day.

A guard roused him at 9 p.m., still dazed, his mouth and face swollen and bruised, when he was led upstairs, locked into manacles and under guard escorted outside to a truck waiting in the dark.

A light drizzle began to fall as someone helped him climb over the tailgate, when he noticed that excluding the driver, there were three guards. One up front and two with him in the rear, all well armed. After a moment's delay the truck moved off as Douglas toyed hopelessly with his restraints.

With the canvas back flap of the truck down, it was impossible to guess where they were taking him, but he reasoned his captors were not suitably equipped for the very long journey to Oslo by road. Therefore, the only alternative would be the railway, and the night train. But he never discovered if he was right or wrong.

Oblivious to external events Douglas felt the truck slow down at the sound of voices, German voices, and eventually stop.

"We're checking all vehicles. There's been reports of resistance activity," someone shouted. "Norwegians masquerading as Germans."

"Ha!" retorted the driver. "So what you looking for? Someone dressed up as Hitler?"

"How dare you be so disrespectful to our glorious leader! I'll put you on a charge if you're not careful! What's in the back?"

"Sorry, Sir. Only a prisoner and two guards."

"Check." Ordered the voice.

Two pairs of footsteps could be heard moving to the back and suddenly the flap was thrown aside and the shadowy figures of two Germans appeared.

"What's this?!" queried one.

"A prisoner for interrogation in Oslo," a guard told him.

"I can't see. Let's have you all outside. Quick, we have lots to do tonight."

The two guards jumped down and Douglas followed as a voice called from the front. "All in order?"

"Yes, Sir!" shouted back one of the men. "Two guards, one prisoner."

"Good -------------- night!"

The word must have been a signal, for suddenly there were a number of muffled pistol shots and the two guards next to Douglas fell silently to the ground, simultaneously as the scene was repeated at the front of the truck where the guard and driver slumped forward in the cab, dead.

"Get back in the truck. Quick!" One of the men shouted at Douglas giving him a hand up, then turned to help the other man pick up the lifeless bodies of the guards and throw them unceremoniously back into the truck, jumping up after them, pulling the flap closed.

"What's going on?" queried Douglas, bewildered.

"You'll see soon enough," and the man banged twice on the back of the driver's cab and the truck accelerated sharply away.

"We've come to set you free." The man told him in a matter of fact voice.

"What? Who are you?"

"We're Norwegian, not German."

"We're the ones masquerading as filthy Germans." The other man added with a laugh.

"Norwegians!" Douglas couldn't believe what he was hearing. He was almost in tears. "Dear God."

The truck sped through the town without further hindrance but not to its original destination.

"Now listen carefully," Douglas was told "in a moment we'll be at the docks where we'll take you down to the boat that'll take you to England."

"England!" The word had never sounded so good.

"But you must do exactly what we tell you." As he spoke, the other Norwegian was already undressing one of the dead guards.

"We'll dress you up like us, German guards, but we anticipated you'd be cuffed so you can't put the tunic on. Put the trousers on and the jacket around your shoulders and the other man's jacket can go over your hands to cover the chain. When we walk, stay close and we'll cover you."

"I can't believe …….." Douglas was still in a daze.

"Dress now, quickly."

Within a few minutes they had arrived at the port and the truck pulled to a halt. The driver came round to the back and lifted the flap and spoke quietly in English.

"Are we all set?"

Douglas immediately recognized the public school voice.

"Silverthorn!"

"Hello old boy. Like a lift home?" He was dressed as a German officer. Douglas had to fight back his emotions.

"Don't worry old son, soon have you sorted out." He looked around. "Only German speaking now."

"We're ready." The Norwegians told him.

*

Dressed as best he could, Douglas concealed himself between the two guards with Silverthorn in front and the four walked purposefully towards the beginning of the fish market docking area where two sentries were stood on duty. The light drizzle had strengthened into steady rain and Douglas shivered as drops ran off his steel helmet and down the back of his neck.

Silverthorn went ahead and spoke to the sentries as the other three passed by, catching them up after a moment.

"I told them we had received reports of a disturbance on the waterfront," he said quietly "and we're here to investigate. There shouldn't be anyone about at this time, it's after ten."

With little sleep, cold and exhausted by physical and emotional traumas, Douglas had not realized how weak he had become and began to stumble.

"Nearly there now old man, don't give up."

Suddenly two more guards appeared unexpectedly from around a corner a little way ahead and Douglas fought to suppress his dread of dying in the rain. 'Not here. Not now. Please'.

"Do you know any German songs, Lieutenant?" whispered Silverthorn sharply.

"Do I what?"

"Do you know any German songs, man?!"

"Yes a few. But why ever … ?"

"Well sing as if you're drunk and we've arrested you."

"Good evening, Herr Hauptmann." One of the Germans greeted Silverthorn, and saluted eagerly as the groups converged. "Heil Hitler."

"Heil Hitler," Silverthorn responded convincingly, over Reid's bawdy singing.

"Underneath the lantern, by the barrack gate … darling I remember the way you used to wait … "

"What are you doing here?" Silverthorn questioned the men.

"This is our regular patrol, Sir."

Douglas's slurred, drunken performance was utterly convincing.

"Good, good. Well be sure not to end up like him. He's under arrest for drinking on duty."

"Of course not, Herr Hauptmann."

"A disgrace to the Fatherland. Carry on then. Carry on."

And with that the two men walked obediently on.

"Good night darling!"

"Alright old boy, don't over do it," he muttered. "You might even get a job on the stage when you get home."

"That's about all I'll be good for after this." But the illusion had sapped his last remaining ounce of strength and the Norwegians had to support him the final part of the way down to Captain Olsen's boat, which was purposely docked along the darkest part of the quay. He was there, ready and waiting.

"English Harald. Come, we take you home."

"Was it you …who told them?" He asked, feeling the Captain's strong arm around him.

"Ya, was me. Captain Silverthorn already in Shetland waiting."

As the darkened boat slipped silently away from the quay with Douglas and Silverthorn safely aboard, the two Norwegian resistance fighters also slipped unseen into the night knowing that once the bodies of the four dead Germans were discovered, a dozen or more Norwegians would be indiscriminately rounded up and publicly executed by way of reprisal.

In London the file on 'Operation Goliath' was officially closed.

CHAPTER EIGHT

The town of Horsens at the mouth of Horsens Fjord, on the east coast of Jutland, Denmark, looks out to the islands of Samsø, then Zealand beyond. Once an ancient Viking settlement, before the war it had been a busy commercial centre, but since the arrival of the armies of the Fatherland all that had changed.

There was little traffic that June afternoon 1941, with petrol rationing and travel restrictions meant journeys were undertaken only when absolutely necessary; so with no stops, the taxi soon completed its fare and once paid drove off hurriedly, anxious to be free of the frightening looking German, leaving Major Claus Muller alone on a deserted flat stretch of road, the driver having assured him that this was where he had asked to be taken.

It was late in the afternoon of a heavy, muggy day and already threatening clouds were building in the east. A strong breeze blowing off the Baltic caused tall dense evergreens nearby to tremble nervously and Muller began to wish he had left the visit until the following morning. Glancing up and down the narrow road, he realized he was entirely alone as there were no dwellings in sight, except the one he was to visit just discernable through plentiful thick foliage. Dark storm clouds continued to gather as he made his way towards the house, along a lengthy winding track thick with weeds and brambles. Try as he might to dismiss it, a sense of foreboding surrounded him.

Stumbling over uneven cobbles and cursing he eventually arrived at the house, a wooden single storey building almost hidden behind thick neglected bushes and, as would have been immediately obvious to any stranger who might inadvertently have strayed onto the property, in dire need of extensive repairs. Or better still, demolition.

He mounted three steps onto a wooden veranda which gave out disconcerting creaks under the sudden weight and knocked on the door dislodging flakes of paint sending them flying off into the wind. He waited, but there was no response, so knocked again, sharply, sending a grey cat on the opposite end of the veranda scurrying off into the undergrowth.

Not a sound could be heard from inside and Muller regretted not having written first to announce his arrival. He tried peering through the windows, but not only were they filthy but curtains covered them completely, causing him to move to the back of the house in search of better luck. But the rear of the property had been completely given over to nature. Two or three cats were fighting in the long grass over what appeared to be the remains of a bird. Muller went around to the far side of the property and found a side door under a small porch. He banged on it hard, frustration beginning to surface. Noises could be heard from inside but they were unrecognizable noises and he banged again, eventually achieving some response. A voice that sounded as if it belonged to an elderly woman called out something followed by sounds of shuffled movement and after some delay the door opened, but no more than an inch.

"Go away! … I don't want anyone." The voice was weak, croaky.

Muller understood a little Danish but the woman's reaction still took him by surprise. He could not see her properly, her face mostly obscured by the door, but she appeared to be in a nightdress of sorts and had exceptionally long, matted hair falling untidily about her shoulders.

"Madam De Roehmers? I have come to talk with you."

"What?!"

"I've come to talk …" he repeated louder.

"What? Go away!" And she went to shut the door but Muller was equally quick with his foot at the same time letting out a sigh of exasperation. This was going to be difficult.

"I wish you no harm Madam, I only want to talk."

"He's asleep," she answered confused "that's all, asleep. Go away!"

On the porch roof above his head, heavy rain drops began to beat their warning of the approaching storm.

The woman would not open the door any wider but Muller was equally determined not to have come all the way from Paris for nothing and pushed it gently, forcing her to step back.

"Help!" she cried in alarm, as two cats dashed past outside.

"Please Madam, I wish you no harm. I only want to ask you some questions." Once inside, Muller was immediately struck by the most appalling, foul smell and for a moment had to physically restrain himself from throwing up there and then, as bile rose into his mouth. The stench was disgusting and as his eyes grew accustomed to the dim light, he began to understand where the smell was emanating from.

The door had opened directly into a small room which was relatively normal except that it was alive with cats; scratching, fighting, purring, stinking cats. They covered every available surface. Every chair, the small settee, even the mantelpiece and table top moved with them. Cats of every colour and breed glared back at the stranger, their eyes glowing like the headlamps of a car in the light of the single oil lamp. Some hissed at him, some came directly and rubbed against his legs, crying for attention whilst others hugged the skirting board meowing, terrified by the intrusion.

Even in the poor light it wasn't difficult to establish the source of the smell, for everywhere cat faeces were as plentiful as cat hair. Almost overcome with revulsion, he quickly covered his nose with a handkerchief. Turning his attention to the woman for the first time he got a good look at the De Roehmers he had come so far to interview. The slight old woman was stood leaning against a chair, dressed only in a thin and tattered nightgown obviously distressed by his arrival but not moving. He could see how long her hair was – very long and straight and grey. It fell about in thick, filthy strands, matted together with food or something worse. Her face had sunk with emaciation, leaving the eyes standing proud and staring wildly, filled with fear and uncertainty. She did not try to speak but let him look at her which was when he noticed her skin which sickened him most. It looked like flakes, dry and lifeless, clinging to her scrawny frame like the scales of a dry and dying fish. And then he caught sight of her bare feet, the toenails so long they had curled back on themselves, and the desiccated skin caked thick with the excrement of a hundred or more cats.

He reached for the door and flinging it wide, took a deep breath of fresh clean air noticing for the first time that it was raining heavily, rumbles of distant thunder heralding the gathering storm that would clear the air. But it would take more than fresh air to clear this evil stench.

With the door open, cats came and went freely, anxious to grab the opportunity, some making a dash for freedom, others too fearful of the unknown, never having ventured outside. Muller turned back to the woman who had not moved but continued to watch him with a wild and unpredictable expression. She went to speak but no words came out. Instead she raised a bony arm, and with a finger like a crumpled horn, pointed to a door he had not yet noticed in the far wall.

Eager to leave the room, he quickly opened the door which lead into a small kitchen but which proved to be no better than the previous room. Cats abounded here too, along with flies and cockroaches, both feeding off abandoned cat food left littering the uneven wooden floor. And then he noticed the sink which was full of crockery green with bacteria and crawling with insects.

A sudden flash of lightning crackled outside sending an eerie shaft of light through thin patterned curtains hanging above the sink, at the same time lighting another door at the opposite end of the kitchen. Hastily passing through, holding onto the handkerchief over his mouth, cats scattered wildly as he tried to ignore what he might be treading in and cautiously opened the door to another room.

The smell in the other rooms was bad enough, but what greeted him now was overpowering. He staggered back into the kitchen, sending cats in every direction and pulled the curtains apart, raising a cloud of dust, and lifting the catch to the window punched it hard. Eventually, it gave way, allowing fresh air to stream in as he gulped at it hungrily.

Yet the additional light only highlighted the filth, and waves of nausea sent sickening shivers throughout his body, just as curiosity combined with determination forced him to return to discover whatever it was the room contained, while thunder continued to rumble nearer and nearer.

Breathing as shallowly as his lungs would allow, he kicked the door wide and peered into the darkness, pausing at the threshold to allow his eyes to accustom to the gloom. He could just make out the outlines of a few simple pieces of furniture and a large bed, but there appeared to be someone in the bed. Could this be what the woman meant when she said 'he's asleep'? Intuition warned him this was more than simply a man in bed asleep.

The storm was directly overhead now, and another flash of lightning revealed where the windows were, but when he tried to draw open the curtains, they disintegrated into shreds and dust in his hands. The sight that met his eyes as he turned around though was to remain with him for the rest of his life.

Suddenly, a gigantic thunder clap shook the dilapidated old house following twin forked- lightning that streaked across the sky, filling the room with piercing light. Muller jumped, seeing clearly there was someone in the bed though whether a man or a woman, he could not be certain because the face was a seething, writhing mass of maggots.

The lightning appeared to petrify and hang in the sky, illuminating the scene just as Muller's stomach could contain itself no longer and he threw up over the floor, trying to steady himself against the first piece of furniture he could grab.

Eventually the lightning faded, but the late afternoon light was sufficient. Wiping a hand across his face cold with sweat, he forced himself to look again at the decomposing corpse.

Where once eyes had moved, their sockets now crawled with maggots gorging themselves on the soft tissue. The mouth was four or five times its normal size where flesh had been eaten away, revealing old, yellowed and broken teeth, and holes in the cheeks had become highways of activity for the burrowing larvae oblivious to Muller's stare.

One arm protruded from under the cover but even that had not escaped the invasion of hungry mouths; the fine bones of the hand picked clean and white were clearly visible. What was going on beneath the sheet could only be imagined. He must have laid there for months. The sheet was pulled up to just under the chin and it was then that Muller noticed the grey stubbled jowls that could only have belonged to a man. But was this De Roehmers?

Suddenly he realized there was something missing from the room that made it different from the rest of the house. Of course, cats. There was not one feline to be seen in the room at all, no doubt the stench of death kept them away.

Thunder continued to clap and rumble overhead and torrential rain beat down upon the ancient house, gushing down the roof and over the eves like waterfalls. A distant, weaker flash of lightning broke across the sky, enough to lighten the room momentarily when he noticed a bookcase above a low bureau against the wall on the far side of the bed. Moving around the room his heart started to beat rapidly as he read some of the titles and for the first time since he had arrived, he actually forgot the appalling smell.

'Famous Diamonds', 'Jewels of the Nobility', 'Famous lost treasures of history', and others, all relating to diamonds and jewellery. Brushing aside the cobwebs he removed 'Royal Jewels' and blowing the dust off, flipped through it. Could it be that the man lying dead just a few feet away genuinely had some connection with the Great Mogul diamond? Was his ancestor Pepin De Roehmers, the man who accompanied Tavernier on his world travels? If only the dead could speak.

He replaced the book and pulled out another, 'Gems of the World'. The pages were yellow with age, some were stuck together and green from damp. Finally, he glanced through a copy of 'Gems of India'. The book had beautiful colour plates of many famous stones – the Taj-E-Mah, Nizam, Hope, Regent, Nassak – and he moved in front of the window to catch the light when he noticed an oil lamp standing on top of the bureau. The lamp appeared to be in good order. He struck a match but the wick was too low. After making the necessary adjustments he tried again and the room suddenly filled with an eerie yellowy glow.

Averting his eyes from the bed he continued to flip the pages of the book, eventually arriving at an entry headed 'The Great Mogul Diamond'. Reading quickly through he learnt nothing fresh but he noticed that someone had penned notes in the margin. Holding the book up close to the lamp, he tried to read the writing, but the ink had all but faded with time and it was impossible to make out anything except the occasional word. But then something fell from the book onto the floor. It was a postcard of a mountain scene somewhere in Switzerland and postmarked 17th April 1940, only fourteen months earlier, but it was the wording which was still clearly legible that set Muller's pulse racing.

Addressed to Ehren De Roehmers in Horsens, it read:

> My dear brother,
> No longer need we live under the curse. The stone is safely hidden forever beneath the everlasting arms.
> Our love to Fran.
> Best wishes.
> Hermann & Ebba.

Suddenly the long journey, the cats, the filth, the corpse were all worth it. Here was proof that the cadaver was that of De Roehmers and pointed to a connection between De Roehmers, Switzerland and a 'stone' which hopefully would prove to be the Great Mogul. The impossible quest he had been ordered to instigate, to trace the untraceable, now suddenly looked as if it was indeed within the realms of possibility. But whatever were the 'everlasting arms'?

Pocketing the postcard he checked the book held no further clues then rummaged through the bureau just in case. But other than old bills, receipts and letters it contained nothing he needed, and picking up the lamp, with one final swift glance at Ehren De Roehmers, he left the room closing the door respectfully behind him.

The storm had moved on and was now no more than intermittent distant rumbles and the rain no longer pounded the roof but had eased to a gentle drizzle. Even so, it was still dark inside the old house and thankful for the lamp he carried it before him as he carefully made his way back to the front room stepping over numerous cats surprised by the sudden light.

The woman must have shut the door and he knocked on it gently before entering, not wishing to cause alarm. She was standing where he had left her, holding onto a chair.

"Fran," he addressed her loudly but not without compassion. "You must be Fran, Frances."

Suddenly, and for no apparent reason, she sprang at him like a demented demon, her vacant eyes flashing wildly and taking him completely by surprise, knocking the lamp from his grasp. Instead of falling directly to the floor, it fell forwards, spilling the oil down the front of her gown. Instantly the tiny flame ignited the oil as it spread into the material and before Muller had time to think, the whole front of her nightdress was a mass of flames which leapt higher with panic speed, until her long matted hair was also alight, flames crackling and licking around the narrow scrawny face like a deadly halo.

At first, disbelief kept her silent, her aged mind unable to grasp what was happening, but realization dawned soon enough and she began to scream, terrified, as Muller grabbed a cushion, the nearest thing to hand, and beat at the flames as best he could. The old woman lifted her arms as if imploring help from some unseen deity, but the flames in her hair ignited the material and soon her arms were like two flaming torches reaching Heavenwards.

The cats were going berserk, running around the room and in and out of the kitchen in a frenzy of fear as Muller relentlessly pounded the flames before they engulfed her back as well, but her ancient body could take no more and she staggered back against the chair, then tumbled to the floor as Muller fought to save her.

Lying quite still, charred and blackened, he thought she was dead but then her eyelids flickered and she tried to speak. Kneeling down beside her, he held his ear close to the scorched skin, trying to catch her words but she managed only one " ... Fran ... " And then her eyes looked at death and her chest sank for the last time as she surrendered her final breath.

Gently, he wiped his hand down her face closing her eyes, the lashes singed and stiff, and then wearily raised himself upright, exhausted. The smell of burnt flesh hung in the air as another nightmare aroma was added to the list in this house of horrors.

Cats cautiously edged nearer now that all was still, but soon withdrew, finding the smouldering body repugnant even to their primitive senses. Muller looked about uncertain what to do next. Cats peered up at him instinctively knowing nothing would ever be the same, and he flung the door open, angry that what had started out as a simple enquiry should end in such drama.

Some of the cats made a run for it as Muller stepped over the old woman's body and crossed the room to extinguish another oil lamp standing on a table nearby before leaving, but as his fingers moved the wick trimmer, a sudden thought crossed his mind. In a strange way it would be the kindest thing to do, and without further deliberation he pushed the lamp off the table, watching as it smashed into pieces and the oil burst into flames flowing quickly across the wooden floor.

He went back to the old man's room, opened the door, and made sure the door to the kitchen would stay open. With the front door wide open a good draft was established and already flames had crept off the floor and were licking at the curtains. Within an hour or less the old house would be a pile of ashes, a cremation pyre where the couple could rest in peace together.

The cats must have sensed what he was about, for by the time he had taken one last look at Fran De Roehmers' charred body, all of them had fled.

The rain had stopped and nature was still once more. As he reached the end of the track by the road he turned back and, wiping his shoes in the long grass, watched as smoke rose high into the twilight sky and ochre flames danced behind windows in a farewell performance.

Inspecteur Rosare had been proved right, but even his policeman's intuition could not have predicted such disturbing events.

*

Returning home from Germany, Douglas Reid needed time to convalesce as well as a course of counselling to help him deal with, and live with, the treatment he had received at the hands of his interrogators, but when he was sufficiently recovered he was called to give a detailed account of what really took place.

His tales of love and deceit were viewed as reckless and thoughtless, as well as dangerous, foolhardy and guilty of endangering the lives of others. He was severely reprimanded, not so much for what he had done, but for deliberately not informing his superiors of the truth earlier. Any promotion which may have been forthcoming was put on hold and he was told, in no uncertain terms, to disappear for two weeks whilst they decided what to do with him because as a future overseas agent, he was now completely useless. With such a scarred face he would be recognizable anywhere, instantly.

Ashamed, he went home to Guildford, armed with a suitable tale to cover the real reason for his disfigured face, but the moment Hanna saw her son's mutilated features she burst into tears in his arms. His father said at the least they should be thankful to have him home. Many parents were not so fortunate.

There was so much Douglas wanted to share with his parents, his meeting with Churchill and so much more, but it would all have to wait until the war was over. As for Douglas, he spent his time brooding over a mental picture of Astrid lying across her bed covered in blood. Wherever was she now?

*

Before returning to Paris, Major Claus Muller called at the Amsterdam workshop of Willem Beck to check on the progress of the facsimile diamond.

Work on cutting the large piece of colourless corundum was proceeding well and the stone was beginning to take on characteristics of the real Great Mogul, but there was still considerable work to be completed before the stone would be ready.

"As you can see Major, the basic shape has taken form," Beck explained. "The high crown is there, but as yet every single facet has to be ground and polished individually to achieve perfect symmetry. The person who cut the original had a comparatively easy job compared with mine, you understand."

"In what way?"

"He was not working to a specific weight goal whereas I am. The finished article must weigh 280 carats."

"Yes, that is very important. The weights must match exactly."

"They will, but it takes time. With every new cut and polish, more of the stone is removed and I have to constantly calculate how much to remove, how much to leave. It's not easy."

"I'm sure it isn't."

The huge stone sat on top of a cutting block like an unfinished piece of sculpture waiting to be born, its embryo shape still crude but recognizable.

"What are all the black lines drawn on for?" asked Muller.

"That's Indian ink. Those are lines of natural cleavage I follow in cutting. That's why it's so important to study a stone thoroughly before cutting can begin, otherwise you could end up in very serious trouble, which is, I suspect, what happened to the original cutter."

"The weight of the original stone in the rough was 789 carats."

"There's my point exactly. Only a butcher would reduce a stone from 789 to 280 carats."

"An Italian cut it."

Beck smiled. "Italy never was a diamond cutting centre. Even the British called in a Dutchman, Voorsanger, to cut the Koh-i-Noor for Queen Victoria."

"So how much longer do you think?" He got in quickly before Beck drifted into a history lesson.

"I have decided to saw the bottom off instead of cutting it."

"Which means what?"

"Which means it will take longer, but it's much safer. For the stone to split now would be," he shrugged "the end, literally. I'm sure you're aware that corundum has a very different crystal system to diamond."

"You mean its crystalline structure?"

"Exactly. Diamond falls into the cubic system whilst corundum belongs to the trigonal or rhombohedral system, which means the cleavage lines I have to follow are completely different from that which I'm used to working with. And as I say, for the stone to fracture now would be terrible, so I'll saw it flat. Don't worry, it'll still look like the original after it's polished."

"Have we made the right choice in choosing to go with corundum and not zircon?"

"Without a doubt, and besides, whereever would you get a zircon as big as this, especially during wartime?"

"I have no idea."

"Well, there we are. Mind you, zircon would be easier to cut, because that belongs to the tetragonal system which is similar to diamond."

"But how long will it all take?" Muller asked again.

"Well, it takes five eight-hour days to saw through a ten carat diamond, so you can work it out from there."

"But corundum's softer than diamond."

"Yes, but only a little. And then every facet has to be polished."

"So how long?!" Muller was impatient.

"Contact me again in six to eight weeks."

"Yes, I will."

"There's another thing we haven't mentioned. The inclusions."

"The inclusions?"

"The marks that were in the original stone."

"Yes, of course."

"Going on the information you left me last time, there was a small speck internally and a flaw at the bottom."

"There's nothing you can do about that surely?"

"The internal speck no, but I can leave you a flaw near the bottom. Fortunately nature has provided us with one."

"Willem. You're the best."

"I told you I would do you a good job, but it all takes time."

*

Anxious not to be summoned again to face the Führer in Rastenburg, Muller compiled a brief progress report on his return to Paris which he forwarded via Major Baum, stating that his investigations were proceeding and were finally beginning to produce encouraging results.

He still found it difficult to believe himself that after all his initial scepticism, he really was now on the trail of the missing diamond, yet still thankful that he had been prudent enough to have Willem Beck cover his rear with an insurance.

*

The report was welcomed by Major Walter Baum.

"So where is he now?" he questioned his aide.

"He told the desk he was going to Switzerland for a while, Sir."

"He gets around doesn't he? Denmark, Switzerland wherever next? Any news from Obernhof, Muller's daughter?"

"Nothing to report, Sir."

*

It was not difficult for Muller to trace the origin of the postmark on the postcard he had found in Denmark, which lead him to the village of Einsiedeln in the Canton of Schwyz, northern Switzerland, corresponding exactly with Rosare's excellent report. According to the map, the village was 20 miles south-east of Zurich and sat in a green valley at a little over 1,000 metres above sea level, at the foot of the Glarus Alps.

Muller sat pensively in the narrow carriage of the small train as it puffed its way up the mountain, making himself as comfortable as possible on the wooden seat, listening to the cogs and teeth beneath his feet bite into the corresponding track to ensure the train did not slip backwards. The train continued to climb higher and higher until eventually it broke through the treetops. A vast expanse of mountain scenery stretched before him in a kaleidoscope of form and colour, and for as far as the eye could see, snow-capped mountains basked in the crystal clear air. A small lake surrounded by woodland sparkled in the sunlight as pleasure-boats cruised along undisturbed by a war, which could well have been a million miles away and yet, was in fact, just the other side of the border.

Eventually, the train juddered to a halt amid clouds of steam at Einsiedeln's neat little station and Muller, wearing civilian clothes, alighted. A taxi driver did as he was asked and took Muller to one of the village's two small hotels. After checking-in and a wash, he took a stroll around the village, which proved to be nothing more than a typical Swiss mountain community concerned primarily with farming, exhibiting pleasant cheerful houses dotted here and there along the valley floor, or clustered together around the few shops which made up the centre.

Yet this village had one ingredient which set it apart from all others in the district. Facing east/west, and to one side of the village's perimeter although still extending into the centre, stood the grand and predominant building of the Abbey Church of the Benedictine Monastery. For hundreds of years the clean, white, four-storey walls dotted with countless windows, under a red tiled roof, had stood as a monument to devotion and learning

Built on a long-sided, open rectangle, the vast building was dominated by two huge bell-towers reaching over 100 feet into the sky, which stood either side of an impressive bow-fronted entrance, as if guarding the spiritual welfare of the occupants. Just a little way from the front of the edifice, a broad crescent of arch-fronted kiosks traded various religious articles and aids for the faithful, who regularly journeyed from all parts of the district to worship. When viewed from the surrounding hills, the Abbey dominated the village skyline standing proud and important at the very heart of the community.

Though it was not until one ventured inside could its true splendour be fully appreciated. Pure white marble and gold dominated everywhere, interspersed with elaborate murals and paintings. And then, at its very core and clothed in virgin white, standing life size on a raised white marble altar, decked with garlands of flowers and countless candles, set in a cloud-burst design of pure gold, stood the magnificent statue of the Black Madonna of Einsiedeln. Our Lady of the Hermits. Her black skin-like marble radiant, immaculate, unsoiled by time or events, her expression forever calm and serene amidst the storms of life.

However, it all left Muller as cold as the marble he trod. He had come to Einsiedeln for one reason, the Great Mogul diamond and was determined to leave either with it or at the least with some clear indication as to its whereabouts.

That night he did not sleep, going over and over in his mind Rosare's report which he had studied so thoroughly he knew almost by heart, and the terrible events at the old house in Denmark. Had he got there sooner he might have learnt something from De Roehmers which might have helped.

In so small a community, tracing the De Roehmers family was not difficult, in fact the proprietor of the hotel recognized the name at once. After breakfast, Muller took a taxi out to the family home, a small farm on the south facing slope of the valley overlooking the village.

Once the taxi had left, Muller tried the door of the wooden farmhouse but raised no response. He wandered around but there was nothing to see that was out of the ordinary. A typical Swiss farmhouse, old, but as could be seen through the windows, clean and tidy within. It fronted onto a yard with a few chickens, and some ducks making a lot of noise in a small pond close to a barn, which also proved to be empty. But even though everything was as one would expect, there remained a sad, run-down, neglected air about the place, as if it had all seen better, happier, times.

It was mid-morning, and already the sun was hot as Muller walked around to the back of the house which enjoyed views across pasture-lands rolling down into the valley. Some way off he saw a man and a woman working at cutting grass with slow, rhythmic, sweeps of a scythe, and made his way over to them.

With their backs to the house as the man cut, and the woman gathered, neither saw nor heard Muller's approach. He cleared his throat when almost upon them and they swung round, startled and surprised, when they saw the stranger sporting an eye patch and an awful scar.

"Who are you?! What do you want?" demanded the man, sharply swinging the scythe round so that it came between them. He was a little taller than Muller and broader, but a good fifteen or twenty years older. He still had a full head of thick, dark curly hair and a face that was deeply lined and tanned. Bushy eyebrows grew over deep-set dark brown eyes and an unkempt moustache under a bulbous nose.

His short, yet ample wife, eyed the stranger suspiciously, for although Switzerland had remained a neutral country, it was still a hot-bed of international intrigue. Before the man opened his mouth it was plain he was neither Swiss nor tourist.

"Güten morgen," began Muller politely. Stranger he may be, but he was still quite handsome, and the woman quickly tucked stray strands of grey hair inside her headscarf and removed her apron.

"My name is Muller, Claus Muller. I have journeyed a long way to see you both."

"And why might that be?" The man was still on the defensive.

"Do I have the honour of addressing Hermann and Ebba De Roehmers?"

"That's who we are. State your business Sir."

"Hermann, you're forgetting your manners." The woman smiled courteously and her round face dimpled. "You must excuse us Herr Muller, but we don't get many visitors these days and these are dangerous times." She was slightly out of breath.

"Of course, I quite understand. You must forgive my startling you like that."

"So what is it we can do for you Herr Muller?" The man slowly lowered the scythe.

"It's a long story and I can see that obviously I have not called at a convenient time, but I can tell you I have just returned from Horsens, Denmark ….."

The woman looked shocked suddenly and alarm filled her gentle blue eyes. "Oh!"

"The home of Ehren and Fran De Roehmers," finished Muller.

"Do you have news?" Ebba's concern was obvious. "Only we haven't heard anything for a very long time."

"I have news." Muller told them slowly, pausing before continuing and glancing up at the sun. "It's getting hot," he loosened his collar. "Perhaps when you have finished your work we might … "

"Surely this can wait Hermann? If this gentleman's come all this way to see us with news?"

"Yes," responded her husband simply. "Come, Herr Muller. Let us go up to the house." And the farmer swung the lethal scythe over a broad shoulder.

*

It was cooler inside the farmhouse which was simply, yet comfortably decorated with the many items of furniture displaying typical hand-painted Swiss designs. As Muller sipped his strong black coffee and eyed the very ordinary couple seated opposite, he could not help but wonder how these country folk could possibly know anything of the Mogul's great diamond. Surely he had to be wasting his time.

"So tell us, Herr Muller," De Roehmers began "what news from Denmark?"

"I shall be pleased to tell you everything, but I think perhaps first, I should explain myself."

The farmer nodded.

"I am an archaeologist, and for some time I have been doing research for a book I hope to produce in the not too distant future, on gems of the east, particularly those of India. And it was whilst I was researching the origins of one particular piece that I continually met with the name Jean-Baptiste Tavernier. And almost every time his name appeared another appeared along side, that of Pepin Udo De Roehmers."

All the while Muller was speaking, he watched for any reaction, but the old man's face revealed nothing. Yet right from the outset, no matter how hard she tried to conceal it, Ebba's expression told him all he needed to know. He was about to continue when Hermann spoke.

"I would have thought this was a strange time for a German to be writing a book?"

"On the contrary," Muller responded quickly, "the Führer is most anxious for his people to pursue the arts and culture, history and the like. And besides," he fingered his scar "one- eyed soldiers aren't in great demand."

"Let Herr Muller continue Hermann."

"Danke. So I made some enquiries as to the name of De Roehmers in the hope that any living kinsfolk may be able to help my research, and I found the couple living in Horsens whom I went to see. Sadly however the news is not good at all."

"Oh dear, how are they?" Said Ebba.

"Tell me Mein Herr," persevered Muller "am I correct in assuming that Ehren De Roehmers was your brother?"

"Ya, my elder brother, by nine years. There's only ever been just the two of us."

"I thought so. And when was the last time you heard from him?"

"I can't remember, a long time anyway."

"More than a year, I'm sure," put in Ebba.

"Yes, more than a year. But you just said 'was' my brother?"

"Yes. I'm so sorry to have to tell you but your brother Ehren is dead."

Hermann let his head fall forward. "I knew it," he said sadly "I just knew it. I've felt it in my bones for a long time. We weren't particularly close but somehow I just knew he'd gone."

"Oh dear, dear, dear. I'm so sorry, Hermann. More sad news," and she squeezed her husband's arm," as if we haven't had enough already. But what of Fran? She hadn't been well for a long time. I'd have thought she would have been the first to go."

Muller chose his words carefully. "I can only tell you that when I arrived there, Fran De Roehmers was in a dreadful state, and alone of course."

"Oh dear, dear. When was this?"

"Just ten days ago. She was very weak when I got there, literally hanging on to life by a thread. I doubt if she had eaten anything for weeks and she was very confused. The house was in a dreadful mess."

"Oh, the poor soul."

"I can assure you I did what I could for her but I had only been there a short while when she died in my arms."

"Oh how terrible!"

"I must tell you it was all very distressing. Very distressing indeed."

"Of course, how terrible for you." The couple's reaction was genuine enough.

"Yes, it was. I'm just thankful that I was there. It would have been awful for her to have died alone."

"Yes, of course poor soul, to have died alone with nobody knowing. Their house was very isolated."

"How did you learn my brother had died?" Hermann asked reflecting on what he had just heard.

"I managed to ascertain that from your sister-in-law before, before the end," he answered. "Naturally I had to leave things as I found them when I left but I reported the situation to the authorities when I got back to town, and they assured me everything would be dealt with and in a proper manner. I'm just so sorry to have to bring you such sad news. It's obviously come as a shock to you both. I wasn't sure if you had heard or not, about Ehren that is."

"No," Ebba told him "as I say we haven't heard from either of them for a long time. We weren't close but they were still family after all." And she wiped her eyes.

Hermann turned to his wife. "You know what this means, don't you?"

"No, what?" she said with a sniff.

"That I'm the sole survivor of the De Roehmers family."

"You have no family yourself?" asked Muller.

"We had, Herr Muller, we had," said Ebba. "We had a fine son, Everard. He and his wife and our three wonderful grandchildren were all killed in an accident the winter before last."

"I am so sorry."

"That's their picture over there," she said, pointing to a family photograph on the wall by the fireplace. "They were all out having fun on a tractor crossing the old bridge down by the lake. We had had a very bad winter that year and what with the weight of the snow and the tractor, it was simply too much and the bridge gave way. The tractor crashed through the ice and took them all … with it." She was weeping openly now. "I lost … my whole family … in one day."

"Now, now Ebba, don't go upsetting yourself."

"None of the bodies were ever recovered … the water's too deep."

"I am so very sorry," repeated Muller.

"And now this … It's that damned curse!"

"Ebba!" exclaimed the old man abruptly. "That's enough."

Muller knew at once a nerve had been exposed, but he could wait.

"I think perhaps I have said enough for one day," he told them. "You have had two lots of bad news. Now it is only right I leave you to reflect." But Ebba hadn't heard.

"The bridge was due to be renewed in the spring … but it was too late."

Muller stood ready to leave. "My deepest condolences to you both. It was very kind of you to see me."

The old farmer wearily got to his feet. "It is we who should thank you, Mein Herr, for what you did, and for coming to see us."

"Auf wiedersehen Frau De Roehmers." But the woman was re-living the scene at the old bridge.

Muller followed Hermann to the front door.

"You must excuse my wife, she still gets very emotional."

"I quite understand. I hate to say it, but there are still one or two things I should like to discuss further with you both, if I may. My book, you understand."

"I see." The farmer did not sound overly enthusiastic.

"Perhaps I might call on you again tomorrow afternoon. Would that be convenient?"

"Yes," he hesitated "very well. I don't see that we can be of much help to you but you've been very kind, so I suppose it's the least we can do."

"Until tomorrow then."

"How will you get back to town?"

"It's a beautiful day. The walk will do me good."

*

The following afternoon the scene was repeated, with the exception that the brilliant sunshine was replaced by heavy, low cloud obscuring the mountain tops, which also appeared to determine the mood inside.

Obviously the couple had been talking and they were prepared for Muller's visit, but Ebba was nonetheless cordial.

"You must forgive my outburst yesterday, Herr Muller. I'm afraid it still affects me like that even after all this time."

"Dear lady, I quite understand and you have nothing to apologize for."

"I don't think I shall ever fully recover from it. We miss them all, every single day. Everard used to work together with Hermann here on the farm, but since the accident things have been getting on top of us, haven't they Hermann?"

"We'll manage though," he answered stoically.

"Yes, but for how long, I wonder sometimes. Neither of us are getting any younger and now with Ehren and Fran gone, we really are completely alone. I remember writing to them about Everard and the family but I never had a reply. They must have been too poorly perhaps. Do you know who took care of the funeral arrangements Herr Muller?"

"I believe that was handled by the local authorities in Horsens."

"When did all this take place you say?" asked Hermann.

"Exactly ten days ago, well, eleven now. After I left, I had a few personal things to attend to and then I came directly here."

"How very sad. I doubt if there were many at the funeral. They had no children you know," Ebba told him.

"No, I didn't know for certain, though I did suspect it."

"So you knew about us before you visited Denmark then?" said Hermann.

"Yes I did. I had compiled a list of living family members. I started in Denmark and then planned to visit the families here."

"Well I can tell you now there is no more family. I know for a fact we are the last of the line. Tell me, how did you find us?"

"It was not difficult. You have a very unusual name and everyone's listed somewhere, county records, the electoral register. I knew of a Swiss connection because of Pepin De Roehmer's connection with Jean-Baptiste Tavernier. Together they made numerous visits to this country. But I trust you don't consider I have invaded your privacy?"

"No, of course not." Said Ebba.

"No, but you said yesterday that our ancestor's name continually appeared while you were looking for a particular gem. Which gem?"

At her husband's question, Ebba shifted uncomfortable in her chair which Muller picked up on at once.

"So you are saying that Pepin 'was' your ancestor?"

"We have heard the name before, yes."

"This is very exciting. I've been searching for a long time to find a connection."

"Which gem is it exactly that are you investigating for your book Herr Muller?" repeated Hermann.

"It is called the Great Mogul diamond, perhaps …" he stopped mid-sentence. Mention of the diamond did not meet with quite the reaction he had anticipated.

"Oh dear," said Ebba heavily "just as I feared. It's started all over again," and looked to her husband. "You tell him," she said.

"Have I said something …"

"Herr Muller," began the farmer "you have done well to find us, very well. In fact you are the first, but after all these years we had hoped we had heard the last of it."

"I don't understand. Do you know where it is?" The question just came out.

"We are penniless farmers Herr Muller, even the farm isn't ours. Do you seriously imagine we would live like this if we knew the whereabouts of a large and valuable diamond?"

"Now you're not telling the whole story Hermann. You see Herr Muller we do know where it is but ..."

"You know where it is!" He exclaimed, just managing to stop himself from shouting out.

"Oh yes, we know where it is because we put it there. But it's safe out of harm's way now where it can't hurt anyone ever again."

"Can't hurt anyone?!" Muller was on the edge of his chair. "Can't hurt anyone, I don't understand. Wherever is it?!"

"Herr Muller," said Ebba evenly "you have been very kind to our family in what you did for Fran. Hermann and I agreed last night that if the Mogul diamond was the reason you had come, and with what you said we naturally suspected it was, that because of your kindness we would tell you the whole story. Which I must add, up until now, has always been a very closely guarded family secret."

"So you really do know about the diamond?" Muller could only just believe what he was hearing.

"Oh yes, we've always known right from the start. That's the root of the problem. I think you had better explain Hermann."

"I must warn you, it's a long story," cautioned the farmer.

"That's alright. I have the time and I would be fascinated to hear."

"Do you mind if I smoke my pipe?"

"Please, I'll join you with a cigarette."

Ebba went into the kitchen to make some more coffee. When she returned Hermann had lit his pipe and was sitting ready. When all was still, he took a deep breath and commenced his narrative.

"What you are about to hear Herr Muller," he began, gently drawing on his pipe "was told to me by my father, as indeed it was told to him by his father and his before that, and so on and so on. As indeed I relayed it to my son, but now, well ... It is better that you, as an educated man, know the truth and you may do with the truth whatever you so please. It will certainly make for good reading in your book.

"As I said to you already, you were very clever to find us and indeed you are the first because the name of De Roehmers is not French as one might at first suspect, nor German but Swiss. Pepin De Roehmers was Swiss. And again, you were correct in connecting him with Jean-Baptiste Tavernier who, as I expect you know already, was a French explorer and a wealthy trader of precious gems.

"Pepin was the younger of two brothers, I regret I cannot remember the other boy's name."

"Edsel," Muller told him "the older brother was called Edsel."

"However did you know that?" he asked surprised, removing his pipe.

"It's not important, please do continue."

"Yes, I remember now, his name was Edsel. Their father was a deeply religious man and very wealthy and as the eldest Edsel was due to inherit the bulk of his father's estate on his death. But Pepin had set his mind on higher things. Pepin was a man of the cloth and it's said he was his father's favourite. Yet his father did not want the young man to lock himself away, as it were, in the confines of the church and encouraged him to broaden his mind with travel, and he financed many of the lad's trips. And so it was on one such journey that he met and befriended Jean-Baptiste Tavernier, who introduced him to the world of precious gems. Together they travelled the world for some considerable number of years.

"But whilst in India one time, Tavernier also introduced Pepin to the Princess Rasha, one of the Mogul's daughters. It is said she was the fairest of the fairest of all his daughters with skin like that of a sun-kissed peach." He cleared his throat and drew deeply on his pipe. "Anyway, the Princess became pregnant with Pepin's child and the Mogul insisted she marry him. But how could he, a good Catholic priest? The Mogul was apparently outraged that a daughter of his had been violated and insisted they marry. Yet the Princess Rasha was in love, - not with Pepin, even though she carried his child, - she loved another, and his name I really do not remember. He was a Prince in another part of the country I believe. Yet even though the Mogul knew of his daughter's love for another he still demanded she marry the father of her child. Pepin, of course, was not allowed to leave.

"Anyway, they married. It was an Indian ceremony naturally, and as such Pepin could only hope it would not be recognized by the Church of Rome, yet it was enough to satisfy the Mogul. Needless to say, Princess Rasha was heart-broken, because she was still in love with her Prince, and so hated her father for what he had forced her into.

"Pepin thought he would be able to leave the Princess, his new wife, in India as his secret affair, but no. The Mogul decreed that now they were married she must leave with him, and he banished her from his kingdom forever for the disgrace she had brought on the family, the royal family. Well, that was the last straw. The Princess hated her father so much that when she left she took with her the Mogul's most treasured possession, the Great Mogul diamond itself. She stole it.

"Pepin and the Princess and their new baby, a boy, left India. It was some time before the Mogul discovered the loss of the diamond, but when he did, he was so furious with his daughter, that he swore a curse on the stone. A three-pronged curse that was both terrible and everlasting, because not only had he lost his daughter whom he really loved, but he had also lost his great diamond and his grandson.

"The first part of the curse proclaimed that every time the diamond changed hands, death would be sure to follow, just as the Mogul had died inside with the shame brought on by his daughter. Then, it would bring no happiness to whoever it belonged like the Mogul himself would never be truly happy again." The farmer paused and with a deeply stained finger, tapped the tobacco in his pipe bowl.

"Fascinating," said Muller. "I had no idea. I'm not sure I'm convinced about the curses though."

"You will be," Ebba told him firmly, "there's more yet."

"Oh yes, that's only half the tale. Anyway," resumed Hermann, "Pepin did the only thing he could, and returned to Switzerland, he had nowhere else to go, - with his new bride and baby son - to face the consequences. And he a good Catholic priest remember."

"Or not so good."

"In the meantime, the Princess gave the diamond to Pepin unaware of course, of her father's curse. When they arrived home, needless to say the father was heartbroken that his favourite son should not only have ignored his priestly vows of celibacy, but married a foreigner, and a heathen at that. He was beside himself with grief, inconsolable. So much so, that Pepin decided to present his father with the diamond as a peace offering, still ignorant of the Mogul's curse.

"In time Jean-Baptiste Tavernier learns about the Mogul's curse on another of his journeys and eventually met up with Pepin and warned him. But it was too late. The curse had already taken hold.

"Within a few years of her arrival in Switzerland, the Princess was dead. Remember, she was the first owner after the Mogul himself, even though she stole it. The next to die was Pepin himself. He was the next owner, remember, and he passed it to his father, who in the meantime had lost most of his wealth and was the third to die; they say, of a broken heart. On the father's death, the diamond passed to the eldest son Edsel, who had adopted Pepin's son and brought him up. Edsel fathered other children but he also died. And then the diamond passed to Pepin's son, who died quite young of some terrible disease.

"And on and on and on, down through the generations it passed, leaving a trail of death and sadness in its wake until it eventually passed to me."

"You!!" Exclaimed Muller. "You owned the Great Mogul diamond!?"

"I did."

"But whatever happened to it? You said earlier you knew where it was."

The old man looked at his wife before continuing.

"Yes," she said to her man's unspoken question. "Tell what happened. There's no reason to keep it a secret now."

"Very well." But he appeared reticent suddenly for some reason. "When our son Everard and his wife and children died, that was the last straw."

"You see Herr Muller, we had the opportunity to break the curse once and for all, you understand," said the woman. "So we disposed of the diamond the only way possible."

"You disposed of it!?"

"Hermann went down to the lake and threw the Mogul's cursed diamond into the waters exactly where our family had all drowned."

"Oh no!!" Muller covered his ears trying to block out what he was hearing. "I cannot believe you actually threw it away!"

"The curse is finally broken," announced Ebba "no more will death and unhappiness ruin anyone's life. It should have been destroyed years ago."

"But this doesn't add up. Do you honestly expect me to believe that for nearly three hundred years, no-one in the family thought of selling it or, as you did, dispose of it even? They just kept it along with this curse you're telling me?"

"But you're forgetting the third part of the curse." Hermann reminded him.

"The third part?"

"I told you the Mogul put a three part curse on the stone."

"So what was the third part?"

"That if ever the stone departed from his beloved daughter's new family, their country would be conquered and fall, and its people live in bondage for ever."

Muller slumped back in his chair, speechless, not knowing whether to laugh or cry.

"So you see, Herr Muller," Hermann carried on "it was a terrible, wicked and powerful curse the Mogul placed on his diamond. Whoever owned it would be sure to die, and to whoever it belonged it would never bring happiness and yet it could never be disposed of or our beloved and free Switzerland, our homeland would fall."

"That's why Hermann's brother Ehren ran away years ago to Denmark and married a Danish girl, because he wanted to be free of the curse when the diamond should have passed to him. Instead it passed to Hermann."

"But surely that only goes to prove the curse can't be true, you're an old man so how come the curse hasn't affected you?"

"I can only think that because the stone should have passed to Ehren, the eldest, I'm not its rightful owner. And now you arrived yesterday to tell me my brother's dead, so that makes me next in line."

"But he died an old man."

"But he knew no happiness," put in Ebba quickly "they were never blessed with children."

"But you said you disposed of the diamond, so what about the third part of the curse? Suddenly, you're not bothered?"

"Ah but you're wrong," Ebba told him. "You see we haven't disposed of it in the true sense because we know exactly where it is. It rests at the bottom of the lake with our dear son and his family, the new and rightful owners. Now the curse is broken forever, my son holds it hidden beneath the deep waters where no-one can ever reach it and Switzerland remains safe and free. We know what the history books say, that the diamond went missing in 1747 on the Mogul's death, but we also know what really happened. But now it's all over, finished."

No-one spoke for a moment. Muller felt exhausted his mind reeling. "I've never heard of anything so fantastic in all my life. Princesses, curses, death, gloom and destruction. I don't know what to believe."

"You say you are an archaeologist, so surely you're acquainted with ancient curses, Egypt and the like. Aren't they all real enough?"

"I know that fear of the unknown is real enough. Fear and superstition do strange things to people, but to actually have the diamond and throw it away, that's…. unforgivable!"

"You haven't had to live through what we have all these years, Herr Muller." Hermann came back quickly, annoyed at the German's lack of understanding. "For generations our family has lived with this every hour of every day. You can't even begin to imagine what it has been like. And when our son died that was the end."

"Whatever's gone on before has gone for good," said Ebba quietly, drawing a line under the whole affair. "It's all over now, finished, closed."

It was then that Muller reached inside his jacket and removed the postcard he had found in Denmark, pausing a moment to ease the elastic band of his eye patch from a throbbing vein in his temple. "Then perhaps someone would be good enough to explain to me what exactly are 'the everlasting arms.'"

CHAPTER NINE

The blood drained from Hermann's face just as quickly as if his throat had been cut. Even his deeply tanned skin was unable to hide the sudden ashen pallor beneath. Ebba hadn't noticed the sudden change in her husband's countenance, but Muller had.

"The everlasting what?" she said innocently.

"The everlasting arms," repeated Muller.

"I've never heard of everlasting arms," she puzzled "have you?" And turned to look at her husband. "Why Hermann, you've gone quite pale. Do you feel alright?"

"Yes, yes. I think, reliving the story … Everard and all … It's been a bit much."

"Yes, you poor man, why don't you go and get yourself a drink. Perhaps our guest would like a drink too?"

"That would be most kind," said Muller as Hermann quietly left the room.

"I think he's been overdoing it lately. Ever since Everard died, he has had to do everything himself. I help as much as I can but well, you can imagine, neither of us are getting any younger. What is it that you have there?"

"It's a postcard I found on the mantlepiece at your brother-in-law's house. To be honest it helped lead me to you. It's a view of Einsiedeln."

"How strange."

"It's addressed to Ehren and signed Hermann and Ebba."

"Really, may I see?"

He passed it to her. She read it silently and then looked up at Muller, her expression one of perplexity.

"I didn't know Hermann sent this. I haven't seen it before, whatever can it mean? I can't read the postmark without my glasses. When was it posted?"

"April 1940." Muller told her. "So you've no idea what the 'everlasting arms' are?"

"No, I've no idea. Whatever can it mean? 'No longer need we live under the curse. The stone is safely hidden forever beneath the everlasting arms'. Ah!" She let out suddenly. "I know what it must mean! April 1940, that was soon after the accident. After Hermann dropped the stone in the lake. He must have written to his brother to tell him the curse was broken and the everlasting arms must refer to Everard. It sounds a rather poetic, strange expression though."

Moments later Hermann returned with a bottle and two glasses.

"Are you feeling better, dear?"

"Yes, yes thank you." Some colour had returned to his cheeks and his breath already smelt of alcohol, but he still appeared very uncomfortable. He poured two glasses of pale beer and offered one to Muller.

"Your good health, Herr De Roehmers."

"Yes, good health." he returned hesitantly.

"Hermann, have you seen this?" And she tried to pass the postcard to her husband but he would not take it.

"Yes," he answered quietly, looking deep into his glass. "I have. I know what it is. It's alright, I don't need to read it. I remember exactly what it says."

"But I didn't know you'd sent Ehren and Fran a card, you didn't tell me? I was telling Herr Muller that it must refer to Everard, but it's a strange way of putting it isn't it?"

"Yes a strange way, I suppose. I don't know. I thought dear Everard would forever be the stone's caretaker if you like."

"Whyever didn't you tell me about it?"

"I don't know. I probably thought at the time my brother should know it's all over, that's all."

"Tell me Mein Herr, what exactly happened the day you threw the diamond into the lake?"

"There's not much to tell," he said, looking across at his wife.

"Yes Hermann tell us, you never really told me what happened."

"Well ... ," he began with obvious reluctance "as I say there's not a lot to tell really."

"Where did you usually keep the stone?" prompted Muller.

"We kept it hidden in the barn. We didn't like to keep it in the house did we?"

"No that's right."

"So what happened?"

"Well, I simply took the diamond out of the barn, in its a leather pouch on a long cord, and went down to the lake. I stood on the new bridge ….."

"They'd replaced the old one by then," inserted Ebba.

"Yes, they built a new bridge exactly where the old one used to be, and the Mayor let us put up a commemorative plaque. And I stood in the middle and dropped the diamond into the water. That's about it really."

Muller was closely watching the old man as he spoke, but there was something about his body language that was not in harmony with what he was saying.

"What time of day was this, or night-time was it?"

"Yes, I mean no, it was night-time. I didn't want to be seen."

"You said it was in a leather pouch. What happened to the pouch?"

"I really don't see the point of answering all these questions after all this time. There's nothing to be gained by raking up the past."

"Yes, come on Hermann tell us, please. You've never told me exactly what happened that night; you said only that you threw it in and that was that. I always thought it would have been nice to say a prayer over it or something."

"There's nothing more to tell."

"But what of the pouch.? What happened to it?"

"I can't remember."

"But surely," said Muller "you must remember every minute detail of the stone that had supposedly cursed your family for over three hundred years, and was now going to rest with your son forever. You must remember what happened!"

"I think I threw it away."

"Where?"

"Where?"

"Yes, where? What happened to it? Was the diamond still in the pouch when you dropped it in the water perhaps?"

"Yes, I mean no. I told you I can't remember!" The old man was obviously lying and Muller wasn't alone in spotting it.

"Hermann, I don't think you're telling us the whole truth."

"Of course I am woman!"

"It's a simple question Hermann and I, at least, deserve an answer. What happened to the pouch after you had finished with the diamond?" His wife was determined to have the truth.

Suddenly the old man let out a horrible shriek and cried out in a loud voice. "Oh God forgive me!" He buried his face in his hands. "God forgive me!"

"Hermann, what's the matter?! Whatever have you done?!"

Muller sat back relaxed, confident that at last his patience was about to be rewarded and the truth revealed. He did not try to speak or interfere, but simply allowed the drama to unfold all by itself.

"I knew one day the truth would be told, but I couldn't do it, I just couldn't do it!" Hermann was almost in tears, his whole being trembled.

"What couldn't you do?"

"The diamond, the damned cursed diamond!"

"What about it for Heaven's sake?" cried Ebba. "What couldn't you do?!"

"The water, I couldn't throw it into the water!"

"Herman!" Ebba was on her feet now, standing over him. "Do you mean to tell me that you didn't leave the diamond in the lake with Everard?"

"I couldn't, I just couldn't."

"Hermann! You lied to me. You lied to me. How could you lie like that and deceive me?"

"I'm sorry, but I couldn't just throw it away." The big man was broken. Tears rolled freely down his face and into the bushy moustache. "It was just too ….. valuable."

"Too valuable. You silly old fool. It was worthless to us, do you hear me, worthless. It ruined all of our lives." And Ebba slumped back down into her chair. "How could you deceive me like that?" She was in tears now too. "I'm shocked, deeply shocked."

"So," said Muller quietly. "And where exactly is it now then?"

Hermann turned to him, his eyes red and wet. "The Klostër."

"The Abbey? So you really didn't throw it in the lake." His wife was still in disbelief.

"I told you I couldn't. I just couldn't do it. It was like a power held me back. I wanted to right enough but I couldn't."

"Where in the Klostër?" queried Muller.

"Under the statue of the Black Madonna."

"So what then are the 'everlasting arms'?" He asked concerned to examine every last detail.

"It's a term taken from the Bible. Ehren and I learnt it as boys. I knew he would understand."

"You wicked, deceitful, silly old fool," said Ebba. "You deceived me and lied to me all this time. May God forgive you."

"I'm sorry, I'm so sorry. I just couldn't. I could not do it."

A smile broke across Muller's face. At last the end was in sight. How ironic that when he had walked around the Abbey and looked at the Black Madonna for himself, little did he realize that somewhere beneath her feet sat the treasure he so coveted.

"How did you hide it there yourself?" he asked.

"I didn't, I gave it to Father Braut and he said he would hide it for me. It was he who chose exactly where to hide it."

"Did you tell him the whole sorry tale?" asked Ebba, ashamed.

"No I didn't. Only that it was something very valuable and we wanted to hide it and keep it safe. I thought the power of the church might break the curse."

"Ah! And so we return to fear of the unknown and superstition," said Muller.

"And what exactly do you mean by that?!" asked Ebba, annoyed by his tone.

"It's fear, Frau De Roehmers, that kept the curse alive in the first place."

But she was too upset to pursue the point.

"It is indeed fortunate that I came when I did," Muller addressed the couple "because I am quite prepared to pay you handsomely for the diamond."

"But we can't sell it," said Hermann. "How can we? We can never let it out of the family or Switzerland will fall."

"Herr De Roehmers, be realistic, please. Switzerland is a powerful, wealthy and neutral country. Whilst the rest of Europe is at war, Switzerland is untouched by it all, totally safe and at peace."

"But that's because of the protection of the curse."

"Rubbish!"

"The gentleman's right Hermann, our country is strong."

"I will pay whatever you ask for the stone. You can both retire and need never work again or worry about anything. It's an offer which will never come your way again, never. Alternatively you can grow old alone, up here miles from anywhere and anyone, working until you drop. The choice is yours."

"But I can't just sell it," protested Hermann.

But Ebba had other ideas. "Shut up you silly old fool. You've caused enough trouble already! This is our big chance to escape and take things easy for once, and I'm not going to let it pass us by. I don't care what you say."

"But you ... "

"Not another word!" She turned to their visitor. "Herr Muller, we accept your offer."

*

The following morning found Muller at the village's solitary bank bright and early, and on the use of the code word 'STARLIGHT' made arrangements for the transfer of funds, knowing well that the manager would need to seek authorisation from Paris (Major Baum), and Berlin before any monies could be released. It would take the rest of the day but Muller made no objections. He had waited this long, so a few hours more would make no difference.

He had agreed to meet Hermann De Roehmers on the steps of the Abbey at 10.30 a.m., then speak with the Abbot, Father Braut, the only person who knew precisely where the package was hidden. Together the three of them would remove the great diamond from its holy sanctuary.

Muller was outside the Abbey with time to spare, anxious that nothing should go amiss now that the prize was almost in his hands. He paced up and down like an expectant father.

A little way to the forefront of the Abbey stood the Virgin fountain, so called because of a large statue of the Virgin Mary surrounded by fourteen spouts of water which, according to a sign referred to an old legend. If all fourteen spouts were drunk from, good fortune would be sure to follow. Unable to resist the temptation, he took a sip from each of the spouts but when he had finished and wiped the back of his hand across his mouth, he felt annoyed that he could have succumbed to such religious superstitious nonsense. He spat out the last few remaining drops in disgust, just in time to see Hermann mounting the steps in front of the great doors.

*

A tall, thin monk of around twenty-five years of age, whose head had been shaved completely bald, spoke quietly to them in the confines of the Abbey interior, concerned not to disturb those at prayer and meditation.

"I'm so sorry to have to tell you gentlemen but Father Braut is away today."

"Away!" exclaimed Muller in a stage whisper. "For how long?"

The monk tried to avert his eyes from the stranger's unsightly scar as he answered. "Not long, he's only visiting further down the mountain. We expect him back before dark."

"Well, at least that's something I suppose."

"Could we call this evening and see him perhaps?" asked Hermann respectfully.

"Certainly, I will tell him he can expect you."

*

When they were alone, Muller and the old farmer stood in front of the altar overseen by the life size Black Madonna.

"I wonder where exactly it is?" pondered Muller, running his hands along the cold white marble on top of the altar .

"It's impossible to tell, only Father Braut knows."

"Have you ever considered what would happen if this Father Braut suddenly died and took the secret with him to the grave?"

"Yes," he said "I have thought of that. The secret would die with him and the curse would forever be covered by the power of the church."

"Then let us hope and pray the good Father makes it safely up the mountain, for all our sakes."

*

Before the close of business, all necessary funds had been made available to Major Muller, and on his word could either be transferred into the account of Herman De Roehmers or cashed. Thanks to Father Braut's little expedition however, negotiations had been delayed another day.

*

Just as before, the two men agreed to meet on the steps of the Abbey. By 8.30 p.m. it was almost dark, yet Muller could still make out Hermann's pony and trap as it made its way across the village square and watched as he climbed down and tethered it to a post. No doubt Ebba had made sure he was punctual.

It was the end of a summer's day, and heat still hung in the usually fresh mountain air. A cloudless, starstudded sky looked down on them and from deep within the Abbey came the steady toll of a single bell, summoning the community of monks to Vespers.

Inside it was even warmer, for all day hundreds of candles had burned in silent prayer, lit by the faithful and the atmosphere was hot and heavy with the scent of spent wax. Candlelight danced and flickered around the walls like the wings of unseen fireflies.

Hermann, removing his hat, made the sign of the cross before speaking with a junior priest informing him of their appointment with Father Braut. The man disappeared for a moment only to return and escort them to a different part of the Abbey. Their shoes tapped rhythmically on the marble flooring disturbing the silence, through extensive labyrinths, until they arrived at a long and gloomy passageway, at the end of which stood a low, studded wooden door. The priest knocked twice and without waiting for a response opened the door, allowing the visitors to pass into a small and sparsely furnished study.

Muller put the Abbot's age at anywhere between seventy and eighty. A small man with piercing blue eyes and completely bald, except for a few grey strands. He had a pronounced stoop, accentuated all the more by his dark habit yet it was evident the moment he spoke, that his mind was both quick and alert.

As they stood together and Hermann went through the introductions, the Abbot gave Muller a smile which lifted an otherwise sombre countenance, but his eyes remained static, yielding nothing as they took in the stranger.

"So what brings you to this remote corner of God's creation, Herr Muller? I detect a strong German accent there, do I not?"

"You do Father." He responded, anxious to get down to business. "I have a little business to conduct with Hermann and his wife."

"And whereabouts are you from, tell me?"

"Berlin."

"Ah, Berlin," he repeated deliberately and with a nod "yes, I was there myself in 1939. But so much has happened since then has it not?" And he turned to Hermann clearly not impressed with the foreigner. "And you Hermann my friend, how are you and Ebba?"

"Not so bad Father, thank you."

"It will take time to recover from the tragedy remember, but recover you will. Time is God's wonderful healer."

"I'm sure you're right Father."

"So what is it I can do for you both?"

"Do you remember Father, I gave you a small package to keep for me?"

"I do remember, yes."

"Well, I'd like to take it," he said, nervously turning his hat around in his hands. "If I may."

"Yes, of course you may, but not just yet I'm afraid."

"Oh!" sounded Muller quickly. "Is there some problem?"

"No, there is no problem Herr Muller. No problem except the time. You see, I have hidden your package, Hermann, under our Lady, I believe I told you, and for any of the worshippers to see me remove something from her altar would be considered as good as sacrilege; theft at the least. This is a very small community Herr Muller, as well Hermann knows, and word travels quickly. It would upset them unnecessarily, and I would not do that for any reason. But … now what is the correct time? I'm afraid we are rather short on clocks here."

"Eight forty-five." Muller told him.

"Well there we are then, not too bad. If you can both wait until ten o'clock when the Abbey is closed for the night, I shall be pleased to do as you ask Hermann." He looked Hermann directly in the face suddenly, as if trying to read his mind. "Now I want you to assure me my friend, that is it your true and un-coerced desire to remove the package?"

"Oh yes, Father," he reassured him. "What Herr Muller says is quite correct. We have business together, the three of us."

"Good, then that is all in order."

Muller realized suddenly how well Hermann must have been drilled by his wife not to change his mind, or do anything foolish at the last minute. For a moment he felt a tinge of sadness. He would have given anything to have his own wife back, anything.

"You gentlemen are at liberty to stay or do whatever you wish, and I shall meet you at the altar to the Black Madonna at ten o'clock."

The hour and fifteen minutes they had to wait dragged more than Muller could ever remember, yet eventually at ten p.m. sharp the doors of the Abbey were shut and bolted for the night and Father Braut met them in front of the altar.

As if on cue, an unseen choir suddenly began a hallowed chant of male voices which reverberated into every corner of the Klostër now that all was still at the close of day.

"Actually, I'm quite glad that you are taking the package away Hermann."

"Why do you say that Father?"

"I am an old man and my memory isn't quite what it once was, you know. I might forget where I put it!" He gave a little laugh exposing a gap in his front teeth. "But you'll be pleased to know I haven't forgotten yet." So saying, not without difficulty he bent down, kneeling on the marble floor towards the left hand corner of the altar, and taking hold of the rectangular white corner stone at the base, began to work it backwards and forwards until eventually it came free, revealing a deep cavity behind.

Muller lent over, anxious to see inside, but it was impossible. The Abbot pulled up the sleeve of his habit and inserted almost the full extent of his arm into the aperture and felt around inside.

"That's very strange," remarked the Abbot. "I know I put it here."

"What!" Muller refused to believe his ears and Hermann clasped his hands together in an attitude of prayer, watching apprehensively as the old man felt around inside the altar.

"Ah! Here we are. I have it."

The onlookers let out a sigh of relief and watched as the altar stone was carefully replaced. Father Braut got to his feet slowly, and after adjusting his habit, passed what looked like a leather pouch on a long cord to its rightful owner.

"Here my friend." He was slightly out of breath.

"Thank you, Father," said Hermann, holding it reverently between his hands. "Thank you so much."

"Now if you will excuse me, I have things to attend to before I retire. It's been good to meet you, Herr Muller," he told the German a little too coolly "and you take care of yourself Hermann. Be sure and give my regards to Ebba." And the elderly Abbot shook their hands.

"I will, and thank you again Father."

"Goodnight," added Muller curtly, relieved the episode had reached a successful conclusion.

"When you wish to leave just ask someone and they will show you the side door. God go with you."

Once the Abbot had left, Hermann looked at Muller unsure what to do next.

"Well open it, then!" demanded Muller impatiently, already behaving as the diamond's new owner. "Let me see it."

Without out a word, Hermann loosened the lanyard around the pouch.

It may have been the men's imagination, but at that precise moment the monk's chanting appeared to reach a crescendo, as Hermann gently shook the precious stone out of its pouch and onto the palm of his hand.

Both men stood speechless.

Part of Muller wanted to snatch it from Hermann's trembling paw and run, but the stone held him fast, mesmerized by its beauty. Shaped like half an egg with countless polished facets, each one captured the light of a hundred sacred candles multiplying their fire a thousand-fold, sending rainbow beams of iridescent colour all around the walls of the Abbey. The Great Mogul diamond sat majestic and regal, after millions of years in the making by incredible forces of nature, only to be condemned to three hundred years of obscurity by an angry monarch. But now, at last, it was free.

*

That night, Father Braut slept peacefully, but not before he had determined to pay Hermann and Ebba a visit in the not too distant future. Hermann had not appeared his usual relaxed self at all. It was plainly time for a heart to heart.

Muller also slept well, but not before he had also decided what to do next. The following day the diamond he had searched for so diligently would be his, and though acting as the Führer's agent, his subsequent move would be crucial.

Hermann however did not sleep at all, knowing the cursed diamond was hidden once again only feet away in the barn. Until the deal had been finalized he was the rightful owner. Would death be sure to follow before it exchanged hands? He listened to his wife snoring evenly beside him. She was right, the money they had agreed on with Muller would make their lives easier, a lot easier. But would Switzerland remain safe? Only God held the answer to that.

The following morning, Muller settled his bill, checked out of the hotel, and walked across to the bank where he withdrew 7,000 Swiss Francs from the special account. He then took a taxi out to the De Roehmers' farm and told the driver to wait.

Superstitious to the last, Hermann refused to have the diamond in the house, so the two men followed Ebba across to the barn, and whilst she counted the money Muller examined the stone with an eye glass searching for the two unique characteristic fingerprint flaws that could only belong to the genuine stone.

The light in the barn was far from ideal, but good enough and he soon found what he was looking for; a mark near the base, and a small speck within. This was without doubt the Mogul's great diamond.

Muller had prepared a simple bill of sale and once duplicate copies had been signed there was nothing further to be said or done. They shook hands and Muller took his leave, taking the taxi to Einsiedeln railway station, leaving Hermann and Ebba watching after the car wondering if they had done the right thing after all.

*

Muller toyed with the diamond in its pouch around his neck.

"Curse," he mumbled. "Country peasants."

"Pardon me, Sir?" said the driver.

"It's alright," Muller assured him, "I was just thinking of something amusing, as well as sad in a way."

*

Whilst waiting for the train to take him down the mountain he wrote a brief note to his daughter in Obernhof and posted it in the box on the platform.

*

Muller's use of the code word 'STARLIGHT' signified that the diamond had been found and when Baum received the news in his office in the Loire Valley, he was delighted, but cautious.

" 'Starlight'. Do you know I think he's found it. I do believe he's actually found it."

"Amazing," declared his aide "after all these years."

"However let's not celebrate prematurely. I'll believe it more when I see it. Muller is still an unknown quantity remember. Send a message to his hotel in Paris with my congratulations, but have him contact me immediately on his return."

"Yes, Sir."

"He should be back there at the most within two days. Any news from Obernhof yet?"

"No news at all, Herr Major."

"Well, tell our new man there to keep an extra close eye on the girl, because if Muller does have the diamond, he might decide to do a runner with it and she's our only insurance remember."

*

Major Muller however did not return to Paris with the diamond but journeyed on instead to Amsterdam.

"That's quite impossible!" Willem Beck was adamant.

"I'm sorry but circumstances demand it," Muller told him equally firmly.

"It's physically impossible to polish so many facets in only two weeks. It simply cannot be done! I told you six to eight weeks at the least."

"I know what you told me, but it's got to be ready in two weeks at the very outside."

"Then you must find someone else to do it for you, because I cannot!"

"What about if I doubled your bonus?"

Beck looked genuinely shocked by the offer. "Doubled it?!"

"To 20,000 Reichmarks."

"Good Lord!"

"If you complete the work within two weeks, a top quality and authentic job, I'll pay you 20,000."

"But whyever the hurry?"

"That's my worry."

"But it'll mean working day and night."

"But worth it in the end, surely."

Yet Beck was still unsure. "I'm not convinced that I would be able to do it properly in so short time."

"I have every confidence in you Willem."

"I wish I shared your optimism."

"Well," he pushed "what do you say?"

Beck reluctantly nodded his agreement. "Very well. I'll do the best I can."

"Excellent. I'll leave you alone until fourteen days from today."

"Yes, please do, or my neighbours will begin to think I have become a collaborator."

*

On leaving the stonecutter's apartment Muller called at the bank where he had originally made arrangements for Beck's monthly payments to be transferred from his own personal account, and cancelled them altogether. From there he booked in to a modest hotel in a quiet part of the city, at the same time as the desk clerk at the Hotel Meurice in Paris was posting two envelopes in Major Muller's pigeon-hole. One was from Major Walter Baum, the other from the Office of the Commander of Military Personnel, to inform him that his son was reported as missing in action, presumed dead.

*

Later that night, as Muller considered suitable ways to employ his time during the next fourteen days, Willem Beck was already putting in overtime on the copy of the Great Mogul diamond.

The sawing of the base had been completed satisfactorily, and after further extensive examinations, to satisfy himself that the stone was not in danger of splitting along any natural lines of cleavage during the polishing process, Beck moved ahead and produced a wooden retainer to hold the stone whilst the many facets were being polished on. He already possessed the tools necessary for holding stones up to 10 carats in weight, but any larger required something special and tailor made.

Once a hard-wood retainer had been completed in the shape of a cone, a hole the size and shape of a large egg was carved into the widest part, slightly larger than the stone itself, and of a depth which allowed just a few millimetres protruding. Then a coating of hot wax to line the hole was poured in and allowed to cool.

The counterfeit diamond was then firmly inserted into the wax and the retainer fitted into a lathe, at the opposite end of which sat a turntable known as a 'lap'. The lap consisted of a gun-metal disc impregnated with a mixture of diamond dust and olive oil, which once revolving, acted as the polishing agent for whatever was placed against it. The angle of each facet was controlled by the angle made between the hard-wood cone and the 'lap'. Time, patience and precision is called for at this stage, for if the stone is not at the precise angle to the 'lap,' a facet will appear which is neither in position or proportion to the others, and the stone spoilt.

During the ensuing days, as each new facet was completed, it would be necessary to regularly remove the stone from within the cone, apply more wax and reposition it so that the stone protruded further and further each time thus enabling additional facets to be polished on nearer the baseline.

Eventually, to complete the job, the stone would need to be thoroughly cleaned to ensure no abrasive material was left behind on the surface, and the stone given its final mirror-like polish. This would be undertaken in a similar manner, but a new softer 'lap' would be used, usually made of copper or pewter, and covered with leather and polishing agents such as rouge.

But all this would take time, and time was a luxury Beck did not enjoy.

*

With two weeks convalescent leave behind him, Lieutenant Douglas Reid found himself once again in the familiar surroundings of the offices of S.O.E. Headquarters, Baker Street, but the atmosphere was not as genial as it once was.

"If we had been conducting this interview yesterday, Reid," began M "I would have told you what we had already decided, and that was to give you a choice in determining your own future, because quite frankly, as an agent, you're no good to us at all now.

"You willingly, and I might add most unselfishly, agreed to have the scar on your face, but it does rather put you at an enormous disadvantage now it's all over. You would be recognized by anyone and everyone immediately, and you're already wanted by the Gestapo. So what we had proposed was to offer you the choice of returning to your old regiment with a suitable cover story as to where you had been all this time, or working for us in training new recruits and tutoring them in languages. S.O.E. is expanding daily. We now have agents operating all over the world."

Douglas went to speak but M held up his hand and continued.

"However, as I say, that was yesterday. Now this very morning, we have had earlier reports confirmed of something we have known about for some time," he eased back in his chair. "You may or may not be aware that the Nazis are thieves, insomuch that they take, or loot, art treasures from each and every country they invade. It is our understanding that these treasures, and they're in many different forms; paintings, china, statues and so forth, are either given to top ranking officials or placed in secret stores in various different locations, but all with one very distinct purpose in mind.

"Again, it is our understanding that Herr Hitler is anxious to rebuild his home town of Linz in Austria as a sort of living monument to himself. A glorified ego trip. And to do so, he plans to make Linz the art and culture capital of the world by installing these looted treasures in newly designed museums and galleries.

"Now, the point of my telling you all this, is this. We have received intelligence that as a centre-piece for the whole absurd Linz idea, he plans to build a vault type display - something along the lines of how we displayed our crown jewels before the war - and fill it with the best of the jewellery he's stolen from these unfortunate countries. But the piéce de résistance will be a certain large diamond called the Great Mogul. As a geologist does the name ring a bell with you?"

"I've heard the name of course, but I'm afraid I couldn't tell you anything about it Sir."

"Hmm, that's a shame, but still. Apparently this diamond, and I have no idea what size it is, is big. Very big. It might even be one of the largest diamonds ever found. Now the thing is, it's been missing for years, but we have just learnt that the Nazi's are on the point of rediscovering it. Don't ask me how, because I don't know. But the point is, Downing Street is very concerned that in discovering the diamond and displaying it publicly, with the huge publicity that's sure to follow, the Nazis will score an enormous propaganda victory. Such a coup could well have a serious and detrimental affect on morale over here, once our people see the Nazis being so successful.

"Personally I must tell you, I think they're barking up the wrong tree. I couldn't care less about the looting or Linz or a diamond or anything else. I've far more important things to concern myself with, like winning a war. But the brass are worried and orders, as they say, are orders."

"So where do I come into all of this, Sir?"

"Yes. What we want you to do, is firstly learn whatever you can about this diamond. We consider your geological training would be an advantage. Then bring me a report A.S.A.P. and we will decide what to do next."

"Well that shouldn't be too difficult, I would have thought."

"Good. Then I look forward to receiving your report imminently."

*

As Douglas concerned himself with acquiring knowledge of the Great Mogul diamond, on the other side of the North Sea in Amsterdam, exactly fourteen days from his earlier visit, Major Claus Muller pressed the annoying door buzzer of Willem Beck's apartment for what he hoped would be the last time, but there was no response.

He pressed again. Still no answer. He pressed it a third time, keeping his finger firmly on the button, listening to the buzzer inside, which eventually produced a reaction.

"Ja, ja. I'm coming." It was Beck's unmistakeable voice, but he sounded as if he was ill and it was some time before the door was finally opened.

"Oh, it's you Claus. I'm sorry I was asleep." Beck looked terrible. If it's possible for someone to grow old by years within just fourteen days, then Beck was proof. There were heavy dark rings around his eyes and the eyes themselves were red and swollen; his silver hair wild and unruly, the normally trimmed beard unkempt, his clothes heavily creased and he appeared to be stooping even more than usual.

He rubbed a hand over his face in an attempt to wipe the sleep away. "I'm sorry, please do come in." As Muller passed through, he caught the Dutchman's body odour. It was obvious he had not washed in days and the smell had permeated the whole apartment.

Muller walked directly into the workroom.

"So," he began impatiently "have you finished it?"

"Finished?" he sounded bewildered.

"The diamond man, the diamond!"

"Oh yes, of course," he wasn't fully awake. "I'm sorry, I've hardly had any time for sleep these past few days and as soon as it was ready I just collapsed on the bed. I didn't even bother to undress."

"So you have finished it then?"

"Yes, yes just as you ordered."

"Excellent ... Well, may I see it?"

"Of course."

Moving around the pieces of machinery in the cluttered workroom, Beck crossed over to the bench and carefully removed his work, wrapped within a white cloth and stood back for Muller to view it. "Here, just as you ordered," he said "an exact copy of the famous Great Mogul diamond. Perfect down to the last detail." He was awake now, and by the look on his face, the old man was obviously proud of his accomplishment.

At that moment, sunlight coming through the fanlight directly overhead, reflected on the many faceted surface and instantly colours burst all around, brightening the dreary workshop. As the only living person in Amsterdam to have seen the original, Muller knew at once he was looking at the Mogul's twin.

"It's wonderful," he said leaning closer, his mood changing instantly. "Just wonderful. You are a real craftsman."

"Here," said Beck offering him a loop. "Take a glass and examine the inside. You'll see the flaw near the base, but as I told you before, there's nothing I could do about the speck in the original."

Carefully lifting the stone with one hand, and the eye glass in the other, Muller focussed his eye inside the stone turning it until the natural inclusion was visible. "I see it … it's good."

"It's a perfectly natural flaw. No-one of course knows what the original flaw looked like, so you'll have no problems in that direction."

"Ah, but there you are wrong, my friend," he declared, carefully replacing the stone on the cloth.

"I don't understand."

"I will show you something very few people have ever seen." So saying he undid his jacket and shirt front, and slipped the cord over his head, gently placing the leather pouch on the work top.

Beck's curiosity was aroused. "What's this?"

"Tell me what you think it is." He placed the real diamond side by side with the copy.

Willem Beck stared at the two stones, his eyes flicking from one to the other in complete disbelief. Eventually he spoke. "Do you … Do you mean to say …"

"Yes, that's right."

"It's real?!"

"It is the real Great Mogul."

Beck was lost for words, his jaw moving silently up and down.

"Have a look inside," encouraged Muller, amused at Beck's reaction. "You'll see how similar the flaws are, but don't muddle them up."

Reverently, and for a some minutes, the Dutchman examined the diamond in silence, carefully replacing it again on the cloth when he had finished.

"Fantastic, fantastic," he exclaimed. "But whereever did you get it from? Very few people have ever seen it. Hasn't it been missing for hundreds of years? Mine is remarkably similar."

"That's right, hundreds of years."

"But if you had this all along, whyever didn't you let me … "

"I only very recently acquired it, otherwise you could have used it."

"Only a trained eye could spot the difference you know. Look at them. What a pair. What a magnificent pair!" The old craftsman was excited.

"Indeed they are," agreed Muller and replaced the real diamond in its pouch and safely inside his shirt. "Now," he said "I need all the paperwork I left you, everything."

"Yes, that's all ready for you, right there on the table."

"And the mould?"

"The mould too."

"And the plaster cast you showed me?"

"That's right … here," he said, removing it from a drawer.

"So you're quite certain that's everything I gave you?"

"Everything."

"Good," said Muller, slipping his hand into the pocket of his jacket which Beck noticed at once, pleased he was about to receive his well earned reward.

"I still can't believe you actually found the original," he said scratching his head. "And I, Willem Beck, saw it. Fancy that."

"Did you tell anyone what you have been working on?" Muller asked directly.

"No-one, I assure you, no-one. I kept my word, in fact I've hardly seen anyone to talk to."

"That is good."

"It's been a difficult as well as an interesting challenge, yet I enjoyed it. I've worked so hard though, I think I've taken years off my life in the process."

"How strange you should say that," said Muller removing a mother of pearl handled pistol from his pocket.

"What … "?! But Willem Beck never completed his sentence. Muller brought the pistol down swiftly and hard on the old man's head. Beck collapsed instantly in a heap at his feet. Leaving him on the floor, Muller collected a cushion from the lounge and wrapped it as best he could around the gun, then holding it directly next to Beck's head, fired a single shot. The sound was audible but muffled sufficiently enough not to have been overheard next door or outside.

"I'm sorry," he said standing over the body "but no-one must ever know the truth."

The small circular hole in the crown of Beck's skull was already oozing thick dark blood into the silver grey hair, and trickling down the side of a face frozen with horror, into his beard, but Muller failed to notice. He wrapped the fake diamond in the white cloth and put it in his pocket. Then, taking hold of a wooden mallet, proceeded to smash the plaster mould of the stone into tiny fragments and swept them onto the floor grinding them to powder beneath his feet.

Collecting together all the notes and papers which he had originally lent the Dutchman to work from, he glanced around, making sure he had not left any incriminating evidence behind. With a final look at the man he had just murdered, he pocketed the pistol, switched off the hall light and left, closing the front door quietly behind him.

CHAPTER TEN

Within ten days of meeting with M, Lieutenant Reid had submitted his report on the Great Mogul diamond, which included not only what he was able to discover in the time, but also his estimation of the chances of its rediscovery.

Two days after M had read the account, Reid was summoned.

"So you consider the Germans are bluffing?"

"I do, Sir. Going on what I've learnt, the chances of them finding the Great Mogul after all this time are simply incalculable. The whole story is shrouded in uncertainties and foggy legends. There's no concrete point from which to even begin a search. It's more than likely, as I mentioned in my report, that as a whole it no longer exists at all, but has in fact been cut into any number of smaller stones."

"What sort of value would something like this be worth do you think, presuming, of course it was rediscovered?"

"You could not put a price on it at all, it would be beyond valuation. A museum piece."

"Which of course is exactly what he plans to do with it, and as a piece of propaganda it would be priceless."

"I'm not sure I go along with that, Sir, if I may say so. I think the people of this country are more concerned with staying alive and winning the war than lost diamonds."

"I felt the same way too, Lieutenant when I first heard about it, but second thoughts are often the best you know, and the powers that be do have a valid point. If our intelligence is accurate, and they are indeed on the verge of finding it, once the British people hear about the Germans getting the best of everything, i.e. the biggest diamond in the world, it could well undermine morale, and at this point in our nation's history, that is the last thing we need. Especially now that Crete has fallen and the news from North Africa is far from encouraging."

"I'm afraid I have still yet to be convinced, Sir."

"Well, convinced or not we have a little task for you Lieutenant."

"You're not going to ask me to find the diamond Sir, are you?"

"No, we won't do that, besides we don't have the time for treasure hunts, but we do want you to arrange a copy of it. An exact copy in some other material than diamond, of course."

"But whatever for Sir?"

"I'll sit on the answer to that for now, but do you think a copy could be put together and reasonably quickly?"

"It's something I haven't considered but in theory I expect so."

"I see in your report you mention a French chappie who actually saw the diamond."

"Tavernier, yes."

"Did he describe the diamond or illustrate it at all?"

"I haven't seen drawings but I believe they are available, Sir."

"But would they be good enough to work from?"

"I'd need to investigate that further before I can answer."

"Then do that because we would like a copy within a month."

"A month! But that's impossible, Sir. Whereever would I find a lump of … I don't know what, to make a copy from? And then who's going to cut it?"

"I don't know Lieutenant, but I am sure you will find someone. And remember when you do, be sure to keep this secret."

"I'm not even sure where to begin."

"Then don't let me detain you. Time is precious."

*

On leaving Baker Street, Douglas immediately caught the train for the west coast of Wales and a return visit to Aberystwyth University Arts Centre, where valuable books formally housed in the Reading Room of the British Museum were stored for the duration. Having gained special access, he continued the investigation that had already provided so much information.

*

At his headquarters in the Loire Valley, Major Walter Baum was purple with rage.

"It's been over two weeks since he withdrew the money, and still there's no sign of him!" Baum was pacing the floor of his ornate office like a caged tiger, desperate to pounce but unable to. "And now this. Of all the incompetent fools. Where do you find these people? I told you I wanted the girl watched twenty-four hours a day."

"It's very difficult to keep an unobtrusive watch on someone all the time, Sir." Baum's aide had gone quite pale.

"Difficult! What do you think we pay these people for, for goodness sake. She was our, no she was my, only insurance, do you understand? I'll be the laughing stock of the entire army, or worse, I'll be shot! I authorized the withdrawal of 7,000 Swiss Francs to purchase the Great Mogul diamond and he's run off with it! Run off with it, do you understand what that means? Do you?!"

"Yes Sir."

"No you don't you cretin, otherwise you'd be more careful who you choose to work for you. I've got to tell the Führer, that the man I, I chose to find the diamond for him, found it alright but he's run off with it and disappeared along with his daughter!"

"He could still appear Sir," the aide put in nervously.

"Still appear? There's more chance of my grandmother appearing than him and she's been dead twenty years!" Baum dropped deflated into the chair behind his desk. "I always knew there was something rotten about him, right from the start. I should have listened to my sixth sense. Why I chose him, God only knows. Hitler was right, he did look menacing. Menacing outside and rotten inside. Rotten to the core. We'd better get a warrant for his arrest but no doubt he's already hidden himself away somewhere safe. This was all very well planned."

He paused and took a deep breath, releasing it slowly. It did not help. "I'm finished, finished. After all my loyal faithful service. If I'm not shot I'll be sent to some hellhole at the Russian front and you my friend," he added menacingly "will accompany me!"

Before the troubled aide had time to respond, there was a knock at the door. If the Major even noticed it he ignored it, leaving his aide to listen to the brief message from his Unteroffizier.

"Sir!" He shouted excitedly, almost springing back into the room. "Major Muller's on the telephone!"

"What!" Baum leapt out of his chair almost knocking the telephone to the floor, and had to make a grab for the receiver.

"Muller! … About time, where the hell are you? Just who do you think you are, behaving like this? You're still under orders remember. I've got a good mind to put a warrant out for you … Don't you dare tell me to calm down, I haven't got a lot to be calm about, thanks to you. Do you realize the trouble… What!" The purple flush of anger slowly began to fade and for the second time he dropped back heavily into his chair.

"So … so the money for the diamond … Switzerland, yes … here … " The Major was composed now, every word coming through the receiver like a calming melody. "No, of course not. I never doubted you for a moment. I knew I had chosen the right man for the job … direct here … Yes that's excellent, then I can take it to the Führer. He'll want to meet you I'm sure, and there's bound to be a decoration in it for you at the least ... Yes, yes I quite understand you deserve a few days rest ... see your daughter, that's nice ... But why have you taken so long to contact me? Tested ... and it's authentic of course ... of course yes ... Yes we must get together and celebrate. I can't believe you have actually found it after all these years, you'll be famous ... you should write a book ... I want to hear the whole story some time ... Well done, very well done Major ... within three days, right. I can't wait to see it ... excellent, excellent ... Yes, goodbye Major and congratulations once again ... goodbye."

Slowly and deliberately he replaced the receiver in its cradle and looked up.

"Everything's alright. He's got it," he said, unable to believe his own words. "What a relief."

"He's found it!" The news hit him afresh. "He has actually found the Great Mogul diamond! The Führer will be ecstatic! The crowning glory for his Linz project! Go and fetch some champagne; we must celebrate. It'll be here within three days. He's having it delivered by special secure messenger, then he's spending a few days with his daughter. That's why she left Obernhof ..... simple as that."

"Why hadn't he contacted you before, Sir?"

"Simple, the man's a professional archaeologist. He was having the stone tested to be sure it's the real thing."

"Surely it would have been more prudent to have arranged that before the purchase. Where is he now?"

"I don't know, I forgot to ask him. Still it doesn't matter where he is now, does it? He said he'll stop over in Paris and tidy up a few loose ends and then come down here with his daughter. I'm still in shock you know." He grinned. "I still can't believe that after hundreds of years, the lucky swine has actually found one of the biggest diamonds in the world."

"It is amazing, Sir."

"There'll be promotion in it for all of us, I'm sure. Oberstleutant Walter Baum. Sounds good doesn't it?"

"Yes it does, Sir, but just one thing."

"Now what? You're like a wet blanket!"

"Why do you suppose Major Muller's daughter left Obernhof in secret, purposely avoiding our agent?"

"I don't know do I? Who cares now anyway? We've got the diamond and that's all that matters. You worry too much."

*

In response to her father's letter, Astrid Muller was waiting when he arrived at the family home in Berlin. It had been a long time since they had seen one another, and there was a lot of catching up to do.

"So how did you manage to get away from Obernhof without being seen?"

"I did just as you said. I waited until midnight and crept out of the house. I walked all the way to Lahn in the dark and caught the train from there in the morning. I left a letter for Aunt of course."

"Well done."

"But why were they watching me? It's horrible to think someone was watching everything I did."

"Without going into it all now, I knew they would be watching you to indirectly keep an eye on me. That's why I told you to move in with your aunt in the first place, away from here. I knew they would find you eventually though wherever you were."

"That's horrible! But why was I being watched at all? Have you done something wrong?"

"No, of course not, and you were quite safe. I knew they wouldn't harm you. But don't worry about it now, all will be well I assure you." He looked at his daughter and felt pleased at how much she resembled her mother. It was like looking at the bride of his youth all over again. She shared the same bright golden hair, mannerisms, expressions. Whatever happened to all those teenage years? So many lost opportunities.

"I can't believe how you have grown up, my dear. You've grown into a very beautiful young woman. It won't be long before some knight in shining armour comes and sweeps you off your feet."

"Well, it's funny you should say that, Father," she said shyly.

"Oh!" He smiled. "Tell." But he could see immediately that all was not well. And so Astrid began the sad tale of Frederic Kutzner, the agricultural salesman from Minden who was his spitting image, and of how they had met and fallen in love when he had shut his hand in the door of the Klostër.

"We only had hours together, but we just knew we were meant for each other," she told him reliving every precious moment. "Our souls had found their mates and we both knew it. He was so like you to look at, seeing you now is painful in a peculiar way." She told her father how he had left quickly but returned later and of the terrible night when a stranger in the village, a madman had burst in on them and taken Frederic away.

"Shot you!!?" She showed him the scars on her thigh left by the bullet which had passed straight through, and told how she had hobbled to a neighbour's house and called the doctor, as Frederic was escorted to Berlin, suspected of being a spy. Her eyes welled up as she continued.

"I tried to find out what happened to him, but it was ages before I discovered the train was bombed and there were no survivors. Not one. They were all killed."

"I am so sorry, my dear. But you say he was suspected of being a spy?"

"He was no more a spy than you are. He was lovely, and for just a brief moment in time he was mine." And she buried her face in her father's strong shoulder as he held her tight.

"I can see I have been away too long my dear, far too long. But it's all going to change now believe me. Everything's going to be different."

Later, over supper they discovered that neither of them had heard from Astrid's brother for some time.

"I do hope he's alright," said Astrid. "I couldn't bear it if anything happened to him."

"Oh I'm sure he is, you know what Stefan's like about writing letters. I'll get someone to run a check and remind him he has a family. He should be due some leave soon, I would have thought."

"Talking of leave, how long are you home for?"

"Well, I've come home initially to see you of course and also to arrange to send a parcel off," his voice was very 'matter of fact,' "and then I have made arrangements so that you and I can immediately disappear to Sweden."

"Sweden!" she repeated. "Whatever for? What have you been up to?"

"I can only say that one day I will explain everything, but for now it's better that you don't know. But it's the right thing to do. You will just have to trust me. We'll enter via Norway."

"I do trust you, but Sweden? What about the army, won't they shoot you? That's desertion isn't it?"

"Then we must make doubly certain that they don't find me. Trust me dear. I've told some people I'm returning to Paris, but I'm not. Instead, you and I and eventually Stefan, will stay in Sweden until the war is over and then we'll be richer than you have ever dreamed."

"Rich?"

"Yes. All our worries will be over and we'll be able to start a new life, put everything behind us. New friends, a new beginning for all of us, but I cannot do anything until the war is over. We'll just have to lie low until then. It can't go on for much longer now anyway. Churchill will eventually persuade the Americans to join in and then it's only a question of time."

"But I thought you were loyal to the Führer, fighting for his victories. That's what you always taught us."

"I am, but something's happened and now we have to leave."

"But why? I have a right to know, surely."

"I told you Astrid. I'll tell you more when it's safe for you to know."

"But Sweden? It's all a bit sudden isn't it?"

"Maybe yes, but I know it's the right thing to do. Later I want you to sort out what you need to take with you while I attend to my parcel."

The girl studied her father as he continued. He had got older and she was right, it was painful to look at him. Just the sight of his face brought back unhappy memories, but whatever was he was holding from her? Running away to Sweden? Still, Sweden did sound attractive, away from the war and a new beginning. She needed a new beginning now that her soul mate was lost.

"Whatever happens," he continued "my parcel must leave here tomorrow. Special couriers will be calling early in the morning to collect it and once it's signed over, we must go too. We dare not delay once it's left."

"What's in this parcel that makes it so important?"

"Trust me, I just ask you to trust me for now that's all."

*

Behind thick black-out curtains in the semi-detached house that was the Muller home, not far from Berlin's central railway terminal, Claus Muller was completing a brief letter to Major Baum which, along with the bill of sale, would accompany what Baum would accept as the Great Mogul diamond.

The two stones sat like identical twins before him on the desk in his study, which was cluttered with artefacts that only a trained archaeological mind could appreciate.

On receipt of the parcel, Muller knew that Baum would do one of two things. He would either take Muller at his word and believe that the stone was authentic, or more likely have the stone tested for himself prior to presenting it to the Führer. Once a trained eye examined the colourless corundum, Muller would be in serious trouble. A wanted man.

His suitcases were standing ready in the hall while Astrid, excited now at the thought of a new life, busily finished packing, unaware that her father's carefully constructed plans were to be thwarted by nothing more complicated than the bomb-door release catch under the belly of an English Wellington bomber.

*

Muller read his letter through and signed it at the same time as air raid sirens began their mournful wail, warning of yet another attack.

Ignoring the warning, indignant that these Britishers should return yet again, as if they hadn't caused enough damage already, he deliberately folded the polite yet non-committal letter and placed it at the bottom of a velvet lined trinket box that had belonged to his late wife. It pleased him that she should play her part. If she had lived, she would have been going with them.

The sound of anti-aircraft fire was ignored along with the ever increasing drone from wave after wave of over three hundred and fifty bombers. Suddenly the house began to shake as the enemy unloaded their cargo.

The study door burst open. "Daddy! We must take cover."

"It's alright, they're still some way off," he reassured her, quickly covering the stones. But her eyes moved faster than her father's hands.

"What on earth are those?"

"They're … paperweights," he told her.

"What are you doing with Mummy's jewellery box?"

"I have to send one of the weights, this one," he said pointing to Beck's copy, "to an important friend of mine, and I thought it would be nice if your mother was involved in some way, as we're on the verge of a new life, so I thought I'd send it in her jewellery box. You don't mind do you? Think how pleased she would be for us all."

"It's a nice thought but couldn't you have sent it in something else?"

"I wanted the paperweight to look special."

"As you wish. What about the other one?"

"That's coming with us. It's quite valuable and to be sure it doesn't get lost I wear it around my neck in a pouch."

"I hope you don't think it's that which is going to make us rich," she said "because it doesn't look worth much to me."

The house continued to shake and the lights flickered as each explosion vibrated against their ear drums.

"I don't like it at all. Are you sure we're safe? I think we should take cover."

"Relax dear, I told you they're not overhead. You can always tell by the drone of the engines."

"Well they sound close enough to me. I'm not used to air raids. We didn't get them in the country."

He tried to divert her attention. "I've just got to put this in the box and seal it along with a letter in the secure bag ready for the couriers. This must leave here tomorrow no matter what. Have you finished packing?"

"Almost," she told him drawing closer. "I really don't like all this noise Daddy."

"If anything ever happens to me Astrid, be sure to save this other paperweight for yourself and your brother. Do you understand?"

"Yes, yes," but her concerns were elsewhere. "I really don't like this at all Daddy, they're getting closer now surely, aren't they? Listen!"

"Alright," he said pushing back his chair. "I'll go out to the air raid shelter and open it up. Give me a moment and then come and join me. Happy now?" He added, not liking to see his daughter so fearful.

"Yes," she said "thank you. Please don't be long."

"Relax. In a few minutes they'll be gone and it'll all be over."

Leaving the two stones covered over, he left Astrid alone and went out into the garden.

*

Jack Cowley had flown his Wellington out from R.A.F. Feltwell near England's East Anglian coast earlier that evening with a fully loaded bomb bay. He was relieved that they had just completed their final run over the target and could turn for home before their luck ran out. But a voice in his ear brought him up sharp.

"Skipper. We've got a problem." It was the voice of the Bomb Aimer.

"What's wrong?"

"One packet hasn't released itself. It's dangling, caught by the tail and now the doors won't open. The hydraulics jammed."

Jack didn't answer at once as his imagination immediately gave him a picture of them trying to land with an unexploded bomb dangling from the aircraft. It meant certain annihilation.

"Is it live?" he asked.

"Yes."

"Can you get at the fuse?"

"No. I've tried."

"Alright," he responded coolly "well, as I've no plans to call in on St. Peter's rest home for retired airmen just yet, one way or another we're going to have to get rid of it."

"How Skip? It's jammed real tight."

"Have you got any rope back there?"

"Any what?" The constant thud and boom from flak batteries exploding all around made it difficult to hear.

"Rope!" he shouted into his oxygen mask.

"A bit, yes."

"Well get Nobby to tie it around you, and hold on tight. You'll just have to boot it out yourself."

"Oh, thanks."

"Don't you go and fall out now. With your ugly mug you'll frighten poor Jerry into surrendering before we've all had a chance to win a medal."

"I'll remember that on the way down."

"Good luck. I'll ease back on the air speed as much as I dare."

Following his Captain's instructions, the Bomb Aimer tied one end of rope firmly around his waist, whilst Nobby secured the other end and held on to it tightly.

Positioning himself directly over the half open bomb bay doors, he waited until there was a change in the note of the engines, then gingerly lowered himself down into the bay, watching the dark earth flashing past thousands of feet below, all the while fighting to retain a hand hold against the constant rush of cold air being forced up through the damaged doors.

The tail of the bomb was clearly visible. Six or so inches had failed to clear before the doors had closed properly and it was now sticking out from the underbelly of the aircraft like a nose on an ugly face.

Knowing well that too hard a boot could send them all to oblivion, he decided instead to kick out at the door itself. He checked the rope was fast around his waist, and glanced up at his mate who gave him the thumbs up.

Cautiously at first, he kicked at one of the pair of half closed doors, but nothing budged so he tried again, only harder. Still no movement. In desperation he lifted his knee high and brought his foot down as hard as he possibly could. Suddenly the steel door gave way, allowing the bomb to fall free, at the same time as the rope pulled on his waist as Nobby stopped him from tumbling out after it.

Without a thought as to where the bomb would land, he climbed back in, shaken and chilled and spoke to his Captain.

"The bombs gone Skip, thank God."

"Well done!"

"But now we're got a half door swinging wide open instead."

"Rather that than a bomb, wouldn't you say? It'll slow us down some and it's going to get mighty chilly back there, so you'd better tell the boys to wrap up warm. It's a long way home."

*

As the relieved aircrew headed for home, the final piece of their lethal load fell silently and indiscriminately through the darkness to earth, precisely as Claus Muller opened up the air raid shelter at the bottom of his garden. With so much on his mind, he only became aware of the all too familiar whistling sound when it was too late.

It had been raining on and off for some days before, and the ground was wet and pliant. Consequently the bomb penetrated deeply into the soft soil before it exploded, otherwise the damage would have been far more severe. Even so, it was bad. When finally it did explode, shock waves radiated outwards with such force they were felt miles away. At the same time a huge crater appeared, flinging out tons of earth, rock and red-hot shrapnel in every direction and removing all trace of the existence of an air raid shelter.

Miraculously the house remained standing, but every window back and front was blown in, ripping curtains to shreds with flying splinters of razor sharp glass. Every chimney was instantly swept clean, sending clouds of thick black soot billowing out into the rooms below and two chimney stacks broke off, crashing through the tiled roof into the attic, leaving gaping holes open to the sky. Every shelf was wiped of ornaments and books, every cupboard burst open, their contents scattered, and the fuse box in the cupboard under the stairs exploded with a flash of sparks.

It was some time before all was still once more.

Astrid had been standing near to the door leading out to the garden waiting to join her father. The blast had lifted her off her feet and thrown her headlong across the kitchen and out into the hallway knocking her senseless.

Gradually she regained consciousness, but was unable to think coherently or to move and she had completely lost all sense of hearing. Calling for her father, her mouth moved silently up and down but her words remained soundless and she lay there quite still in the inky blackness. It was some minutes before her senses eventually returned and lifting herself up, she immediately started to cough and choke in fog-like clouds of dust and soot. As quickly as she was able she stumbled her way to the back door, crunching over broken glass and crockery, only to fall over a toppled chair, landing heavily and grazing both hands.

The door was broken in the frame and yet had somehow managed to stay on its hinges. The small kitchen window had been blown out, but the room was still suffocatingly short of air and, unable to breath properly in air heavy with ash from the boiler, she struggled with the door, pulling on the handle until at last it gave way and the kitchen was flooded with life-saving oxygen.

She could breathe now, but what met her eyes outside sucked the breath out of her once again.

Even by the cloudy moonlight, it was still possible to see the shocking devastation. The garden had gone. The next-door neighbour's garden had also gone, replaced instead by an enormous black and bottomless hole, already filling with water from a ruptured main.

Peering across the crater to where the shelter should have been a surge of dread suddenly struck her with a force equal to that of the explosion. From head to foot, her slim body started to shiver uncontrollably and she began to cry, deep heart wrenching wails of grief. As her legs turned to jelly, she fell to her knees amongst the rubble and screamed as loud as her dust-choked lungs would allow. "Dad-eeeee!!!!"

*

The first light of dawn saw the horizon streaked with smoke from fires burning across the city and saw Astrid clambering over mud and rubble at the edge of the crater, searching for signs of her father. The night had been full of misery and self recrimination. If only she had listened to him and not been afraid, and not bothered with the shelter. If only he had stayed indoors. As it was, she was now alone. No mother, no father, and a brother miles away, only God knew where. And Frederic. Frederic. Frederic, if ever she needed those strong arms around her, it was now.

During the long night hours she had eventually collected herself with the aid of a neighbour who had also suffered much, and now with a sooty and tear streaked face, Astrid scoured the area for her father's body. But there was no sign of it at all. The explosion had completely obliterated all suggestion of him, or the shelter, ever having existed.

*

Later during the morning, the local authorities arrived. She reported the death and they secured the house from looters with boarding over all the windows and any damaged doors, checked the electricity was properly disconnected and turned off the water. It was at that point that Astrid decided what she had to do for the future, for she certainly could not stay there. They offered her temporary accommodation but the offer was declined.

After tidying herself up, she collected her luggage which had been ready since the night before and standing her father's cases to one side, with a final glance around, opened the front door.

To her surprise, two military personnel were just getting out of an army vehicle parked in front of the house. They stood momentarily, looking the house over, one shaking his head at what he saw.

"Can I help you?" she called to them, annoyed at the delay now that her mind was made up.

"Frau Muller?" asked one, a tall young man with a very square jaw.

"Fräulein." she corrected.

"We have a parcel to collect from your father." He told her walking up the path.

"A parcel? I'm afraid I don't know anything about a parcel. We were bombed last night as you can see and my father ….."

"It's to be a special delivery," he interrupted, checking the paperwork on a clip board. "To be delivered personally to a Major Baum in France."

Suddenly she remembered the two crystal paperweights and what her father had said.

"Oh yes," she said "I do remember now. Wait a moment."

"Of course, Fräulein."

Leaving the door open, she went into the study which was in a very confused state and, kicking aside rock samples which had fallen from a display, lifted the cloth on the desk revealing the two paperweights. Selecting the one her father had pointed out, she dropped it gently into her mother's trinket box and shut the lid. Next to the box was the special security bag and with the box inside, she sealed it tight and returned to the man waiting on the doorstep.

"Here," she said, eager to be rid of it and be away.

Checking the address on the outside corresponded with his instructions, he wrote something on a form and tearing off the bottom half, issued her with a receipt.

"Danke Fräulein Muller. Delivery will be the day after tomorrow."

"Er … good, thank you."

"I see you had a bad time last night," he said, always ready with a word for a pretty girl.

"Yes, we did. Very bad."

"Those English," he began and then spat heavily into a flower bed. "Still, soon we shall be marching along the London Bridge."

"Yes," she agreed, disinterested "soon."

The young man knew he was wasting his time with her.

"Danke Fräulein," he said with indifference "Heil Hitler."

"Auf wiedersehen."

Once they had driven away, she returned to the study and placed the other stone into its leather pouch and hung it about her neck, tucking it inside her clothes as her father would have done. At least it was something of his to keep.

Again, with a last look at the appalling mess that was once a home, she picked up her cases and stepped outside, knowing she could return at any time and sort things out properly, along with the funeral. But for now it was best to get right away from it all, the memories, the trauma, leave them all behind and return to the country, and Obernhof. There was nowhere else to go.

With tears in her eyes she locked the door and left.

*

During the morning in the reading room of Aberystwyth University Library, whilst reading V. Ball's translation of Jean-Baptiste Tavernier's book 'Voyages en Torquie, en Perse et aux Indes', Douglas Reid made an important discovery; that Tavernier had indeed made sketches of the Great Mogul diamond along with details of weights and measurements.

'It should be enough to work on', he estimated 'but whatever do I do now'?

He sat there impatiently tapping his pen against his bottom lip seeking inspiration, allowing his mind to return to his university days, when they had studied diamond simulants. 'Zircon!' he exclaimed. 'And I know exactly where I can lay my hands on a piece'.

Once back in London, it was some time before he could organize a requisition order, but when eventually he did, he went at once to his old place of work in the Department of Geology at the British Museum, and much to the despair of the head of department, removed a large example of white, colourless zircon, from an unprotected exhibit which would be more than adequate for any competent cutter to work on.

From the Museum, with the stone safely packed in a small box, he took the underground to Chancery Lane, and walking down to Holborn Circus turned left into Hatton Garden and right into Greville Street. Almost at the end of Greville Street, on the right hand side sat Bleeding Heart Yard, where Douglas made his way up several flights of worn wooden stairs to the top floor and the offices of Abraham B. Rosenburg and Sons, diamond dealers and cutters. He waited to be introduced to a gentleman who should be able to get things moving, seeing that time was now of the essence.

After a few minutes, a man appeared from a workroom, unable to conceal his surprise at the sight of a uniformed officer with a serious scar, sat waiting to see him.

"Lieutenant Reid?" His voice was thick and guttural and even though he had spoken only two words, it was immediately obvious he was no Englishman. Due to a deformity, he was unable to raise his head fully, and he studied Douglas over the top of powerful spectacles perched on the end of a generous nose.

"Mr. Janovitski?"

"I am he, how do you do? Mr Rosenburg has told me all about you." His head was a mass of confused grey and unkempt curls, yet there was something about him which gave the impression he was younger than he appeared. He gave Douglas a wry smile. "It's not every day the British Army choose to call on me."

"Is it convenient to talk? Mr Rosenburg told me I could call at any time and see you."

"Of course, but I hope you haven't called to enlist me?"

Douglas laughed, immediately taking to the man.

"I know, let me say it for you" he said "you're not that desperate yet, eh?" Deep laughter lines appeared around kind brown eyes. "Am I right?"

"And yet," began Douglas "there is something we would like you to do."

"Come into my workshop, young sir and we'll talk." He put a finger to his lips. "Schhh, walls have ears. Isn't that what you English say?"

"You can never be too careful."

They found some chairs in the disorderly workroom and Janovitski asked Douglas how the army had heard about him.

"I spoke to one of the directors at Asprey's. You come highly recommended."

"Aspreys I know," he remarked, with a characteristic lift of the palms and a shrug of the shoulders. "What can I tell you? I'm famous."

"And Mr Rosenburg also told me you are the best cutter in London."

"Mr Rosenburg is a very nice man. He exaggerates sometimes, but I can live with that. So what can this now famous old diamond cutter do for the British Army, I wonder?"

"A special commission for His Majesty's Government."

"A special commission? Special commissions I like. Keep talking, the price is going up all the time."

"It needs to be completed very quickly."

"That's good, the price is climbing still." But there was humour in his eyes.

"Forgive my asking this but as a follower of the Hebrew faith ….."

"A Hebrew! Now however did you guess I'm a Jew, I wonder?"

Douglas gave him a smile. "I have to ask you, but as a Jew would you have any objections to working on something directly related to the war effort, in view of what's happening in Germany at the moment?"

"Objections? Why should I have objections? Do you think I'm a pacifist or something just because I don't march up and down with a gun; you think I have objections to fighting Nazis? Young man I must tell you, the only good Nazi as far as I'm concerned is a dead Nazi and if you're offering me a special commission, as you call it, to help in some way defeat the Nazis, I'll take it! Whatever it is."

Douglas was about to speak but the man stopped him.

"Listen, young sir, and I will tell you a story, and every word on my life, a true word." He paused thoughtfully and removed his glasses, cleaning them before continuing.

"You're right of course I am a Jew, a German Jew, my name is Isaac. I am one of two sons born to German Jewish parents. I was born in Munich in 1881 and my brother Victor was born in 1897. Our father was a watch and clock maker, as was his father before him. We weren't rich but we wanted for nothing. My father so wished for me, as the eldest, to continue the family tradition and carry on the business but I didn't want to. I had been raised around clocks remember. Ticking clocks, chiming clocks, cuckoo clocks, every day all around me, waking us up at all hours and they held no appeal for me at all and I told my father so. Sadly we fell out, so much so I left home. What can I tell you, but I broke my mother's heart? But there's nothing I can do about that now.

"So I came to England in 1906, when I was twenty-five and trained in what I always wanted to do, cut diamonds. And now today, you tell me I'm famous," he allowed himself a grin "so I think perhaps I chose the right profession after all.

"My brother Victor stayed at home, and took over the business. I was pleased for him. We weren't that close, there was sixteen years between us remember, but he was still my only brother and I loved him.

"But then the Nazis came to power, and in January '33 the German people made a mistake they will live to regret I'm sure, in electing Hitler as Chancellor. How I begged Victor and his family to leave and come and live here, but they wouldn't listen." He stopped talking for a second and his face took on an expression of immense sadness.

"Then one day I got a letter from his wife, his widow. He had been murdered."

"How terrible!"

"If only that were all. He had been beaten, gagged and tied up with an S.S. necktie and then hung upside down and left. When finally they took him down, he'd had a Star of David cut into his forehead."

"I've never hear of anything so barbaric!"

"Yes. So you see, young man, I will do anything, in my limited way, anything to help defeat the Nazis. Whatever you are asking of me I'll do and I'll do it for Victor because soon, very soon the ordinary decent German people will wake up to their terrible mistake. But for Victor, it will be too late." His eyes were full of memories. Neither of them spoke for a moment until eventually he said. "So, that's my story."

"And very moving it is. Thank you for being so honest."

"Yes," he nodded "and now you can tell me something. However did a fine young gentleman like yourself get a scar like that?"

"Fighting Nazis, indirectly."

"Then," and he leaned forward "it's a mark you can wear with pride young sir. Pride!"

"I'll remember that, Sir. Thank you."

"Now tell me something else. What is it you need for me to do for His Majesty's Government?"

For answer Douglas opened the box and removing the contents, carefully placed the large piece of un-cut stone on the table next to him.

"Zircon." he announced proudly.

"I wondered what it was you had in the box. I thought it might be your lunch. So what's it for?"

"I, we, want you to cut it into an exact replica of the Great Mogul diamond."

*

"You are absolutely certain it's real?"

"There is no doubt whatsoever, Major Baum. This is a diamond."

"Will you stake your life on it?"

"Better than that," the pert little man in his winged collar and tailcoat answered him boldly. "I will stake my reputation on it!"

"Let us hope it won't be necessary to gamble with either."

"You may rest assured Monsieur, I guarantee this is a genuine diamond." As if to confirm his own experienced judgement, the Parisian jeweller whom Baum had arranged to authenticate the parcel received from Muller, held the stone up to the light and looked once again deep into its crystalline interior with a powerful lens.

"Real," he said at length. "Without a doubt."

"Then I am obliged to you Monsieur, for coming all this way and giving me the benefit of your experience. Needless to say, what you have witnessed here today will remain secret. Is that perfectly understood?"

"I am the soul of discretion, Monsieur."

"I hope so," added Baum, knowing full well that once back in the capital it would be impossible for the jeweller to contain the fact that he had seen and handled the legendary diamond. Yet it wouldn't matter if he talked because soon the whole world would learn of its reappearance.

"My aide will see you out, and there's a generous reward for your trouble."

"If I may ever be of service again ... "

"Yes, yes, thank you. Goodbye."

So it was all over, he thought to himself when alone. Muller had played it straight after all. That was a surprise, and he glanced through the letter and bill of sale. All that was necessary now was to inform the Führer of his success and reap the rewards.

When his aide returned, Baum told him to send a communication to Berlin and dictated the following:-

"Address it personally to the Führer and be sure to use all of his titles. 'Heil Hitler. I am delighted to report that I am in possession of the Great Mogul diamond my ... no, better put your, your quest having been successful. May I offer my most heartfelt congratulations and await your further orders, et cetera, et cetera.' Send it off right away."

"Herr Major."

Later that night at great personal risk, an Unteroffizier on Baum's staff relayed a message to London.

*

"So how did he react when you told him?"

"His jaw hit the floor, Sir. After telling me he would do anything to avenge the death of his brother, I think he rather regretted the promise. Yet to his credit, he did say that if it helped defeat the Nazis then he'd be willing to try."

"And in the time?" M questioned Reid.

"As best he could."

"You've done well to get this far this quickly, but from now on, you're going to have to keep the reins very tight, because we have just received inside information that the Germans have definitely found the Great Mogul."

"Good Lord! So the reports were true then."

"Indeed they were."

"How on earth did they manage it after all these years?"

"I have no idea."

"But how do we know it's the real thing? They could easily be bluffing."

"Apparently, it's been confirmed as the genuine article, but the all important thing now is we're very pushed for time. You asked me before why we wanted a copy made, well I can tell you now that they have actually found it ..."

"We're going to swap them over."

"That's right."

"I thought so. And who's going to do that, Sir?"

"Well it certainly won't be you, that's for sure." he told him firmly. "We know where the diamond is at this precise moment, but it's to be transferred to Berlin soon, so we have got to make the switch before then. Once it reaches Berlin it'll be impossible, quite impossible."

"I see."

"Our man inside is willing to try the switch, but he's quite junior in rank, an Unteroffizier, and the only access he'll have is before it leaves for Berlin."

"And when exactly is that, Sir?"

"Unfortunately we don't have that intelligence yet."

"Well if it's only a matter of days, then it's out of the question. There isn't a person alive who could cut a copy in so short a span."

"I appreciate that, but until we know when it's leaving, you're just going to have to hound your cutter man, night and day."

"I'll do my best but he's no spring chicken. He's a nice enough chap but push him too hard and he'll crack, I know he will."

"Time, Lieutenant, is of the absolute essence here; you must not let us down."

"You mean like I did before, Sir?"

"I did not say that."

"No, you didn't have to Sir. I know I let the side down badly before, but I'll do my best with this one, but you must realize diamond cutting is a very precise art."

"I appreciate that, but we've got a lot riding on this, not least our agent's very life. He's code named 'Oakleaf' for your information. A very brave young man working right in the thick of it, for a man named Major Walter Baum. A so called treasure hunter."

"I can well imagine how the poor chap's feeling," said Douglas standing ready to leave.

"We know the Germans are going to rename the stone 'Light of the Reich'."

"Let's hope 'Oakleaf' can dim that light in time then Sir."

"Quite. Incidentally, how much is this work going to cost?"

"I spoke with Mr. Rosenburg himself about that, and he estimates …"

"On second thoughts, don't tell me I don't want to know. You can take that up with the finance department yourself."

"There's just one other thing, Sir."

"Which is?"

"The original diamond had natural internal inclusions, flaws."

"And?"

"And the copy won't have, it's impossible."

"Just do the best you can. Practice the art of deception."

*

Douglas immediately returned to Mr Rosenburg in Hatton Garden, and careful not to divulge any secrets, explained the urgency they were under suddenly.

An intelligent and astute man, Mr Rosenburg fortunately had the solution. Unbeknown to Douglas, Mr Janovitski had been training Mr Rosenburg's son Reuben (who wasn't fit enough to join the forces), for years in the art of diamond cutting and polishing to the point where he was now competent enough to work on his own. Once Mr Janovitski had cut the stone to shape, Reuben would be able to polish on the many facets as zircon was much easier to work with, being that much softer than diamond. Reuben could work through the night and let Mr Janovitski work the day shift, thus achieving twenty-four hour production and reducing completion time by fifty per cent.

It was the best solution anyone could ask for, but even so the man refused to commit himself to a fixed time scale. It would not be finished before it was finished, and until such time all those concerned would just have to be patient.

*

It was four days before Major Baum received a reply to his announcement. Both he and Major Muller were to report in person to the Berghof, with the diamond, for a special reception on the 7th of September.

*

On the evening of 30th July, the shortest of messages was received in London. It read simply, 7 Sept 41. OAKLEAF.

*

Douglas Reid was summoned to M's office early the following morning. M was uneasy. "No matter what, the stone will have to leave here on the 1st of September at the very latest."
 "That gives us exactly one month, thirty-one days."
 "Can it be done?"
 "It'll have to be."
 "Exactly. We have to smuggle it into France first of all, and then allow 'Oakleaf' time to set up the exchange which won't be easy."
 "I had better inform our friends at once."

*

When Mr Rosenburg was told of the deadline he was far from pleased. "Isaac has been with my company since I cannot remember when," he told Douglas "he's the best cutter in London and though there is no work now, when the war's over and things return to normal please God, he'll be invaluable to me. I don't like to put him under such a strain. It's not good for anyone, let alone him." He shook his large head, deeply dissatisfied with the news. "I'll let you have the pleasure of telling him yourself, but I'm not pleased. Not pleased at all."

*

"Can you reassure me, my young friend," the craftsman addressed Douglas determinedly "that what I'm wearing myself out to complete for you, is in some way helping to bring the Nazis down?"
 "I can give you that absolute assurance, yes Sir."
 "Then for the memory of my dear brother Victor, I will do it. And may God help me."

*

On the 1st of September a special courier codenamed 'Magpie', carrying the substitute stone concealed in the base of a Thermos flask, left S.O.E. Headquarters, and under cover of darkness was air-dropped into North Western France in the countryside on the outskirts of Rennes, Brittany. He was met by members of the Resistance and immediately concealed in the specially designed false bottom of a truck, and driven to within walking distance of the château in the Loire Valley used by Major Baum.

On the night before the Great Mogul diamond was due to leave France for the Berghof, it was successfully exchanged for the worthless zircon substitute.

*

On the 7th of September 1941 on the wide veranda of the Führer's Bavarian residence in brilliant afternoon sunlight, a delighted Adolf Hitler was photographed being presented with what was believed to be the famous, and long lost Great Mogul diamond, still in the velvet lined trinket box belonging to the late Frau Muller.

Major Walter Baum was promoted to Colonel and awarded the War Merit Cross 1st Class. He reported to his leader the tragic news that Major Muller had been killed during an air-raid over Berlin.

Major Claus Muller was posthumously also awarded the War Merit Cross 1st Class which was eventually forwarded to his daughter Astrid, in Obernhof.

Some time later, Astrid received another official communication, addressed to her father, which had been posted months earlier and redirected from the family home in Berlin, informing her that her brother, Stefan Muller, had been killed in action. He had died a hero for the glory of the Fatherland.

*

7th December 1941:
Pearl Harbour.

6th June 1944:
'D' Day. Allied forces land in France.

20th July 1944:
Assassination plot on Hitler at Wolfsschanze (Wolf's Lair). A bomb concealed in a briefcase fails to harm him.

25th August 1944:
Paris liberated. The military governor of Paris, General Dietrich von Choltitz, allowed himself to be arrested at the Hotel Meurice for having refused Hitler's direct order to destroy the city.

30th April 1945:
Russians report that Adolf Hitler committed suicide by swallowing a cyanide capsule whilst dressed in a new Nazi uniform and seated on a couch in the bunker of the Reich Chancellery, Berlin. This however was never verified and his death remains shrouded in uncertainties, many being of the opinion that he escaped to South America and lived out his days in obscurity.

8th May 1945:
'V.E. Day'. Victory in Europe.

20th August 1945:
Catching the dawn sailing from Dover, Douglas Edward Reid left England for the Continent and slowly made his way through war ravaged France and Germany, eventually arriving at the village of Obernhof.

Once Astrid Muller had recovered from the shock, Douglas claimed his bride, and ten days later the couple made their way up the hill to Kloster Arnstein, and were married by the kind, elderly priest Father Brant.

Special courier 'Magpie' however, having successfully executed part of the mission, failed to rendezvous with the Resistance and return to London.

CHAPTER ELEVEN

" 'The Princess Elizabeth is to marry Lieutenant Philip Mountbatten R.N. on 20th November 1947 at Westminster Abbey'." Astrid read slowly, following each word with her finger. "That is a happy picture of them both I think. What a nice couple they make, don't you think, yes?"

"Don't you think, so," Douglas corrected her. "Yes, I do think so, they make a lovely couple."

"Oh, this language. I'll never be good."

"Yes you will, of course you will. Look how far you've come already, and so quickly. And how well you read now too."

"I think so yes. We think so. They think so."

Standing behind her, Douglas wrapped his arms around his wife as she sat over the newspaper spread out on the table, and moving aside her long golden hair kissed her tenderly on the back of the neck. "We all think so," he said "all of mankind thinks so, everyone in the galaxy thinks so, yes please and thank you very much."

"What is gal … , something?"

"Forget it, it's not important."

"This Philip, he is very beautiful I think so."

"No he isn't."

"Yes I think so he is."

"Men are not beautiful. Women are beautiful, like you," and he kissed her again. "Men are handsome."

"Yes, Philip is handsome man."

"A Royal wedding is just what this country needs right now. Lift us all from the 'slough of despond'."

"The what?"

*

With the war two years past, life in Britain was slowly returning to some resemblance of its former self. The victory may have belonged to the allies, but the cost was high. The country was still bleeding from many a wound and would continue to do so for some time to come as food rationing, the economy, industry and commerce all struggled to realign themselves to a pre-war situation.

Following the operation with the Great Mogul diamond, Douglas spent the remainder of the war years as an instructor/tutor with S.O.E. in operational procedure and languages, achieving the rank of Captain, until it was disbanded in January 1946 when, for the first time he was able to tell his parents the truth of his war time exploits. Yet through it all his heart was in Obernhof.

Douglas returned to his former position in the Department of Geology at the British Museum. Yet now, with two mouths to feed, his meagre salary would not support a flat in Bayswater (which had miraculously escaped the bombing), as well as a wife, so he rented a small basement flat in Lady Somerset Road, Kentish Town, North London. Here there was good access to town via the Underground, as well as the feeling of making a new beginning. A fresh start on the adventure of their life together.

Yet life in post-war England for a German national, however beautiful she may have been, was not easy, and to avoid any unnecessary, and yet at the same time understandable unpleasantness, it was decided between them that to all who met her, Astrid was Swiss. And as such, Astrid Reid from Switzerland, took a job at Leighton Road laundry.

*

Set back from the line of adjacent buildings as if the builder had wanted to hide the structure from public gaze, the laundry was built on three floors, and Astrid was assigned to the pressing room on the top floor, where she spent most of her day standing in a hot steamy atmosphere, bent over an ironing table trying to make gentlemen's shirts from the wealthy Highgate area, look as good as new.

The other women, ten in all, a mixture of English and Irish and mostly married, proved nice enough to begin with, and looked upon the foreigner in their midst as something of an agreeable oddity. And sometimes in the mornings when the boy was late returning from his rounds collecting the day's work, they would encourage her to tell them stories of mountains and lakes and snow and places they had never heard of, as if trying to fulfil a need to be taken out of their ordinary routine lives to a better place.

For Astrid this presented a unique, if not amusing problem at first, which she solved by joining the local library and familiarizing herself with Swiss life. With Douglas's help, she invented a cover story which brought a touch of excitement to her otherwise monotonous days. Yet when questioned as to whatever possessed her to leave all that behind, she would answer quite truthfully, love.

Astrid and Douglas were as happy together as they could be, and though life was difficult and often hard, it was good. Though never did his wife learn that Douglas had once been intent on killing her father. Some things were best left buried.

*

The day of the Royal Wedding came and went. Although cloudy and cold it was a day of celebration and crowds, street parties and laughter, all helping the nation to forget almost six years of bitter conflict. Eventually the calendar clocked off the end of another year.

With every passing day Astrid's command of the English language improved, until it became obvious that her level of education was far superior to that of the other women at the laundry, and over their heads the proprietor offered her the post of Manageress. Knowing this would cause friction she rejected the position, which in turn strengthened her standing with the staff, but the boss persisted until finally with an offer of better pay and conditions, she relented.

About this time, Douglas decided to help himself up the ladder of promotion by studying for an M.A., in the belief that promotion would be sure to follow. It would mean an enormous amount of work but with the Museum's support and Astrid often late at the laundry, he could study in the evenings and at weekends, and with their combined salaries it would not be long before they would be in a position to put down a deposit on a home of their own, in a better area.

It was also about this time that Astrid's employer had a routine visit from a representative of the Immigration and Nationality Directorate of the Home Office, when the truth of Astrid's nationality was exposed. This left her employer feeling both annoyed and unsure. Annoyed at being lied to, and by a German at that, he was unsure about knowing what to do for the best. Ever since he had promoted her, the laundry had never been run so efficiently with the introduction of a number of sensible working practices he had overlooked himself. She also had an excellent telephone manner which went down well with the toffee-nosed clients, and now that he was looking to expand into lucrative hotel contracts, customer relations would be paramount.

Astrid had not broken any law by misleading her employer, for everyone knew she was a foreigner, but if he kept her on, her secret would need to remain closely guarded, because if it ever became known that the new Manageress was a 'Kraut', all hell would break loose and her life become unbearable.

The third event around this time was the sudden and unexpected death of Edward Reid, Douglas's father, from a sudden heart attack. The news came as a dreadful blow to Douglas as he knew his bringing home a German bride had grieved his father deeply. He had hoped, in time, when his father got to know her better, he would have seen Astrid for the wonderful woman she was and grow to love and accept her as his daughter-in-law. But it was never to be.

The funeral was a very strained affair, with relations and friends treating Astrid as one might a rare specimen in a zoo; interesting, but best kept at a distance. And to make matters worse, it had rained all day, each drop bringing with it painful memories and awakening old fears and wounds.

Hanna, Mrs Reid senior, had borne up well to the demands of the day and she was polite, even friendly, in response to Astrid's approaches, remembering from her own experiences what it was like to be a foreigner in a new country. Yet still she could not completely disguise the feeling of resentment towards her German daughter-in-law, believing her people responsible for her son's disfigurement, as well as the ravishing of her homeland. Combining the pain of suddenly losing her husband with the disappointment and disgrace Douglas had brought to the family, she proceeded to lock herself away in her own isolated little world in an attempt to ignore the hurt until it went away. But it never did.

Astrid was retained at the laundry, but the news heralded in yet another difficult and painful episode of her life. Somehow, one morning, her secret broke loose and it was discovered that the Manageress of Leighton Road Laundry was not Swiss at all, but a liar, and a German.

*

It started with whispers in quiet corners, and quickly developed into snide remarks, but as the women became bolder, it was just a short step to direct insults and abuse. Astrid did her best to cope, even ignore them, and to a point could understand their hostility for, without exception, every one of them had been touched in some way or other by the war. Yet even so, it hurt. Every word cut deeper, gradually wearing her down. She brought the problem to the boss's attention and he promised to speak to the staff. But he never did, or if he did, it made no difference.

Many a time she was on the point of sharing it all with her husband, but he was so absorbed with his studies, she did not like to worry him. Instead she carried the pain alone, in the hope that as soon as he had passed his exams they could move away. She knew her wages made an important contribution to that end.

As a couple, they rarely went out. Either he had his face stuck in a book or she was on the late shift, and on the occasions when they were home together, there was always the question 'can we afford it'? The thought of coming to the exciting city of London had thrilled her when he had proposed on that unforgettable day in Obernhof, yet she had seen almost none of it.

Suddenly from being so happy, the magic had vanished. Was this how her life was meant to be? She thought of leaving the laundry, but where would she find another job? Who would employ a German?

Somehow, the neighbours got to learn her secret and from being friendly and talkative with the lovely Swiss girl, changed overnight and became either openly hostile or treated her as if she did not exist at all.

The 23rd November 1948 was Astrid's birthday, and in a bid to win the women round, she purchased a large iced sponge cake and left it in the room where the staff took their breaks with a note for them to help themselves. But by the end of the day no-one had mentioned either the cake or her birthday and out of curiosity she went to see how much thy had eaten of her peace offering. They had not eaten any. Instead, it sat exactly where she had left it, untouched, except for a swastika carved into the icing.

It was the last straw. Shutting the door to her tiny damp office, she broke down and wept bitterly.

When she arrived back at the basement flat, Douglas had prepared a surprise, a small celebration. He had cooked dinner, and laid the table for a romantic candle-lit evening together. All Astrid wanted to do was pour out her heart, but after a glass or two of wine and the soothing embrace of Nat King Cole and Bing Crosby, she found the hurt had eased. Later, when she had opened his present and tried on the slinky nightdress, they made love in a way they hadn't for a long time.

*

The strain began to take its toll though. Her working day was unbearable, then she would rush home and prepare a meal, which had been chosen in haste during her lunch-break, only to flop down mentally and physically exhausted at the end of the day. She would watch her husband leaning over his books in silence, not only looking, but behaving exactly like her father had when she was little; rarely affording her any quality time. Seeing Douglas like that regularly brought it all back. How often had she tugged at her father's trousers only to be shooed away? 'Run along and play, Daddy's busy.' How pitiless that history could be repeating itself.

She was too tired to knit or sew, reading English was too taxing and reading German impossible as there was absolutely nothing available. Nor could she listen to the radio for fear of disturbing his studies. On the rare occasions when Douglas enquired after her work, she would make up stories and lie. Astrid Reid began to feel as if she was living under a curse. And now, as if all that was not enough, she knew she was pregnant but was too afraid of what Douglas would say to tell him.

*

One evening, towards the middle of January 1949, feeling thoroughly disillusioned with life, she suddenly announced that she was going out for a walk. Douglas hardly stirred from his books, just grunting an acknowledgement. The real reason was to clear her mind and compose what she would say to him on her return, for as the father he had a right to know, even though it would mean all their plans going out the window. Yet whatever his reaction she had to tell him soon, for she could not hide the bouts of morning sickness for much longer.

It was dry but cold outside, yet wrapped in her thoughts the temperature went unnoticed. She walked the streets as her feet dictated for almost an hour and a half, going over and over what it was she wanted to say.

'The arrival of a baby is meant to be a happy time. Please God, please help Douglas understand and not be cross. Surely I deserve at least some happiness in my life?'

About ten o'clock she made her way home, walking down Dartmouth Park Hill, past the butchers, and turned the corner into Burghley Road but as she did, and before there was time to cross over, she walked directly into one of the women from the laundry. A loud, brash woman, with a man who was presumably her husband. Their breath telltale of an evenings drinking.

"Well, look who it ain't! The little German Hitler 'erself. An' all alone."

Astrid tried to pass but the woman would not move. "'Ere Bert. This is 'er I was telling ya about."

"So you're the one are ya?" started Bert, his speech slurred. "And what gives you the right to come and live in this country? That's what I wanner know."

Astrid made no reply, anxious to get away quickly, but her path was blocked.

"Yeh," joined the woman, egged on by the presence of her husband. "Go back to the rest of 'em filthy murdering Krauts!"

Again Astrid tried to squeeze past, but this time the man barred her way. "Not so fast my pretty little Hun."

She started to tremble and could feel her heart pounding within her breast and, knowing she had to get away, looked around for an escape, or help. But the street was both dark and deserted.

"Do you know," began the man, his breath rising like putrid gas in the chilled air. "I lost my brother in 'forty four?" He was prodding Astrid with his forefinger as he spoke. "He was shot in the back, by German filth!"

"He was a good'un too. Better than any German!" the woman was shouting now.

"That's right. He was. Ask his wife and four kids. They'll tell ya!"

Astrid felt she had to say something and stammered. "I'm sorry, I'm sorry. But I didn't … "

The woman spat into the gutter. "You're all rotten. Rotten to the core," and she pushed her away with the palm of her hand.

The blow rang an alarm bell in Astrid's head and she panicked suddenly, pushing the man out of the way with both hands as hard as she could. With a shout, he staggered drunkenly and fell backwards against a high brick wall, and in the still night air, both women heard the sharp crack as his head hit hard. They stood in disbelieving silence, watching as he crumpled to the pavement.

The woman turned on Astrid and spoke through tightly clenched teeth. "You bitch!!"

"I didn't mean to hurt … " But she was cut off as the woman's hand landed heavily on top of her head. Reeling, she turned to run, but the revenge-charged woman grabbed her coat and simultaneously with her other hand, sunk her finger-nails deep into the side of the German girl's face.

Screaming, Astrid lashed out in defence, but her blows were wild and of little consequence. Her head was wrenched sideways as the woman pulled mercilessly at the golden hair, sending her reeling once again, as she brought her knee up with revengeful force directly into Astrid's face. Astrid dropped backwards onto the ground.

Lying dazed on the pavement, blood began to leak from her nose and her head rang with the rhythm of a steam hammer. Silhouetted against the night sky, the woman came towards her but, powerless to move, all Astrid could do was groan, again and again, as she felt her kidneys being crushed under the woman's violent kicks. And then, quiet.

Slowly Astrid's head was pulled up by its hair and the woman spoke close into her bleeding face. "Go home you filthy German bitch!" Every word was thick with spit. "Go home!!" She slapped Astrid full across the mouth with the back of her hand, and let her head drop to the ground with a thud. Finally she spat directly in a dazed eye.

Turning away, she went and tended to Bert who was still lying moaning on the pavement where he had fallen.

Knowing she had to get away before she was turned on again, Astrid fought against the pain and staggered to her feet attempting to stem the flow of blood, but it was no use and her eyes started to cloud over as she teetered on the edge of unconsciousness.

'I must get home. I must … get home'. And slowly, holding on to anything for support, constantly fighting against the urge to cry out and attract more unwanted attention, she eventually reached the house, almost falling down the worn steps to the basement, landing against the door at the bottom in a heap.

Reaching for the doorbell her arm refused to stretch and she cried out in desperation. "Douglas! Help me!" And thumped the door with her last ounce of strength, before finally collapsing.

*

Astrid never returned to the laundry. In fact, other than brief visits to the corner shop, doing the best she could with necessities still rationed, she did not venture outside for months.

When Douglas had found her unconscious on the doorstep, she was admitted to hospital and kept in under observation for three days during which time he learnt he was to be a father. When she was allowed home, he learnt a great deal more, when finally Astrid unburdened all the trauma and misery she had suffered in silence for so long.

Douglas went to the laundry, and raised such a stink that his voice was heard all over the building. But on mention of bringing in the police, the proprietor became very nervous for some reason, and not only paid Astrid's wages in full, but also gave her an additional £50 in cash to, as he put it, 'buy the little lady something nice'.

When Hanna heard the news, she offered to look after her daughter-in-law and they were on the point of accepting, until she casually remarked that she 'knew something like this would happen; it was simply a question of when'. Somehow the remark added to the divide between them and Astrid chose to stay put.

Life took on a new pattern for the Reids. Douglas left each morning for the museum leaving his wife with an all-consuming feeling of loneliness and isolation. As the months went by and the days grew longer with the approach of spring, Astrid's wounds may have healed, but her inner hurts never faded.

Each day became a tedious repetition of events. A quick trip to the shops in the hope that no-one would recognize her and cause trouble; then back to the dingy flat and the constant ticking of the clock, silenced only by the wireless until supper time, when Douglas studied relentlessly, night after night.

She was comforted by the assurance of his love and the promise of the new life growing within her, but it was not enough.

Try as she might to lift herself from the stranglehold of depression that tightened its grip with each day – the rejections, the insults, the days of utter loneliness speaking to no-one with only her thoughts to torment her; the awful memories of the night in Berlin when her father had been blown to pieces; the way her mother's life was snatched away so cruelly, and her brother Stefan killed fighting for a lost cause all took their toll. By the time June arrived, with her pregnancy clearly evident, her self-worth had deteriorated to a point where she had started to let things go, and with no signs at all of any maternal instincts of preparation for the arrival of their baby, Douglas got his first suspicions that something was wrong.

The flat was not kept quite so clean as it once used to be; the washing was a day or so behind; the bed unmade. But then the evening meal would be late, sometimes very late and on occasions there was nothing to eat at all, when she couldn't be bothered to go shopping. And things went from bad to worse.

*

One evening in early summer when the air was weighed down with humidity and the promise of rain, after a particularly bad day at the museum and a difficult journey home, Douglas arrived to find Astrid asleep, slumped uncomfortably across the kitchen table. The flat was as untidy as when he had left that morning. In front of her sat an unopened letter with a German postmark, alongside a German bible open at Matthew's gospel.

He knocked on the table and called sarcastically. "I'm home dear! Anyone in?"

Gradually, her eyelids lifted, revealing two red and puffy eyes. She had obviously been crying, and it was clear she had given no thought to her appearance.

"Hello," she responded surprised, sitting up "home already?"

"Just what's going on here?!"

"What? What's the matter?"

"What's the matter? Look at you. Look at this place," he said, glancing around "it's a tip. Whatever have you been doing all day?"

"I must have fallen asleep," she responded, wiping her face. "It's so warm. Please don't be cross with me."

"Don't be cross with you! For goodness sake, you're going to be a mother in a few weeks and our child's going to be totally dependant on you for everything. But by the look of you now, God help him. Or her. You need to pull yourself together Astrid, for the child's sake as well as your own."

"I do my best." She told him, toying with a lace handkerchief.

"Well, you'd better start doing a whole lot better than you are now. I know it's difficult at the moment with only one wage coming in, and until I get my degree it's going to be tough with three of us. But if we're careful we'll be able to manage alright."

But Astrid only continued to toy with her handkerchief.

"For goodness sake! Have you been listening to one word I've been saying?"

"Of course I have. You think I should have stayed at the laundry. I feel sometimes you think more of the money than you do of me."

"I did not say that!"

"No, but that's what you think. I know." She wiped her eyes.

"Oh please don't start crying, that's all I need. I've had a lousy day and I don't expect to come home to all this. You should be taking care of yourself, and the home, and everything. This is a mother's special time."

Astrid twisted the handkerchief nervously around her fingers. "And how would I know about that? I don't have a mother. This was my mother's. It's all I've got of hers, a tiny lace handkerchief. Not much is it?"

"Well, that's ... " He paused, and thought before speaking again. When he did his tone had mellowed. "Well that's very sad, I'm sorry."

She did not say anything but stared at the handkerchief, remembering, as the tension between them eased.

"What's the bible for?" he asked eventually. "You're not getting all religious, are you?"

"No. Well ... I just feel I've neglected my faith recently, that's all. And I needed some words of encouragement. I was looking at what Jesus said", and proceeded to read. "'Come to me, all you who are weary and burdened, and I will give you rest. Take my yoke upon you and learn from me, for I am gentle and humble in heart, and you will find rest for your souls.' And to read something like that gives me ... I don't know. Strength. I've been praying too. For you, for me, the baby. All of us. Our future."

"I see. Well if it helps ... "

"Has anyone ever prayed for you Douglas, do you know?"

"Not to my knowledge ... No wait," he added promptly, remembering a dawn on the Shetland Isles, when Hamish had committed him into God's care. And his attitude softened at remembrance of the man's kindness. "Someone did pray for me once, during the war. And now that you mention it, I prayed for myself once too. When I was captured," wincing at recollection of time spent in a Gestapo prison cell.

"And were the prayers answered?"

"Yes, I suppose they were," he acknowledged, with a nod to the memory of 'the best of times; the worst of times.' "It's so easy to forget, isn't it?"

Astrid looked at her husband. How like her father he was, the likeness was quite uncanny. He used to have a faith; they had gone to church together often enough, especially after her mother's death. But all of that was before the war. The war changed everything. The Führer promised them so much. Too much.

"What's the letter from Germany?" he asked after a while.

"I know what it is, you can open it. I know what it'll say."

His interest aroused, he opened it quickly and read through the official looking document. "It's from a firm of solicitors," he told her, surprised. "They say there's going to be a considerable delay in dealing with your claim for compensation for the family house in Berlin which has now been demolished, and in settling your father's estate as all the necessary papers were destroyed when the city was taken by the Russians. But they say they will contact you again just as soon as they can." He passed the letter across the table. "So what's all that about?"

"I knew that's what they would say. I wanted it to be a surprise; that's why I didn't say anything about it before. My father wasn't a rich man, but he had a little behind him. And then there's the compensation for the house; but proof of ownership could go on for years. I thought the money would help us. Now that Stefan's dead that makes me … what do you say?"

"Sole beneficiary."

"Yes. I did my best for us, darling."

"I had no idea you'd been so busy."

"It's nothing, a few letters. I thought it might help us, that's all. I cleared the house out in Berlin and sold off the furniture long before you returned, but I hardly got anything for it all. So now all I'm left with to remember my family is this lace handkerchief. How sad is that?" Her eyes began to fill with tears as she spoke. "My father even gave away my mother's jewel box."

"I'm sure he had good reason."

"Just to put a paperweight in, that's all. A silly glass paperweight for Major Baum. I really wanted the box myself."

Douglas studied his wife for a moment uncertain of what he had just heard. "What did you say?"

"Please don't be cross with me. I'll try and be a better wife. Really I will."

"No, no. You just said a name." And he took her hand in his, feeling guilty suddenly for all the pain he had put her through in bringing her to his country. "You just mentioned a name, someone's name. What was it?"

"The paperweight, it went to Major Baum."

"Baum, you're sure?"

"Yes, I sent it myself."

"You did?" he queried.

"I was just about to leave the house when two messengers arrived asking for a parcel. My father was dead but I knew about it. He had told me the night before. So to save a lot of questions I did it up and gave it to them. I just wanted to be rid of them quickly and get away."

"Fancy hearing that name again after all this time."

"Did you know Major Baum then?"

"No not at all, but I knew of him."

"Has it got something to do with deceiving me and pretending to be German and looking like my father?"

"No, and please don't bring that up again. I've told you about it so many times. My pretending to be Frederic Kutzner was simply a secret service matter which all came to nothing. The fact that I look like a younger version of your father is nothing more than an accident of nature."

"What about the scar?"

"I've told you. I got that from flying glass in an air raid."

It was the story he told her originally and he saw no reason why she should be hurt any further by the truth.

Astrid stroked his damaged cheek but her hand was damp and clammy to the touch. "It's not as bad as it was when I first saw you in Obernhof."

"It'll always be there. But you never told me what your father did exactly during the war," he said, anxious suddenly to hear more.

"Oh, do I have to?"

"Yes Astrid, please."

"I'm hungry aren't you?" She told him, more concerned with food suddenly than war stories.

"Yes, I'll get some fish and chips in a minute but firstly tell me what your father did during the war."

"I know he was in tanks for a while. I remember feeling very proud of him. I had a photograph over my bed of him standing on top of a tank looking very pleased with himself. That was before his accident."

"But he didn't stay in tanks did he?"

"No, he was moved to intelligence in Berlin. I didn't see much of him after that, but he did write. It was always nice to hear from him. Then he became involved with some sort of treasure hunt he called it, with Major Baum."

"A treasure hunt, you say?"

"That's what he called it, don't ask me why."

"Do you remember where the parcel you did up went to?"

She thought for a moment, still clutching her mother's handkerchief.

"No, I can't, sorry. Somewhere in France that's all."

"France, you're sure?"

"France, yes. I can't tell you where though. I was in a bad way after the bombing. Can we have something to eat now? I've hardly had anything all day."

"Well, in that case you've been very naughty, especially in your condition," and he tapped the back of her hand "but you've got a good memory, so I'll forgive you on one condition."

"And what's that?"

"You must try and pull yourself together. Promise?"

"I promise. I'll do my best." And she smiled at her man, thankful for his love.

"You have a cool drink and tidy yourself up, and I'll get us some fish and chips."

"I didn't mean what I said," she told him, still holding his hand. "I know you love me. Kiss me before you go. You're all I've got."

He did as he was asked and kissed her softly on the forehead. "I love you too," he told her "remember that. I always will."

*

Walking to the fish shop, his mind was occupied not with supper but with the chances of hearing the name Baum again after nearly four years, and learning that his father-in-law worked together with him on a so-called treasure hunt. How very strange! Was that why Muller didn't show that night in Berlin, because he was already working for Baum?

Standing in the queue at the fish shop, suddenly an understanding of the truth hit him with such energy he called out. "The paperweight!"

"Yes mate, you'll just have to wait like everyone else."

But Douglas hadn't heard the fishfryer. 'Of course,' he thought 'the paperweight wasn't a paperweight at all but the Great Mogul diamond! Dear God. I don't believe it! And Astrid actually gave it away while I was making a copy in London. What an incredible coincidence. I must ask her what it looked like'.

*

The receding light had helped to lower the temperature, but the air was still sticky and damp as he made his way back to Lady Somerset Road. He kept going over the war years and the business with the Great Mogul Diamond. Surely it was too much of a coincidence that the man he had been instructed to eliminate and impersonate, was also the man behind the diamond's rediscovery. But on descending the steps to the basement flat however, he was suddenly brought back to reality.

Voices. A man's voice, talking to Astrid. It wasn't possible to distinguish what they were saying, but there was something about the tone that made him pause before turning the handle.

'Who could it be?' he thought. 'The rent man? No, paid him last week. The milkman? No, he only calls in the morning. Local tradesmen?' He turned the handle decisively and pushed open the door that led directly into the sitting room.

The stranger was seated with his back to the door, but on hearing it open, he stood up sharply and turned around. "Hello, old boy!" said the man, adding a salute-like wave. "Long time no see!"

Douglas gasped. "Good Lord! I don't believe it!"

"Yes, it's true, my old chum. The proverbial bad penny reporting for duty."

"Captain Silverthorn. After all these years."

"Put it there, my dear friend," said Douglas, dumping the supper on the table as the two former secret service men shook hands energetically.

"I'd recognise you anywhere."

"With a scar like mine, that wouldn't be difficult."

"It's healed up a good bit though, I see."

"But whatever brings you to this neck of the woods?"

"Oh, a bit of this, a bit of that. Business, pleasure, you know how it is. All chasing an honest crust."

"I'm still in shock. What a day this has turned out to be! How many years has it been?"

"Since the old S.O.E. days? It must be at least five years, give or take a month or two."

"But however did you find me?"

"I knew you'd gone back to The British Museum, so a word in the right ear. It wasn't difficult."

But as Douglas looked into his friend's deep set dark eyes, above cheekbones that protruded far more than they used to, he instinctively knew that something was wrong. He may have been his usual jovial self, but he had lost a lot of weight; the double-breasted pinstripe suit hung a few sizes too large; the hair had thinned to a limp salt and pepper grey. Yet his face still lit up when he smiled. "And I've had the pleasure of meeting your gorgeous wife."

"Yes of course, forgive me," said Douglas, regaining himself. "You haven't met before."

"There was a knock at the door just after you left," explained Astrid. "Captain Silverthorn told me you knew one another in the army."

"That's true enough," added Douglas. "We certainly did."

"And, correct me if I'm wrong, but there's shortly to be an addition to the family," said Silverthorn.

"Yes," Astrid smiled, running a hand through her hair. "In September. Our first."

"Well, my heartiest congratulations to you both. The first of many, I'm sure."

"Thank you so much. Pull up a chair, Alex. Make yourself at home. What a wonderful surprise!"

"I'll put the fish in the oven," Astrid told them. "You'll stay to supper, Mr Silverthorn? I can easily open a tin of something. Make it stretch."

"Please dear lady; I'm Alex to my friends. And thank you, but no. I won't be staying. This is only a swift social call." Yet straight away he produced a packet of cigarettes, offering them to Douglas, and they settled back as Astrid moved into the kitchen, leaving the two comrades alone.

"So I presume this is the beautiful daughter," he spoke quietly, "of Herr Claus Muller?"

"That's right. As you know, soon after the end of the war I went to Germany to get her."

"Well, you sure can pick 'em, old boy. I'm not surprised you fell for her. She's absolutely gorgeous. If I may say so, that is?"

Douglas laughed. "Yes, you may. And yes, she is. It hasn't been easy though. There's been quite a few problems I can tell you. But what about you, Alex? What have you been getting up to?"

"Well, I never got round to marriage, if that's what you mean?"

"There's still plenty of time, you're still young. Would you like a drink by the way? It's so humid isn't it? I'm afraid we've only Guinness in. If I had known you were coming I'd ... "

"No. Not for me. Thanks all the same. I mustn't. It clashes with my medication."

"Oh? A cup of tea then; coffee?"

"No really I'm fine. I'll come straight to the point Douglas, and then I'll be on my way. Leave you two love-birds to a quiet evening." When suddenly his countenance changed, as if a menacing cloud was passing across his consciousness. "I'm dying, Douglas," he announced in a matter of fact tone. "Brain cancer. Tumour. The big C. I've known for some time."

"Oh Alex! I could see something was wrong. I am so sorry."

"Yes, thanks. To be honest I haven't got long without expensive treatment, very expensive treatment. In fact there's only one Swiss clinic which holds out any hope for me at all. They reckon the treatment should give me another few years. Strange how you cling to the slightest straw in a storm."

"You poor man."

"But sadly, an old soldier's pay doesn't stretch to expensive Swiss clinics," he drew on his cigarette, "and that's why I've come for the diamond," and exhaled slowly.

Douglas looked blank, convinced he had heard wrong. "I'm sorry? What did you just say?"

"Oh come now, old boy, don't try the big film star routine on me," he said, tossing his cigarette into the fireplace. "You're no actor, and you never will be. You know perfectly well I'm referring to the Great Mogul Diamond."

Douglas stared at Silverthorn open-mouthed. "Are you serious?" He said after a moment. "You've got to be pulling my leg."

"I know you've got it, and I want it. I deserve it."

"Oh come on Alex, you're not making sense. Do you honestly imagine that we'd live in a place like this if I owned a diamond the size of the Great Mogul?"

"So you remember how big it is then?"

"Of course I do, for goodness sake. I arranged a copy. Remember?"

"Oh yes, I remember alright. And then 'Magpie' smuggled your copy into France and 'Oakleaf' exchanged it for the real thing."

"Exactly. And nothing was ever heard of 'Magpie', or the diamond, from that day to this. 'Missing presumed dead', was the official line. Or he ran off with it. But either way, it vanished into thin air."

"That's what you had everyone believe, certainly, but now, now it's time to come clean and confess to what really took place."

Douglas shook his head. "I don't believe this is happening," he said "surely you remember the terrible stink it caused at the time."

"But you were in league with Magpie. Admit it!" cried Silverthorn, pointing a finger of blame at Douglas as he moved to the edge of his seat.

"What! Are you mad? He probably did a runner with the diamond immediately after the swap. No-one knew where he'd disappeared to. No-one."

"Except you!" yelled Silverthorn accusingly, his eyes flashing and wild.

"Oh come on man, this is absurd. I gave the best years of my life to the interests of the S.O.E. And my face! I stayed on after that and worked for them 'till the war ended. Remember? Hardly the actions of a ... of a thief, now is it?" Douglas stubbed out the remains of his cigarette aggressively.

Silverthorn waved a hand in dismissal. "An excellent little deception. All part of a well conceived plot. Who would suspect someone of owning a million-dollar diamond working for a pittance for the intelligence service? What are you going to do? Give it a few years and then do a runner?"

"Don't be so bloody stupid! And it wasn't a deception. I didn't have it! I've never even seen it. I knew nothing of it's whereabouts, then or now. But what about Oakleaf? Have you considered his part in it all?"

"He did what he was supposed to do, and swapped the stones. I know he's not involved. Some months later the Germans discovered he was working for us, and shot him."

"I didn't know that. Poor bugger."

"I tell you, Reid, I've laid in bed night after night thinking about this, and the more I think about it, the more I'm convinced you're at the bottom of it. You're hiding something that belongs to Her Majesty's Government!"

"Oh Alex, please. Since when have you been a representative of the government? Look, I'm genuinely sorry to hear that you are so ill, but what you're asking is ridiculous."

"Let me tell you something, Reid. You were always useless. Right from the day you started, to the bitter end. One hundred percent useless. I had to nurse you like a baby. I nursed you on your first mission, holding your hand all the way to Shetland and back, then I wet nursed you and wrapped you in cotton wool as you prepared for the assassination mission, which you completely cocked up. So much so, I was ordered to put my neck on the line and go to Norway and bail you out. And then you have the audacity to treat the S.O.E. with utter contempt by plotting with Magpie to steal the diamond."

"I've never heard such rubbish in all my life!" But Douglas was deeply worried. Obviously the cancer was affecting the man's power of reason.

There were footsteps, and Astrid entered just as Silverthorn was getting to his feet; his face sweaty and flushed. "What is all this, Douglas? I thought you would be pleased to meet your friend again after all this time, not argue together. It's horrible to have to listen to you both."

"Ah, yes of course," observed Silverthorn. "Claus Muller's beautiful daughter rescued from the smouldering ruins of the Führer's glorious Third Reich."

"Whatever do you mean? Did you know my father, Herr Silverthorn?"

"That's Mister Silverthorn to you! If you don't mind."

"We're just having a disagreement dear, that's all. And you keep my wife out of this, Silverthorn. It's got nothing to do with her at all." Douglas was on his feet now.

"Know him? repeated Silverthorn. "Oh yes, I knew him alright. We all knew him. We knew him better than you did."

"Enough!!" Douglas was enraged. "I told you to keep her out of it."

"Whatever are you saying?! Just what is this all about? I demand you tell me!"

"My pleasure, Frau Reid. You see, your husband's got something which I want. But he's being very silly insisting he hasn't got it."

"That's enough! Don't you dare drag her into this."

"But whatever is it you want?"

"A diamond," Silverthorn told her.

"A diamond?"

"An extraordinarily big diamond. As big as this," he made a circle with his fingers. "Flat at the bottom, but with a high crown …"

"But … but I've got something just like that. It couldn't possibly be a dia…"

"You've what!!?" exclaimed Douglas.

"My father left me something just like that. I told you. Didn't I? One went to Major Baum and I was to keep the other."

"Oh my God! And you've still got it?"

"Ha! Just as I always suspected. You do have it! You really must think I'm stupid not to see through this little charade."

"But why ever didn't you tell me, Astrid? Where is it, for goodness sake?"

"Under the bed," she told him, surprised by all the drama.

"Under the bed!!" Douglas could not believe what he was hearing. "All this time and we've been sleeping on a fortune."

Douglas hadn't seen Silverthorn slip a hand inside his jacket, but suddenly he was looking down the barrel of a .38 Smith and Wesson revolver, pointed directly at the centre of his forehead; yet far enough away to be out of reach. He remembered Reid was S.O.E.-trained.

Astrid screamed.

"Tell her to fetch it, Douglas, old boy." Suddenly his voice was alive with a newly-found intimidation. It was the voice of someone seriously disturbed.

"It's alright Astrid. Just do as he says. Whatever he says. Just fetch the diamond. Bring it in here."

"And don't try anything foolish, my pretty little German, or your new baby will be fatherless. Understand?"

"Yes! Yes. I understand. Don't hurt him. Please. I'll fetch it."

As Astrid left the room, Douglas made a plea for calm. "Alex, please. Put the gun away. We can talk this through."

"You shut up. And get down on your knees. You're not going to jump me now that I'm so close. Come on! Get on you're knees."

"I knew nothing about the diamond Alex," Douglas told him, dropping to the floor. "And obviously Astrid had no idea of what she was holding."

"I neither know, nor care how, Muller, or the girl, or anyone else is involved with this but it's obvious she's sitting, or rather, sleeping, on the real thing."

"But why is it so obvious? Maybe Muller had a copy made too."

"Come on stupid! Wake up! Do you think he would have left his own daughter a worthless copy?"

All the while Silverthorn never lost his aim; both arms steady, pointing the gun directly at Douglas's head. Crazy enough to fire.

"Here. Here it is," Astrid returned, holding a small cardboard box. "Don't hurt him. Please."

"Just do exactly as I tell you and no-one will get hurt," never for a second did he let his attention slip from his quarry. "Put the box on the table, and open it. Very slowly."

Astrid did as instructed. "There's other things in here too," she told him nervously.

"Just take it all out and put whatever it is on the table. Nice and slow. Remember, your husband's life is in your hands."

Astrid eased back the cardboard flaps and removed the newspaper packing. "There's my father's medals," she said. "And the one the Führer gave him," removing a red, black and white ribbon attached to the medal of crossed swords.

"Just put them all on the table."

"And here's the paperweight," she announced with relief, lifting it carefully in trembling hands. "Well, that's what I always thought it was. Surely it cannot be a diamond, it's much too big?"

"I'll be the judge of that. You just unwrap it and place it very carefully on the table."

Again, Astrid obediently did as she was ordered, knowing Silverthorn was watching her out of the corner of his eye, desperate to get his first glimpse of the magnificent stone. Yet with Douglas watching his every move he knew better than to risk even a fleeting glance.

'Can this really be the Great Mogul Diamond?' Douglas thought to himself. 'Silverthorn's right though, surely. Muller wouldn't have left his own daughter a useless copy.'

Still with his eyes fixed firmly on Douglas, Silverthorn backed away and moved around until the table was between them. "Switch the light on, girl," he commanded. "It's so dim in this dump, and I want to see it in all it's glory. And then move slowly over next to your husband and kneel down beside him ... Right. Now both of you put your hands on your head."

"For goodness sake man! Is this really necessary. A defenceless, pregnant woman's hardly likely to jump you."

"Shut up you!" Silverthorn allowed his eyes their first look at the stone sat unceremoniously amongst old newspapers. "Oh yes! Yes. This is the real thing alright. Salvation is suddenly within my grasp." Whilst the gun remained trained on Douglas, he let his other hand twist the stone around, delighted as pockets of rainbow light danced around the walls. "At last!" And closing a fist around the stone, he jammed it into a pocket of his suit and cautiously began to back away towards the door. "Stay exactly where you are! Not one move. Not one sound. And to think I was beginning to believe you really didn't have it after all. Ha!"

Finding his back against the door, with his left hand, he turned the knob and pulled it towards him, not for one second letting the gun drop. "What a delightful scene. The lovers on their knees in humble repentance for deceiving so many people, for so many years. Just as I told you. Useless."

And suddenly he was gone. Leaving them with nothing but the sound of leather against stone, as he mounted the steps, two at a time.

Astrid collapsed, letting out a cry of relief. "Gott im Himmel! The man's mad."

But Douglas was up, and on his feet. "But don't you see!? He's right. Your father was no fool, he must have left you the real thing for your own good. And now that bastard's just run off with it! Over my dead body!" He'd already reached the front door and without a backward glance raced up the stairs in pursuit.

"Wait! Douglas, no! It's not worth it," she screamed, sensing the danger. "Let him go. Come back. Come back!"

But it was too late.

Outside, the air was oppressively heavy, and the day was fast receding, but looking this way and that, even in the twilight it took only seconds for Douglas to make out Silverthorn's fleeting figure, dodging in and out of the gutter avoiding pedestrians as he made his way up Lady Somerset Road.

"Wait you! Stop!" he yelled. "Stop, thief!" He set off at a sprint, just as Astrid arrived at the top of the steps looking and calling frantically after him.

Silverthorn stopped, turned, and fired a round wildly at Douglas. But missing him completely, the bullet clipped the edge of a lamp-post, ricocheted off, only to hit Astrid just to the left of her sternum.

She clutched her chest and mouthed her husband's name, but no sound came, and glancing down at her already blood-soaked hands, she toppled backwards. Even before her head hit the bottom step, she was already dead.

That was when it started to rain.

EPILOGUE

During the final dark days of World War 2, Adolf Hitler still believed his dream for Linz was possible, and even with the allied armies at the gates of Berlin, he would often refer to a scale model of the city continually making alterations right up to the end, although his bold and ambitious plans for Linz were never realised.

The piece of colourless zircon was examined regularly, yet never closely or by an expert, so jealous was Hitler of his beautiful new possession. As a result the hoax was never discovered.

*

The Mogul's huge, legendary diamond, created millions of years ago by unimaginable forces of nature, remains to this day at a secret location, more than likely in the private collection of a wealthy entrepreneur, or as Major Muller reasoned, re-cut into a number of lesser stones. What is certain though, is that at one point in its extraordinary history, it rose from obscurity to eminence, merely to be despatched unwittingly, following a flick of the hand of fate by Major Claus Muller's daughter Astrid, to Adolf Hitler, but 'rescued' en-route by the British Special Operations Executive agent 'Magpie,' who mysteriously, was never seen or heard of after that day in 1941.

*

Douglas Reid lost his wife, Astrid, and child, in pursuit of what both he and Alexander Silverthorn believed to be the genuine diamond, but was in fact the corundum copy created at the cost of his life by the Dutchman, Willem Beck. Secreted away, possibly in the hands of a Nazi sympathizer, sits the second, zircon copy, made by the German Jew, Issac Janovitski.

Was Astrid's death as owner of what was believed to be the Great Mogul Diamond, nothing more than the Mogul's original curse playing a cruel joke?

It would be foolish to try and speculate, but down through the centuries, history records all the diamond's owners experienced great unhappiness, as well as sad and tragic ends, not forgetting the fall of the Third Reich, all in accordance with the Mogul's terrible curse.

Only time will reveal the true and unabridged tale.

THE END

BIBLIOGRAPHY

Encyclopaedia Britannica.
For references and quotations relating to The Great Mogul diamond and the life of Jean-Baptist Tavernier.

An Outline History of the Special Opeation Executive 1940-1946 (Quoted)
M.R.D. Foot. Published by Mandarin. Reprinted by kind permission of The Random House Group Limited, and the B.B.C.

Famous Diamonds. (Quoted)
Ian Balfour. Published by De Beers.

A Tale Of Two Cities. (Quoted)
Charles Dickens.

Voyages En Torquie, En Perse Et Aux Indes. (Quoted)
J-B Tavernier. (1679) Translated by V. Ball.

Famous Diamonds. (Quoted)
V. Ball. Published 1889.

The Jackdaw of Linz. (Quoted)
David Roxan and Ken Wanstall. Published by Cassell 1964.

S.O.E. In Scandinavia. (Quoted)
Charles Cruickshank. Published by Oxford University Press. 1986

The Holy Bible. (Quoted)
New International Version.

'Lily Marlene.' (Quoted)
Written by Hans Leip and Norbert Schultze.